POMMY BASTARD!

POMMY BASTARD!

by

John H Livings

JANUS PUBLISHING COMPANY
London, England

First published in Great Britain 2007
by Janus Publishing Company Ltd,
105-107 Gloucester Place,
London W1U 6BY

www.januspublishing.co.uk

British Library Cataloguing-in-Publication Data
A catalogue record for this book is available from the British Library

ISBN 978-1-85756-692-5

Cover Design: John H Livings

Printed and bound in Great Britain

For Moira

For advice, encouragement, friendship and the occasional hand-out thanks go to: Jodie and Tony Bailey, Janet Brett, Grant Calton, Gaynor Crawford, Bernadette and Phillip Dagg, Cathy and Mike Hawkins, Garry Heppleston, Fraser Johnston, Jeff Jones, The Laugh Garage, Bill, Pat, Ralph and Ruby Livings, Faith Martin, Clarissa Mattingly, MHYC, Chris and Gale Preston, Natasha Rist at Sisko, Geraldine and John Smith, Rod and Susie Vallis, Michael and Ruth Weisz and Jeannie Leung at Janus.

Apart from umpteen wild embellishments, half truths, outright lies and stuff that I've simply made up because I felt like it, everything contained in this book is the absolute truth as far as I can tell.

Dates and locations may be inaccurate and have been changed in many instances because I've forgotten the real ones and can't be arsed to do the research. And all names have been changed – not to protect the guilty but to prevent yours truly from losing his shirt.

Archibald Winston Spinks
Sydney, Australia, 2006

Contents

WELCOME ABOARD

The Captain, his officers and crew would like to take this opportunity to wish all those passengers who embarked at Southampton,

KALO TAXIDI – A HAPPY VOYAGE.

SEASCAPE

Monday 29th October 1973 En route to Bremerhaven

I stayed on deck for a while and watched the lights of the Isle of Wight drift past. Thoughts of all the ancient mariners, intrepid adventurers and ocean warriors who'd passed this way crowded my mind. Now it was my turn, albeit as crew on a rusty old Greek cruise ship. Freezin' me nuts off, the cold soon drove me inside and back to my cabin. Time to get dressed for my first evening at sea.

You should see my new suit; talk about sharp. Bottle-green velvet with huge lapels and massive flared trousers. It cost me an arm and a leg in Ken' market but what the fuck; with my brand new snakeskin boots and the yellow satin shirt with matching kipper tie from Lord John I look the dog's bollocks!

I had to dress quietly 'cos I was scared to wake Sean. He was still snoring his head off, the fat, lazy bastard. Looks like he'd polished off the whisky, too. The empty bottle rolled about the cabin floor with the motion of the ship and looking at it made me realise that I'd been so excited with all the goings-on of departure that I'd forgotten to be seasick. When I did give it some thought, the combination of the midday bender and the sway of the ship had me feeling real queasy. I tried to put the thought out of my mind and, as requested, reported to Paul's cabin at 7.30 p.m.

I thought I looked good but you should have seen the state of him. He wore a beautifully tailored black whistle with a white silk shirt and black dicky bow. He looked dead posh – if it hadn't been for his bleached blond and back-combed hair and not very subtle make-up, he'd have been a dead ringer for Simon Templar off *The Saint*.

Paul looked me up and down, sighed theatrically and said that I'd have to do. Cheeky old poof! Oh well, have to swallow it for now, so to speak. Being the on-board entertainment director, he is, after all, my boss. Tell you the truth I'm very grateful to the old darlin' for taking me under his wing in the first place. Not only is this my maiden voyage but I have no experience whatsoever with this showbiz caper. Zilch, in fact.

Paul asked me if I knew the whereabouts of Sean. I didn't want to dob my cabin mate in but I didn't see why I should protect the drunken bum, either, and so owned up that I'd left Sean snoozing in his bunk. It's clear to see that there's no love lost between the two. Paul is an outrageous old sodomite and, being teetotal, is none too keen on Sean's excess drinking and frequent bouts of violence. And Sean's rabidly homophobic. Could be a long trip.

Paul shrugged his shoulders in a gesture of resignation. I got the feeling he didn't have the stomach to provoke the wrath of the belligerent paddy on the first night out. Then he announced that I would be calling this evening's bingo. Oh shit! My first night under the spotlight. Now I was really nervous and as the ship started to roll in the channel I wondered how the hell I was going to cope. Listen: I know it was only bingo but this was to be my first experience at public speaking and I was packing it.

The Main Lounge was teeming with about two hundred little old grannies queuing up to buy bingo cards at fifty pence a pop. Paul briefed me on the etiquette of the game and it was eyes down for a full house. I sat up on stage with Nick, the purser, who handled all the cash and worked out the prize for each game. I was surprised that at half a quid a game the top prize of the evening was a measly twelve pounds. I was instructed to explain this away with the lame excuse that all profits went to the Seaman's Mission. What wasn't explained though, was where all the profits really went. This was revealed to me at the end of proceedings when all the loot from the evening's session was divvied up in the Pursers Office.

It was my first taste of a system of graft and corruption that was endemic on the ship. It appears that everyone from the Captain down is working some sort of scam or another. I should fit in well.

The burgled bingo booty was split up with the pursers getting the lion's share and Paul, as entertainment director, receiving a healthy wad. He, in turn, did the noble thing and passed on a few quid to Sean and myself. Considering there's three sessions of bingo a day, I'm on to a nice little earner indeed. Looks like I won't be going short in port.

Following my baptism of fire with the grannies, my duties were over for the night and I spent a couple of hours getting sloshed with a few crew mates in the Outrigger Bar. Ours is the best of both worlds. In the scheme of things, we are regarded as petty officers and have all kinds of privileges denied to the majority of the crew, who do all the shit jobs and spend their off hours well and truly below decks and out of sight. Being on the entertainment staff, I'm not only allowed, but encouraged to hang out and fraternise with the passengers.

It had been a long and eventful day and by midnight the sea was kicking up, causing the ship to pitch and heave in a giddying motion. Showing off to my new pals, I gulped down, with difficulty, the last of umpteen duty-free Bacardis, then excused myself and staggered off to bed. I got lost on the way back to my cabin and, feeling decidedly seedy, ducked into a toilet, which only made matters worse. The place was awash with vomit and, as the deck heaved a tsunami of piss, shit and bog paper raced across the floor and sloshed around my flares. If it hadn't been for my four-inch heels, I'd have been up to my fuckin' knees.

Sean was awake when I finally crept into the cabin and he seemed none the worse for the bottle of Scotch he'd guzzled that afternoon. In his gruff way he thanked me for filling in for him at bingo and handed me a seasick tablet, claiming that it would knock me out in no time. I lay in the dark, my bunk spun and Sean asked me a question:

'How do you get a roomful of old ladies to say fuck? Answer: You get another old lady to say bingo. Boom-Tish! An ancient joke; but not bad, eh?'

'Night, Sean.'

I need a stroke of luck
I need some sort of boost
Now that all my bad behaviour
Is coming home to roost

Anonymous graffiti scrawled on the back of a dunny door in an East Sydney pub.
(I'm buggered if I can remember the name of the pub.)

1

The End

Giddy-up! You're only young once. Trouble is, you're only old once too and right now, as I creep up on this, my fifty-second glorious year on planet earth, I find that I don't have a clue as to what it is I'm supposed to be doing here. I don't know where I fit in – God only knows. And God only knows where the years went. I just wish they hadn't.

Believe me; I didn't plan it this way. Not that I ever recall having a plan, but, at my time of life, at this, the scary and equidistant point of no return, I somehow envisaged myself to be comfortably retired by now. Having magically scored it off, I'm supposed to be ensconced in a large house in the heart of the English countryside. The stockbroker belt, perhaps. Commuting distance from London. Quaint old pubs, antique shops, farms and foot and mouth disease.

I'm supposed to be married to a fashionably thin, raven-haired posh bird who's twenty years my junior and talks with a plum in her mouth. She'd be none too bright but that wouldn't bother me. It would be enough that she looked ravishing and dropped words like 'horrid', 'churlish' and 'beastly' into her increasingly vapid prattle.

So that's me, Lucinda, and a couple of precocious oiks, whom I would never get to know as they'd spend most of their time away from home attending extortionately expensive private schools where they'd learn to resent my slovenly accent and rags to riches blatherings.

I would drive a vintage Jag (British racing green), have a ton of cash offshore and maintain a mistress in the city. On Sundays, I would ride out on my favourite mount before joining my well-heeled chums at the sixteenth-century Ploughman's Forelock, the local pub on the green. They would all be there. A bevy of merchant bankers, British Airways captains and the wily Rupert, who, 'tis rumoured, is something very hush-hush in the Foreign Office.

I can see myself now. Slapping backs, waving a cigar around and flinging money across the bar like confetti.

'So that's four pints of Duftons Old Familiar, a glass of top-shelf Chard' for Hector's new squeeze, make mine a large Brandy – oh, and half-a-pint of shandy and a small sherry for the vicar and his wife, thanks, Thelma.'

Alas, it was never my destiny to grow up to be a rich tosser. Instead, I find myself on the other side of the planet, technically homeless, posh bird-less and, as far as I'm aware, completely sprog-less. Worst of all (and this is the bit I hate the most), I'm just about on the bones of my arse. Just about penniless. Skint, broke, busted, strapped and can't, for the life of me, see any light at the end of the tunnel.

Disenchanted though I most certainly am, I can, if the mood takes me, console myself with the fact that I do not stand alone. My demographic is referred to as 'The Baby Boomers'. You've probably heard of us. We were born in the fifties, grew up in the sixties and, in general, have enjoyed a charmed existence. We've seen and been the impetus for a lot of changes and we've had a lot of laughs along the way. The smart ones amongst us made hay whilst the sun shone. The smart ones amongst us made piles of cash and are now retiring in droves to squander their kids' inheritance. But then there're a large percentage of us who, well before our use-by date, have become Generation Axed. Who would have thought it?

Is it my fault that I don't have a pot to piss in? The answer, I'm afraid to admit, is, in my case, a very resounding yes. The truth is, I'm bloody hopeless with money – hanging on to it, that is. Mark my words; I'm a master at getting rid of it. I'm not kidding! Money goes through my hands, in the parlance of the day, faster than a vindaloo through a geriatric.

The very concept of investing for the future, building a nest egg, and putting something by for a rainy day, has always been completely alien to me. I've never saved a penny, cent or skerrick in my life. Truth is, I'm a hopeless spendthrift, a bit of a wastrel and, though generous to a fault, something of a ne'er-do-well.

The problem is that I never envisaged, for the life of me, the day when I would be incapable of paying for my extravagant lifestyle. For the life of me, I never envisaged the day when the goal posts would not only be moved, but be torn down, chopped up and used for firewood. For the life of me, I never envisaged the day when I would be tossed on the scrapheap like an old, worn-out typewriter.

Maybe I'm being a bit hard on myself. It's not entirely my fault that I find myself up shit creek minus a home, job or career. You see, for most of my life I've worked my balls off and, for the most part, managed to earn moderately fat wads of dosh plying my trade as a graphic artist. I was a good one too. Top of my game, with a natural flair for design and never short of a creative solution. Lickety-split, my services were in constant demand and I was never short of work. That is, until computer graphics came on the scene and, well, how can I put this diplomatically ... totally fucked up my livelihood!

A few of my colleagues (generally the least talented) went over to the dark side and made the transition from magic marker to mouse without too much heartache. I didn't! Believe me, I tried. Really I did. I sat through hours and hours of mind-numbing computer courses, workshops and lectures but I just couldn't get it. Truth is, I didn't want to get it. I was never cut out to spend my days staring at a friggin' computer screen. As it happens, I don't believe any of us were. Not a very popular notion these days but that's just me. Call me old-fashioned. Call me what you will. I didn't get where I am today by being sensible and I didn't go to art school to become a computer nerd. (Come to think of it, I didn't go to art school but that's academic.)

I truly loved being an artist. I felt liberated when I worked on a drawing board. I felt as though I'd found my true calling. I felt as though I had the best job in the world. If you must know, losing my career has left me shattered. Losing my career has left me bereft. Losing my career has just about broke my heart.

Shackled to a computer, I feel trapped, caged and bored out of my skull! Don't get me wrong, I'm no Luddite. I totally accept, hook, line and sinker, that society should bow down in homage to the brave new world of computers, cyberspace, virtual reality and assorted bollocks! That's okay. I understand and empathise. The world is a truly scary place at present. Who in their right mind would choose reality? Better to deadbolt yourself behind a blast-proof door, kick back, log on and surf the mighty net. You can make new friends and lie your tits off in the chat room. You can be short, fat, have a harelip and a hunched back. It doesn't matter if you have a face like a welder's bench. You can even have a beard. So come on all you Internuts – log on! You don't have to look anyone in the eye, shout a round of drinks or pay for dinner. And with physical contact out of the equation, the only thing to worry about is picking up a nasty little virus on your floppy or hard drive, or whatever the fuck it's called.

Honestly, I don't mean to rage against modernity but is it really progress? All this new technology has no doubt created whole new industries, and has no doubt created millions of new jobs. But I ask you. In our rush to slavishly embrace the computer as a fix-all panacea, have we not forgotten the multitude of people who've been totally disenfranchised and left behind in the wake of all this techno babble? Me, for instance!

Is it progress when a talented artisan, such as my good self, can't get a job? Is it bollocks! Thirty years plus in the graphics caper and the only thing I'm qualified to draw is the fuckin' dole.

Back when I was a useful member of society, and back when I was a young gun artist, art studios were wild places stocked with an eccentric array of wonderfully creative lunatics. Walk into your average art studio these days and it's like walking into a morgue – or an insurance office. Box-like workstations have replaced those messy drawing boards and artists are referred to as operators. Operators, for Christ sakes! Suits have taken over the asylum and creativity has taken a back seat to commerce as sponge-bellied bean-counters, art direct, pasty-faced, computer geeks – the bland leading the bland. The meek may not have inherited the earth but they sure as hell usurped my chosen profession, the swotty bastards.

Listen: I've crossed a lot of bridges in my long life but if things don't turn around soon, I could very well find myself living under one.

Oh well, mustn't grumble as they say. Truth is, I can't deny that I haven't had a lot of fun getting to my present precarious position. I've lived life to the hilt, travelled far and wide and, lucky for me, for the past twenty years, it's been my privilege to call Australia home. So I really mustn't grumble. It doesn't do me any favours and, more to the point, being a Pommy, I've learnt that complaining is strictly *verboten* in the lucky country, lest one be labelled with the dreaded moniker of being ... 'a whinger'!

Just for the record, I love Australia and the very thought of relocating back to 'Blighty' (even for a posh bird called Lucinda) fills me with loathing. No! I've lived in the sun far too long and as bad as things get, at least I know I'm home. This is where I turn my turbulent life around. This is where I make my stand. This is where I draw a line in the sand. (Great beaches, too.)

LIFE JACKET DEMONSTRATION FOR ALL
PASSENGERS WHO EMBARKED AT SOUTHAMPTON

At the sounding of the ship's alarm bells this morning, all passengers who embarked at Southampton are kindly requested to assemble at their emergency stations taking with them their life jackets. The assembly station for each cabin appears on a notice behind the cabin door and is either in the Ballroom or the Main Lounge, both situated on the Promenade Deck.

SEASCAPE

Tuesday 30th October 1973 En route to and at Bremerhaven

I slept like a baby last night, as in, I woke up covered in vomit. Peeking out of the porthole, I was greeted with a turbulent ocean of whitecaps to the lightning-streaked horizon. It was pissing down with rain and a cargo ship a mile to port was pitching in the large swell and burying its bow in the boiling sea.

Sean rolled over in his bunk, farted loudly and seemed in no hurry to get up. He appeared dead chuffed when I told him what a shitty morning it was, explaining that the bad weather would keep most of the passengers in their cabins with very few of them venturing out in search of entertainment.

I skipped breakfast and headed off to Paul's cabin to check on my duties for the day. I seemed to have found my sea legs far quicker than most and apart from running a slight temperature and the odd giddy spell, I felt ridgy-didge. I took the scenic route to Paul's cabin and as I tottered along the sloping Promenade Deck, the fresh blast of salty clean air blew all thoughts of seasickness away.

A few forlorn passengers scurried crab-like along the slippery deck and, occasionally, one of these unfortunate crustaceans would make a sudden dash for the rail. With hilarious results, they'd barf directly into the wind, only to have the whole messy lot immediately flung back at them. Ah yes! A life on the ocean waves for me.

Paul was looking very dapper this morning, resplendent in a canary yellow 'Mr Freedom' boiler suit, and around his neck he'd tied a jaunty polka-dot cravat. On closer inspection, I noticed an angry, purple love bite peeking out from beneath his scarf.

My first mission of the day was to tour the ship flogging tote tickets. The deal was for passengers to shell out twenty pence a ticket to guess the ship's mileage from noon one day to noon the next. As we'd sailed at six the previous evening, the tote would be calculated from the Southampton pilot station to noon today. Sean's prediction came true and I only managed to sell about fifteen tickets as the inclement weather rendered the ship virtually devoid of passengers. I was to find out later that on a good day, the tote would turn out to be another joyful way of parting the passengers from a few bob. Of course, all profits went directly to the Seaman's Mission. Another nice little earner, thank you very much.

The ships alarm bells rang to alert passengers to assemble for life-jacket demonstration. Out of interest, I sauntered along to the Ballroom, which remained as sparsely populated as the rest of the ship as most of the passengers had wisely remained holed-up in their cabins, chronically seasick and horribly homesick.

A couple of Greek officers rambled on in broken English and the few poor bastards who had bothered to turn up were shown how to put on a mildewed life jacket.

My next job of the day was supposed to be fun and games with the kiddies on the Sports Deck but as it was now blowing a gale, this activity was mercifully cancelled and so endeth my first day on the job. We'll be docking at Bremerhaven this evening and welcoming aboard a consignment of German migrants to amuse, abuse and do battle with the English on the long, slow voyage down under.

I was excited to be setting foot on my first foreign soil. Don-the-Slot (looks after the one-arm bandits), Tiny-Tom (ship's printer) and Bunger (works in the duty-free gift shop) said I could tag along with them to some good bars they know. Unfortunately, my plan of chasing down a bit of foreign puss' were thwarted by Paul, who insisted that Sean and I join him for a bonding, get-to-know-you dinner in a better part of the town.

Sean was mortified, stepping off the ship with us two. Me, with my long hair and white Afghan coat, and Paul in a full-length mink that some adoring old duck had bought for him. Turns out that Paul, apart from being a screaming queen, is also a very successful and sought-after gigolo. Going by his mink coat, expensive jewellery and impressive collection of Patek Philippe watches, he must be a fuckin' sex machine.

We caught a cab to *Am Markt* – the city centre. Being one of Germany's major ports, Bremen would have had the shit bombed out of it during the war but I was pleasantly surprised by the cute cobblestone streets. Several ornate buildings vied for attention and a big, old, medieval cathedral dominated the town.

It is interesting to note that in 1794 Duke Ferdinand Von blah, blah, blah ... Not interested in a history lesson, Sean and I scoffed down our dinner and Paul acted hurt when I declined his offer of a tour of the town's gay clubs. He minced off in a huff and Sean and I took off in search of the other boys in the sleazier, though hetero, part of town.

After several bars, we managed to track down the three stooges and a night of mayhem and merrymaking followed. Sean got horribly pissed on schnapps and got into a fight with a German bloke who took umbrage at Sean's unwanted advances towards his fräulein. Not very creatively, Sean called the guy a Nazi and the whole bar turned on us. From what I remember, we were lucky to get out of the place alive. I vaguely recall staggering back on board at three in the morning. I was very seasick that night, even though the ship was tied up at the quay. I'm doing my best to keep up with the drinking habits of the more experienced crew but these guys are the biggest piss-heads I've ever met. I've got no chance.

My name is Archibald Winston Spinks and with an 'andle like that, it's imperative that one has a sense of humour. Lucky for me, I do. There's no doubt about it. I like a laugh, me. I like a bit of fun – you can ask anyone. And, to be honest, it's my jocular disposition as much as my rabid technophobia that has led me ultimately down the slippery slope to the scrap heap of unemployment and hideousness.

It's true. Seriously. I must be nuts! If I had just been content with my lot I wouldn't be on my tod right now, staring down the barrel of an uncertain future. Take it from me, fun can be a very expensive paramour.

Just listen to this: it was sometime back in the mid-nineties when things started to unravel for me. (If this was a TV soap, the screen would now wobble cheesily so as to alert the viewer that they're about to witness a flashback. For extra emphasis ... bung in a harp). To all intents and purposes, my life, predictable and safe as it was, was pretty much hassle-free and hunky-dory. I had a well-paid, secure job, managing the art department in one of Sydney's largest advertising agencies and, with a combination of hard work and a bolshie attitude, had held the position for eight years.

Eight bloody years and I was ashamed of myself. I sat at a big, shiny desk in my very own office, with my very own couch, my very own pot plant, and my very own sparkling view of Sydney Harbour. Ye gods! I was a bona fide advertising wanker! The pissy lunches and corridors full of long-legged lovelies was no reason for me to stick around as long as I did. Take away the perks, and I was going nuts, running what had become nothing more than a collection of soulless workstations ... a cemetery with desks. I deciphered briefs from the suits and trafficked work to my staff, 'the operators', who bathed, boggle-eyed, in the blue hypnotic loom of their screens. Docile drones, all of them, mesmerised, subservient and besotted with their 'Power Macs'. God, it was starting to do my head in! And it was certainly no place for the artist that I'd once been. The whole industry had fallen madly in love with computers ... tap–tap–tap ... save me.

I was doing the job standing on my head but the work lacked any creative buzz. I was a cog in a wheel churning out inane ads promoting anything and everything from frozen foods, beer, washing powder, paint, shampoo, refrigerators, vacuum cleaners, cars, hi-fi's, TVs, sofas, toys, tampons and assorted cobblers. There had to be more to life than coming up with a snappy new way to flog bog rolls, for Christ sakes!

Anyway, in spite of everything, believe it or not, I worked hard at my job. I was respected and popular with my staff but, at the end of the day, I felt empty and unfulfilled. My bohemian ethics, long dormant and denied, were now increasingly in conflict with my yuppie pretensions and I began to have the sneaking suspicion that my contribution to the well-being of the planet was nothing more than immense piles of junk mail, drivel and bile. The way I saw it I may as well have been an overseer on an assembly line in a shit sandwich factory!

The only fun I was having was the never-ending battles with the suits over their ridiculously impractical deadlines. And boy, doesn't a suit love a meeting? They live for meetings. Endless meetings. Meetings to plan meetings. Meetings to discuss previous meetings. And seminars, think tanks and workshops. Workshops? Where I come from, workshops were industrious places ... where work got done. Where things got produced – or at least repaired. Where I come from, workshops were generally devoid of tossers!

The umpteen meetings that I was obliged to attend generally descended into bitch-fests. They were mere blame-storming sessions; the sole purpose of the waste of time being to ascertain which department, or better still, which individual, could be held responsible for the latest monumental cock-up. It was all politics and bullshit and I didn't want to play any more.

As in all good office dramas, there happened to be one particularly loathsome sycophant who'd been slithering up the corporate ladder for a number of years. The odious creep had never done a day's work in his life but spent what little energy he did possess busily kissing arse, back-stabbing, lying, cheating and sucking up to the powers that be. And he drove a beige car. Beige, I ask you!

Inevitably, the day came when the slimy pillock was rewarded for his grovelling and promoted over my good self for the sole reason that he played golf on a regular basis with the creative director. I kid you not! Golf. A game played by men with very small balls!

That was it for me. High time I turned my back on the wonderful world of advertising. Time to strike out and do something more worthwhile and, ultimately, more fulfilling with my one and only life. Not that I intended jacking my job in. That would have given my new *oberführer* exactly what he wanted and I couldn't have that now, could I? No. I would bide my time. Take the slings, arrows and knives courageously in the chest whilst I searched for something to assuage the desperate mid-life crisis that I was enduring.

But it was a time to tread softly for I'd already dabbled disastrously with the more traditional diversion. Listen up chaps: let me just say here and now that if for any reason whatsoever – be it boredom, excitement or just plain lust – you ever decide to have a fling, do not, at any cost, do as I did and choose, as the object of your desire, your beautiful, long-term, long-suffering girlfriend's best friend. I'm not kidding. It just ain't worth the grief.

If you're kept awake all night, tossing and turning with disturbing fantasies of your significant other's best chum, then take some evasive action immediately! I dunno! Nip it in the bud! Slam the bugger in the fridge door! Chop the fuckin' thing off! The girlfriend's best mate must, at all costs, be given the widest of berths and avoided like the blackest of plagues.

What a bloody disaster. And to make matters worse, when the whole tawdry business finally blew up in my face ... when I got caught ... I actually admitted to the truth. Arghhh! Wrong! Wrong! Wrong! Deny! Deny! Deny! Too late for me but I thought it worth mentioning as a note of caution for the unwary. Mind you, she was fuckin' gorgeous.

Guilty as charged, your honour. In way of defence, I would just like to point out to the court that I am, after all, only a mere bloke and consequently have no control whatsoever and, indeed, am in no way responsible for the dastardly behaviour of the downstairs department and said love trumpet.

Not surprisingly, my girlfriend promptly became my ex-girlfriend and the best friend of my girlfriend, or rather the ex-best friend of my now ex-girlfriend got all weepy and pissed off with me. She just couldn't get her head around the fact that now freed up to do so, I showed no interest whatsoever in wanting to commit to a more meaningful, more permanent arrangement. Tears and accusations flowed, hair was torn out, clothes ripped asunder and furniture and hearts broken.

'But you said you loved me, you lousy bastard,' etc, etc. Um, well, technically that's true but may I once again respectfully point out to the ladies and gentlemen of the jury, that I am, after all, only a humble bloke and, therefore, emotionally incapable of bearing any responsibility whatsoever for anything said or suggested – when getting one's end away.

Now I wasn't dragged kicking and screaming into this little tryst and Helen, the yummy inamorata of my desire, didn't exactly play hard to get, either. We pounced on one another one hot summer's night when, by accident or design, we found ourselves alone together and full of vino. The taboo of our intimacy made the whole sordid entanglement all the more intoxicating and following that first frenzied night we went on to fuck each other's brains out at every stolen and delicious opportunity.

Being a recovering Catholic, I suffered from terrible guilt at cheating on my girlfriend, whom I loved and whom neither Helen nor I had set out to hurt.

'It just sort of happened, M'lud.'

We tried in vain on several occasions to break off our dalliance but the forbidden sex was so fanfuckintastic that it would have been an easier task to give up food. Or alcohol, even! From that first night, our fate was sealed in a vice-like embrace. Destined to run its traitorous course until the day when the shit would inevitably hit the fan.

HELP! HELP! HELP! HELPERS!

Singers, dancers, or any passengers wishing to participate in our forthcoming shows – meet Paul, now! No experience necessary. All ages welcome. 3.00pm, Ballroom.

SEASCAPE
Wednesday 31st October 1973 En route to Las palmas

We'd already put to sea when I woke at nine. I had a quick shower, shovelled down a greasy breakfast and then joined Paul at the entertainment office, where he was gleefully adding to the bulging coffers of the Seaman's Mission.

At a refundable deposit of a quid, passengers can hire board games, darts, table tennis bats and assorted crap and hang on to the stuff for the duration of the voyage. In reality, it was yet another way of fleecing them as most of the stuff gets lost, ruined or tossed overboard and only a small percentage is ever returned. By the way, today's prize for brain of the ship goes to a young man from Hull who wanted to know if there was a pool table on board?

Following my morning stroll around the ship flogging tote tickets, it was time for fun and games with the kiddies again. The weather had abated and a hundred or so migrant brats were eagerly awaiting me on the Sports Deck.

This turned out to be not as stressful as it sounds as most of the little buggers were happy enough to kick a football around for an hour or two. All I did was split them into two teams, chuck a ball in the middle, blow a whistle, light a ciggie and watch fifty-a-side footy take its bloody course. When some of the little girls complained I bunged them a couple of skipping ropes and left them to it. And that's about as far as any organised deck games went.

I would soon learn that the majority of the kids were excited enough by just being on the ship and had no trouble amusing themselves. And I would be pleasantly surprised at how much I enjoyed their company. Without trying very hard, they seemed to take to me, too. I'm twenty years old but small for my age; I look about fourteen, so most of the kids see me as an elder brother and they follow me all over the ship like I'm the Pied fuckin' Piper.

Not counting the band and Harry, the ancient ship's pianist, that just left Paul, Sean and me to organise the on-board entertainment so we would be calling on volunteers amongst the crew to help out in the upcoming shows. We also advertised in the daily Seascape newsletter for volunteers amongst the passengers. These cat-calls are a complete farce but with the long days at sea, you'd be surprised at the number of passengers who eagerly queued up to make twats of themselves.

Come three, the Ballroom was packed and Paul didn't fuck about when casting for shows. He simply picked the least worst acts and the best-looking boys for his chorus line. Best of all, he let me choose the birds. Next, he lined up all the new recruits, me included, and taught us a few simple moves. We had to learn quickly as the first show was scheduled for three nights hence and we rehearsed every afternoon for a couple of hours. Step, kick, step, kick, step, twirl, mince, step, kick, step!

2

A Recipe for Disaster

Helen was married to Ken, a loud-mouthed, pugnacious, rugby-playing twat who was ten years my junior and as wealthy as a skunk. He liked to guzzle malt whisky and, of late, had taken to using Helen as a punching bag when in his cups. Ken was some sort of lawyer – a legalised bandit who specialised in setting up overseas tax havens for fat cats and corporate crooks. We'd never been friends but, unfortunately, due to the fraternity of our respective partners, I often found myself in his overbearing company.

Helen and Ken were in the tenth winter of a union that had seen more than its fair share of ups and downs. Their helter-skelter marriage was way past its use-by date but, like too many well-heeled couples, they remained stubbornly shackled together. Why? Helen and Ken remained stubbornly shackled together, not by a state of real love, but by a love of real estate. Not by a state of real love, but by a love of real estate. (I thought it worth repeating.)

Sharing the palatial home were their two children, Caitlin, seven, and nine-year-old Barnaby. They were intelligent, well-adjusted and likeable kids, despite having their work cut out refereeing their parents' numerous brawls and altercations.

Poor old Ken. For all his knockabout, male-bonding pursuits, I don't think he had any real friends and he'd welcome me into his home like a long-lost brother; something I found disconcerting in the extreme once I'd started shagging his missus. What a cad!

Ken liked to get me down in his dark, musty den. Two good ole' boys together. After plying me full of Chivas Regal, he would thrash the pants off me at pool whilst boasting of his wheeling and dealing. This would inevitably lead him to pontificate on his favourite subject – the share market. Once he got bangin' on about money, I switched off. For all the sense he made to me, he may has well have been slurring in Swahili. I'd try in vain to change the subject, even feigning an interest in the many framed photographs of Ken and his mud-spattered rugby cohorts that jostled for wall space alongside his impressive collection of antique swords. Ken was very fond of his swords.

Oh, what a mangled web we weave. It was a Saturday and as my girlfriend was at work and I knew that old Ken would be huffing and puffing his considerable bulk around a rugby pitch (followed, no doubt, by a communal bath with his team mates), I decided to skulk around to Helen's to erm ... borrow a book.

Helen dragged me through the kitchen door and, between frantic breaths, explained that the coast was clear as young Barnaby was at the movies and Caitlin was across the road at her best friend's birthday party.

Apart from Helen giving my balls a massage with a stockinged foot at dinner parties, we didn't, as a rule, make a habit of fooling around in her house but as we hadn't fucked each other for about twenty-four hours, we threw tongues, hands, legs and caution to the wind. Grunting and groping, we ended up in the laundry and shagged, wedged up against the washing machine.

The kitchen door crashed open and Caitlin came bowling in, followed by one of her little friends. The two girls, dressed cutely as fairies, flashed past in a pink blur and their footsteps receded into the house and banged up the stairs. We froze on the spot. I zipped-up and Helen hurriedly buttoned her dress, scooped her panties off the floor and threw them in the dryer out of sight. Then we hid behind the laundry door.

For two little fairies, Caitlin and her friend, were making a hell of a racket and minutes later, we heard them descending the stairs like a pair of sugar-plum elephants. Clutching a handful of dolls, the two girls, mercifully oblivious to our presence, skipped across the kitchen and out through the door in a spasm of shrieks and giggles.

Fast-forward to Monday morning, and I'm sitting in my office, staring out of the window and looking forward to popping around to Helen's for a 'nooner' at lunchtime. The phone rings and it's the lady herself. The balloon's gone up!

Between sobs, Helen blubbed that, over breakfast that morning, little Caitlin had shattered the usual silence by spectacularly announcing that she'd seen Mummy kissing Uncle Archie...and, that Uncle Archie had had his hand up Mummy's dress. Ken apparently pebble-dashed the table with regurgitated cocoa pops, then dragged Helen down to his den. All the better to extract the awful truth. Helen knew the situation was hopeless...she knew her goose was cooked. Putting up little resistance, she promptly spilt the beans.

According to Helen, Ken, apart from a bit of justifiable cursing, was strangely calm in the face of his wife's infidelity. Paralysed with the devastating news, he became strangely composed and, mercifully, fisticuffs were not employed. Ken took off to work and Helen drove a confused Barnaby and Caitlin (the supergrass) to school.

Before hanging up the phone, Helen enquired, disturbingly, as to what 'I' intended to do about the dire situation that 'we' now found 'ourselves' in. Ugh? To be honest, I'd been so dumbstruck during the whole tearful exchange that it hadn't dawned on me that I was in some way involved. After all, technically, I wasn't the one who'd committed adultery.

My fantasy of innocence lasted all of five seconds, for as soon as Helen was off the phone, my girlfriend was on the blower, demanding to know what the fuck was going on. She'd just got off the phone from Ken, who had blabbed what he knew of the whole sordid affair.

What could I say? Sorry seemed a tad inadequate under the circumstances. She was screaming and I was squirming but doing my valiant best to answer her umpteen questions with the truth and nothing but the truth, your honour. Alright, I may have bunged in a few white lies when bombarded with a litany of 'how longs', 'how many times', 'wheres', 'whys' and 'what fors'. (Give me a break. I was under extreme duress.)

Feigning a migraine, I took the rest of the day off and hid out in a dark and gloomy bar where I drank myself into a stupor, took up smoking after nine years of abstinence and, ironically enough, developed a real migraine. What a shame it all had to end in tears.

Liberally zonked, I mused on one of life's more perplexing conundrums. Are we, as a species, as human beings, cut out to be monogamous? Is the concept of shagging the same person till death us do part, a completely illogical ask?

Fan that I am of David Attenborough docos, I know that the animal kingdom is not run along such impossibly stringent lines. Sure, it's thought there are a few exceptions; it's believed that certain species of penguin shack up for the duration but, as they all look identically alike, why wouldn't they? And research shows that the mighty albatross mates for life. However, the male albatross is only found on land during the breeding season. The wily bastards spend the rest of the year at sea, out of sight and out of mind, no doubt getting up to all kinds of deviant mischief. Free as a bird, so to speak. (I briefly attempted to research the above on the Internet but, being such a technophobe, I gave up after five minutes so, in all probability, I could, as usual, be talking out of my arse.)

But come on. What did I have to feel guilty about? It was only sex. And great sex at that, I'll grant you. Glorious, forbidden, promiscuous filth. Maybe it's just me but as far as I know, nothing comes close to the heart-pumping rush of sneaking off to a no-tell motel for an afternoon of euphoric, toe-curling rutting with someone else's significant other. And, strangely enough, the prospect of being caught only heightens the thrill. I dunno. Maybe it is just me. Maybe I'm just old-fashioned. Maybe I've got issues?

Surprisingly enough, old Ken never did come after me but he and Helen promptly split up. Three months later, Ken was shacked up in a new home with a young car chaser from his office who, it turned out, the despicable swine had been bangin' for the past year. Helen got the kids, the house and, finally, the picture that what had gone on between us was not half as much fun now that we didn't have to sneak around.

When the dust had settled, we saw each other a few times and shared some romantic dinners together. We held hands in the movies like a proper couple and spent some deliciously dirty weekends away in various B&B shag nests in the country. Champagne, candles and big, fluffy pillows. For a brief while it was like being in an episode of some hideous daytime soap.

It was a novelty to spend a whole night together, but the sex soon lost its steam now that we didn't have to worry about an enraged Ken catching us 'at it' and decapitating the pair of us with his prized five- hundred-year-old Samurai sword.

We were never cut out to be a couple and Helen soon got pissed off with my total lack of commitment. She took up with a gentle, friendly, honourable chap who was completely nuts about her and, within no time, they were shacked up and planning a sparkling future together.

As for my ex, she was gone in a flash. Or, to be more accurate, I was given my marching orders. I boxed up my books, CDs, clothes, vintage Batman comics and assorted toot and moved out of our warm, comfy home into the cold, stark, solitary world. She took up with a gentle, friendly, honourable chap who was completely nuts about her and, within no time, they were shacked up and planning a sparkling future together.

I rented a shit box to start with and got drunk a lot. Later on, I half-heartedly pulled myself together and managed to scrape up enough of a deposit for a bank to foolishly grant me a hefty mortgage on my very own minute bachelor pad. Down at the end of a lonely street and squashed in a block of fifty identical units, the real estate blurb described it as a 'New York-style loft apartment'. In reality, it was a tiny bedsit with a ladder leading to a small shelf where the bed went. But it was my bolt-hole. A place to crash, contemplate my lot and occasionally lure women back to.

For my own sanity, I kept busy and threw myself into my hobbies like never before. Sailing, scuba-diving, skiing, drinking, chain smoking, reading on the toilet, watching a lot of telly and, a new one on me ... cooking. Delighted and surprised by my prowess in the kitchen, I quickly mastered the microwave and was, in no time, handling a tin opener like a pro. Fuck it! With Christmas looming and with nothing better to do, I had a go at making a cake.

Archie's Christmas Cake
Works for me every year!
Ingredients:
1 cup of water. 1 cup of brown sugar.
1 tsp baking soda. Lemon juice.
4 cups of flour. 4 eggs.
1 cup of sugar. 2 cups of mixed nuts.
Cup of butter. 1 quart of Irish whisky.
1 tsp salt. Half quart of brandy.

Open the whisky and brandy to ensure quality and freshness. (A big glass of each is recommended.) Take a large mixing bowl (usually found in a cupboard under the sink) and add two to three fingers of whisky. Test the whisky again to be sure. Add two to three fingers of brandy and taste-test the brandy again. Turn on the mixer and blend the whisky and brandy. Check taste. Not all of it! Start again.

Add flour to the large fluffy bowl and beat in one butt or cuppa. Add the sugar and more whisky. Check the quality of the whisky before and after adding. Beat again. Try a cup of brandy. Add some to the mix as well. Turn off the mixerer. Break 4 leggs and add to the bowel. Chuck in the dried fruit. Check the whisky and brandy again. Mix onb the turner. If it the dried fruit gets stuck in the beateres, have a brandy or a whisky or both and pry it loose with a drewscriver. Check the whisky for tonsisticity. Sift two cups of anything left over. Or something. Strain your nuts. Add one table. And a spoon. Chuck in anything else. Finish the whisky. Not in the cake.

Greash in the oven and piss in the fridge. Turn the cake tin 360 degrees. Beat off the tuner. Throw the bowl through the fuckin' window. Finish the brandy and piss off to bed.

Season's Greetings, etc.

WORLD NEWS IN BRIEF.
According to an American ear specialist, sexual intercourse, heavy drinking, or a combination of both, can cause severe deafness. Dr F. Blair Simmons of Stanford, California, said these activities can cause a rapid build-up of pressure in the inner ear, which results in loss of hearing.

SEASCAPE
Thursday 1st November 1973 En route to Las Palmas

The Kioni headed out into the Bay of Biscay to our next port of call, Las Palmas in the Canary Islands. The sea has kicked up but shipboard life is settling down. Old codgers busy themselves playing bridge and canasta or sit on deck snoozing under a blanket or sipping bouillon. I get on well with the old ducks and they're my best customers when it comes to flogging tote tickets. Mind you, if I fuck up the numbers at bingo they can turn on me like a pack of hyenas.

The many pissheads amongst the passengers have formed drunken alliances in the bars and shipboard romances blossom. Dolled up in their finest uniforms, the Greek officers patrol the public rooms like sharks. Some of them have even taken the trouble to shave. Shagging is in the air.

There's a ton of eligible pussy on board but there's also hundreds of horny blokes so the race is on to pull a good one before they're all snapped up. Having a uniform appears to be a definite chick magnet but being part of the entertainment staff doesn't do me any harm, either. The problem, as I see it, is that I'm forced to spend a lot of time in the camp company of Paul and I get the feeling that it's assumed I'm his punk. Course, he doesn't help matters by openly referring to me as 'Maude'. I know for a fact that the majority of the Greek crew presume that I'm a shirt lifter and I've soon learnt what the word *pusti* means.

Two sisters, Annie and Sarah, came along to the audition and, in spite of having four left feet between them, I've persuaded Paul to put them in the show. Talk about gorgeous – especially Annie. She's very pretty, with a mischievously suggestive smile. As it happens, she looks like a slutty version of Marie Osmond ... but with tits!

The two sisters are travelling out to Australia for a holiday with their mum, a wonderful, liberated old piss tank called Emma. Sarah, the eldest, is engaged to some bloke back in Croydon but she's already been chatted up and chased down by Spiro, a notorious root rat who plays drums in the ship's band. Turns out old Emma can't stand Sarah's boring boyfriend back in Croydon and is actively encouraging her toothsome daughters to have a good time and let their hair down. I only hope she's actively encouraging them to let their pants down, too.

Sharing a cabin with Sean poses a bit of a conundrum when it comes to the bedding of young Annie, for when Sean's not working or bludging drinks off gullible passengers, he spends his time hibernating in his bunk like a grumpy old bear. Annie is eighteen. I know she likes me and if I can just convince her that I'm not being rogered senseless by Paul, I reckon I'm in like Flynn.

Meanwhile, I continued to work my balls off at the agency – all the better to show up my spineless boss. Hangover or not, I'd be in the office at eight every morning and he would slink in at 10.30 a.m. and do nothing more than get in the way, kiss arse and position himself nicely to garner kudos for my, and my staff's, considerable labours. For all the use he was, he may as well have stayed at home for, apart from his elevated title and extortionate salary, I was still running the show and having to put in twelve-hour days to meet the increasingly pressing deadlines.

At the end of a long day, I'd head straight for the nearest boozer and proceed to get legless whilst talking shop to like-minded reprobates who, like me, had no reason or desire to head home until last orders. The journey from pub to pad a mystery, I'd wake on the couch at 3.00 a.m., dry-mouthed, stiff-necked and fully clothed but for one missing shoe. Home sweet home was a coffee-table clutter of crumpled notes, piles of coins, a congealed, half-eaten pizza, an overflowing ashtray and a bottle of wine at low tide. A rabid TV evangelist would be barking at me from the tube that never sleeps.

This would not stand. I wasn't exactly living life to the full. Things could be worse but things had been a lot better. I was living a half-life and I knew it. It was time to get off my arse, get my head together, and get sorted!

A fellow barfly, another lost soul in similar dire straits, suggested that I might like to join him at his male support group. I gave it some thought for all of about two seconds. To be fair, I didn't really have a clue what a male support group got up to but I imagined, with horror, that it may involve bizarre male-bonding weekends in the woods. The very thought of running around half-naked, daubed in war paint and a feather up my arse didn't exactly appeal. And sitting around a camp fire listening to a bunch of doomed, disillusioned forty-somethings pour out their inner child angst and then having to hug a fat bloke with a beard called Jeff was definitely not my style.

Another drinking buddy, another first-class clown, suggested I may like to join him and a few pals for an exhilarating weekend of paint ball. He enthusiastically raved on about the joys of togging-up in pseudo-military garb and the thrill he got from firing his toy gun. Fuck that! It sounded to me like yet another dumb-arse game played by men with very small balls!

No! This would just not do. What was required to shake me out of my torpor was a challenge. Something truly scary. Most importantly, it had to be something that would awaken my long-dormant creativity. It had to be something crazy and it had to be something truly different – an uncharted rocky road, travelled only by the brave or mentally deranged.

Like I said before, I like a laugh, me. I like a bit of fun. The solution to my problem had been staring me in the face for years and I'd been too blind drunk to see it. What transpired next, I feel, is best illustrated with a short story.

Here's one I prepared earlier.

Boom! Boom!

A Short Story I Prepared Earlier

A fat red sun hovers over the harbour bridge, then sinks slowly and reluctantly into the western suburbs. Down at Circular Quay, a majestic cruise ship slips from its berth, and up on the phalanx of decks, flocks of bejewelled coffin-dodgers wave listless, arthritic claws at the glittering city.

A storm is brewing out at sea. Lightning flashes dramatically on the horizon, the sky grumbles and, within an hour, a bank of angry black clouds roll up the harbour bringing gale-force winds and torrents of driving rain. Working stiffs scurry from blue glass towers, brollies blow inside out, shops close down, bars fill up and traffic grinds to a halt.

In time, buses, trains and ferries ferry the sodden folk home where they flop, shagged, in front of the telly. Whoopee Doo! Another titillating evening of soapies, sitcoms, sports updates, crap movies, game shows, cooking shows, slimming shows, reality shows, big blubbers and assorted bile. 'It's life, Mr Spock, but not as we know it!'

Meanwhile ... in the front bar fug of a down-at-heel hotel, situated in one of Sydney's less salubrious suburbs, sit half-a-dozen up-and-coming comedians. A veritable untapped cesspool of questionable talent, they bemoan their fate and chosen obsession. The talk is predominantly that of killing and dying, of triumphant shows, and of bad gigs endured and survived.

'Did you see so-and-so at "The Basement" last week? He died in the arse.'

'What about wotsisname, he killed last week at "The Store", and now he's scored a gig on "The Footy Show".'

'Thieving arsehole!' someone chirps in. 'What he didn't steal from us he nicked off the Internet.'

Nods and hurrumphs all round.

Old jokes are regurgitated and new gags blabbed optimistically. The latter, more often than not, greeted with derision and scorn, especially if they happen to be funny in any way. The ribbing is merciless amongst the group but the sense of camaraderie is plainly strong. There is a peculiar *esprit de corps* honed under duress in the battle zone of stand-up comedy.

Tonight is just an open mic night; no big deal, no big stars, not even any small stars and, what with the weather and the crummy venue, it's highly likely that there will be no audience. But it is a chance for up-and-comers to grab some precious stage time, try out new material, gain confidence and build an act. Who knows? With a bit of luck, maybe one day some of them will be accomplished enough to jack-in their hated, dead-end day jobs and join the proud ranks of the professional comedian. Eureka!

The MC ricochets in the door and is greeted with cheers from the group. He is balding, speed thin, soaked to the skin and would rather be anywhere than this stinking 'toilet' on a wet Monday night. But he has no choice. He really needs the hundred and fifty bucks appearance fee.

Poor bastard. He's been in the business for eighteen long years and is worn out, jaded and cynical. His rising star has long since plummeted to earth and his last TV appearance was a spot on The Midday Show sometime back in the late eighties. He can't be arsed to write new material so he ekes out a paltry living these days by pasting on a fake smile a few nights a week and regurgitating the same old shit for every show.

He survives on a diet of ciggies, booze and amphetamines and the money he makes is perfectly adequate. Perfectly adequate that is, just so long as he doesn't plan on actually buying anything. But he keeps going. Stumbling towards oblivion. What the hell else is he going to do?

He salutes the up-and-comers with the finger, snarls a passing 'get fucked!' and then walks to the bar and orders a beer.

Over in one corner sits a lone, dejected soul. The new kid on the block. A first-timer. A 'virgin'. He's totally ignored by the more experienced rabble for, until he has proved himself on stage, it is only right and proper that he be treated like a war criminal with leprosy. He is made to feel about as popular as Gary Glitter in a child-care centre. As welcome as Pauline Hanson at a *corroboree*.

The poor, deluded fool. Egged on by his uni mates, whom he never fails to crack up, he's decided to give stand-up a whirl. But he didn't expect to feel so alienated, or so scared shitless. Right now, he's wondering what the hell he's let himself in for and, like the old pro propping up the bar, wishes he were somewhere else.

Half an hour to show time, and 'The Booker' shimmies into the bar on a pair of vicious red stilettos. She is resplendent in leopard-skin tights, a black leather mini skirt, tight satin blouse and a fun-fur jacket. The whole magnificent ensemble is topped off with her finest feature, a long, shimmering mane of hair, dyed slut-black.

Hers is a defiant but sadly bygone beauty. Sure, men still fall at her feet but only when they're too drunk to stand up. She couldn't give a rat's arse. She's seen it all and done it all, has three very successful marriages behind her, and is as hard and sharp as her manicured nails. She enjoys quiet nights at home, black and white movies and, occasionally, when the mood takes her, rough sex with strangers.

She plops a kiss on the MC's cheek and then totters over to the new kid and warns him of the cardinal rule ... not to exceed his allotted five-minute time slot. He nods obediently, gulps down his beer and makes a dash for the toilet.

The Booker approaches the up-and-comers and they fall momentarily silent, for she has the power. She also has the almighty list; the running order for tonight's show. Nobody wants the tough spot of going on first, when the audience isn't warmed up; and nobody wants to hang around for two hours and go on last, when the audience is getting bored and restless. They all want to go on somewhere in the middle, when the audience has had a few drinks and is 'into it'.

They bitch and squabble and The Booker lets fly with a torrent of abuse, cigarette smoke and halitosis.

'You'se'll go on where I tell you'se to! It's my room and if you'se don't like it you'se can all rack off!'

Thus mollified, the whole sorry bunch of would-be troubadours is hustled, still grumbling, into 'the theatre'.

Welcome to the glamour of showbiz. 'The theatre' is a large, gloomy room at the back of the pub with a bar running the length of one wall and a small stage shoved in at one end as an afterthought. Dog-eared rock posters dating back to the punk era adorn the bare, brick walls and strung above the bar is a promotional banner for Jack Daniel's. 'Jack Lives Here,' it proclaims proudly ... a somewhat pretentious boast considering the grim surroundings.

With no backstage area, the up-and-comers take up position at a table to one side of the stage. There is no sign of the new kid and bets are taken as to whether he's 'done a bolt'.

In a sound booth at the back of the room, squats a mangy, dishevelled character. He has long, greasy hair, a ratty beard, and the complexion of a cadaver. He doesn't smell too good, either. He picks his nose and flicks the spotlights off and on, off and on. He scratches his beard, twiddles a few knobs and then shuffles on stage to test the mic.

'One tu ... tu, tu ... one, tu one ... one tu ... two Jews walk into a bar.'

The only response to his lame attempt at a joke is a loud howl of feedback.

Ten minutes to show time and, for what it's worth, the audience is let in. Only fifteen brave citizens have turned up this evening. They look slightly bewildered and a little anxious as though they have come to witness an execution. In many ways, they have. They order drinks, fan out about the room and try to make themselves as comfortable as possible on the sort of chairs usually only found in hospitals and prisons. In a vain hope that more paying punters will show up, The Booker makes the decision to delay the start for half an hour.

An hour later, all is ready. The crowd has swelled to twenty-two, plus a couple of belligerent bikies who refused to pay and have taken up position at the bar. The house lights are dimmed and the first few bars of the Star Wars theme blare out incongruously from the speakers. Show time!

An up-and-comer leaps on stage and before he can get the mic out of the stand, he is heckled by one of the bikies. Wisely ignoring the insult, he launches into a heartfelt but ludicrously fictitious diatribe.

'Good evening, ladies and gentlemen. It gives me great pleasure to introduce to you your MC for this evening. One of Australia's finest comedians and twice winner of the prestigious Perrier award at the Edinburgh Comedy Festival, recently returned from wooing audiences in America! I love this man like a brother and I know you will, too. "Bought" to you at great expense, direct from Caesar's Palace, Las Vegas ... go wild; go crazy; and please welcome to the stage the one and only Mr Buuuuuussster Hymen.'

There will be much carnage as the evening wears on. Some will do better than others but tonight, nobody will kill. It's just not that kind of night. Yet, in a strange way, everybody will get what they came for. The punters will enjoy an evening of cheap and cheerful humiliation. The MC will pick up a few bucks. The Booker will pick up a bikie, and the up-and-comers will gain some precious stage time. As for the new kid ...

Halfway through the show, the MC ducks into the dunny for a leak and a line and discovers the new kid quaking with fear and throwing up in the sink. He's literally too green to know that alcohol and stand-up are a ruinous mix for the uninitiated and the poor, doomed sap has tanked himself up on Dutch courage. He splashes water on his mug and the MC, in a rare moment of benevolence, tells him to relax.

'Just go out there and have fun, mate; they're not such a bad mob tonight.'

Sweating like Elvis at his last concert, the new kid wipes his mouth, attempts a lopsided grimace in the cracked mirror, and then goes completely to pieces when he notices that his whole routine, painstakingly scrawled on the back of his hand with a biro, has now been rendered an indecipherable sweat-and-vomit-stained mess ... and he's on in two minutes.

The MC is back on stage and briefing the crowd that the next guy up is 'doing it' for the first time. The new kid has made his way to the side of the stage and is bemused by the lack of feeling in his legs and by the fact that his balls seem to have shrunk and now appear to be heading on a long, sickening journey to the floor. Seconds before he is about to go on, one of the more depraved up-and-comers saunters over and with a wink, hands the new kid a note. The new kid opens it with trembling hands and reads: 'You will die! You will die! You will die!'

The new kid is vaguely aware that his name has been called and, with great difficulty, manages to get his leaden limbs to carry him up the few steps to the stage. He has the demeanour of a young man stepping up to the gallows. The MC hands him the mic, pats him on the shoulder and disappears down the steps, leaving the new kid feeling more alone than he ever dreamt possible.

He squints into the spotlight and is surprised, but strangely relieved, by the white blinding wall that separates him from the small crowd. The only people he can see are the few faces in the front row who gawk up at him expectantly.

'Make us laugh you sad twat!'

This is it! Nowhere to run; nowhere to hide. Slowly, he brings the mic to his mouth. So close to his mouth, in fact, that what he is about to spout will be totally obscured by distortion and feedback. Words tumble out in a jumbled confusion and his first woeful punch line lands on the stage with a dull, wet thud. It is greeted with silence. Deafening silence.

Not exactly the reaction he had hoped for or anticipated whilst rehearsing with gusto in front of his bedroom mirror that very afternoon. God, how he wishes he were back in his bedroom now. In a desperate attempt to win the audience over, the new kid decides to hit them with one of the few sure-fire gags in his limited schtick. The one that never fails. The one that always cracks his uni chums up, no matter how many times he tells it. Unfortunately, it's a gag of vaudevillian vintage and is met with loud, painful groans.

Time stands still. The room expands, cavernous and cold, yet the stage lights burn bright into the new kid's sweating brow. If silence is truly golden, the new kid has just hit Lasseter's Reef. He's now past the point of no return. Way beyond recovery. But he keeps going. Stumbling towards oblivion. What the hell else is he going to do?

Fear sharpens the senses and within the roaring silence, the new kid becomes aware of whispers, coughs, and the uncomfortable scraping of uncomfortable chairs. The rain beats down on the roof and he can hear traffic in the street. A cop car wails, a plane drones overhead and somewhere, suburbs away, a dog barks in the night.

Things go from bad to worse. The new kid is whimpering now.

'You're not funny, mate!' yells Bikie One.

Not to be outdone, Bikie Two, another budding Einstein of repartee, pitches in with an enthusiastic, 'Faarrkk orf ya' arse'ole!'

The up-and-comers snigger and kick each other under the table.

Finally, after the most gruelling five minutes of the new kid's young life, a spotlight flashes, signalling time up. He mumbles a thanks to the audience (presumably for not lynching him) but now his hands are shaking so badly that he can't get the damn mic back in the stand. The MC materialises on stage and snatches the baton from the new kid who slinks off stage, completely spent. He heads straight for the bar, meekly asks for a beer, lights a cigarette, drags deeply, and then lights another from the tip.

A few of the up-and-comers drift over and introduce themselves, tell him it wasn't so bad, tell him nobody does well their first time up. They don't hang around long, though. They don't linger, for fear that what they have just witnessed with such obvious glee may be contagious in some way ... but not in the same way that laughter is said to be.

The new kid sculls his beer then skedaddles out of the door. Boom! Boom!

WELCOME CABARET
Compere: Sean Tierney Music by: Evris and his Athenians Featuring: Paul and his Dancers. First Performance 9.00 p.m. Ballroom. Second Performance 10.30 p.m. Ballroom. Dancing to the music of Evris and his Athenians will commence after the show until 1.00 a.m.

SEASCAPE
Saturday 3rd November 1973 En route to Las Palmas

Our supreme leader, Captain Tsakos is rarely seen. I'm told he hates to leave his cabin and does so only when absolutely necessary – greeting customs, obligatory show's, cocktail parties, fatal collisions and the like. The officer who really runs the ship is the Staff Captain. His name is Coucoulakis but behind his back, everyone calls him Cocksakis so I will, too.

Cocksakis strikes fear into the whole crew and his rule is law. I'm told he likes to party and chase women the same as the rest of us but

I've also been warned not to cross him. Doing so risks disciplinary measures that include the imposing of heavy fines and, in severe cases of malignancy, being thrown off the ship with a one-way ticket home. It is said that Staff Captain Cocksakis often comes down heavy on new crew just so as they know who's boss from the outset. I had my first run-in with him today.

I was mincing along the Boat Deck on my morning tote ticket round. Admittedly, I looked a bit of a prat, dressed as I was in clogs, very flared loon pants and a multi-striped polo neck sweater. Cocksakis was walking towards me, accompanied by Stuart Pike, the Master at Arms.

'So you're the new *pusti*,' Cocksakis bellowed.

I laughed at the insult to my manhood, which, going by his scowl, I immediately knew was the wrong thing to do. Cocksakis has been working on the cruise ships for donkey's years and his command of English is exemplary. In no uncertain terms, he told me to smarten myself up and not prance about like a big girl's blouse.

'Shape up or get the fuck off my ship!' he barked. As a parting shot, he snarled at me, 'Get a haircut!'

Stuart hung back and warned me that I'd better do as requested ASAP.

After lunch, I changed into some far more respectable clobber and took off to the Beauty Salon on A Deck. I've been advised to steer well-clear of the ship's barber as he's said to be a bit of a butcher who hates long hair.

There are two hairdressers on board. A young Welsh bloke called Phil and a hilarious old French fag called Henri. The many old ducks on board love Phil and Henri and the salon is always full of old biddies baking under a dryer or having their thinning hair dyed blue.

Phil's worked on the Kioni for a couple of years and, though well liked, is said to be a notorious tightwad. Old Henri has worked on the ships forever and has clocked up thousands of sea miles and boyfriends. The current love of his life is a young Greek plumber called Georgios. Henri adores Georgios and tells all and sundry that he dreams of the day when he can have his love child and hopes he hasn't left it too late in life to conceive.

Phil and Henri make a formidable team and are very funny together. They are the best of friends but are forever squabbling like an old married couple. Phil is hetero, likes to shag a lot and won't tolerate Henri dragging trade back to their shared cabin. Henri and Georgios bed down on an air mattress in the hairdressing salon at night and I can't help but laugh when I think about it. The little old ladies who worship Henri would have kittens if they knew what he got up to on the salon floor of an evening. As Phil is the younger and hipper stylist, I got him to give me a haircut as instructed by Staff Captain Cocksakis. He gave me a perfunctory trim, having been on board long enough to know how much length I could get away with.

There was a full dress rehearsal this afternoon and I, along with the other greenhorns, got to try on our costumes for the first time. We all took ourselves very seriously and overlooked the tatty showbiz garb we were forced to wear. Sweat-stained from a thousand shows, buttons missing and ill fitting, held together with safety pins and first night nerves, we put on a brave face.

Show time. Billed as *The Welcome Cabaret*, the show was a combination of old-time musical numbers and passenger talent (or lack of it) quest. Sean was compere and opened with a barrage of ancient and offensive jokes. Next, the ship's band, Evris and his Athenians, launched into *That's Entertainment* and Paul leapt on stage, scaring the willies out of several children who were seated on the floor at the foot of the stage. Fabulously turned out in a pair of black skin-tight pants and white puffy shirt, he was followed, hesitantly, and far less magnificently, by his troupe of timid amateur hoofers.

We did our best but the swell was up tonight and every time the ship rolled, the entire chorus line skittered across the stage and ended up bunched together in one corner. Paul glared at us and herded us back to the centre of the stage, muttering under his breath to 'get it together, Maude' and pinching me on the arse for good measure.

Between costume changes, Sean lambasted the audience some more and, when heckled by a Germaine Greer disciple who accused him of being sexist, got a huge laugh when he shot back 'What? Me, sexist? How would you know, love? You're only a woman.'

For further insult Sean went on to introduce a menagerie of brave, though misguided, performers. A drunken Scotsman with a bad ginger wig played the bagpipes off-key. A precocious nine-year-old tap dancer who fucked up the lyrics to *Somewhere over the*

Rainbow and ran off in tears. An old Aussie in an Akubra hat bored the arse off everyone by doing bush ballads. Some old git from Yorkshire murdered *Stranger on the Shore* on his mouth organ and, not to be outdone by the English Morris dancers, a couple of Krauts in lederhosen slapped each other around the arse for a bit.

The show eventually closed with the whole cast on stage performing a triumphant rendition of *There's No Business Like Show Business*. In all honesty, we had no business in show business.

Surprise, surprise, the captive audience went wild and we left the stage to a thunderous applause. Most of the passengers are simple working-class folk who seem to be revelling in what, for a lot of them, is the first holiday in their lives. Then there's the old ducks who haven't seen a show since vaudeville days. And the late show turned out to be an even bigger triumph as the audience, along with most of the performers, were well and truly sozzled. We were fuckin' stars!

I was so hyped up after the show that I decided to put the hard word on Annie. Liberally oiled with a few litres of duty-free pant remover, she was all over me, the dirty little cow. The problem was I had nowhere to take her to seal our lust. Sean had crashed immediately after the show and Annie shared a cabin with her mum and sister. Guess what? Seeing my dilemma, Paul showed his true colours and, taking me to one side, slipped me the key to his cabin and whispered:

'Darling Maude, if you insist on wallowing in such sordid and unnatural behaviour, I'd feel far more comfortable if you did it in the safety of your mother's house.'

With that, he kissed me on both cheeks and told me to have fun – what a trouper. (I found out later that Paul spent the night in the amorous embrace of an engineer called Anatoli.)

To be honest, I'm still a bit green when it comes to matters of the leg over. Lucky for me, Annie reinvented herself once I got her in the sack. All her inhibitions dropped away and she turned out to be a right little shag monster. She also turned out to be my first experience with 'a screamer'.

Leaving Paul's cabin in the early hours of the morning, we had to skulk past the Radio Room and it was obvious that the officer on duty had been trunking in; he couldn't have avoided the racket that Annie made if he'd tried. He leered at us approvingly, winked, and bade us *kalinichta*. Annie blushed and I felt like a stud.

The public bars closed at two so, after escorting Annie to her cabin, I made my way to the crew mess where I found a party in full swing. It was three in the morning but, as the Kioni would be spending all day and the following night in port, I, and the majority of my crew mates, were officially off duty for the next twenty-four hours. No excuse not to party the night away.

I can't believe all that's happening. I'm twenty years old and off to see the world – and being paid for the privilege. Sure, I put in long hours but my cushy duties can't exactly be termed as work and nobody seems to give a rat's that I don't have a clue what I'm doing. I'm making loads of new friends who, like me, revel in getting drunk every night for virtually nothing. Bar tariffs on board are duty-free but being crew, we're issued with vouchers, which means we pay half what the passengers are charged. A can of beer works out to be eight pence and if we want to buy in bulk from the victualling purser, a bottle of spirits sets us back a mere quid. On top of all that, it looks like I've a regular shag all the way to Australia. Bonzer!

Dawn was breaking when the party finally petered out. Don-the-Slot pulled me to one side and, with Bunger in tow, we made our way up to the Crew Deck situated behind the aft funnel. I was feeling a bit average after the long, eventful night and figured that what I needed was some fresh air. The deck was deserted and the lights of Las Palmas twinkled on the horizon a few miles off the bow. With the coast clear, Bunger pulled a fat joint from his pocket, lit up, then took a few tokes before passing it to me.

'I presume you smoke, old boy?'

Fuckin' A! Floating along on this rusty old tub, a head full of dope and the sky turning orange, I was in heaven.

Bunger's a strange cat. He speaks with a very clipped, upper-crust accent and is evidently the black sheep of a well-heeled family whose background he doesn't normally discuss. As the dope took effect, he opened up and revealed a little of his rebellious background. Turns out his old man is chairman of one of England's largest banks. It was fully expected of Bunger that he follow in the family tradition and spend his life accumulating vast wads of other people's cash. Alas, it wasn't to be and, after being expelled from several prestigious public schools, including Harrow, Bunger failed miserably to gain entry to university.

31

Sick of the constant battles with his old man, Bunger ran away from the stately home when he was eighteen and lived in various squats in London. When not working sporadically in West End bars, Bunger spent his time pursuing his one true passion. Gambling. For the next few years, he squandered every cent he could get his hands on, eventually running afoul of a dangerous loan shark, who he still owes a considerable amount of cash to.

Bunger is, if nothing else, well-connected and managed to secure himself a job with the company that has the franchise to run the duty-free shops on board several ships. Bunger's been on the Kioni for eighteen months, is only twenty-two, but looks a lot older, and is one of the craziest people I've ever met. He's highly intelligent with an amazing head for figures, is always up for a scam, but has a complete disdain for money. He struggles to hold on to any cash for longer than about five seconds and squanders it as fast as possible or simply gives it away.

The nick name 'Bunger' derives from the fact that whenever he enters a restaurant, he immediately 'bungs' the head waiter or *maître d'* a bundle of cash. Not content with this, he's been known to disappear into the kitchens where he'll seek out the head chef, thrust a large wad of cash at him and say, 'Look after us, old boy.' Oh yeah. And he's the only person I've ever known who actually uses the term 'old boy'.

3

Dying for a Laugh

And so it was that on the 16th of January 1996, at the ripe old age of forty-two, I stepped boldly on to the stage at Sydney's Comedy Store and died spectacularly in the arse. (How about that for a mid-life crisis.) But never mind, I had found the thing I'd been searching for. That night, under the spotlight, I was revitalised, reenergised, reinvented and recycled. Better late than never, I had found my true calling. This was it. I would become a stand-up comedian. Wow! What a top idea! Move over Billy Connolly – you Scottish twat!

With a name like mine, I didn't have to piss about with a stage name and since that memorable (unfortunately) first night, Archie has been making audiences laugh, cry, squirm and, at times, demand a refund in all the major (and not so major) comedy venues from Sydney to Melbourne, Adelaide and Perth, plus a host of small towns in between.

I was immediately hooked and got right into the scene, going out and performing three or four gigs a week. In the main, during that first year, most gigs were just five-minute open mic spots, begged or bribed from jaded bookers who begrudgingly dolled out precious stage time like stale sweets. And, like all budding comedians, I died the death of a thousand cuts at first. Those early gigs were not so much a performance but more a form of humiliating target practice with yours truly as the woeful bull's-eye. But fuck it! It was, in no small part, the scary step into the adrenaline-fused unknown that I was getting off on. I was dying for a laugh.

I got heckled a lot but in no time at all, I found that I could usually shut the offending yobbo up with a well-aimed and brilliantly executed put-down – 'oh yeah, well why don't you fuck off, too?' (it was early days).

And then there were nights when I would have welcomed an abusive heckle or two. The bad nights. The worst nights. The nights when a crowd of punters decided, as one, that they didn't think much to the diminutive Pommy git who's lambasting them with his rapier-like wit and sparkling repartee. I don't know of anything more humiliating and degrading than standing on stage, alone and exposed, and nothing – and I mean nothing – you say is working. It gives me the heebie-jeebies just writing about it.

The weird thing is, that even when I was dying in the arse, I'd never felt so alive. Coming off stage, I'd make it to the bar in record time as the crowd would part like the proverbial Red Sea. I'd down a few quick drinks to calm myself then – to avoid further embarrassment – bolt out of the door! Home sweet home. Exhausted, beaten and dejected, I'd drop my clothes on the floor and flop, face down on the bed, drop off quickly and dream of killing the bastards next time. Always next time.

Though, admittedly, few and far between to begin with, I did have the odd killer night and, strangely enough, these were the nights when I found it almost impossible to sleep. Endorphins kicking in like a speed jag, I'd sit up late into the night watching any old crap on TV. I'd swill Scotch and chain-smoke, then make lengthy overseas calls and ramble on into the early hours, boring the arse off distant friends in the UK.

'You should have been there ... I was brilliant ... honest ... I kicked arse ... comic fuckin' legend, me!'

So the good gigs made up for the bad. The deaths salved by the kills. And even the bad gigs didn't seem so catastrophic once I'd become accustomed to being treated like Osama bin Laden at a bar mitzvah. In my limited experience, the trick seemed to be to keep going out on a limb. If material did work, I'd file it away then try out some new, risqué shit and see how far I could push a crowd before they turned into a howling lynch mob baying for my blood.

When I first started making a complete tit of myself on stage, I soon realised that my bolshie attitude, intended to portray cool self-confidence, could often be misconstrued as yet another smart-arse Pommy bastard airing a litany of complaints in the colonies. As mentioned previously, being a Pommy down under can be fraught with peril when it comes to venting one's spleen in public.

Pommies, infamous for their constant whingeing and finding fault in just about anything under the sun (which, by the way, is far too hot in Australia), meant that I had my work cut out for me as soon as I opened my big mouth.

To combat this, I found that if I opened with a bit of self-deprecating Brit-bashing – i.e.: 'You can probably tell from my posh accent that I come from England. I hope you won't hold that against me, it's just backpackers and the Royal family that give Poms a bad name,' (thank god for the Windsors', a veritable mother lode of material) – Aussie crowds would appreciate where I was coming from and would be open to a bit of slagging off when their turn came.

Aussie crowds generally enjoy a bit of baiting but it can be a precariously fine line for a Pommy comedian. I know loads of Aussie comics who crack audiences up on a regular basis with routines based on a *smorgasbord* of grievances. This is considered brilliant, observational comedy. Try too much of that shit as a Pommy, and you could be entering a world of pain. Not that I'm whingeing, you understand.

Now I'm no expert on stagecraft, that's for sure. And it took me years of treading the boards before I hit my stride. Stand-up can be a long and brutal apprenticeship and I only got into it in the first place to have a laugh and exorcise some crazy shit from my noggin. (In retrospect, it would probably have been less painful if I'd had a lobotomy.)

Starting as I did at forty-two, I was well aware that I'd perhaps left my run just a tad late to turn my strange new hobby into a full-time career. But I gave it my best shot and in that first year, for better or worse, clocked up over a hundred gigs.

The unforeseen spin-off that came my way on the tight-knit comedy circuit was all the eccentric and deviant new friends that I made. Performing stand-up on a regular basis meant that, within no time, I knew just about every comedian in Sydney. This came in very handy on tough nights when it became well and truly 'us against them' and, apart from getting a huge blast from one another's deaths, the sense of camaraderie came as an unexpected bonus.

When I first began schlepping on stage, I used to get so nervous I could hardly piss straight. Walking towards the stage, I felt as though I was being led to the gas chamber. (Not a bad name for a comedy club, as it happens.) I still get a bit towie prior to going on, but these days it's become a far more familiar sensation, an anticipated pre-show rush that, once harnessed, can be a positive and dynamic tool. Strangely, no matter how jittery I may be, as soon as the spotlight hits, all anxiety miraculously drops away and I find myself in a different energy-charged zone.

I've seen comedians use an array of novel techniques to combat stage fright. Contrary to popular belief, getting pissed isn't one of them. You won't see much drinking backstage; not pre-show, and certainly not by anyone who is serious about their craft. Most guys just pace up and down like caged circus animals. Running through their routine for the umpteenth time, they chain-smoke, quaff down gallons of water, and swap war stories and gossip with friends. Some meditate. Some do push-ups. I even know of one screwball who performs an elaborate series of unconvincing and half-baked karate moves.

Another crackpot, a piss-funny pal who's currently a regular at the London Comedy Store, uses a simple affirmation that he recites before hitting the stage. Calmly, he points to himself and says 'comedian'. Then he points towards the curtain – in the general direction of the audience – and says 'cunts'. He repeats this dark incantation over and over for a minute or two.

'Comedian ... cunts, comedian ... cunts, comedian ... cunts.'

Then, when his time comes, he strides on stage and, nine times out of ten, blows the fuckin' roof off! You do whatever it takes. Whatever gets you through the night.

In August of '97, I scored my first tour and, with three other unbalanced freaks, played to small, hostile crowds down the south coast of New South Wales. Kicking off in Wollongong, we moved on to Nowra, Batemans Bay and on down to beautiful Bega – home of cheese and unemployed loggers.

The four South Coast gigs were just a precursor for the main tour, which was a ten-day jag up to far north Queensland. I was taken along as the lowly fifteen-minute warm-up dupe, so, although all hotel and travel expenses were covered, there was basically bugger all money in it for me. Fiscal inducements aside, the chance to perform on a nightly basis for two weeks solid was too good an opportunity to pass up and as I was overdue for a respite from the rigours of advertising, I launched into the tour with impetuous zeal.

From Sydney, we flew to Rockhampton where we picked up a mini-van and, for the next ten days, performed in a variety of far-flung tropical toilets as we worked our way up the coast to Cairns. From Cairns, we flew inland to the mining town of Mount Isa. The highlight of the dog-leg into the desert, was landing at the small community at sundown. Hardly a tree in sight and red earth stretching to the horizon, it was an awesome sight. Truly amazing. Like Mars but with less atmosphere. Mercifully, we were only in town for a one-night-stand at the 'prestigious' Mount Isa Civic Theatre. I remember it being an arduous gig with a sparse crowd of only fifty sullen punters in the eight-hundred-seat theatre.

The tour, though not exactly 'a stormer', turned out to be a wild experience. The four of us sharing the thrill of the road. And the flat tyres, breakdowns, miles of monotonous cane fields, and a diet of McDonald's and KFC, gave birth to a flood of gastro-enteritis and new material. We shared laughter, tears and hangovers and when not driving, performing or drinking, we took refuge in run-down budget motels, uniformly depressing dumps with floral wallpaper, plastic furniture and breakfast thrown in.

Treading the boards in pubs, clubs and community centres, we were afforded a whiff of some very rancid backstage facilities and we managed to upset at least one cantankerous RSL club manager. A grizzled alcoholic geriatric, his idea of funny ran to Carry On films and The Goodies. Naturally, he was rendered apoplectic by the language and subject matter of our show. A show that he was solely responsible for booking.

As I recall, we had a big turnout that night and the crowd were with us all the way. Everything was going along swimmingly until our headline act – a particularly filthy bastard – launched into his infamous routine that dealt explicitly with the 'ins and outs' of anal sex. Without warning, the mic went dead and the stage lights blacked out. The manager stormed backstage accompanied by a pair of local goons and we were unceremoniously thrown out of the club. The old fucker refused to pay us, too!

Apart from this one bleak spot, the shows were generally well-received and appreciated in the small, entertainment-starved communities that we played. Dead chuffed, we returned to Sydney in triumph whereupon I was promptly sacked from my lucrative day job.

6.00 a.m. – SS Kioni is Expected to Arrive at Las Palmas Pilot Station.Passengers, please note that there is usually an interval of approximately 2 hours between arrival at the pilot station and the time when the vessel actually docks.In order to avoid congestion, passengers are requested to remain on the open decks, in the public rooms or in their cabins until an announcement is made over the public-address system advising them when to proceed ashore.

SEASCAPE

Sunday 4th November 1973 At Las Palmas

With stoned reptilian eyes we watched the pilot boat motor out to greet the ship, then disappeared below for an early breakfast before going ashore to explore the island. Michael, the chief steward of the mess, was going nuts over the carnage left from the previous night's celebrations and as we walked in, he let rip with a salvo of swear words – English mixed with Greek:

'Fuck, bloody, *pusti*, *malakas*, cunty, buggery, *sta arhidia mou!'*

We took his point and helped the poor old bugger clean up the worst of the mess but failed to budge Reg, the ship's photographer, who'd passed out under one of the tables. He stayed there, obliterated and oblivious, throughout breakfast and was finally roused from his slumber by his frantic assistant, Dirty Charlie, who reminded him that they had only a few minutes to get set up on the quay for the very lucrative gangway shot. Passengers love the gangway shot.

I had a quick shower, dressed quietly so as not to wake Sean, and then went ashore with Bunger and Henri. We ambled around the markets for a while, basically biding our time until the bars opened. Bunger stocked up on litre-bottles of Spanish plonk, Henri bought some clothes for Georgios and I bought a flick knife. Then it was off to the Rex Bar for a liquid brunch.

The Rex turned out to be an infamous gay bar that's been home away from home for legions of seagoing sodomites. Legend has it that Christopher Columbus dropped in for a piña colada on his way to discovering the new world way back in fourteen hundred and something or other, or some such drivel. It was only midmorning but the place was doing a roaring trade as old friends from around the world traded gossip and make-up tips. They all seemed to know Henri but he sat, morosely, guzzling Pernod, bemoaning the fact that his beloved plumber, Georgios, had been forced to stay back on the ship and work.

Following one too many unwanted propositions, I took off on my own and wandered around the small town, marvelling at the sights and sounds of this, the second country I had ever visited. The temperature was only about 25° Celsius but more humid than the hottest day in England and I thought it all very exotic.

But, by now, I hadn't slept for something like thirty hours so I made my way back to the ship with the intention of crashing out for a few hours. The next thing I knew, I was being shaken awake by Sean, who demanded to know where the fuck I'd been as I'd missed out on an almighty bender and ensuing punch-up ashore. Damn!

Sean was completely legless and within minutes, he was sprawled, face down, on his bunk and snoring his fuckin' head off. I was wide awake by now and as the ship wouldn't be sailing until eight the next morning, I got up and dressed with the intention of heading ashore. I was shocked when I noticed it was already past midnight. Shit, I'd slept the day away. So much for exploring the island. Not relishing the thought of listening to Sean snoring all night, I went ashore anyway.

I found a wharfies' bar at the end of the quay and spent the night drinking and getting to know some of the ship's stewards, cooks, cleaners and below-deck rank and file. Just before sailing, I scribbled off a postcard to Judy, just to make her jealous when she realised what an international bon vivant I was becoming. The cow!

The enemy had been unusually industrious in my absence. Forked tongues had been a-wagging.

'Who does he think he is using his time off to make people laugh?'

My 'crime' was considered completely outside of the square. Holidays were for camping and fishing, or a trip to Hollywood on the Gold Coast with the kiddies, or doing a bit of DIY around the house. Even playing bloody golf was considered honourable.

Most of my work colleagues knew of my nocturnal obsession and, though bemused, supported and admired my bravado. But I was always acutely aware that upper management took a far dimmer view.

They saw that what I was doing was, in some way, divided loyalty. All it had taken was a scheming smear campaign from my snivelling boss and I was a marked man – destined for the chop.

The truth is, I in no way deserved to get the bullet. In spite of all the late nights spent on the comedy circuit, I had been careful not to let stand-up interfere with my duties at the agency. But getting the boot had nothing to do with my performance at work. In fact, since discovering stand-up as an outlet, I was a lot happier and healthier and was working my balls off like never before. No, the problem was that I out-performed my boss in every way and, shock-horror, I was actually popular with my staff. I knew it was only a matter of time. I had to go. And I was happy to oblige.

The poor, sad, phoney old kipper actually had tears in his eyes when he attempted to explain the complexities of 'down-sizing' and how, regrettably, he was being forced by the board to make some cuts. He waffled on some more about how he was under extreme duress, being forced to restructure the department and in so doing, my position was to become redundant. Unfortunately, I was being 'let go'. I didn't let him drone on for too long for I had no interest in listening to his bullshit so I simply told him (not very creatively, I must admit) to stick the job up his arse and hand over my fuckin' envelope.

As I'd been with the company so long, I received a whacking great severance pay-out which had been nicely topped-up with a few months' guilt money – this designed to dissuade me from questioning the reason for my dismissal. On top of that, I had a few shares, which I was obliged to cash in on departure, plus a sizeable percentage of superannuation, which (much to the horror of my accountant) I took as cash and rolled over into my now bulging bank account.

For the first time in years, I was cashed up, sorted, and as free as a bird. A week later would find me sitting on the beach in Mexico with a joint in one hand and a great big drink with an umbrella in it in the other.

(I can't resist this postscript – I deserve it.)

True to form, my boss had been lying when he'd informed me that my position was being made redundant. Soon after my departure, he replaced me with a notoriously incompetent pisshead who'd worked for short periods in just about every agency in town.

The guy lasted a month before being fired for coming back legless from lunch one afternoon and making unwanted sexual advances to the CEOs PA. What a tosser!

My boss was then genuinely forced by the board to make my position redundant and he had no choice but to uncharacteristically get his hands dirty and attempt to really run things. Woefully inadequate and now vulnerable, it took him all of six months to run the department into the ground. Three-quarters of the staff walked out, profits began to plummet and, eight months after giving me the chop, he, himself, was given the old heave-ho. He failed, miserably, to attach himself limpet-like to another agency and the last I heard, he was earning a pittance mowing lawns on the Central Coast. Sucked in!

WARNING!

Despite several requests, it has been noted that certain passengers who use the ship's public rooms and decks late at night do so with disregard for their fellow passengers. *UNDUE NOISE AND UNRULY BEHAVIOUR WILL NOT BE TOLERATED.* The Master at Arms has been informed and has full authority to stop such activities.

SEASCAPE

Wednesday 7th November 1973 En route to Cape Town

When I'm not partying or shagging Annie, I'm rushed off my feet doing my bit to keep the passengers amused. If I'm not flogging tote tickets or calling the bingo, there's deck games to organise, swimming tournaments, bar room singalongs, bingo, old-time dancing for the codgers, and discos for the teenagers. There are dart competitions, bingo, fancy dress parades, funny hat parades and knobbly-knee contests. Then there's bingo, ping-pong tournaments, scrabble tournaments, chess tournaments, treasure hunts, quiz shows and bingo, bingo, bingo.

Of course, not all the passengers are enamoured with such naff distractions. There's a contingent of young Aussie backpackers on board – homeward bound after their obligatory year in Europe. They're harmless enough and call us English, Pommies or Poms. I don't think it's meant as an insult; in fact, it's more a term of endearment, especially if the word 'bastard' is tagged on the end.

In the main, they stick together in the bars, drinking all day and night, content to spend the whole trip in a drunken stupor. And who can blame them? The majority appear to be harmless young pissheads but according to Stuart Pike, the Master at Arms, he's been receiving complaints regarding a less benign element and it looks like he's gonna have to start bangin' a few heads together. Maybe loosen a few teeth.

It's Pikey's job to maintain discipline on board and with seventeen hundred passengers and six hundred crew members, he has his work cut out. Pikey, a very tough hombre who relishes his role, is backed up by Zeno, the Greek Master at Arms who's said to be a bit of a psycho. And if things get really out of hand, the two MA's have been known to call on the huge Somali sailors – and nobody wants to mess with them. Enormous to a man, with rows of platinum or gold teeth set in blue-black heads the size of bowling balls, they make for a very scary lot indeed.

I'm told that if a fight does break out, no quarter is given and the misguided troublemaker, after being beaten senseless, is more often than not thrown in the ship's brig for the night. And if that fails to cool their heels, there's always the padded cell. A tiny, airless dungeon – reserved for serial agitators, loonies or anyone endangering themselves or others – it appears to be Pikey's favoured mode of stomping out any dissension or mutinous conduct.

I'm not normally claustrophobic but a couple of nights ago, I was down in the kitchens knocking back a late night ouzo with some of the cooks when Stuart dropped by on his rounds. Much to the amusement of my new shipmates, he spun me round, slapped a pair of handcuffs on and dragged me along a corridor then down a set of metal stairs before locking me in the padded slammer. There's a tiny slot in the centre of the door so as to monitor the loony within. I was only banged up for about five minutes but I squeezed my face up against the slot and pleaded and howled to be let out. Hilarious!

It just so happens that last night, Pikey got to use his torture chamber for real as a particularly feral and permanently pissed young Aussie, who'd been causing trouble since Southampton, went berserk and beat up a Filipino cabin steward. Eventually subdued by a few well-aimed kicks to the head, the drunken jerk, minus a few teeth, was thrown, semi-conscious, into the padded cell where his punishment was only just beginning.

Seeking justifiable retribution, the Filipino victim and his pals kept up an all-night vigil and, taking it in shifts, took turns hurling abuse, piss, shit, lit cigarette buts and a live rat through the tiny slot in the door. According to Pikey, the guy looked very haunted when he was let out this morning and is not expected to cause any more trouble.

Pikey's turning out to be a bit of a hoot who likes to partake in a hit of dope as much as I and the rest of the expat crew. Not many of the Greeks are into dope but as long as we exercise a bit of caution, we run little risk of being busted.

Same goes for the passengers as it happens. It's obvious that several of the young Aussies are not only drunk, but permanently stoned out of their heads. If they're cool, behave themselves and do nothing to upset the harmony of the ship, then Pikey turns a blind eye. Failure to adhere to this simple edict can result in a surprise visit from him late at night. If the dope is not immediately handed over, he'll tear the fuckin' cabin apart to get at the stuff.

Caught red-handed, the unfortunate chump will then have the riot act read to them with dire threats of being thrown off at the next port of call. And special emphasis is given to all of the horrors that may result in being incarcerated in a foreign jail on drugs charges. They will also be informed that (for their own good) their stash is being confiscated and will be disposed of overboard. This last snippet of information is not technically true as what Pikey doesn't keep for himself, he sells on to his dope-smoking pals amongst the crew. Funniest of all, I'm even hearing stories that it's not uncommon for passengers to unwittingly buy their own dope back – buy it back, that is, once it's been recycled throughout the ships unscrupulous and ever burgeoning drug network. Excellent.

4

'Donde estan los banos por favor?'

Acapulco had recently experienced a devastating earthquake and, not exactly in a charitable mood, I headed for the sunburnt splendour of Cancun on the Caribbean coast. The searing white beaches, turquoise ocean and laid-back locals quickly blurred any resentful baggage that I may have been shouldering and within days I had slipped into a far more sedate state than the one I'd left behind.

I was an Englishman abroad. Casually elegant, sanguine and cavalier, with a bursting wallet and without a care in the world. I half fancied myself as a sort of vertically challenged, cockney-flavoured James Bond. Albeit, minus 007's flash motor, licence to kill and legendary pulling power – in fact, bugger all like James Bond. (But that's okay. I wouldn't be seen dead drinking that Martini shit.)

I'd wake early, go for a run and then catch an eight-thirty scuba-dive. Returning for a late breakfast, I'd hit the beach till three and then retire to a favourite bar for a few hours of casual drinking and serious perving.

One such serene afternoon I met Megan and Pamela, two drop-dead gorgeous sisters from New York. We were soon joined by their two travelling chums, the equally breathtaking Kerrie and Louise. The girls, all four in their early twenties, were far too young to be interested in me but being the rare gentleman that I am, I good-naturedly offered to discount the yawning generation gap (just this once, you understand). Not surprisingly, the girls declined my good-natured offer; we did, however, become firm friends as only possible when travelling. They appeared to enjoy my company and I became something of a chaperone, escorting the girls to night clubs and pouring gallons of tequila down their young necks. And so what? It didn't do my battered ego any harm to hang out with such toothsome strumps.

I was having a ball. Drunk as a skunk with my very attractive harem in tow and, just for old time's sake, stoned off my head on powerful Mexican grass. I should have known better regarding the latter. The stuff I scored was so potent that following a brief sensation of giddy euphoria, 'the fear' would set in. One night, I became gripped with such heart-pumping paranoia that I gave my stash to the girls, who appeared to suffer no such ill effects, and henceforth spent every waking hour in a beatific gonzo trance.

Ten days of blissful lunacy later, and the girls returned to breaking hearts in the Big Apple and I trekked off to visit the Mayan ruins of Chichen Itza. The temples and pyramids built slap-bang in the middle of the jungle are mightily impressive but what really blew my mind was the ball court, a huge arena with temples at either end and bounded on either side by towering walls with areas for spectators on top.

From the many stone carvings and reliefs, it is thought that the object of the game was for two opposing teams to run about like silly buggers whilst passing a hard rubber ball about using feet, knees and, specifically, hips. (Come on my son, on me hip!) To score a goal, the ball had to be shot through one of the small stone hoops cemented high up in the centre of each wall. Being extremely difficult to achieve, a nil-all draw would have been the norm. On the rare occasion when a goal was scored, it bought the team immediate victory. Some experts believe that the captain of the winning team then had 'the honour' of being ritually beheaded. Now that's what I call a game. I can only hazard a guess at the cap's pre-game, locker room pep talk.

'Right lads, gather round ... listen up. Now, these Guatemalans shouldn't cause us too much grief. They're a bunch of pussies. They've got no game plan and their defence is a shambles. We're far superior in the air, plus, of course, we've got the home crowd on our side. Right, that's it! Let's get out there and kick some arse! ... Oh! Just one more thing, lads ... erm ... whatever you do ... don't even think about scoring a fuckin' goal. High-fives' all round.'

All very interesting, but following a couple of days of traipsing around the jungle and crawling over ancient Mayan rubble I got a bit towie for the ocean and so headed back to the coast. Destination Cozumel, a small island that lies near the northern end of a magnificent barrier reef of coral that is second only to Australia's (which, of course, is 'Great'). Cozumel is world renowned for its excellent diving, with waters of crystalline clarity and an ocean temperature warm enough to dive *sans* wetsuit.

I checked into a small hotel in the backstreets of the bustling little seaport town of San Miguel and, for the next few days, lurched in and out of the many bars and restaurants in search of adventure. To my chagrin, I soon discovered that San Miguel is a favoured port of call for an armada of cruise ships that transform the little town into a large retirement village as the seafront clogs up with an army of shuffling, geriatric tourists. And then I met Michelle.

She was sitting alone in the beach-side bar, frowning into a book and stealing occasional sips from a bottle of Corona. Bathed in the pink glow of sunset, her raven hair gleamed in the gentle evening breeze. Occasionally, she would push an errant strand back from her face with a small, delicate hand. She was very pretty and looked to be closer to my own age than the New York minxes (she looked to be in her late twenties). She sensed my ogling and turned full-face to reveal mischievous amber eyes, perfectly framed by the beautiful twin smudges of her sculptured black brows.

Squinting into the setting sun, I threw my best 'James Dean' smile, sculled my beer, and then stood up to show off my towering full height of five-foot-six. Unfortunately, I'd been sculling beer for the past three hours and, unsteady on my pins, I banged a knee painfully on the underside of the table and sent a glass crashing loudly to the floor. Now the centre of a lot of unwanted attention, I traversed the short distance to Michelle's table and, without a clue what to say, completely lost my bottle and limped out into the balmy night like a rebel without a brain.

Early the next morning, I was sitting in the bow of a dive boat listening to Carlos, the swarthy Mexican skipper. Bitching about the punctuality of the half-dozen divers yet to show, he stopped jabbering mid-moan, winked at me, then leered at the vision swinging down the dock towards us. Though wearing a baseball cap and with her eyes hidden behind a pair of designer shades, I immediately recognised her as the goddess who'd sapped my courage the previous evening. God, she was just my type. Short – about five three – stunningly cute and most important of all ... female.

I leapt up from the deck and rushed aft to catch the kitbag that she tossed aboard, then made a fool of myself yet again by attempting to take her hand as she negotiated the yawning three inch gap that separated the boat from the wharf. Brushing my hand aside, she leapt aboard and laughed in recognition.

'You're zee guy from zee bar last night. Ow's zee knee?'

Blimey. Music to my ears. A Frog. I thanked her for her concern and assured her that there was no damage done (save for my ego, which I'm sure she'd already sussed).

While we waited for the other divers, she joined me in the bow and we sat in the sun making tentative small talk and watching a towering cruise ship glide past and head out to sea. The decks were lined with crowds of old duffers who waved a chivalrous goodbye to a large chunk of their children's inheritance – recently fleeced from them by the local bandits who posed as shopkeepers. Not so cynical, Michelle waved back and even ventured a good natured *'bon voyage'* or two.

The other divers eventually showed up and on the ride out to the dive site, I learnt that Michelle was not French but Swiss. She didn't give much else away and, doing my damnedest to remain cool, I didn't push her. As it was, the boat was howling along at such a clip that communication was rendered impossible beyond a shout and so we sat, contentedly, side by side, half-hypnotised by the lazy pitch of the boat as it sped over the long, smooth, aquamarine swell.

Our destination was Palancar Reef, a chain of spectacular coral made famous by Jacques Cousteau that, in parts, drops steeply into mile-deep troughs. We were split into two parties of six with a divemaster assigned to each group. The majority of the divers were couples so it was natural and fortuitous that Michelle and I should buddy-up together.

As I was doing the right thing and going through a pre-dive safety check of our well-used hire gear, Michelle conceded to being a little nervous as she'd only obtained her PADI certificate the previous year and had done no open water diving since. Valiantly, I promised to keep an eye on her. Truth is, I couldn't keep my eyes off her.

We stepped off the stern together, adjusted masks, got comfortable and floated on our backs as we waited for the rest of the group to join us. When everyone was ready, Felix, our divemaster, gave the thumbs down and we descended into the awesome submarine world. The vis' was in excess of thirty metres so dropping down the dazzling coral wall was akin to a free-fall-flight. As I looked around to check on Michelle, she laughed into her regulator and gave me a reassuring okay signal.

The dive plan was simple. Descend to twenty-five metres, level out, then simply float along in the strong current and watch the fairy-tale world drift by.

Felix led the way and appeared so in his element that he drifted along with his arms folded and his knees tucked in front as though reclining in a favourite armchair. It took the rest of us a while longer to get comfortable but once I'd sorted out my buoyancy, I simply went with the flow and allowed the current to do all the work. Halfway through the spectacular dive, I was sufficiently zoned-out to adopt an upside down attitude and, facing backward so as to keep an eye on Michelle, I marvelled at the bewitching, chameleonic changes of the reef and the taut athletic figure of the best-looking buddy I'd ever been paired with.

The crystal-clear waters teemed with life. Delicate blue angel fish, black and white striped majors, multihued parrots, clowns and strange, bug-eyed squirrel fish. A shoal of inquisitive barracuda stalked our every move and followed us throughout the dive. We drifted past coral gardens so eerily beautiful as to be adjective-less and past waving sea anemones and lace-like, fire-red gorgoneia. Faced with such stark, natural splendour, I briefly rediscovered religion and thanked God for the wonder of it all. (I don't talk to him much but when I do, it's usually to beg for something.) We were joined by a large, graceful turtle and towards the end of the dive, a huge manta ray came flying along the reef, dropped a wing and veered off into the steely depths like a stealth plane on a secret spying mission.

All too soon, Felix signalled a halt, pointed to his watch, and then gave the thumbs up, indicating that it was time to head for the surface. Michelle banged into me and it was then that I became aware that she was having trouble with her buoyancy. As we began our ascent, she seemed to be having difficulty dumping air from her BCD (Buoyancy Control Device) and was beginning to accelerate to the surface dangerously fast. Checking my depth gauge, I noted that we'd exceeded our planned twenty-five metre depth limit and had bottomed out at thirty-two metres. We'd been down way too deep and way too long for safe recreational diving and a slow, controlled ascent rate was imperative to prevent serious injury from the bends.

She flew past me with a look of panic behind a mask that was fast fogging up and, with more luck than judgement, I reached out just in time, grabbed her legs and pulled her down towards me. Her BCD was now fatally inflated and as Michelle frantically tried to dump air, I noticed that the control on her deflation hose (designed to dump air) was not responding to her increasingly frenzied attempts. Locked together as we were, I realised, with horror, that buoyed by the over inflated BCD we were now a worrying six metres above the rest of the group and rising faster with each passing second. I shook Michelle and looked into her eyes, which were bulging and red with fear. She was shaking her head from side to side and breathing way too hard. Gulping air, she was starting to lose it.

I looked down at the other divers, now an alarming ten metres below us. Felix was waving his hands, desperately – a signal for us to level out; to stay down. Thanks, pal. At any moment, Michelle was going to break free from my grip and rocket to the surface, possibly getting herself killed in the process.

As luck would have it, I knew what the problem was and how to fix it if she would just keep still for a second. I grabbed hold of her hands, reached up and, with one quick motion, pulled sharply down on the toggle attached to the 'dump valve', specifically designed for quick deflation. I grabbed Michelle in a bear hug, squeezed the excess air from her BCD and our upward motion ceased in seconds. She stopped jerking around, her breathing slowed and she put her arms around me as we drifted in the current and waited for the rest of the group to join us.

Throughout the dive, the boat had followed our progress along the reef and now hovered above with a safety bar dropped over the side. We ascended, ever-so-slowly now, eventually grabbed the bar and hung there for a good five minutes so as to assist the body in eliminating excess nitrogen.

Michelle was coming around. She was breathing easy and smiling now. Best of all, she wouldn't let go of my hand. I reached over to her BCD and tried pressing the troublesome deflation hose control valve and, just as I had suspected, the damn thing wouldn't budge. I gave it a couple of twists, pressed it again and it worked fine. I knew what had happened as I had experienced a similar equipment failure the previous year, though at a shallower ten metres. In no danger, I bobbed to the surface like a cork and discovered the problem was nothing more than a small pebble that had lodged in the mechanism. Not an uncommon problem, especially when using dodgy, worn-out hire gear. The real danger is that when things go wrong underwater, they go wrong fast. Once panic sets in, things can turn catastrophic very quickly and spin out of control to disaster.

When we clambered aboard the boat, Felix was pissed off with Michelle but relieved that his lucrative client was none the worse for wear. No mention was made of the poorly maintained equipment or the fact that we'd been literally out of our depth. None of this mattered. Michelle was safe. She was fine. And what could I do? The poor disillusioned girl was smothering me with kisses and jabbering on about how I'd saved her life. I may well have averted a disaster but I was no hero. I'd merely got lucky in identifying the problem and managing to keep my head. But who was I to argue?

That evening, Michelle insisted on buying me dinner and we arranged to meet in a restaurant close to her hotel on Avenida Melgar – the waterfront boulevard. I arrived early, secured a good table, ordered a beer and watched an ancient mariachi band shuffle on to a small stage and crank up their instruments.

Michelle walked into the restaurant and the band skipped a beat. Dressed simply in a white linen blouse and a pair of favourite, faded Levi's, she looked stunning. Over steaming plates of spicy Mexican food and well lubricated with a couple of bottles of fine Californian vino, we exchanged stories.

Michelle worked in a bank in Geneva so I don't imagine she was ever likely to find herself lacking for a gig. It turned out that she was several years older than she looked and, presumably, proud of the fact as she quite unnecessarily volunteered her true age before we'd got to the main course.

'Yes, I am sirty-five.'

I was genuinely shocked and said words to that effect, which, going by her smile, was the spot-on, correct response.

She was a bit of an amateur history buff and, obsessed with anything Mayan, raved on enthusiastically about the past three weeks she'd spent clambering up and down pyramids in Honduras, Guatemala, Belize and Mexico.

We were getting along famously and the effects of the wine sent giddy, erotic fantasies racing around my brain and down to my trousers. She laughed deliciously at my jokes, which were, in truth, a best-of compilation filched from some of Sydney's most talented comedians. Then, over coffee and cognac, she suddenly came over all weepy and dropped a bombshell.

She wasn't wearing a wedding ring but she suddenly took my hand, looked me in the eye and revealed that she was married. (Bollocks!) However, she was unsure of her feelings towards hubby (sounds promising), who was back in Geneva (better still) looking after their six-year-old son.

Blubbering now, Michelle fished a photo from her wallet and I oohed and aahed appropriately at the picture of a cute, little kid sitting on a sledge and grinning, gap toothed, at the camera. She continued on with her sad tale, explaining that her marriage had hit the rocks a few months previously (excellent) when her despicable spouse had admitted to a brief dalliance with her best friend (Bingo!).

Michelle had been so traumatised by the betrayal that she'd taken off on a much dreamed-of sabbatical to the Yucatan Peninsula and all things Mayan ... which is where I came in. I gripped her hand tightly and assured her that I understood her pain ... nay, shared her pain. Understood completely as only a kindred spirit could. Understood as one only too familiar with the stinging lash of betrayal.

She stopped crying and was all ears as I proceeded to divulge my own pitiful saga of deception. Holding nothing back, I told her all about my long-term girlfriend and how she'd broken my heart by having an affair with my ... sob ... sob ... very best friend. About the fateful day when I'd got the call at work and the humiliation of having to learn of the whole torrid tale from 'his' wife. About how they had been witnessed 'doing it' in the laundry of all places.

With bottom lip a-tremble, I dropped my head and gave the shoulders a good old shake. Then, for good measure, scooped a napkin off the table and wiped a flood of imaginary tears from my lying eyes. Though I say it myself, it was, if not an Oscar-winning performance, certainly deserving of a Logie. Michelle was hungry for more details and, on a roll, I went on to explain how the treachery had blown my aching heart asunder and how I was unsure if I could ever put my trust in anyone again.

We sloshed back a couple more cognacs and then Michelle called for the check, then stood up and tottered off to the lavvy. It was as I watched her weaving unsteadily to the back of the restaurant that I realised how drunk she was. As it happens, I was feeling a bit shabby myself.

She was gone for some time and when she finally returned, she looked pale beneath her tan and said sheepishly, 'Archie, I sink I drink too much; I feel 'orrible. Please, we go to my 'otel now, yes?' (Oh alright then; if you insist.)

She fumbled in her purse in a gracious gesture at paying the bill, which I'd already settled, and we tumbled out on to the crowded sidewalk. Sidewalk being the operative word we propped one another up and staggered the short distance to her hotel like a pair of disorderly, though very attractive, hermit crabs. Two steps forward, two to the side, one step back, then start all over again.

Michelle was staying at an up-market joint on the seafront and as we entered the bright, neon lobby, we were greeted by a herd of overweight Yankee tourists who were jostling for attention at the reception desk. Fortunately, Michelle had her room key with her so we skirted the mob and lurched into a waiting elevator. The doors sighed shut and we were in each other's arms. Our tongues met for the first time and we kissed long and furiously, bumped and banged around in the confined space and finally became wedged in one corner.

I stroked the back of her head and slim neck. Caressed a breast, her slender waist, then down to grab her ripe, denim-clad arse. She arched her back and moaned and I pressed my groin into her. She lifted her feet off the ground and wrapped them around me, and we kissed, and sucked, and slurped, and groped, and dry-humped our way up to her floor. The lift doors opened and we reeled out into the corridor and slithered down the hall to Michelle's room. Once inside, she took off to the bathroom, slammed the door and left me to recover from the brief sexual frenzy, and to ponder the fleshy pleasures to come.

My head was spinning and I had a raging hard-on so, in an effort to calm down, I plundered a brandy from the mini bar, kicked off my shoes, flipped on the TV and flopped on the bed. I fiddled around with the light switches in the headboard until satisfied with the right ambience, turned the TV off, and found a radio station playing suitably South O' the Border tunes. I then sculled the brandy and helped myself to another, walked out onto the small patio and sucked on a cigarette. Came back inside, drew the curtains closed, then opened them again. Sat back down on the bed, stood up and sat back down. Turned off the radio and drained the rest of the brandy. I was as jumpy as a sixteen-year-old on a first date. And what was keeping her?

Eventually, the bathroom door banged open and Michelle emerged looking lovely but decidedly green about the gills. Her blouse was open and the top two rivets of her Levi's were undone revealing a tantalising glimpse of lacy, white panties. She staggered uncertainly towards me and then flopped, face down, on the bed, mumbled something in Froglataire, then passed out – dead to the world.

I sat beside her on the bed for a long time, stroking her hair and watching the gentle rise and fall of her breathing. When I was certain she was out cold, I carefully reached beneath her and eased her blouse off her shoulders and tossed it on the floor. I lent over her, kissed her neck, and gave her shoulders a gentle squeeze.

Michelle sighed in her sleep and, after removing her sandals, I gently peeled her jeans down over her perfect, heavenly arse and slid them off. I stood up, picked her blouse off the floor and hung it over the back of a chair along with her jeans. I looked down at Michelle and she looked so gorgeous I felt as though I would, at any moment, expire of a massive heart attack. It was hard but, working quickly, I grabbed a clean sheet from the wardrobe and covered her up to prevent her from being eaten alive by mosquitoes. I scrawled my hotel phone number on a scrap of paper and placed it on the bedside table, then, bending over, gently kissed the back of her head goodnight. The mere scent of her threatening to sap the last of my strength, I turned the lights off and let myself quietly out of the room.

The lobby was deserted now apart from the frazzled employee on reception who eyed me suspiciously as I schlepped out into the night. Alone with my thoughts and a lingering erection, I was far too wired to sleep and stopped in a bar on the way back to my hotel.

The next thing I knew, I was waking, fully-clothed, in my room. The bright Caribbean sun was pouring through the blinds and the band-saw buzz of a mozzie droned in my ear. I sat up and the room spun. I closed the blinds, struggled out of my clothes and went straight back to bed.

The phone woke me at noon. It was Michelle, full of apologies for getting so trashed and full of thanks for taking care of her. We met for lunch but were both so hung over we just sat holding hands and downing gallons of mineral water. We spent the afternoon on the beach, swam in the surf and snoozed in the shade of a palm tree. Michelle didn't wear a bikini but favoured a plain black, backless, one-piece number. She looked so beautiful. Then again, she would have looked great in a hessian sack. That night, we slept together.

The next day, we checked out of our respective hotels and caught the ferry to Puerto Morelos. Relatively free of tourists compared to most resorts along the coast, we checked-in to a quaint little hotel situated right on the talcum powder beach.

I took Michelle sailing and she dragged me around the shops. We couldn't keep our hands off each other, even when we were scuba-diving. In the evening, we had long, candle-lit dinners and powwowed on about everything under the stars. We got drunk. We went dancing. And we fucked like weasels all night long and made love as the sun came up. For a few brief days, we were in heaven. In fact, apart from all the fun and fantastic sex, we were, to all intents and purposes, just like a regular couple.

We had five blissful days and nights together until reality reared its ugly head and the time came for Michelle to head back home and attempt to sort out her marital hassles – for better or worse. Reluctant to say goodbye, and for the sake of an extra night together, I cut my Mexican sojourn short and accompanied Michelle to Los Angeles.

We sat in the crowded bar at LAX, miserably holding hands as we waited for her flight back to Europe to be called. We promised to write – to stay in touch. We even hatched a plot to meet in Paris in the not-too-distant future. But we both knew it was bullshit. We'd had a fantastic and truly memorable time together but, whether we liked it or not, it was time to go back to our respective lives. She had a lot of crap to take care of and I was in no position to start bandying promises of commitment about.

Surprise, surprise, we never did meet in Paris and I don't know if I'll ever see her again. We've spoken on the phone a few times but getting together for even a quick boisterous bonk seems highly unlikely. The last time I spoke to her, she said she missed me and thought of me often but was endeavouring to salvage her bruised marriage for the sake of her kid. Best of luck, my darling. As for me what the hell was I playing at? I had no business falling in love. Been there, done that. In movies and books, people give up everything for love. I'm afraid they don't in my book, though. Sorry.

Wherever I travel, I always do my utmost to respect local mores and customs. As I was in LA, I thought it only prudent to do as the locals do – so the first thing I did was to buy a great big fuck-off gun. (Not really.) No, but what I did do on my very first night in town was to score a couple of grams of not-half-bad coke from the affable barman in my hotel.

I'd been to LA before and as I was only planning to stay in town for a few days, I dispensed with all the usual tourist crap and, so as not to stand out, hired a hot red Mustang convertible. I had a fine old time tooling around town with the top down and a Doors greatest hits CD for company. The coke did nothing for my navigational skills but did help in putting a far more positive bent on the recent loss of Michelle.

With wheels and brain cranked to overdrive, I spent a couple of carefree days getting hopelessly lost on the spaghetti freeways and, one day, wound up in a very dodgy part of South Central LA by mistake.

Another day, I cruised down to Venice Beach and followed the Pacific coast highway to Santa Monica and on to Malibu, where I stopped for a solitary lunch. On the way back to town, I became completely disorientated and found myself up in the Hollywood hills. Screeching around hairpin bends – just like in the movies – I half-hoped I'd get pulled over by the highway patrol just to make the experience all the more authentic. Of course, there's never a copper around when you want one.

I like the States but the almighty dollar rules like nowhere else on the globe. Consequently, I've always found that so long as I keep shelling out endless wads of cash then I'm, more often than not, treated with great decorum and respect. The laying down of the old Pommy patois has never done me any harm, either.

One night I was hunkered down in a bar on Sunset Boulevard that swung to the sounds of Frank Sinatra and Dean Martin. It was a strange but friendly joint and I struck up conversation with the old duck who ran the place. She had a bright-orange helmet for a hairdo and beneath several layers of pancake make-up lurked the looks of what once could have been a much fought-over 'Rat Pack' squeeze. She slung me free drinks all night for no reason other than she dug my accent.

'Oh my God, I love your accent,' she croaked, in a voice cured by decades of gin and Marlborough Lights. 'You're so lucky; I wish I had an accent.'

On my last night in town I paid homage at the LA comedy store – bought the T-shirt – then caught, of all people, Men at Work at the House of Blues across the road. The next day I flew to London.

DECK QUOITS AND SHUFFLEBOARD TOURNAMENT
Anyone willing to organise these tournaments please contact Paul or Archie at the Games Desk between 11.00 a.m. and 12 noon, today.

SEASCAPE
Friday 9th November 1973 En route to Cape Town

As we head south, the weather's becoming warmer and if I do manage to snatch some time off I like to lie out on the crew deck and catch some rays. This is the first time in my life that I've ever had a suntan and I love it. You should see the state of me. I'm burnt to a fuckin' crisp.

I get a buzz out of simply staring at the vastness of the ocean, too. With the attention span of an ant, it's about the closest I'll ever get to meditation and I'm surprised and inspired at the strange mesmerising effect it has on me. My favourite look-out is up on the observation deck above the bridge – the highest accessible part of the ship.

Yesterday, I watched, enthralled, as a lone albatross skimmed effortlessly two feet above the white-crested dips and valleys of the ever-changing waves. And today I looked down to see a pod of dolphins motoring along in the bow wave of the ship that was doing in excess of twenty knots. Sea life abounds and so far, I've seen whales, a couple of sharks, a sail fish, turtles, thousands of dancing flying fish, a giant squid and umpteen unidentifiable sea monsters. My horizons are expanding, the sky is getting bigger and the lump of hash I scored off Pikey last night is fuckin' phenomenal!

As far as I can make out, we're about halfway to Cape Town and have crossed the equator. This morning the pool deck was packed with passengers, there to witness the time-honoured ritual of the crossing the line ceremony. Sean, with false beard, a majestic cape of rubber seaweed, cardboard crown and trident, made for a splendid and noble King Neptune. Paul played the role of 'the doctor', enthusiastically performing various initiation rights on the dozen or so virgin line-crossers who'd volunteered, with glee, to be humiliated in front of their fellow passengers. For a royal entourage, we dressed our chorus line in bathing costumes and crêpe paper and for his queen, Sean chose his current bonk, an elegant, silver-haired old dame in her late forties who Sean chatted up after she had won the glamorous grandmother quest a few nights ago.

The troupe tromped out to the pool with much fanfare and banging of drums and the crowd went mad. Sean, doing a not-half- bad impression of Charlton Heston playing Moses in The Ten Commandments, silenced the crowd and in a booming voice, announced:

'I, King Neptune, my gracious Queen and court, have boarded this vessel to baptise subjects who are crossing, for the first time, the borders of my kingdom commonly known as the equator.'

I was initiated first and found myself manhandled by a pair of strapping, Antipodean 'pirates' who, after roughing me up for the delight of the crowd, laid me prostrate on a trestle table in front of the King and Queen. Sean rattled off some salty mumbo-jumbo and Paul, dressed in nothing but a minuscule pair of sequinned hot pants stepped forward and, with a flourish, tipped a bucket of jelly all over me. Squealing with excitement, he proceeded to rub the lime green gunk all over my body. The crowd hooted with delight and didn't seem to find Paul's obvious concentration on my genitals in the least bit disturbing. Paul then leapt nimbly on to the table, squatted over me and proceeded to rub his boney old arse up and down my bare chest. For a finale, he fished a foot-long, evil-smelling fish from another bucket, slapped me around the face with it a few times and then shoved the thing down the front of my bathers. King Sean, affronted by such obvious breach of etiquette, jabbed Paul in the arse with his cardboard trident and ordered my release. Paul shrieked, called Sean a brute, hopped off the table and I was thrown in the pool by the two pirates. A dozen more victims were 'baptised' in similar fashion, the girls receiving a perfunctionary dousing of jelly and the boys having to endure the old faggot's unwanted groping of their privates.

Tonight there was another dreadful show. Billed as 'The King Neptune Show', we used the same chorus line and basically fucked up the same simple dance steps but to different, hackneyed Broadway numbers. Paul got a bit carried away during *Life is a Cabaret* and, feeling the tempo needed speeding up, screeched at Evris, the band leader, to 'pick up the pace!'. Evris, a very precious personality with a large Zapata moustache and a head of jet-black, back-combed hair, swans about the ship as if he's Demis fuckin' Roussos. Needless to say, he didn't take kindly to having his musical direction questioned by a prancing old poofter like Paul. Evris glared at Paul, called him a *pusti*, unplugged his bizouki and stomped off the stage like the petulant pop star he isn't.

His highly unprofessional behaviour was, according to Sean, nothing new and something he'd seen the 'Greek God' act out on previous voyages. The show carried on without him but at the end of the evening, a huge catfight took place backstage and Sean had to get between the two errant entertainers before they scratched each others eyes out.

Thankfully, the barney did nothing to dampen the after-show party and I managed to get enough free grog into young Annie to coax her up to my cabin for a night of rumpy-pumpy. I knew we'd have the place to ourselves as Sean was entertaining the glamourous granny, aka Queen Neptune, in her Upper Deck suite.

I took Annie on the scenic route and we stopped to blow a joint on the Sports Deck. It was a beautiful, crystal-clear night and we gazed in wonder at the constellations that swayed serenely above as the ship rolled on to Africa.

Annie hadn't smoked much before and she giggled hysterically when I found a piece of chalk and scrawled our names on the deck. Huddled as we were under the steps leading up to the Crew Deck, I explained that our names were now written under the stairs. Annie just about sprang a leak at my stoned humour and I made a mental note to use the same lame gag on other young, vulnerable girls on future voyages.

By now, Annie was completely off her face and, once inside crew quarters, lost the ability to walk. I was feeling a tad shabby myself and to the accompaniment of loud Greek music emanating from the chief engineer's cabin, I dragged her like a sack of potatoes on the final leg of the perilous journey.

As we approached the chief's cabin, where it was obvious that a raucous party was in full swing, the door swung open and Staff Captain Cocksakis stepped out, blocking our way. The rule about taking passengers into crew quarters was flouted and ignored by all but I was sure that I was about to get blasted, convinced as I was that Cocksakis had it in for me. Surprisingly, he said hello to Annie, who smiled sweetly back at him, then stepped back to let us pass. Annie momentarily regained her footing and as we continued on our way, I looked back at Cocksakis who, still standing in the doorway, smiled and nodded his head in approval. I think he's pleased to see that I'm straight, as he hates *pustis*.

Annie came to life once I got her in my cabin. We were both as horny as fuck and I tore her clothes off in about five seconds flat. Meanwhile, Annie had whipped my satin body shirt off but had difficulty unbuttoning my white flared trousers, which are so claustrophobically skintight they leave little doubt that I'm not of the Hebrew persuasion. She finally got the job done and we tumbled, naked, into my small bunk. I worked fast and was inside her warm young pussy in an instant.

Annie stayed the night and we didn't get much sleep. Not, I have to admit, due to my Herculean skills in the sack but more to the fact that my minute bunk makes it virtually impossible for even two child-sized adults to sleep together.

Sean stomped in the cabin at eight and Annie dressed awkwardly under the covers. When she'd left, Sean remarked on her prettiness and congratulated me on pulling such a good-looker. He then went on to spell out, in colourful and lurid detail, his night of passion with the granny. Looks like he'll be spending most nights in her suite, which suits me just fine.

5

Return to Devil's Island

Being a Sunday, the tube out of Heathrow was merely jam-packed as opposed to chock-a-block full. Tired and jet-lagged, I stood with my nose squashed against a grimy window and peered out at the foggy autumn vista and wondered what the fuck I was doing back in Blighty.

Backyards full of junk rattled past. Broken swings, discarded washing machines, abandoned toys, bird baths and garden gnomes. An old man – probably called Fred – stood, bent and bow-legged, puffing on a dog-end in his vegetable patch. Runner beans, potatoes, cauliflowers, brussels sprouts and rhubarb for afters. God. It was all so depressing I was relieved when the train ducked underground and all I had to contend with was my own maudlin reflection, which I silently cursed for ever leaving Mexico.

Billeted at a well-heeled chum's Chelsea pad, I spent the first few days running around town, revisiting old haunts and getting pissed with a retinue of old cronies. I squandered tons of cash, looked up an old girlfriend and hooked up with a mate from the Sydney comedy scene.

Toby had launched himself into the fickle world of stand-up roundabout the same time as myself. A comrade-in-arms, we had witnessed one another's deaths on numerous occasions. At thirty-seven, Toby had left things relatively late to embark on such a challenging vocation. Not as late as myself, I'll grant you, but he was doing it tough.

With his girlfriend, Josie, he was holed up in a fully furnished dustbin above a Chinese takeaway in Hammersmith. Somehow, Toby had got it into his baldy head that to make it as a comedian, it was necessary for him to starve to death in London for a few years. The deluded fool probably had some sort of point to make but, having recently sacrificed my job to the comedy gods, I had no desire to emulate him. Toby had lined me up a couple of gigs.

'They're really good clubs. You wait and see.'

We came out of the tube at Stockwell and trudged the wet pavements, heads down, ever alert for dog shit. Some learned chap once claimed that the streets of London are paved with gold. Well, not anymore, they're not. As for the pavements...Bullshit! Or rather, dog shit! With the possible exception of Amsterdam, London has to be, without doubt, the undisputed capital of the turd world. I kid you not. A minefield of gigantic, steaming barkers' eggs make walking a London pavement akin to negotiating a dog shit slalom course. You've gotta be Jean Claude Kille just to make it down the shops!

We continued on down the boulevard of broken teeth, past countless rows of cheerless shops with Fort Knox grills and doorways full of garbage and lumps of homeless humanity.

'You just wait; you're gonna love this place,' said Tobes optimistically.

We ambled past blocks of drab council flats, flung up in grey abandon sometime back in the sixties. Not for the first time, I wondered what had happened to architecture back in, what was, the most creative of decades. Music, fashion, literature, art, Northern Ireland and Vietnam – everything was exploding. Did the architects of the day miss a meeting? Take the wrong drugs? Didn't take enough drugs?

I took in the glum surroundings and thought of the diamond light of Australia. The pristine beaches, wide open spaces, fresh, clean air and swarms of sun-kissed rumpy-pumpy. I wasn't lucky to have emigrated. I was lucky to have escaped!

We made it to the gig unscathed. A dusty room in the back of an old, stale pub grandly named 'The Grosvenor Palace Hotel'. The pub stood guard at the entrance to a dark and menacing park. A burnt-out car was dumped out front and a stroppy kid in a pork-pie hat was brazenly dealing drugs at the door. I scored some wicked speed.

Predictably, it was just an open mic night with what turned out to be a dead-pan but brutally funny bloke called Brian Damage billed as feature. The MC was a piss-funny old coot of about eighty years old, fresh from his veggie patch and now kitted out in a soccer referee's outfit. For any of the acts who were truly tragic, he'd perform the coup de grâce by trotting on stage, blowing a whistle, flashing a red card and yelling at the poor, doomed turkey to 'Faarrkk orf art of it!'

Toby got on early in the proceedings and, considering his threadbare material, did okay. (To be honest, he was about as funny as a kick in the nuts. I'm just covering all bases in the wafer-slim hope that I happen to get this masterpiece published and he happens to read these words by candle-light in his Hammersmith hovel – highly unlikely, I know.)

I went on last and killed. (No, I really did. I'm not making this bit up.) Not that there were many witnesses to back my claim of theatrical triumph. I guess there were only about thirty people in attendance but ten of them were wannabe comedians. The rest were a very dishevelled lot, half asleep and, by the looks of them, recently evicted from a shop doorway up the road. Oh well, mustn't grumble. As bad as the night turned out to be, it was, after all, my London debut.

Two nights later found us at a karzie in Islington called 'The Purple Turtle'. Talk about the glamour of showbiz. The Purple Turtle made The Grosvenor Palace look like the Albert bleedin' Hall.

We arrived late and what passed for a show was already in full swing. The place was at least full up but, as Toby and I soon discovered, this was only because there was no cover charge. The place was packed full of pissheads, there to get blind drunk and share in the merriment of jeering at a few hapless comedians.

The Purple Turtle was a truly horrible establishment. Not even a proper pub, it was nothing more than a scummy old dive that sold grog. Featuring a floor to ceiling plate-glass window by the front door, the place looked like it had once been a shop or some sort of discount carpet showroom. A beer-soaked bar ran the length of one wall and the pissed punters perched on stools or crammed around several small tables jammed in with barely enough space to walk between.

The location of the tiny stage made for an interesting and challenging set as it was squashed immediately inside the door. On stage, it was possible to keep up a running commentary of the comings and goings of the inebriated punters and wave at the bewildered passengers on the umpteen buses that rumbled to a halt at the stop outside.

What a laugh. As it happens, I fuckin' killed. (No, seriously. I really did. And I'm not making this bit up, either.) It's strange how sometimes the biggest shitholes can turn out to be the best of gigs. Coming off stage to a huge, drunken cheer, I was immediately accosted by a very young, but very scary, waitress. She was a goth-looking thing, with long lacklustre hair and black lipstick. Her pasty face was embellished with a nose ring, an eyebrow ring, and what appeared to be a large metal spike skewered beneath her bottom lip.

Thrusting a sticky glass of warm, flat beer into my hand, she screamed above the crowd (who were now baying for blood as a first-timer was being introduced):

'Well done, mate, you sure as fuck gave it to these cunts!'

Praise, indeed; shame about the rough head.

But two killer gigs in a row. What was going on? I'd only been in London a week and, not wanting to push my luck, I decided on a little side trip to blessed Ireland.

MISSING LUGGAGE:

One dark-brown zipped bag with the name **Mrs Crotch,** Southampton – Auckland, Cabin 546. If any passenger has found the bag would they please contact the B-Deck Pursers Office.

SEASCAPE

Thursday 15th November 1973 At Cape Town

Leaving Annie to sleep, I got up at six and went on deck to catch my first glimpse of Africa. We were only a couple of hours from docking and Table Mountain loomed large in the early morning light. An immense pink cloud covered the top of the mountain and spilled over its edges like a cascade of candyfloss. The old hands amongst the crew had briefed me on the town itself, its limited delights and the harsh, oppressive laws practised by the apartheid government. That aside, I was awestruck by my first sight of Cape Town but felt a certain guilt when we passed Robben Island, where Nelson Mandela is banged up.

Annie was going off on an organised tour with her mum and sister, which left me off the hook to go exploring with some of the boys. Sean, Bunger, Don-the-Slot, Tiny-Tom, Reg the photographer, Phil the Welsh hairdresser, Henri and Georgios made up the nucleus of our landing party. With this posse of pissheads, perverts and drug fiends, I was relieved when Rebecca, the nurse, decided to tag along with us. Rebecca has an on-again, off-again thing going with Tiny-Tom. Poor cow. Tiny-Tom has something going on with just about every female on the ship, the dirty, big, lucky bastard!

Dressed in our finest threads, we cut a fine jib. Unfortunately, the local Gestapo at customs was less than impressed and hassled us for an hour just because they could. Don, Phil and I were taken into a back room and searched and Henri was miffed when he was forced to empty the contents of his Gucci shoulder bag. Thankfully, nobody had been dumb enough to be carrying anything and all Henri had in his 'man bag' was a ton of make-up and his purse. Mid-hassle the unfathomable realities of the apartheid system smacked home when, looking around the customs hall, I noticed a 'whites only' sign on a bench. Fuck it! I think I'll stand!

Eventually waved through customs, we stepped outside and made our way across the quay. After ten 'gruelling' days at sea, it felt good to be on terra firma and, it being such a fine day, the consensus was to begin our shore excursion with a trip up Table Mountain – take in the magnificent view, maybe enjoy a drink or two.

We commandeered a couple of cabs and drove through the bustling rush-hour traffic to the base of the mountain. The ride up in the cable car was just like the guide books boasted – breathtaking. But Georgios had to hold Henri's hand the whole way up and whisper to him not to be afraid. It was quite touching, really.

Most of the gang had been up the mountain before and headed straight to the restaurant, eager to begin the day's liver damage. Don and I ambled off for a short stroll, snapped a few photos and then sat on a bench (whites only) to take in the view.

The pink cloud of early morning had burnt off and the Atlantic stretched to the far horizon, melting in a flawless vignette with the deep blue of the sky. The traffic hum from the city was barely audible and a thousand metres below, the Kioni looked like a toy, tied up with other miniature boats in the port. It seemed inconceivable that the stark, natural beauty of this country is marred by such vicious injustice and suffering. There's so much about this place I don't understand. I wonder how long the bastards can get away with it.

We rejoined the rest of the troops and, after several beers in the sun, caught the cable car back down and split up in search of our own nefarious pursuits. The ship was sailing at midnight so we made arrangements to rendezvous at an up-market bar for evening cocktails.

I spent a very arduous day bar-crawling with Bunger and Reg so the last thing I needed was another drink but when we turned up at six, the place was heaving with crew and we did as required and got stuck into partying along with everyone else.

Situated on the top floor of one of the tallest buildings in the city, the bar was a very swanky joint that appeared to be not only the favoured hangout of half the ship's crew but also the haunt of the town's silverbacks. Grey-haired geezers in penguin suits and old matrons in diamanté cocktail gowns rubbed shoulders uncomfortably with a swarming mass of loudmouthed, inebriated, seagoing rabble. For sure, the only reason we were tolerated is because we were throwing so much dosh across the bar.

I got completely hammered and, in my own personal protest against the apartheid regime, spent the entire cab ride back to the port with my head stuck out of the window as I sprayed the mean streets of Cape Town with vomit. Unfortunately, the black taxi driver was completely underwhelmed by my magnanimous sacrifice and I was forced to hand over double the fare just to shut him the fuck up.

On our walk across the quay, Bunger bumped into an old acquaintance he knew from previous trips. Jacob was a powerfully-built black wharfie with a bald, shiny head whose sparkling eyes lit up when he spotted Bunger weaving unsteadily towards him. His broad smile revealed half a mouthful of very white teeth. Missing alternate gnashers, Jacob had the appearance of having a midget keyboard wedged in his gob. After being introduced, the two went into a conspiratorial huddle and Bunger instructed me to go on ahead as he had some 'business' to attend to.

I crawled up the gangway, stumbled to my cabin and crashed, fully-clothed, on my bunk. Alas, sleep was impossible for as soon as I'd lain down, I was gripped with the dreaded whirling pits. I threw up in the small sink and then went outside to the Crew Deck hoping the fresh, night air would revive me. Standing at the rail, I stared out at the twinkling lights of the city that ended abruptly at the black ramparts of the great mountain. High above, the table top cloud had descended once more and shone, fluorescent-white, in the moonlight.

I nodded off, exhausted, in a deckchair. I don't know how long I slept but when I woke, we'd sailed. Bunger was standing above me and jabbering excitedly as he pulled me out of the chair and dragged me down to the cluttered cabin he shared with the other three shop boys.

Boring Graham was, as usual, akip in his bunk. Boring Graham is only twenty-two but seems to miss the whole point of working on the ships. He's the only one of the expat crew who actually takes the whole thing seriously and is only at sea to squirrel away as much money as possible so as to marry his bird back in Blackburn. And he's so cheap that he makes Phil, the Welsh hairdresser, look positively philanthropic. Boring Graham takes no part in the day-to-day or night-to-night partying on board and he didn't even bother going ashore today. From the looks of the many car mags strewn about, he'd spent an enthralling day alternately drooling on pictures of MGBs and tugging himself over the umpteen snapshots of his beloved Brenda that were taped to the wall above his bunk.

Boring Graham is also a bit suss in that he lives in mortal fear of the multitude of shirtlifters on board, convinced that they're all bent on having their wicked way with his young self. So terrified is he that he even takes the trouble of getting fully-dressed for the ten-yard walk to the communal showers whilst the rest of us prance about semi-starkers or wrapped in a towel. Because of all his paranoid fuss, he's teased mercifully by the queens who blow him kisses, tweak his arse and, on more than one occasion, slide into his bunk in the middle of the night.

'Fookin' queers,' he says in his dull Lancashire accent.

Listen: Boring Graham is so boring that he doesn't even pursue any of the legion of passenger crumpet or crew birds that everyone knows are all gagging for it.

'I'm saving meeself for Brenda,' he drones.

Unlocking his wardrobe, Bunger retrieved a large package wrapped in newspaper and held together with string. After closing the curtain on Boring Graham's snoring form, he laid the package on his own bunk and, with great reverence, unwrapped it to reveal the largest stash of grass I've ever seen. The fuckin' thing was the size of a small Christmas tree.

Bunger had scored the stuff off his man, Jacob, who apparently does his bit for race relations by supplying dope to trusted crew members from all over the world. With a flash of his crew pass and his customary idiot's luck, Bunger had walked the stuff through customs and smuggled on board a wonderful stash of very powerful Durban poison. Being the gentleman that he is, he filled a plastic bag full of heads and 'bunged' it to me gratis. The perfect end to a fun-packed and enlightening day.

I caught an early train to Swansea and a Greek-owned ferry took me across the Celtic sea to Cork – last port of call for the Titanic and birthplace of my long-dead granny on my mother's side. After checking into a small hotel in the city centre, I went out and walked the cobblestone streets of my ancestors and, anointed with several pints of Guinness, felt the familiar, melancholy glow that always descends whenever I journey to the Emerald Isle.

Not a wholly original observation, I grant you. These days, everything Irish is considered cool and people are coming out of the woodwork to lay claim to Irish blood coursing through their veins. And what with Ireland's economic boom and the worldwide success of Irish bands, theme pubs and *River*-bloody-*Dance*, it's nowadays considered downright trendy and, indeed, *de rigueur* to boast of Irish ancestry.

Course, it wasn't always that way. Be Jaysus! When I was growing up, I kept dead shtum about my Paddy connection. Looking back, I recall my Irish rellies as being a bunch of savages. Sporadically employed on building sites, they wore donkey jackets and mud-caked wellies with the tops turned down. They smoked rollies and drank like...well, they drank like Irish navvies. Once pissed, the singing would start. Then the fighting.

That night, I happened upon a pub in Tuckey Street where, instead of the usual diddley-dum music, there was a stand-up show in progress. I sat on my own in a corner and allowed the laughter of the crowd to wash over me like a soothing balm. I felt right at home.

The next day, I hired a car and headed west. Following the coast road to Clonakilty and Skibbereen, then up through Bantry and on to Killarney, I stopped at the end of the day in the postcard-perfect village of Dingle.

Now, how could a place called Dingle be anything other than wonderful? Even the name rings a bell. The narrow streets lined with whimsical, multihued houses painted turquoise, yellow and pink. A small, bustling harbour with a working fishing fleet and a stray dolphin called Fungie who turned up in the early eighties and has been a permanent resident ever since. Best of all, Dingle boasts about five million excellent pubs, a large majority host to a swag of great live music from traditional to rock. So content was I that I stayed in Dingle for the next week.

One unusually fine day, when the soft rain eased and the sun came out, I went scuba-diving. The guys who ran the dive boat thought I was nuts and the skipper made the following observation:

'Now let's get this right. You live in Australia. You have the best beaches in the world, the Indian and Pacific oceans, and The Great Barrier Reef, and you come all the way to Ireland to go scuba-diving.' Then, with emphasis, 'And we have jokes made about us for being tick!'

Point taken, I clambered aboard.

Fungie escorted us out of the harbour and on the way to the dive site, we spied a pair of minke whales basking lazily on the surface. It was an interesting dive through a forest of eerie kelp beds but apart from being spooked by the biggest and ugliest motherfucker of an octopus that I've ever seen, uneventful. After having recently been diving in the Mexican Caribbean, I hadn't really been expecting much and had only decided on a dive in Ireland for the hell of it – for the craic.

Stupid me. What I hadn't bargained for was the icy Atlantic chill. I was wearing a five mil' wetsuit and was only in the water for about thirty minutes but by the time I scrambled back in the boat, I felt as though my dick had shrunk to the size of a peanut. Teeth chattering, I was turning blue with cold so severe that it took half a bottle of Jameson's whiskey before I could stop shaking. The guys on the boat had another good old laugh at my expense.

Yet another fine day, I caught the ferry from Dunquin over to Great Blasket Island, remote, haunted and uninhabited since the fifties and now home to a flock of hardy sheep that cling, stubbornly, to the steep hills. The only other sign of life was a colony of slick black seals that snoozed on the beach like a gang of jumbo slugs.

Apart from the crumbling remains of the small, deserted village, there was bugger all to see on the island but the roller-coaster ride over the emerald waves made the trip worthwhile. I'd been travelling for over a month now and the salty Atlantic spray blew the last remaining cobwebs of corporate bullshit from my soul. Turning full face to the wind, I gulped in the briny air and whooped with the sheer joy of living life to the full and the luxurious indulgence of tooling aimlessly around the globe.

On my last night in Dingle, I was getting well-oiled in what had become a favourite hangout down by the pier. An exceptional band – guitar, bodhran, whistle and uilleann pipes – were making such a wonderful racket they were threatening to lift the roof off Murphy's Bar.

The packed pub was going crazy and, as I sloshed back another Guinness an attractive woman, who looked to be in her mid-forties, sidled over and tapped me on the shoulder. I looked at her and a flicker of recognition stirred in my alcohol-addled brain.

'Don't you recognise me, Archie?' she said. 'Have I changed that much?'

Then it hit me all at once. Incredibly, the woman now smiling at me was an old flame from my dark and distant youth. She was, in fact, one of my first loves, or rather, one of the first women to have granted me an 'access all areas' pass. I remembered her now and if my memory served me right, she used to be a dirty little thing.

But that was a long time ago. Aeons ago. My God, thinking about it, I realised that I hadn't seen her for the best part of thirty years. Her name was Kirsty and we'd had an on-again, off-again thing going way back in '69. The chances of bumping into her all these years later in a small pub on the West Coast of Ireland was truly incredible. We hugged for a long time and then she dragged me through the crowd to a table at the back of the bar, keen as she was to introduce me to her hubby. (Bollocks!)

Her husband, Brian, was an impressive-looking bugger. When he stood up to shake my hand, he towered a good foot above me. Barrel-chested, with an enormous gut, he had the menacing look of a man wholly capable of snapping a neck like a stick of celery. And, with his long, blond, windswept hair and penetrating blue eyes set in a weathered face, his Viking ancestry was never in any doubt. Gripping my hand in a huge, meaty paw, he appeared delighted to meet me. To save any confusion, Kirsty had introduced me as 'an old friend' from her days in London. Thankfully, Brian didn't press for further details but slapped me on the back and took off to the bar to fetch me a pint.

While he was gone, Kirsty sat me down at the crowded table and explained that Brian was the owner and skipper of a fishing boat. The other revellers at the table were his crew and introductions were made all round.

Kirsty was so pleased to see me and, somewhat tipsy, kept giving my leg a squeeze and smothering my cheeks with several wet kisses. She rambled on about old times.

'What was the name of that club we used to go to?' ... 'I wonder whatever became of those freaks who lived in the flat above you?' ... 'Remember the time we went to see The Bonzo Dog Doo-Dah Band and you got me so drunk I threw up on the tube on the way home?'

Brian returned from the bar cradling six pints of Guinness in his ginormous mitts. Accepting the pint, I held my breath thinking, with dread, that, at any moment, Kirsty was going to recall the time she'd let me shag her up against a tree in Hyde Park. To my relief, she snapped back to the present in the presence of her very significant other.

I was thinking how well Kirsty had weathered the years, especially when she informed me that she and Brian had five children. With this, she reached inside her husband's jacket, fished out his wallet and proudly presented me with a photograph of her brood. I never really know what to say when people show me pictures of their offspring.

The best I could come up with was a wan, 'Oh, they're lovely. You're so lucky.'

I vaguely recall leaving the pub way past closing time and, arms linked, crawling up a steep hill with Brian's crew and their respective wives and girlfriends. Kirsty, Brian, and their offspring, resided in an old, very lived-in house overlooking Dingle Bay. The band from the pub had trudged up the hill after us and a huge messy party, apparently in my honour, continued into the wee hours.

I woke on their couch the next morning, my head throbbing from the previous night's excess and from the several blows I'd copped from Aidan – their youngest oik – who was standing over me brandishing a plastic light sabre. He whacked me across the head one more time for good measure and laughed when I tumbled to the floor.

After sharing breakfast with the large happy family, Brian, apparently none the worse for wear, crushed my hand one last time then headed off to the harbour to darn some nets or whatever it is fisherman do when they're not fishing. One-by-one, the kids took off to school and I was left alone in the kitchen with Kirsty.

Over umpteen cups of tea, she once more journeyed down memory lane, recalling, with apparent relish, the time she'd let me shag her up against a tree in Hyde Park. We talked some more and Kirsty seemed distressed with the news that I'd never married and truly saddened on hearing that I was childless.

Time for me to be moving on, we hugged, swapped addresses, promised to stay in touch and said a tearful goodbye. I must admit, I'd felt slightly uncomfortable when left alone with Kirsty. I imagined, with horror, an irate Brian, returning early from his chores, having got it into his head that I, just for old time's sake, had been less than honourable with his adored wife (just as if).

Tempting though it was, I perished the thought and shuddered at the dire consequences. Brian's wrath would know no bounds. Waiting until nightfall, I'd be dragged aboard his boat and trussed up in an old burlap sack. Once clear of the coast, I'd be tossed into the cold, dark sea and weeks later, my rotting remains picked over by hungry gannets on a rocky outcrop somewhere off the coast of Iceland.

Leaving Dingle, I spent the next week driving all over the West Coast and thrashing the shit out of the hire car (which is what hire cars are for). I stayed in a different B&B every night and, once or twice, an ancient, converted castle with suits of armour standing guard in the hall and a satellite dish affixed to the east-wing turret.

Before heading back to the UK, I had one last task to perform. A mission to complete. For some obscure reason, my mother, now in her dotage, had got it into her befuddled head that the kissing of the Blarney Stone was, to people of Irish ancestry, akin to what a once-in-a-lifetime pilgrimage to Mecca is for a Muslim. In fact, she'd been nagging me for years to perform this bizarre ritual for which, she assured me, I would receive 'the gift of the gab'.

On previous trips to Ireland, I'd managed to come up with all manner of excuses so as not to lower myself to such undignified tourist behaviour. Taking a wrong turn on the way back to Cork, I found myself driving into the village of Blarney and, on a whim, decided to get the thing done and shut the old duck up once and for all.

In truth, I was pleasantly surprised by the beauty of Blarney Castle and its surrounds. Sure, the village was full of tourist buses and had more than its fair share of gift shops stocked full of tea towels, shillelaghs and plastic leprechauns. But on the upside, it had several welcoming pubs.

Over the obligatory pint of Guinness, I struck up conversation with a young Aussie larrikin from Perth who, to silence the bleating of a distant Paddy relative, was on a similar crusade to myself. Kevin was backpacking around the world and gave off the spicy aroma of long days on the road between showers. He was rake thin and his sunken cheeks were covered with a patchy growth of dirty ginger stubble. For one so young and scrawny, Kevin possessed an impressive Australian appetite for alcohol and we whiled away several happy hours swapping travellers' tales and knocking back vast quantities of the black stuff.

Now I find Guinness to be a precarious and somewhat hazardous tipple. The first couple of pints slip down with deceptive ease and, seemingly, little effect, resulting in a devil-may-care tendency to knock back a few more.

'Yum yum ... I think I'll have another one of them ... and another ... same again please, squire.'

And so on into the fuzzy afternoon.

Too late and the damage done, I found myself staggering around atop a fourteenth-century castle, swearing and yelling encouragement to my new best friend, Kevin, who is hanging upside-down beneath the Blarney Stone. Gyrating his bony hips, sticking out his hideous yellow tongue and slurring:

'Oh yeah! Give it to me, baby. You know you want it, you dirty slut.'

Egged on by me, the drunken fool was having a pretty good go at shagging one of Ireland's major tourist traps. My mum would have been so proud.

The next day I skedaddled back to Blighty to catch a flight to India.

Afternoon Tea will be served on the Promenade Deck, port and starboard sides, on Boat Deck aft in the swimming pool area (weather permitting), and in the Waikiki Dining Room.

SEASCAPE

Sunday 18th November 1973 En route to Fremantle

When Pikey, the Master at Arms, isn't beating the shit out of the passengers, locking them in the slammer or relieving them of their drugs, he's tossing the occasional old codger overboard – no, really! On every trip, there's at least one elderly passenger who pegs out mid-voyage. More often than not travelling alone, their next of kin are contacted and offered the choice of having granny shipped home at considerable expense or simply dumped over the side for nix.

No prizes for guessing the favoured option. (I don't pretend to understand the ramifications of shipping stiffs around the globe but, apparently, all kinds of health issues, red tape, taxes and bullshit make it a very costly enterprise. A bit futile, too, if you ask me.)

The day after leaving Cape Town, an old duck was found dead in her cabin on C-Deck. She happened to be travelling with her son- and daughter-in-law and, not wanting to bugger up their trip, they wisely opted to have her buried at sea. Very few of the passengers are aware of this practice as the short ceremony usually takes place at dawn. Pikey told me all about it at breakfast this morning.

As the relatives were present, the proceedings were conducted with a touch more decorum than normal. The Captain made a rare appearance, along with Staff Captain Cocksakis, the Chief Purser and the ship's doctor. Four sailors stood to attention, flags fluttered at half mast and, as a further mark of respect, the ship's speed was reduced to dead slow.

A Protestant minister who happened to be on board mumbled a few prayers and then commended the body to the deep. This was Pikey's cue to up-end the custom-built wooden plank and tip the weighted corpse over the side. Unfortunately, the plank hadn't been used for some time and, having been stowed on the rain-swept Rope Deck, had become waterlogged. Granny refused to move. With the distraught couple looking on, Pikey was forced to shake and jiggle the plank as though he were emptying a wheelbarrow full of bricks. Still the old duck stubbornly refused to budge.

Pikey, who had spent a sleepless night humping a very athletic New Zealand girl who's on her way home to get married, was eager to get this added early morning duty over with as fast as possible. Exasperated, he simply reached under the shroud covering the body and with a good shove, sent the old girl tumbling head over heels into the Indian Ocean. He swears she executed three perfect somersaults before piercing the water in an expert, head-first entry.

This fascinating bit of tattle sparked a heated debate amongst the other diners, with Sean – always the wag – suggesting a novel way of spicing up these generally gloomy proceedings.

His brainstorm involved having a few select crew members on hand to act as judges. As Sean saw it, each judge would hold up numbered cards as to the style of the drop, adding or deducting points for execution and difficulty of manoeuvre. Instead of the ceremony being a sombre affair, the event would be a wonderful celebration of a person's life. A right royal send off attended by the entire ship's company. Bunger would be on hand to act as tout, taking bets for points scored and reaping a sizeable profit on the outcome of the final plunge into the abyss (with all profits going to the Seaman's Mission). 'Evris and his Athenians' would play an upbeat, reggae version of *The Funeral March* and at the final moment, the ship's whistle would sound and a huge cheer of farewell would ring out.

Pikey appeared morbidly taken with the idea. His eyes glazed over and, for a moment, I shuddered with the thought that he was seriously considering pitching the concept to Cocksakis. Pikey's worked at sea for something like six years and reckons that in that time, he's chucked a total of twenty-eight stiffs overboard. The weird fucker keeps count!

6

Lonely Planet, My Arse!

India. Mother India. Vast teeming cities, deserts, jungles and the majestic glory of the high Himalaya. India. Home to a billion souls and ancient birthplace of Buddha, Gandhi and Sir Cliff Richard.

I set off happy and full of the buzz and anticipation that a new adventure always brings. And I was pleased to be getting out of the UK and heading to warmer climes as the bleak northern winter was fast approaching.

I'd known plenty of people who raved about India and since my hippy days, had harboured an inkling to go take a geek at the age-old, spiritual subcontinent. Unfortunately for me, making the trip some thirty years too late was a God-awful mistake. I should have known better.

I was too old, too pampered and too steeped in creature comforts to take on such blighted, suffering soil. Being in India sucked all the humour out of me and replaced my customary jocular disposition with a deep, despondent gloom. Some days I felt ashamed to be on holiday in India – as though I were vacationing in a huge, festering rubbish tip. For the life of me, I couldn't see past the pollution, grinding poverty, deprivation, disease and despair. Suffice to say, after blundering through such a bleak, apoplectic landscape for three horrendous weeks, India would wreak gruesome retribution and make me very ill indeed.

I flew into Bombay (yes, I know, the city has been officially renamed Mumbai by the government of Maharashtra State but travellers and locals alike still refer to it as Bombay – so I will, too) at midnight and spent my first two hours in India squashed in a scrum with thousands of fellow doomed travellers as we queued, hot and hung-over from the long flight. Eventually clearing passport control, I joined another queue and finally retrieved my bags from the large pyramid of luggage plonked haphazardly in the centre of the dimly-lit arrivals hall.

Clearing customs without too much hassle, I exchanged a pair of pristine one-hundred-pound notes for a wad of threadbare rupees and then elbowed my way outside. Immediately descended upon by a yowling swarm of ragged touts who all claimed to be my friend, I was seized upon and pulled in the direction of a row of battered black and yellow taxis. Managing to break free from the mob for a second, I lobbed my bags in the back of the nearest cab, jumped in and slammed the door on the melee. The crowd's angry jabbering continued unabated and I was left alone to swelter in the fetid night air. Minutes later, the driver's side door creaked open and an ugly old buzzard who was swathed in a dirty bed sheet peered in at me, smacked his toothless gums and eased himself, with difficulty, into the cab.

I'd done a bit of research on Bombay and knew that hotel rooms were at a premium and so had pre-booked my first couple of nights from London. Even so, my grizzled driver was having none of that. The concept of simply delivering a passenger to their desired destination appeared completely alien to him. In his few words of English, he informed me that my chosen hotel was 'very bad' and assured me that he knew of 'a much better place'. (No doubt, the 'much better place' being an establishment where he would receive a hefty middle-man's baksheesh.)

By now, it was close to three in the morning and, completely trashed, I was in no mood to haggle so I reached for the door as if to get out. My gesture seemed to have the desired effect on the old git and, at the risk of losing his precious Western client, he noisily cleared his throat, gobbed out of the window and coaxed his antique wheels into life.

Once on the move, the driver started haggling over the fare. The cab had a meter but it appeared to be broken and unused. Furthermore, I'd read that after midnight, negotiating a rate was the norm. I was booked into a hotel at Juhu Beach, only a half-hour drive from the airport, and after much wrangling, I settled on a price with the old bandit and he left me alone to take in the sights.

The guide books informed me that Bombay was India's most populous and affluent city but there was little to see as the streets were badly lit, if at all. Indeed, it was as though Bombay was experiencing a blackout. As we cruised the broken roads, minefields of potholes and foot-deep puddles, I couldn't help but wonder if the guide books had got it all wrong when referring to Bombay as affluent, effluent being the word that came to mind when musing on my first impressions of Bombay.

We made it to the hotel whereupon the driver, in a last-ditch attempt to fleece me of as much cash as possible, demanded twice the agreed fare and the haggling began all over again. By now, I was past caring and coughed up the required rupees, to which he coughed up a large ball of phlegm.

'You very bad man. All Christians bad,' he croaked, as I got out of the cab.

Old fucker! I was at a complete loss to know what I'd done to upset him. If I hadn't been so knackered I would have taken great pleasure in wringing his scrawny neck.

There were yet more hassles checking in. The surly dude manning the reception desk claimed to have no knowledge of my reservation and it was only after I'd agreed to pay an extortionate one hundred and eighty dollars US a night that I was miraculously found a room in the hotel that, moments before, I had been assured, was fully booked.

Welcome to India. It was nothing like the brochures, that's for sure. Fuck me! I'd been in the country for less than three hours and already I'd been ripped off twice and mercilessly slandered into the bargain. Alas, I was to learn that the ripping off of Westerners was so endemic and prolific it was like a national sport. Westerners, it appeared, were viewed by the general populous as walking Christmas trees, fair game to be tricked, screwed, swindled, shafted, hoodwinked, conned, duped, bamboozled and chicaned at every twist and turn.

I slept for a few hours then made my way downstairs for breakfast. The hotel was a sinister joint with a gun-toting guard on each floor. The air conditioning rattled on and off sporadically and a hideous barrage of piped muzak tormented guests night and day. Bad enough in itself, what made the muzak even more unbearable, was the fact that there were always two songs playing at once. As I stuffed down a greasy breakfast that tasted vaguely of gasoline, I was serenaded with the schizophrenic sounds of the theme from *The Good, The Bad and The Ugly* and a medley of ABBA hits played on a xylophone.

Pommy Bastard!

Still shagged from the flight and the previous night's hassles, I decided to crash out at the beach for a few hours. Work on my tan. Relax a bit. Ha!

Garish hotels ran the length of the strip, evaporating into the smog in both directions. Clustered incongruously between these overpriced joints, were huddled hundreds of shanties, jerry-built from cardboard boxes, packing crates, sheets of rusty corrugated tin and old tyres and roofs made from a patchwork of dirty plastic sacks.

From these prime beachfront slums gurgled rivulets of stinking raw sewage that snaked down the brown mud to the brown, insipid sea. Oblivious to this toxic shitscape, throngs of happy locals paddled, knee-deep, in the sludge and out in the scummy surf, a bevy of Bombay beach-babes shrieked and giggled as they skinny-dipped ... Indian style ... fully clothed.

I stumbled on, slack jawed, past heaps of rotting garbage, pursued now by a howling mob of hawkers, urchins and beggars. Beating back the crowd, I figured I'd give the beach a rain check for now.

I hightailed it back to the hotel where, outside the gates, sat a pile of rags that, incredibly, turned out to contain a human being. A pair of spindly arms that ended in blunt, black stumps held up a begging bowl and two slits for eyes peered out, imploringly, from a hideously ravaged face ... a horrific face, a face that looked like it had been set on fire and put out with a shovel. I dropped a wad of cash in the bowl and took off for the pool. I found out later that the poor bastard was a leper.

Oh, I do like to be beside the seaside. But not in Bombay, I didn't.

Mercifully, the pool area was segregated from the bedlam of the beach by a ten-foot-high fence, topped with razor wire and broken glass. To ensure added privacy from any gawking riffraff, rows of banana palms had been planted and swayed pretentiously in the sharp, rancid breeze. Perched up in the trees were a flock of large, opportunistic crows that would swoop down and steal scraps of food whenever a guest's back was turned. It was only mid morning but what the fuck! I ordered a beer, buried my head in a book and wished I were somewhere else.

The sensory overload from my morning stroll made it hard to concentrate so I gave up on the book and studied my fellow guests, predominantly well-to-do Indian families and lone Pommy businessmen – podgy, white and jaded.

I got chatting to an old American couple, Clem and Alice, who bitched loudly about the horrendous week that they had just endured. They seemed only too eager to share their tale of woe. Back in the US, they had booked an organised tour of India's sacred sights, travelling in what they were assured would be a modern, air-conditioned coach, full of like-minded codgers and chaperoned by experienced guides. Met at Bombay airport by a flunkey from the tour company, they were horrified to learn that, as the sole punters to have booked the tour, they were to be shunted all over India in a clapped-out minibus. Their driver and 'chaperone' turned out to be a chain-smoking teenager who spoke no English apart from a few guttural phrases picked up, parrot fashion, from celluloid hero and speech therapy doyen, Sylvester Stallone. Clem and Alice had tried to put a brave face on their predicament and in an attempt to salvage what was supposed to have been the trip of a lifetime had endured a week of hell on wheels before throwing in the towel in Agra and catching a train back to Bombay. They were flying out that night, back home to Des Moines, Iowa, where Clem wanted some answers. He got all heated up at the prospect of revenge and his face turned puce and puffed up like a bullfrog.

'When I get hold of that goddamn travel agent sonofabitch I'm gonna kick his butt. Goddamn it, I was in Korea!'

Alice patted his arm tenderly.

'There, there, dear, at least we got to see the Taj Mahal.'

'Goddamn rag heads,' muttered old Clem, darkly.

Alice fished in her handbag and handed Clem a pill, which he gulped down obediently.

'Come along, dear; it's time for your nap.'

As they got up to leave, Alice whispered to me that her husband wasn't supposed to get too excited as he had high blood pressure. Poor old sods.

They shuffled off to their room, the old soldier leaning heavily on his faithful missus, who appeared the stronger of the two. Alice looked back and, being a sweet old duck, I guess she couldn't help herself.

'Have a nice day, dear,' she squawked.

Next up was a couple of local comedians who appeared to have lifted their entire routine from Laurel and Hardy. It was with growing horror I watched as two lackadaisical workmen lugged electric cables around and over the pool then placed two large speakers atop a pair of teetering tripods at either end. Moments later, the relative peace was shattered by a crescendo of Euro disco followed almost immediately by a loud bang then silence.

The Indian families hurriedly gathered their startled children about them and the Pommy businessmen, believing one of the armed guards had gone berserk and was taking pot shots at them (Jihad style), dived for cover.

The speakers crackled and fizzed and sent twin smoke signals racing after the flock of crows who had fled their tree-top eyrie. A grisly bone fell from the burnt blue sky, bounced off the diving board and plopped into the pool. I spilt my beer.

A uniformed *maître d'* came running, anxiously wringing his hands, tut-tutting and wiggling his head from side to side in the Indian way. He apologised to guests and chewed out the two hapless clowns who, after dismantling the ruined sound system, were hustled off to less hazardous duties.

Enough fun for one morning; I decided to see what delights downtown had to offer. I'm not real big on sightseeing but as I didn't intend staying in Bombay for too long, I figured I should make the effort. There was bugger all else to do.

Following some habitual haggling, I hired a cab for the afternoon and bravely sallied fourth on a whiz-bang tour of the steaming metropolis. The sights, sounds and, in no small part, smells of Bombay completely overwhelmed me. The streets, jam-packed with a hooting, honking crush of bumper-to-bumper traffic. Thousands of wheezing clunkers, packed to the gills and held together with bits of string and gaffer tape. Whining auto-rickshaws, taxis driven by hot-tempered zealots, umpteen bicycles and entire families, complete with befuddled granny, balanced precariously on belching motorbikes. Bullock carts and camel carts and decrepit donkeys, heads bowed and labouring under stupendous loads. Saddest of all, clapped-out double-decker buses, choking in the heat and dust, homesick for London.

The cab crawled along at a snail's pace, past rows of perplexing, half-built, or half-demolished, buildings and on the broken pavements trudged a motley soup of humanity, fighting for air and space with a menagerie of mangy wildlife. Goats, pigs, chickens, dogs, scrawny cats, rats and sacred cows all picking and pecking through mountains of fermenting, fly-blown garbage.

Bunged up atop some of the larger, soot-blackened buildings clung massive gaudy billboards advertising the latest Bollywood flick. Variations on the same theme, they more often than not featured a savage-looking brute with his shirt torn off and brandishing a huge, smoking gun, whilst in the background, cowered a ravishing damsel, mouth agape and hands up, dramatically, either side of her tousled head. The giant posters, rendered as they were in a childlike, heavily retouched fashion, made it hard to ascertain whether the damsel was, in fact, in distress or merely a willing, seductive sidekick, playfully pulling a funny face at the baddy whilst his back was turned.

We pushed on, dogged constantly by an army of beggars who risked life and the few limbs that they had left, dodging in and out of the traffic, grovelling and wailing for a handout. The driver, whose name was Ramesh, snarled at the rabble and ineffectively attempted to shoo them away. Then he barked at me to close my window and told me to ignore the pathetic tide of poverty.

Easier said than done, for the majority of the beggars were very young children, filthy and barefoot, with innocent grime-streaked faces that made my eyes sting. More to the point, when I did attempt to wind the window up the handle came away in my hand. I waved it feebly at Ramesh and he growled and rattled off a litany of unintelligible curses.

We rolled on, slow-mo, through the unrelenting, miserable streets, each passing scene a snippet of hell on earth: a young boy, wearing nothing but a pair of tattered Y-fronts, a huge tumor growing from the centre of his chest like a large wobbly tit, a legless beggar on a skateboard and an ancient skeletal crone, so emaciated she would have made the average bulimic supermodel look positively obese. And we drove around a mini-slum, constructed, believe it or not, on a traffic island. Sad as it was, I couldn't help but imagine the estate agent's spin. 'Charming one-room hovel, mud floors throughout, city views.' And the additional tantalising inducement, 'Close to transport.'

First stop, 'The Gateway of India'. A sort of scaled down 'Arc de Triomphe' built down by the port by the Poms in 1924 and now one of Bombay's premier landmarks. A must-see for even the most reluctant tourist, I soon learnt that the monument and its environs were consequently the favoured hangout of the now familiar gang of beggars, vagrants, rip-off merchants, pimps, trinket touts...you name it! I hopped out of the cab and was immediately accosted by a tall, slap-headed holy man who, unsolicited, anointed my forehead with yellow paint, then stuck his hand out for a donation. I was starting to get somewhat peeved with this constant panhandling and so brushed the fake fakir aside, stomped on his bare foot and waded into the fray. I spent the next happy hour doing battle with the beggars and politely declining the many kind offers of 'You want hashish?' and, tempting though it was, a chance to have my photograph taken with a rabid monkey. I knocked back a henna tattoo, passed on having my ears cleaned and reluctantly refused an introduction to a nice Hindi girl, 'very clean ... very young ... you fuck!'

Back in the cab, Ramesh drove me the short distance to the Prince of Wales Museum, famed for its fine collection of dead animals and chock-a-block full of musty artefacts, dodgy works of art, bric-a-brac and various assorted booty that had miraculously escaped being shipped back to Blighty during the glory days of Empire – a bit boring, really.

Next stop, a lovely, rambling old house, for many years the Bombay residence of Mahatma Gandhi and now a shrine to the man oft dubbed the 'Father of the Nation'. Photographs of the old boy in various poses graced the walls and there was a ton of books written by and about the great man. His bedroom has been left, supposedly, just as he left it, with his bed roll and a few meagre possessions: his sandals, a bowl, a few pieces of cutlery, a broken toothpick and a spinning wheel for weaving popadoms.

Next, Ramesh drove me to the Hanging Gardens, high above the city on Malabar Hill. Yippee! A public hanging. What a perfect way to top off the afternoon. No such luck. The gardens turned out to be a crowded, rubbish-strewn park; the main attraction being rows of scraggly bushes vaguely clipped in the shape of, what looked like, obscure Disney characters.

Ramesh and I retired to a bar opposite the park, grabbed a couple of beers and plonked ourselves at a table with sweeping views over the damaged city. Ramesh had struck me as a miserable sod but over a few beers, he loosened up and gleefully regaled me with tales of the many years he'd spent working on cruise ships and travelling the world. Evidently his halcyon days, he'd only returned home to do the right thing by his family and, following an arranged marriage, he'd dutifully done his bit for India's population explosion and banged out half-a-dozen sprogs.

We prattled away contentedly, drank copiously and watched a magnificent crimson sun slink slowly into the Arabian Sea. Rarely had I witnessed a sunset so breathtaking. How unfortunate that the stunning light show was the result of the polluted, crud-filled atmosphere.

The traffic was considerably lighter on the coast road back to Juhu and Ramesh, a happier and far more relaxed driver with a few gallons of beer inside him, expertly tore up the corniche, merrily screaming abuse at anyone who got in his way. We screeched to a halt outside the hotel and, following a congenial twenty-minute haggle, we settled on a fare, which included a tip large enough to put all of Ramesh's six kids through med school. We shook hands, and he weaved off into the early evening chaos and I weaved off to the bar.

On my way, I passed by the same pitiful pile of rags still huddled outside the hotel gates. I wanted to bung him some more cash. Really I did. Unfortunately, when I checked my pockets, I found that I didn't have a rupee to my name. I felt really sorry for the poor bastard. He'd been sitting there all day whilst I was being swanned about all over town and whingeing about it, too. Still, I suppose it just goes to prove the age-old adage that a leper never changes his spot.

The next day, I flew to the capital, Delhi. Basically more of the same minus the polluted beach. After a couple of days of the now-familiar hassles, I made the wise decision to avoid the major cities like the plague and determined to boldly go in search of the real India. For the next few weeks I haphazardly criss-crossed the country, never staying in one place for too long.

I journeyed by train to Shimla, the favoured hill station, a retreat from the heat and summer capital in the days before independence. I liked Shimla. It was scruffy but mercifully cooler than the cities and the hassling was less intense. I stayed two days, did some trekking and, rejuvenated by the fresh mountain air, headed back to Delhi where I caught a flight to Jaipur.

The pink-walled, bustling capital of Rajasthan, Jaipur was also the place where a good friend of mine had come to grief five years previous. Sonia was a beautiful, totally wild and free-spirited girl. A talented artist, she'd worked for me at the agency in the early nineties before heading off overseas. Fit as a flea with an unquenchable thirst for adventure, she was travelling alone around India and, unlike me, appeared to love the place.

One day, I received a postcard from her, which raved on about what a mind-blowing place Rajasthan was and how excited she was to be taking off into the desert on a camel safari. The very next day, I received the tragic news that she was dead. To her peril, she had contracted a very rare form of malaria, which killed her within a week. She was fit, healthy, full of life and dead at thirty. Felled by a mozzie.

I gobbled my malaria tablets diligently. Had taken all the right precautions. Had all the right shots. Insisted on bottled water with my Scotch and never got in any serious strife until the third week of my Indian odyssey.

I found myself holed up in a beachside hovel in Anjuna, Goa, with a hideous dose of the squits. God knows what was wrong with me. I rarely get ill and being a bloke, I'm not very good at it. I've travelled far and wide and have a cast-iron stomach. I've eaten from street vendors in Cairo. Been right through Africa, no probs. Believe it or not, I've even survived a British Rail breakfast!

I never did find out what was wrong me but something wasn't right. I was running a temperature, couldn't stop shaking and was bent over double with excruciating stomach cramps. Most worrying of all, I had blood coming out of places that blood is not supposed to come out of. I was sick as a parrot and I was a bit scared, too.

With thoughts of my friend Sonia's sticky end, I managed to find a friendly local quack who checked me out. Doctor Patel examined me and, to my relief, pronounced nothing serious. Just some strange malady that apparently only attacks 'soft-bellied' Western tourists. He prescribed some antibiotics, told me to rest and advised me to get checked out once back in Australia.

Bollocks! It was time to be heading home anyway. I would be missing out on a planned trip to Nepal and a trek to Everest base camp but I felt it was time to be getting back to Sydney. See what the future had in store.

Once I'd made the decision to head home, I wanted to get out of the place as fast as possible. To tell you the truth, I was a bit spooked by my condition. I made a few calls (not as easy as it sounds in India) to check out flights back to Australia. Picking up an international flight out of Bombay would be no problem but I was stuck down the coast in Goa. When I checked out domestic flights to Bombay, I found that they were booked out weeks in advance. And I'd been on enough packed, rickety trains over the past few weeks for the novelty and romance to have well and truly worn off.

The antibiotics worked wonders and in no time I was fighting fit, though several kilos lighter. Deserving of a bit of well-earned pampering, I moved down the coast and checked into a lavishly expensive joint that overlooked the old Portuguese fort at Aguada Beach. (One hundred and sixty US dollars a night and the electricity packed it in three times a day.)

It appeared that the Pommy package tourist had also discovered Aguada, as swarms of tattooed bricklayers from Huddersfield, and their wives, baked on the beach and bemoaned the fact that 'the coories are mooch better back 'ome'. Once I'd worked out what they were saying, I was forced to concur.

I'm afraid I was bored shitless in Goa. Whatever charms the place had once held had, by the time I got there, sadly got up and gone. I could see that at one time it would have been paradise. But that was probably back in the sixties and seventies when I should have made the trip. Admittedly, Goa was Shangri-La compared to the rest of the country but it looked as though the locals, in their haste to grab the tourist dollar, had done immeasurable damage to the environment. The water was horribly polluted and all along the coast, thousands of palm trees had been ripped out to make way for hotels, half of which appeared to have been abandoned mid-project and were now inhabited by herds of goats or, in some cases, herds of squatting hippies.

I checked in with a travel agent and, for a substantial bribe, managed to secure passage on a ferry that ran between Panaji and Bombay. Great ... a sea voyage ... just what I needed to revive my flagging spirits. I envisaged sunning myself on the sweeping decks as the great subcontinent slipped past to starboard. Sipping G&Ts with a stiff-upper-lipped plantation owner in a pith helmet. We would discuss tiger shoots and Kipling, the spiralling cost of onion bhajis, and debate, at length, a favoured episode of *It Ain't Half Hot Mum.* Then I'd have my way with his nympho daughter before joining the captain in the first-class lounge for pre-dinner cocktails. The captain, a rum-soaked rapscallion on his last voyage, would grant me permission to climb up into the bow and scream into the setting sun (DiCaprio style) 'Cor blimey. I'm the King of the World!'

Alas, the ship of dreams turned out to be a rusty, Scandinavian-built hydrofoil. No sweeping decks and not a nympho in sight. My fellow passengers were predominantly Indian families and burnt-out Western freaks taking the long way home.

Sailing time was scheduled for 3.00 p.m. and we sat, sweltering, together in the departure lounge, a tin shed with several large ceiling fans that, like our mode of transport, refused to budge. Eventually, a couple of hours past three, we were herded aboard, the doors were sealed shut, the air conditioning was cranked up to eleven and blankets were passed out to stave off the sub-arctic cold.

I was travelling club-class, which was the same as economy but with a bar that sold a tantalising selection of warm fizzy drinks and warm beer. It was to be a freezing-cold seven-hour trip and I fell into conversation with some of my fellow shipmates.

A German couple, good people, told me of the fun time they'd been having. They were in India to adopt a two-year-old girl for which they'd diligently secured all the required paperwork back in Düsseldorf. Or so they thought.

Having arrived in India, they'd spent three frustrating weeks being shuffled from one court to the next, the purpose of which, according to them, was to bribe various corrupt judges. At their wit's end and almost out of cash, they were eventually granted permission to take the kid out of the country. The little bundle of joy nestled between her proud parents, dribbling, drooling and, by the smell of it, shitting herself with ecstasy.

The sun went down and a movie came on. I quite enjoyed it the first time around but, on a continuous loop, the damn thing was screened three-and-a-half times throughout the trip. Two hours into the voyage, and I was going nuts and praying that we would hit an iceberg or be gobbled up by a giant sea monster. Anything to put an end to the misery.

Luckily, I got chatting to Vikram (call me Vik). An Anglo-Indian in India to trace his roots, he loathed the place. He'd been fleeced by his relatives in Madras and couldn't wait to get back to his house, his dry-cleaning business and his bird in Doncaster. He produced a photograph of a heavily made-up blonde slapper draped, provocatively, across a motorbike. (Nice body – I think it was a Ducati.) Vik also produced a bottle of cognac and we whiled away the long hours drinking, bullshitting, chain-smoking and watching, over and over, Men in Black, dubbed into Hindi.

We docked in Bombay at midnight and the next day, I flew back to Australia.

If you happen to be Indian, or, indeed, a fan of India, then I apologise for bagging the shit out of the place and admit that maybe I missed the point. I just didn't get it. Millions of souls living in abject squalor whilst banging away producing more sprogs. I read an article the other day that claimed that the population of India increases by the size of the population of Iceland every three days, and by the size of the population of Norway every three months. That's a fuck of a lot of mouths to feed, don't you think? And, despite India's booming economy, more than eighty per cent of its desperate citizens somehow scrape by on the equivalent of less than two Aussie bucks a day. Oh yeah, and India has more people with HIV/AIDS than any other in the world.

Meanwhile, their leaders pour millions into a nuclear weapons programme to rival their next-door neighbour and arch-enemy, Pakistan (another mega-rich nation).

I don't pretend to have a clue as to how to solve the myriad problems that burden India. Yes, India is teeming with life but then again, so is a rubbish tip. Yes, India is steeped in history and I saw some amazing sights. And yes, India does have a way of getting under one's skin – a bit like scabies.

And I met some good people, too. Not everyone tried to rip me off and, in spite of everything, I'm glad I made the trip. I think maybe it was good for me.

These days it makes me wince when I hear some of my wealthier, still-employed friends, banging on about how tough their lot is. They consider themselves impoverished if they don't upgrade their car once a year. Hard done by if they don't make it to the snow at least twice during the season. I let them prattle on for a while. Then I recommend a trip to India.

Lonely planet, my arse!

OLD TIME DANCING
With Harry and his organ. 9.00 p.m. – 10.00 p.m. Main Lounge

SEASCAPE

Friday 23rd November 1973 En route to Fremantle

Groan! Midway between Cape Town and Fremantle, it was show time again. This time, Paul decided to slaughter the Rodgers and Hammerstein classic *Oklahoma* and the whole chorus, including me, were dressed as cowboys and cowgirls. Oklahoma happens to be one of Paul's favourites and, as the wind came sweeping down the plain, he had a fit when he noticed I was managing higher kicks than him. For the late show, I was relegated to the back row and he hissed at me.

'Watch your stepsss, Maude!'

We sailed on across the Indian Ocean. The sea was as calm as a lake and the sun beat down, hotter with each passing day. The lily-livered Pommy passengers, who'd never seen the like of it, baked themselves on deck, turned lobster-red then limped, painfully, to the ship's surgery for sunburn ointment.

We're two days away from Fremantle and the young Aussies, excited to be getting home, have upped their alcohol intake. For the Pommies, the last few days of the voyage are taken up with immigration formalities. Briefings and slide shows are conducted in the Main Lounge by two on-board immigration officers who have spent the voyage billeted in the best suites the ship had to offer – government freeloaders that they are.

The Pommies appear agitated and homesick for England. Their holiday is coming to an end and the unknown looms, ominous over the horizon. Reality is setting in and a lot of them are wondering if they've done the right thing in travelling to the other side of the world in search of a new life.

There's been loads of presentations for the umpteen competitions and hotly-contested tournaments that have taken place throughout the voyage. The rarely seen skipper even emerges from his cabin for these joyful occasions and appears to get a genuine kick out of dolling-out the tacky prizes. Ashtrays, lighters, key rings, packs of cards, ties, towels, T-shirts and caps, all emblazoned with the Cyclades logo, are much sought-after souvenirs.

Last night was the farewell cocktail party. A strict dress code was enforced and Pikey stood guard outside the ballroom to ban entrance to any passengers not properly attired. Young Aussies were forced to wear socks for the first time in weeks and the Pommies, dressed in their finest, queued obediently to shake hands with the Captain and his officers, who stood in line to greet them at the door. Evris and his Athenians played suitable tunes of *The Girl From Ipanema* oeuvre and waiters served unidentifiable *hors d'oeuvres* and watered-down cocktails that tasted like something usually used to remove rust.

Fuelled by the free syrupy grog, a festival atmosphere took hold. As hundreds of passengers seemed reluctant to return to their stifling cabins, the Chief Purser, in a bid to fleece them of their remaining British currency, made the decision to keep the slot machines and bars open until 4.00 a.m.

The cocktail party being my last duty of the evening, I went in search of Bunger and we retired to the calm of the crew deck to see how wasted we could get. Babbling gibberish into the long, warm night, it would have been sometime around 3.00 a.m. when we detected movement down on the darkened Boat Deck. With our night vision shot to pieces by the potent grass, we could just about make out the strange sight of three characters struggling under the weight of what appeared to be a long, rolled-up carpet. With whispered curses, they staggered to the ship's rail and heaved their burden over the side. Peering down, we watched the strange exercise repeated twice more before deciding to investigate further.

So stoned we could barely stand, we took a short cut and, on rubbery knees, negotiated our way, with difficulty, down a rickety ladder to the Boat Deck below. We crept along on all fours and were attempting to stand when a steel 'crew only' door creaked open and three dark shapes emerged. Startled by our presence, they dropped their heavy load on the deck and the largest of the three stepped forward menacingly.

Thankfully, the trio turned out to be friends of ours. Barry, Pete and his twin brother, Jim, were three cockney carpet layers who'd been put on the ship in Southampton by their company, which held the contract to supply carpet to the Cyclades fleet.

Barry, Pete and Jim – 'The Three Carpeteers' as they were affectionately known – had a simple brief. A certain amount of carpet had been loaded aboard at Southampton and all they had to do was keep laying the stuff until it ran out. Their mission complete, they'd be flown back home to England. A straightforward task, the job should easily have been completed prior to arriving in Australia and their flights had already been pre-booked from Perth. The problem was that with no supervision, the boys had been somewhat lax in their duties and had spent the major part of the voyage drinking and partying with the crew. In fact, they'd laid more stewardesses than carpet.

But in spite of all the fun the boys were having, they were very much landlubbers and keen to get back home to their manor, their mates, their boozer and their beloved Millwall FC. At their current rate of production, they'd calculated that the stock of carpet wouldn't be depleted until sometime halfway through the northbound voyage. They'd be lucky to be finished by Panama and were concerned that they wouldn't make it home for Christmas.

Musing on their predicament, they put their heads together and came up with the simple solution of tossing several thousand quid's-worth of Axminster into the Indian Ocean. They figured that nobody would be the wiser as the little work that they had managed to complete was the carpeting of several hundred feet of the ship's corridors. To the untrained eye, it appeared as though they'd been working like Trojans.

Sharing a joint, the three swore us to secrecy and Barry, a scary, pugnacious type with a large scar down one cheek, 'subtly' threatened violence if, by chance, their little secret ever got out.

'If, by chance, our little secret ever gets out, I'll hunt the both of you down and chop your fuckin heads off,' he quipped.

To prove our loyalty, Bunger and I implicated ourselves in the crime and spent the next hour assisting 'The Three Carpeteers' to donate the remaining bales of expensive shagpile to Davy Jones's locker.

7

A Tale of Two Sitcoms

Flying out of India on Qantas was a unique experience. Airline food had never tasted so good. And, as always, one of the highlights of travel is the return home; this especially if one's home happens to be Sydney. It was great to be back.

Christmas was approaching so jobs were scarce. No one was hiring and, to be honest, I considered the prospect of re-entering the corporate world to be totally abhorrent. At least for the time being. I still had enough dough to not have to worry about working for some time to come, so why not kick back and enjoy life in the best city in the world?

I worked out at the gym every morning and then had breakfast at the beach, which is where I'd remain for most of the day. At night, I threw myself into stand-up like never before. By now, I was starting to feel so at ease on stage that I found I could depart from my contrived set list and attempt a bit of ad-libbing. Sure, I ended up down a few comedy cul-de-sacs but I was far more natural and free-flowing and my act was all the better for it.

The festival of greed came and went and towards the end of January, I banged into an old friend of mine. A thoroughly decent chap and one of Australia's finest advertising copywriters – for what it's worth. He was also, like me, between jobs and, like me, totally disenchanted with all the bullshit that had sucked the creativity out of our industry.

Greg got a kick out of the fact that I did stand-up and he'd been to see me perform on several occasions. Being a bit of a wag himself, he would, when appropriate, attempt to inject a humorous spin into his copywriting. Unfortunately, Greg would attempt to inject a humorous spin into his copywriting when it was least appropriate. This erratic behaviour spoke volumes for his patchy employment record.

It was over the course of several beers that Greg first broached the idea of the two of us putting our heads together and writing a sitcom. Wow! What a top idea. Move over Jerry Seinfeld – you American twat!

As the afternoon wore on, our ideas and excitement grew to the point where we wouldn't be merely writing a sitcom but had decided to cast and produce our very own pilot episode. For technical support, we would call on the expertise of another old advertising crony; another out of work lunatic – but a lunatic with over twenty years experience in producing TV commercials. And for cast, we would tap into my many contacts on the stand-up scene. My comic pals. How could we fail? This is it! We're going to be rich! Rich, do you hear? Wealth beyond the dreams of avarice – whoever he is.

Surprise, surprise. Things weren't to turn out quite like that. The whole painful project took us almost eight months to complete. Greg and I tore each other's hair out as we attempted to flesh out plausible scenarios. Eventually, after much blood-letting and umpteen drafts, we had a shooting script.

Alex, our producer pal, produced cameramen and soundmen, and gaffers and grips, and best boys who all donated their time for mates rates or next to nix. Casting turned out to be the least of our problems as every comedian in town wanted to be in on the act. When it came to selecting our stellar ensemble from the hundreds of hopefuls, we employed a straightforward method and simply typecast.

The lead character was a foul-mouthed Jewish megalomaniac who had seen better days. We had simply cast a foul-mouthed megalomaniac of the Hebrew persuasion who had been a star for a bit in the eighties.

There was a part for a stereotypical Italian restaurateur with a bad accent and one eyebrow. We simply cast a stereotypical Italian stand-up comic with a bad accent and one eyebrow.

The part of the laconic, street-wise, black leather-clad satanist was played by a laconic, street-wise, black leather-clad comic and the part of the fat bastard was played with gusto by an even fatter bastard.

The part of the bird with big tits was played by two very good friends of mine and the part of the typical bronzed Aussie surfer went to a young Chinese guy fresh out of drama school. Confused? So was he.

Last but by no means least, the pivotal role of a short-arsed, loud-mouthed Pommy git was played with flair by none other than yours truly.

Several well-meaning people with considerable experience in film and television production questioned the wisdom of casting comedians. 'Comedians can't act,' they would bleat. 'Oh yeah! Ever heard of Robin Williams?' we would sneer back. (I recently read a Robin Williams biography and, egg on my face, discovered that he was a trained actor long before he got into stand-up.)

But we had stars in our eyes and greed in our hearts. There was no doubt in our minds that what we had produced was going to have TV executives drooling at the mouth and reaching for their cheque books. We imagined a bidding war. With such a brilliantly conceived concept, how could we miss? What a cast! What a crew! And, unfortunately, what a fuckin' waste of time.

Looking back, I must concede that if it hadn't been for a dogged blind faith in the mess that we had begun, we would never have been able to keep going through some very turbulent times.

Greg and I ended up writing thirteen scenarios and, under extreme duress, managed to shoot our pilot episode. Luckily for us, an editor friend joined the fray and, with much skill and patience, managed to hack around the forest of atrociously wooden acting.

For an original music score, we roped in a musician friend – an advertising jingle writer. Our brief to him was that we wanted a soundtrack for a sitcom that didn't sound anything like a soundtrack for a sitcom. With zero budget, he jumped through hoops, delivering the goods and some. An untamed cacophony of dirge guitars, crashing drums, organ, whistles and his favoured instrument, a screeching electric violin. For scene segues, our mad maestro sampled police sirens, squealing tyres, screams, howls and the sound of breaking glass. The finished soundtrack sounded like ACDC meets The Clash, with both bands ripped off their tits on high-powered blotter acid. We loved it!

We were breaking all the rules, including the one about canned laughter – there wouldn't be any. We were arrogant advertising wankers and, sick of what we saw as the dumbing down of anything creative, it became our mission to shake things up.

The project wound up costing Greg, Alex and myself a lot of dough. Not so much in production costs, as we only had to shell out for film, props, hire of lights plus a few thousand dollars' worth of alcohol to pacify cast and crew. What really cost us an arm and a leg was the time that it took us to complete the enterprise. Owing to the fact that all involved were donating their time for basically fuck all, we were not in a position to get heavy when it came to shooting schedules and it became a logistical nightmare to coordinate the availability of fifteen or so people at the same instant.

The cast were no problem as the majority of comedians are lazy bastards. Nocturnal creatures, they don't do much during the day except sleep, get stoned or sit about bullshitting and bemoaning their fate with other comedians. But the crew were professional people and we always had to shoot around their availability. The trouble was that, during this time, my two partners and I didn't work in the conventional sense – as in going to a specific place of work and doing some work. There was no money coming in, only flowing out, and we lived off our dwindling savings.

Eventually, we had our masterpiece. For all the effort that had gone in, it didn't look much, physically. A half-hour VHS pilot episode and an A4 document. The document contained a series outline, character breakdowns, support characters, proposed locations, future episode outlines, brief bios on the cast, and information on myself and my two partners – the grandly titled executive producers. After much deliberation and at least one punch-up, we named our epic *Road Rage*.

Why *Road Rage*? Well, briefly (and I mean briefly, as just writing about *Road Rage* makes me want to vomit), the premise of the show revolved loosely around a bunch of oddballs who, communicating via two-way radio, work for a very shonky courier company. The business, fast going down the gurgler, is owned and operated by Luke (played by the foul-mouthed Jewish megalomaniac), whose favoured motivational line to his lacklustre employees is, 'I give the orders. You take 'em.'

Luke's drivers are a motley group of individuals from a variety of socio-economic and ethnic backgrounds thrown together by fate and circumstance. And they'd rather be doing anything than working in the courier business. Through the drivers, we get to see the other side of Sydney and its rich diversity of culture and subculture. The drivers weave in and out of a serpentine plot of twists and take us on a journey through the city not seen in the tourist brochures.

Luke operates his business from a one-room hovel above a takeaway joint run by our stereotypical Italian friend and it is here, at the end of a long day, that the drivers meet to cool their heels and attempt to make sense of the confusing and ludicrous scenarios that their creators had sent them on.

So we were all set. Ready to take on the arduous task of hawking our show around town. Alex had a lot of contacts at the networks and the first one we approached seemed very interested and mightily impressed that we'd gone to the trouble of producing our own pilot. It was only when they'd viewed the fruits of our labour that things went pear.

It had been decided that Alex alone would pitch the show and Greg and I retired to a pub around the corner from the TV station where, between drinks, we composed our Emmy acceptance speech. An hour later, Alex showed up and instead of waving a cheque triumphantly above his head, looked beaten and drawn. After guzzling a large Scotch, Alex ran through what had transpired.

Two execs had listened patiently to Alex's spiel and then deigned to view the tape. Ten minutes into it, the head suit had stood up, thanked Alex for his time and, in no uncertain terms, spelt out that *Road Rage* was not for them. Thanks but no thanks and Alex was shown the door.

Somewhat stunned by the rejection, we retired to the toilet where the three of us squeezed into a cubicle and hoovered up the two grams of coke that we'd earmarked for a perceived celebration. As the afternoon wore on, we took it in turns pouring scorn on the network that had knocked us back and pledging that the bastards would rue the day they'd let a piece of television history slip through their fingers.

Unfortunately, the TV industry is a village in Sydney and I can't help but think that our disastrous first pitch had put the hex on us. They all know each other's business and, over the coming weeks, it became abundantly clear that word had got around about the three advertising wankers who had cobbled together a pilot and now had the gall to think that somebody would actually buy it.

Alex trundled the thing from one network to the other and basically got the same short shrift. Some were more polite than others but the message we got was the same: 'You guys have got to be joking! Thanks but no thanks! Fuck off!'

It appeared that the Australian public were not quite ready to invite such a bunch of dysfunctional deviants into their homes. Not quite ready for a new genre of sitcom with such honest, though colourful, language. (In the pilot episode, four 'get fucks', two 'stick it up yer arses' and a 'bollocks' bunged in for an expected UK audience.) It appeared that there was no way we could compete with the current insipid fodder being spewed up on TV.

Fuck the networks – we belong on cable! And so it was that Alex worked his way down the food chain of production companies and eventually got a nibble. As it happens the nibble was more like a great big bite in the arse, for the company in question were so excited by our show that they immediately nicked the idea and went into production with their own watered-down version. In fact, the cheeky bastards were so impressed with our pilot that they tried to poach our cast. Ha! How they underestimated the unflagging loyalty of our troupe who, to a man, informed the thieving arseholes exactly where they could stick their offer. (Except for one snivelling Judas who, like the production company, must remain nameless.)

We had no choice but to hire an entertainment lawyer. Umpteen letters went back and fourth and veiled threats were bandied about. Now we were throwing good money after bad. We owned the copyright and contents on *Road Rage* but were completely unprotected if, as had happened, some unethical bastard decided to simply nick the idea.

By this time, Greg, Alex and myself were thoroughly sick of the whole affair and increasingly arguing amongst ourselves. It was patently clear that we had all run out of energy. We had certainly all run out of funds and simply couldn't afford to become embroiled in any lengthy litigation. Every time our lawyer sneezed, it cost us money.

The game was up. All our efforts had come to nothing and our dream had turned into a nightmare. Of course, the only way to deal with a nightmare is to wake up. It was time to face facts and the fact was that we had done nothing more than waste a lot of time and money. Admittedly, I've never had so much fun going broke but we'd been kidding ourselves in thinking that we could ever get our effort to screen.

As for the bottom-feeders who poached our concept: they went on to produce their own doomed pilot, then burnt more time and money promoting the thing before eventually admitting defeat and throwing in the towel themselves.

The worst thing about the whole painful episode is that it soured the relationship between Greg, Alex and myself and I rarely see them these days. The last I heard, Greg had a semi-regular job writing real estate brochures and Alex managed to land a gig as an in-house producer at an ad agency. As for me, it was back to the drawing board. Trouble was, I didn't have a drawing board to go back to.

The Entertainment Staff wish to thank all those passengers who participated in the various activities on-board during the voyage.

SEASCAPE

Sunday 25th November 1973 At Fremantle

We arrived off the coast of Western Australia early this morning. According to the blurb in Seascape, Fremantle was founded in 1829, when a bloke called Charlie Fremantle landed here on his ship, HMS Challenger. Fremantle is the port of the city of Perth, a further seven miles up the Swan River ... blah, blah, blah.

At first glance, Fremantle didn't look too enticing. Dull, low warehouses sprawled out blandly to the small town that nestled below scrubby baked hills. The many Pommies who'd be disembarking looked bewildered, nervous and wan as they lined the rails, squinting into the bright diamond light at this strange new land down under.

We were a hundred yards from the quay when a young Aussie larrikin stripped down to his soiled underpants and leapt from the Promenade Deck. The ship's props had been disengaged and tugs were shunting us in so there was no danger of him being sucked through the screws and turned into chum. Even so, the silly bugger was lucky not to have got himself killed when he hit the water with a resounding smack. Disappearing momentarily, he resurfaced to a huge cheer from those lining the rail and the hundreds of well-wishers onshore – there to meet the ship. Acknowledging the crowd, he punched the air, trod water for a minute then struck out for shore with an impressive crawl. When he reached the steps to the wharf he was hauled from the water by a pair of laughing coppers and led away to an unknown fate.

Skipping breakfast, I went ashore with Don-the-Slot and Bunger. It was only eight in the morning but the sun already had some bite in it and a full moon was clearly visible in the bluest sky I'd ever seen.

Keen to soak up some Aussie rays, we caught a cab the short distance to Cottesloe Beach. Only ever having savoured the questionable delights of Britain's pebbly shores, I was completely knocked out by the vast expanse of golden sand that greeted us. The incandescent emerald surf beckoned but, before going in for a dip, Don-the Slot warned Bunger and me to watch out for something called 'rips'.

We dashed down the hot sand and into the welcoming cool of the water, Don diving expertly under the first giant roller that seemed in a desperate rush to get ashore. The wave slammed into me like a brick wall and sent me tumbling backwards in an uncontrollable tumult of skinny arms and legs. The force whipped my new bathers down, shoved half-a-ton of sand up me jacksie and then dragged me under where I gasped and gagged for air. Disorientated, I fought my way to the surface only to be sucked out into deeper water. Bunger had suffered a similar fate and, bobbing to the surface beside me, we clung together as we headed off to Antarctica. Don swam over and, laughing, instructed us to 'stop freaking out like a couple of girls' and follow him as he swam parallel to the shore and out of the strong undercurrent. Easier said than done, it took us ten minutes of intense effort before we managed to crawl, exhausted and bedraggled, out of the surf.

Fuckin' hell! I had no idea waves behaved like that. The waves I was familiar with were of a far more sluggish breed, that came ashore reluctantly at dumps like Clacton. Only about a foot high and brown in colour, they come moping up the excuse for a beach, as if to say 'Oh, I can't be arsed, really. Fuckin' freezin', I am. Bored, too. Think I'll just have a little lie down'. After which they curl over, collapse and die in the mud and rubble. Australian waves, however, appear to harbour a far healthier attitude. Six, eight, ten foot high and, having travelled thousands of miles, they can't wait to get ashore and come screaming in as though they want to shag the beach!

We spent a pleasant few hours alternately baking and trying not to drown, then took off in search of lunch. Don, hailing from Sydney, was pleased to be back in Australia and proud to show off the delights of this corner of his gigantic homeland. Trouble was, it being a Sunday, the place wasn't exactly pumping. Furthermore, Don assured us that there was no point going into Perth as the city was dead on a Sunday. According to his expert opinion 'like a fuckin' morgue with shops – all closed'.

We hailed a cab and left it to the driver to find us a restaurant. The old cabbie was a sullen-looking alkie with a large blue nose shot through with veins. He didn't say much but pointed out places of interest along the way with his swollen, varicose conk. The baking-hot noon-day streets were so devoid of life that I felt like I was in a scene from *On the Beach*, the sixties film starring Gregory Peck, which was shot in Australia and concerns the lonely quest of Peck and his crew of submariners as they searched for signs of life following a nuclear conflagration. The places of interest along the way were all pubs and it seemed the old pisspot couldn't wait to finish his shift, plonk his arse on a bar stool and continue to sup his life away.

He pulled up outside a restaurant called the Tum Tum Tree, a cook-your-own-steak joint on the outskirts of Fremantle, and, after palming Bunger's large tip, bade us farewell with a friendly, 'Good on ya, boys.'

The steaks at the Tum Tum Tree were gigantic and, it being my first experience with the famed Aussie barbie, I managed to burn my jumbo-sized piece of flesh to a crisp. Having been raised on a paltry, working-class Pommy diet, I was as full as a doctor's wallet in no time and only managed to get through a quarter of the thing before admitting defeat and giving up.

We trudged the deserted streets until the pubs finally opened at four; universally run-down dives full of wharfies, frontier types and sad, broken Aboriginals bludging drinks. Worse still, the draconian licensing laws meant that the bars had to shut up shop a mere three hours later at seven ... seven! We ended up in the first (and last) pub in Australia, which is just a short stagger across a wooden footbridge from the quay. Last orders were called and we were back on board ship soon after.

The vast majority of the expat crew take the precaution of putting a little distance between themselves and their chosen illegal substances prior to docking in any port. Certainly, it's a wise move to ensure that one's cabin is 'clean', as Customs always target crew quarters, turning over selected cabins at random. I stashed my grass along with Bunger's, in his favourite (top secret) hidey-hole. Far from prying eyes or sniffing dogs, located in a seldom-visited part of the ship, our precious dope lay secreted in a rusty cavity behind an air-conditioning duct, high in the superstructure between the funnels.

It being unwise, if not downright bad form, to retrieve any drugs prior to departure I, for want of nothing better to do, went in search of Annie. She'd be disembarking in Melbourne so was still mine for a few days. I found her out by the pool, where she was sharing a bottle of cheap Aussie champers with her sister and mum. Annie looked an eye-full; scantily clad in a tiny strawberry-pink top and matching miniskirt, she was very tanned from a day spent cycling around Rottnest Island.

A stiff breeze blew the last of the heat out of the day, a blood-red sun disappeared over the horizon and Annie snuggled into me. Emma, Annie's mum, handed me a glass of the warm, sticky wine and, as I took a sip, she waved the bottle menacingly at me and squawked out of the blue:

'I hope you've been taking precautions with my daughter. She's not old enough to be a mother. More to the point, I'm too young to be a fucking grandmother!'

Spluttering on the cheap champagne, I assured her that I had, indeed, taken every precaution with her young daughter. Unfortunately, Annie wasn't on the pill and, though I hate the damn things, we must have gone through a rubber plantation of condoms since our first tentative shag in the Bay of Biscay. Emma burst out laughing, as did Annie and her sister Sarah, pleased with my obviously uncomfortable reaction to the forthright question. Annie elbowed me in the ribs, bit my ear and snuggled in closer. Horny now, I dragged her back to my cabin for a brisk fuck before dinner. And, yes, I took precautions.

Oh fuck! It was time to get serious. The game was up and I was left wallowing in the fallout of disastrous optimism. The past year had certainly not been without incident but when I looked back, all I had to show for it was an extortionately expensive globetrotting bender and a crude home video starring a bunch of drunken idiots. I'd just about blown all of my agency bunce and the sitcom had sent my umpteen credit cards into meltdown. There was nothing else for it. I would have to do the unthinkable and get a job!

Putting my wounded pride to one side, I chased up every headhunter in town. The very same headhunters who, up until a year previous, had kept up a non-stop barrage of fawning phone calls begging me to hire one of their artists. I was in a position of power then but now that the boot was well and truly on the other foot, it was all most of them could do to return my calls. I didn't get one interview in two months of grovelling. Things were closing in. Life was imploding and I didn't know where to turn.

What to do? Inertia was setting in and, as I pissed my last remaining shekels up the wall, a grim acceptance that life may never be the same again. No overseas trips. No squandering money on designer clobber. No expensive restaurants. No posh birds and, perish the thought, the bleak realisation that I may never smell that new car smell again. What to do?

Now there's nothing I'd like more than to claim that my next brainstorm was in some way heaven-sent. A bolt out of the blue, so to speak. The truth is that, with bugger all else to do, I decided I'd write a book. Wow! What a top idea. Move over Jeffrey Archer – you toffee-nosed old lag!

But, seriously. Why not write a book? Writing a book can't be that hard, can it? Surely its just a matter of bungin' down a load of words, one after the other. The only tricky bit, as I saw it, was making sure that the words were actually arranged in some semblance of order. How hard can that be? And bollocks to a structured narrative.

And so it was that in the spring of '98 I bought a clapped-out laptop and began pecking away at my magnum opus. I got right into it, too. I got right into it for about three days before the novelty wore off and I realised that there might just be a bit more to this writing caper than I'd first thought. It had never occurred to me that writing might actually be hard work!

Luckily, I had an easy out. Life got in the way and my literary pretensions were plonked on the back burner as I gradually began to pick up the odd bit of freelance. One thing led to another and all too soon I found myself once more embroiled in the hurly-burly world of advertising. Desperate for cash and not in a particularly strong bargaining position, I wasn't picky when it came to assignments. I worked on all kinds of rubbish just to keep the wolf from the door. Meanwhile, my clapped-out laptop gathered dust in a cupboard.

Sandwiches, Meat Pies & Potato Chips are available from the Marine Bar (weather permitting).
Sandwiches, 8 cents. Pies, 10 cents. Chips, 12 cents.

SEASCAPE

Saturday 1st December 1973 En route to Sydney

A fierce storm lashed us in Bass Strait last night and it looks like we'll be late into Sydney. The new passengers who'd joined us in Fremantle, Adelaide and Melbourne turned every shade of green through to grey and once more, the decks, foyers, passageways and public rooms became a hideous skating rink of stinking vomit. Several old codgers went arse over tit and the ship's surgery was kept busy dispensing seasick tablets and mending broken bones. Don-the-Slot was nearly killed when a slot machine became dislodged and crashed into a glass display cabinet, missing him by inches.

The storm kept most of the passengers in their cabins but I was amazed how many old biddies managed to hobble along to bingo. Now that we're well and truly in Aussie and heading north, the official ship's currency has changed from British sterling to Australian dollars and bingo costs a buck a game.

Prior to the storm, the last few days have been uneventful and, apart from flogging tote tickets and calling the never-ending bingo sessions, I don't have much to do. The new passengers are left alone to settle into shipboard life and the old passengers ready themselves for disembarkation.

It was pissing down with rain when we pulled in at Adelaide early on Wednesday morning. We were only scheduled to be in port for six hours and, with no particular plans, I got off the ship with Bunger, Don, Phil and Henri with the intention of simply going for a short walk. Typically, we got as far as the nearest boozer, an early opener that catered to the thirsty wharfies and waterfront workers who'd been loading and unloading ships all night long.

Several large gentlemen wearing moth-eaten singlets and faded shorts lined the bar. They eyed us suspiciously as we walked in and laughed in unison when one wag slammed his beer on the bar, wiped the foam from his beard with the back of a gnarled hand and roared:

'Jeez! Check out the Sheilas!'

Henri made to leave but Bunger saved the day by laughing even louder and promptly shouting them a round.

They turned out to be an amicable, knockabout bunch and we stayed in the pub for hours, swapping stories and sharing ciggies, jokes and numerous frothy ales. As it happens, we only just made it back on board before the ship sailed.

More water under the bridge would find me bidding a tearful farewell to Annie in Melbourne. Along with her sister and mum, she's spending six weeks holidaying with relatives in Australia before catching another Cyclades ship, the Austral Star, back to England.

As it turns out, my older brother, Bobby, will be on board. He's a ship's printer and worked on the Kioni before signing off for the European summer. The last time I heard from him he was having a blast but, just about skint, was looking forward to getting back to sea. His Kioni slot having been filled by Tiny-Tom, he's signed on the Austral Star and will be shipping out in a few weeks' time. I told Annie I'd write to Bobby, assuring her that he'd look after them – show them a good time. She boohooed in my arms, told me how much she was going to miss me and we said our goodbyes. As I didn't have a clue if and when I'd ever see her again, I crossed my heart and told her I'd stay in touch and crossed my fingers and told her I loved her.

Allowing a good half-hour for my broken heart to heal, I ventured ashore to drown my sorrows with Tiny-Tom and Bunger. It was late morning and the dock area was almost deserted. As we ambled up to the customs gate, the bored officers ushered us into their small office.

Seeing we were crew, they decided on a bit of fun and, before allowing Bunger and myself entry to their fair city, ordered Tom to fetch them half-a-dozen 'coldies' from the pub at the top of the hill. Tom did as he was bid and returned, ten minutes later, with six cold stubbies for the thirsty coppers.

We caught a cab into the centre of town, skulked around the shops, got drunk, happened on a cinema showing *Deep Throat* and were back on board by early evening. That night, I crashed out early for once.

I woke the next morning in a cold sweat, having endured a terrifying nightmare in which I was getting married to Annie after putting her up the stick. It was the gentle swaying of the ship that told me we'd put to sea and all was well. Leaping out of my bunk with relief, I was immediately bought back to reality when I stepped painfully on the upturned plug from Sean's stereo that, along with the rest of his belongings – including his clothes – lived on the floor.

Limping down to breakfast, I bolted down the usual fare of greasy eggs and bacon, which, as usual, had been liberally adorned with several thick black hairs from Michael, the steward's, moulting head. The gossip around the breakfast table concerned the platoon of Greek crew who'd jumped ship in Melbourne. Apparently not an unusual occurrence, as Melbourne is said to have the third largest concentration of Greeks outside of Athens – home away from Homer?

8

Close to the Wind

Two years flew past and I scraped by. The freelance work paid okay but it was sporadic and I never knew whether I'd be working from one week to the next. Then I was offered a six-month contract by an ad agency that specialised in retail crap and junk mail. I was put in charge of the advertising for one of Australia's largest electronic goods retailers. Not the most glamorous of gigs but it beat sleeping under a bridge.

When the contract was up, a large salary was waved under my nose and I was offered a full-time job running the art department. Okay, money isn't everything but being broke isn't anything. I decided to take the job for a year – just to get straight, you understand. It turned out to be, without doubt, the busiest and most soul-destroying job I've ever had but, being a greedy little fucker, I did it anyway. Being a greedy little fucker, I did it for the next four years.

The heavy workload typically consisted of at least three brochures (junk mail) with a combined print run in excess of eight million a month. The brochures were supported by point-of-sale ticketing and augmented by magazine and press ads. I was responsible for the day-to-day running of the department, print buying, approval of colour proofs, mentoring and training of staff, creative direction and maintenance of style and branding ... blah, blah, blah ... same shit different shovel.

The constant deadlines were doing my head in and, at times, I was so stressed out I'd throw up after meetings. If it hadn't been for the release that stand-up brought, I think I would have gone nuts. And it was only my morbid fear of poverty that had me stick it out for so long. I was well and truly back on the treadmill. What was I thinking?

I was running down the beach one sharp winter morning when God tapped me on the shoulder. A strong southerly wind was howling across the harbour and flying erratically towards me down the beach was what appeared to be a large flock of multicoloured parrots. Drawing closer, I realised, with growing horror, that the flock of birds was, in fact, umpteen copies of the latest brochure that I'd spent the past month pulling my hair out over.

That stupid brochure represented countless meetings, fights, tears, late nights, panic attacks and thrown phones. And for what? To advertise a bunch of landfill that's been manufactured by slave labour in Asian sweat shops.

I turned around and the flock of brochures swirled mockingly about me and pursued me along the pristine beach. And as I jogged home, every house that I passed had one of the stupid things poking out of a letter box. This was my contribution to the well-being of the planet. I'd gone from a career-high of running my own art studio in the eighties, designing album covers, to churning out junk mail on a computer twenty years later.

Ten long years had slipped past since my treasured drawing desk had been given the heave-ho by technology. On Monday morning, I resigned.

> Whilst In Port, passengers are advised that the Swimming Pool, Ship's Shops, Barber's Shop, Beauty Salon, Shore Excursions Office, Radio Room, Library, Photographer's Desk, Baggage Room, and Playroom, will be closed.

SEASCAPE

Sunday 2nd December 1973 At Sydney

We arrived at Sydney pilot station in the middle of the night and had to wait until dawn before entering the heads and making our slow progress up, the old hands assured me, the most beautiful harbour in the world.

Sydneysiders waved from ferries, yachts and pleasure craft, tugs hooted welcome, and the Kioni replied with several long blasts that reverberated around the harbour. I stood with Paul on the Observation Deck above the bridge and he informatively, though unnecessarily, pointed out various beaches, parks and pick-up joints where he'd been sucked off over the years.

We were tied up at Woolloomooloo by 7.00 a.m. and, scrambling across a wobbly plank that had been precariously positioned between the kitchens and the quay, Tom, Don, Phil, Bunger and I had disembarked even before the first gangway went down.

We made our way through the Customs hall then outside, where we had breakfast courtesy of the United States Navy. The leviathan bulk of the aircraft carrier, USN Kitty Hawk, was tied up alongside the Kioni and, with the Vietnam War still raging, the crew had set up, in a goodwill gesture, several food stalls along the quay. To the chagrin of the nearby established pie cart, Harry's Café de Wheels, a few mangy protesters had magnanimously put their placards to one side and rubbed shoulders with smiling black cooks, who doled out complimentary hamburgers, hot dogs, pancakes and Cokes.

We hung around in the sun and got chatting to half-a-dozen Yankee sailors who, revelling in their short shore leave after several months at sea, pestered Don on the best place to pick up chicks. Don assured the horny mariners that they couldn't go wrong in the pubs of Paddington but once out of earshot, he laughed and let on that 'Paddington is full of poofters'. Rotten sod.

Don buggered off home to Avalon to spend the couple of days we were to be in Sydney catching up with his surf buddies and being pampered by his mum. The rest of us caught a cab to Circular Quay and jumped on a ferry. We had no plans other than to spend the day sightseeing and exploring the intoxicating city. Maybe a bush walk in one of the excellent national parks, visit the zoo or take in a gallery or two. Ha!

Things started out innocently enough with the morning spent sunning ourselves on Manly Beach. Then it was back across the harbour for a boozy lunch in the shadow of the Opera House, followed by a predictable pub crawl around the Rocks. Sometime during the blurry afternoon, we bumped into Nick, my aptly named purser friend, who divvied up the pilfered profits from the numerous bingo sessions.

Midnight would find us in a Greek club in Newtown, gleefully hurling plates at Cocksakis who, *methizmenos* (pissed), was wobbling unsteadily around the dance floor, whooping and hollering and waving a hanky enthusiastically above his head as he lead a conga line of dancers in a sort of Hellenic 'okey-cokey.

I was to learn that the club was a favourite with the Greek crew and it appeared that half the ship had turned out to celebrate the turnaround point of the voyage.

The band grew louder, gallons of beer, retsina, ouzo and Metaxa brandy was sculled and a huge, messy bender of behemothesque proportion was enjoyed by all. I'm afraid I ended up *poli methizmenos* (very pissed).

Well, that was six months ago. I don't have a clue what the future holds but as I'm getting on a bit, I don't intend to waste any more precious time. Sure, I'm going broke again but what's new? Nothin' I can't handle. For what it's worth, my love life is sporadic but mercifully uncomplicated; I'm healthier than I've been in years; have given up the fags and rarely take a drink these days. (I just made that last bit up.) Meanwhile, I've dusted off the clapped-out laptop and, to my surprise, we're becoming quite chummy.

In a week's time I'm taking a break and crewing on a yacht in this year's Sydney to Hobart. (It's my second go at the race. My first attempt a few years back ended in near disaster when the yacht I was on hit a submerged object and began taking on water at an alarming rate. We never made it to Hobart but limped into Eden two days after leaving Sydney.) If I don't get swept overboard in the middle of the night and end up in the belly of a white pointer, I'll keep on pecking away at this book in the New Year. And I swear I'll finish the bugger this time. (The race and the book.) And why not? After all, you're only old once!

'A man hath no better thing under the sun than to eat and to drink and to be merry.' (Ecclesiastes 8:15)

SEASCAPE
Monday 3rd December 1973 At Sydney

Planet Earth and I don't even know how I made it back to the mother ship. I woke up, got up, threw up and crawled straight back to my bunk. Tiny-Tom and Bunger burst into my cabin at noon, insisting that I join them on an excursion to Bondi Beach. Begging to be left alone to die in peace, I told them to fuck off! Undeterred,

Tom assured me that he merely wished to visit the famous beach to check out Australia's national obsession. Sounded healthy enough. And now that I was an expert in the surf, an exhilarating dip in the Pacific could be just the tonic I needed.

A cab dropped us on the seafront but instead of heading for the beach, Tom led the way to a large white boozer on the main drag. Groan! Here we go again. I should have known better. The national obsession Tom was keen to check out was nothing more predictable than the quaffing of gallons of fine Aussie beer. Bunger, completely unscathed from the previous night's excess, shouted drinks for half the bar and, within no time, we were once more aglow with the bonhomie of being young, drunk, cashed-up, footloose and free!

Tom knew one of the curvaceous barmaids. A dalliance from a previous trip, she was a very leggy, very fit young thing, who was clearly pleased to see Tom. Once she'd finished her shift, she joined us at our cluttered table, sculled Tom's beer and then dragged him outside where the two lovebirds tumbled into a cab and disappeared.

Bunger and I decamped to a seafood restaurant at Watson's Bay called Doyles and once seated at the best table in the house (after Bunger had 'bunged' the head waiter a healthy wad), we settled in for a long, leisurely lunch.

My worldly friend ordered the house speciality, a gigantic seafood platter, the likes of which I'd never seen before. Noting my wide-eyed confusion, Bunger explained the various shellfish, molluscs, creepy-crawlies and bottom-feeders that made up the mountain of food. Crikey! The only seafood I'd ever eaten was deep fried in batter and came wrapped in newspaper with chips. The most exotic it ever got was oblong shaped, covered in breadcrumbs and came frozen in a box.

We slouched in the prow of the ferry as it headed up the bustling harbour towards the bridge. The giant clown's face of Lunar Park grinned inanely at the Opera House, whose sails glowed pink in the setting sun. Circular Quay was abuzz with the early evening departure of the QE2, Bunger commenting on how much better off we were working on the lax, though far less luxurious, Greek ships as the British liners were said to be far stricter, treating their crews as though they were in the Royal Navy. We wouldn't have lasted five minutes and would never have never got away with the debauched behaviour that I was becoming accustomed to.

The smell of doughnuts was in the air, lovers strolled hand in hand, toddlers chased seagulls that fought over scraps, buskers gave it their all and a carnival atmosphere abounded. We sauntered over to the Rocks and I followed Bunger into a souvenir shop where he was warmly-greeted by the owner, a friendly Egyptian character called Akmal. Getting straight down to business, Bunger negotiated the purchase of two hundred boomerangs and, following some good-natured haggling, sealed the deal with a large wad of cash. Akmal assured Bunger that the consignment would be spirited safely aboard ship before sailing the next morning and, as we left the shop, ventured a joke, reminding Bunger that it was not possible for the boomerangs to be returned.

The night was young so we toddled up to the Lord Nelson pub where Bunger, having noticed my confused reaction to the strange transaction that had just occurred, let me in on another little hush-hush fact of shipboard life.

Explaining the boomerangs away as 'extra stock', he reminded me that the company he worked for, the company that held the lucrative franchise for the on-board gift shops, were well and truly out of sight and out of mind.

Consequently, with a head office firmly anchored back in London, the shop boys saw it as their entrepreneurial duty to engage in a little wheeling and dealing for themselves.

'What they don't know about won't kill them old boy,' Bunger chirped happily.

So, picking up stock from various shady acquaintances around the globe bought Bunger and his cohorts a healthy, under-the-table bonus each trip. He explained that they always went in for cheap, easy to move tourist trash such as the boomerangs he'd just purchased. Marked up by a hundred per cent or more, he assured me they'd sell like hot-cakes towards the end of the northbound voyage, when disembarking Pommies would queue to grab this iconic memento of their once-in-a-lifetime trip to the land down under.

As we walked into the Lord Nelson, Henri waved us over to a corner table where he was cosied-up with Georgios. Bunger took off to the bar to shout everyone a drink and Henri took the opportunity to proudly show off the clobber he'd bought Georgios on their afternoon shopping excursion. A beige three-piece suit complete with brown velour piping adorning the oversize pocket flaps and lapels, several cheesecloth body shirts, a pair of embroidered, bell-bottom jeans and umpteen sweaters, T-shirts and Y-fronts. For his *pièce de résistance*, Henri rummaged through a plastic bag and whipped out a hideous, paisley-patterned kaftan. Georgios sat, glowing, by Henri's side, reached under the table and gave (I hazard a guess) Henri's hand a gentle squeeze.

Bunger returned from the bar with a tray of drinks and we toasted the happy couple's anniversary. With far too much information, Henri expounded on the happy news that, indeed, it was six months to the day since he and Georgios had consummated their union and 'made love' on a blow-up mattress on the floor of the Beauty Salon. To celebrate, they were off to visit an old friend of Henri's and Bunger and I were invited along.

The cab deposited us outside a quaint, ivy-covered terrace house in Surry Hills. Henri tugged on a brass chain that was attached to a wall and muffled tinkling chimed from within. Moments later, the door was opened by a very gay young man of about twenty, resplendent in a body-hugging, stark white and blatantly mock sailor suit. However, as he postured and preened before us, my immediate reaction was that he'd got lucky with a luckless Yankee seaman and procured the uniform. Another, older, queen came running from the back of the house. Wringing his hands on a tea towel, he shrieked at the sight of Henri and the two old fudge monkeys embraced warmly.

We were led into the small, immaculate house and introductions were made all round with Henri, bless him, emphasising that Bunger and I were a couple of 'straight' friends from the ship. He introduced Georgios as his fiancé.

'Gorgeous,' gasped Roland, the older fag.

His young housemate's name was Jay. He spun on his high-heels and wiggled across the room to silence Eartha Kitt, who was belting out a number from the stereo.

The house was very spic and span, though eccentrically furnished for a purposely kitsch feel. A fake zebra-skin couch dominated the lounge and umpteen curios, knick-knacks and outlandish *objets d'art* vied for attention. Pride of place was a large tropical fish tank that was perched on a red perspex table in the centre the room. Fabulous!

Jay busied himself preparing drinks behind a fifties cocktail bar and Roland and Henri traded gossip. Like Henri, Roland had worked at sea for many years and consequently had a plethora of bawdy yarns to look back on. Now comfortably retired in Sydney, he was a wiry old bugger who, by the looks of him, divided his time equally between the gym and the beach. Deeply tanned with wrinkled, leathery skin, he didn't have an ounce of fat on him and, with his sparse, closely-cropped patch of white hair, he looked like a friendly old reptile.

Daiquiris were served all round and we were led through some sliding glass doors to a small paved courtyard where four snappily-dressed men and two beautiful women lounged on wicker furniture sipping cocktails.

Limp, manicured hands were proffered and then we were introduced to the two girls. Both models and friends of Roland who did their hair, they were clearly zonked on something and barely spoke a word all evening. If they did say anything, it was to each other, or about themselves or their latest wealthy beau, making it perfectly clear to Bunger and me, the only two straight males at the soirée, that we were way out of their league. Stuck up slags!

Bunger and I ignored them and concentrated on getting totally out of it with the Sydney gays, who were a riot of fun. Roland busied himself in the kitchen and laid a table in the garden full of dips, salads, breads and cheeses; then, whipping off his apron, he became momentarily butch and fired up a barbie. The evening wore on, drinks were thrown back in reckless gay abandon, joints shared all around and the music cranked back up.

It was about two in the morning before the party finally began to fizzle. The two girls were passed out on the couch and Jay was snoozing, oblivious, in a flower bed, where he clutched a garden gnome to his chest. Roland had retired upstairs to his boudoir and Henri and Georgios had long ago sneaked off to a back bedroom. The rest of the party had headed home apart from Rick, a waspish, leather-clad homo and font of wisdom when it came to substance abuse, who now suggested we revive our flagging spirits with a few lines of speed. Declining his kind offer, we opted instead for a splendiferous snort of amyl nitrate.

It was getting a bit chilly in the garden so we went inside and Rick handed me his vial of vile-smelling amyl. A first for me, the stuff gave off the vague, mephitic whiff of stinky socks and I was completely unprepared for its effect as my brain went from nought to a hundred in three seconds flat. Bunger took a hit, followed swiftly by Rick and the three of us grabbed on to one another for support as our knees buckled and we crashed to the floor, laughing like hyenas and flaying our legs in the air like upended cockroaches.

The drug wore off after a minute or two but the racket we made roused the unconscious models who demanded their own hit. Bunger sifted through the stack of records by the stereo, bunged on an Elton John album and with a second wind, the partying began all over again. I remember when rock was young but I'm fucked if I can remember what happened next, or the couple of hours that passed in an alcohol-, dope- and amyl-fuelled blur.

It would have been around 4.00 a.m. when I was brought, literally, crashing back to my senses when, making a dash for the garden to throw up, I ran straight through a plate-glass door which some drug-addled nincompoop had chosen to slide shut. It all seemed to happen in slow motion and I don't recall feeling any pain as a shard of glass opened up a deep, ragged gash in my left wrist. Once through the door and into the garden, I was immediately snapped back to the present and, instantly sober, looked down at the blood that was now pumping from my wrist, soaking into my favourite pair of flared Levis and splashing on to my white sneakers.

Jay woke, rolled out of the flower bed, jumped to his feet and dropped the garden gnome, which crashed on to the flagstones of the patio. Somebody had turned the music off and it was suddenly, and eerily, quiet – even the cicadas had ceased their non-stop chirping.

Moments passed, then Jay let out a piercing scream, which probably woke the neighbours but certainly woke the rest of the house. The two girls grabbed their handbags and, without a word, hightailed it out of the front door and Rick quickly hid behind the bar. Henri and Georgios emerged, sheepishly and half-naked, from the back bedroom and Roland came barrelling down the stairs wrapped in what looked like a particularly fetching sari.

Stopped in his tracks midway, he took in the devastating scene. Yours truly, supposedly bleeding to death in the glass-less door frame; Jay, still screaming and clutching the now decapitated gnome; and Bunger, standing in the middle of the room, slopping sludge-green

115

water on to the once pristine, biscuit-coloured carpet from the tropical fish tank that he's holding with difficulty in his spindly arms. 'Taking care of the fish, old girl,' Bunger said, cheerfully.

Ignoring Bunger's confusing remark, Roland sprang into action and, leaping down the remaining stairs, went immediately to work on my damaged wrist. Applying a tourniquet, he managed to stem the bleeding then wrapped the whole thing tightly in a towel. While he worked, he ordered Jay to quit his bleating and phone for a cab.

Bunger accompanied me to the all-night clinic off Oxford Street, where he commandeered a wheelchair and pushed me to the front of the queue. Told to wait our turn, I was eventually attended to by a young, bleary-eyed doctor who, refusing Bunger's attempt at a tip, assured me there was no major damage. I did, however, require ten stitches – a better result than the poor old garden gnome who ended up being tossed, headless, into a dustbin.

It had been a long, eventful night and dawn was breaking by the time we hailed a cab outside the clinic. The ship wouldn't be sailing for another three hours and, with the pair of us exhausted and splattered with congealed blood, we were feeling a tad dishevelled and somewhat sorry for ourselves.

Bunger suggested a detour to the Bourbon & Beefsteak in Kings Cross, where he convinced me an early morning hair of the dog would soon have us feeling our old selves. The Bourbon turned out to be a twenty-four-hour drinking haunt, well-favoured by an eclectic crowd of Sydney's more colourful, not to mention, criminal characters.

I felt about a hundred years old as I trudged up the steps to the bar but was stopped at the door by a huge Maori bouncer who demanded proof of age. Bunger took this as an opportunity to shell out a few bucks, I flashed my crew pass and we were granted entry into the smoke-filled tavern.

Fifty-odd American sailors from the Kitty Hawk were holding each other up in a bawdy scrum and singing along to Don McLean, whose American Pie boomed from the very loud speakers. (Just for the record, I fuckin' hate that song.) A brood of bored hookers looked on, chain-smoking, haggard and sore after a long night, winning the hearts, minds and wallets of some of Americas finest.

Bunger and I found space at the bar and spent the next couple of hours drinking Bloody Mary's, one after the other. Glug! Glug! Glug!

'One for the road.'

Glug! Glug! Glug!

'One for the road.'

Glug! Glug! Glug!

'One for the road.'

There were forty-five minutes left before sailing when we finally tottered out into the blinding, early morning light.

As crew, we were required to be back on board at least an hour prior to sailing but Bunger insisted we had nothing to worry about as the Kioni was parked just down the road at Woolloomooloo – a mere five-minute cab ride away.

We weaved across to the other side of Darlinghurst Road and headed down Macleay Street, looking back all the time, increasingly frantic for a cab. Panicking now, we ran past the fountain and on down the hill and not a bloody cab in sight. In the distance, the Kioni was obviously preparing for departure and we could hear the blasts from her horn as she called her errant children home. When we finally made it to the dock, we had to plead with the old soldier who was guarding the locked gates of the wharf. Lucky for us, Pikey spotted us and hollered to the old boy to let us through. The gangways had long since been taken away and just as we'd first scrambled ashore in Sydney, we left the same way via a plank placed between the quay and the kitchens. Last on board, we'd made it with minutes to spare and the Kioni set sail for Auckland. At over thirteen hundred miles across the Tasman Sea, a bloody long swim.

9

Kaboom!

Apparently, 1953 was a good year. Liz Windsor, who had never done a day's work in her life apart from opening the occasional bridge and driving a truck around for a bit during World War II, got crowned top dog of England, Scotland, Wales, Northern Ireland and the plethora of pink bits that dominated any school atlas way back when in the glorious, but dying, days of The Empire.

For those who give a rat's, England won back the Ashes after a twenty-year drought. Arsenal won the League Championship for a record seventh time, and a gangly Kiwi and his Tibetan sidekick became the first blokes to stand on the roof of the world. A lovely view by all accounts.

Over in America, John and Jackie got hitched and a still svelte Elvis graduated from high school and shelled out four bucks to cut his first demo at Sun Records in Memphis. He would also go on to drive a truck around for a bit, be crowned the undisputed king of Rock 'n' Roll, then die of a massive heart attack on the toilet and end up as a big fat man in a box.

The Korean War ground to an end and, over in Russia, Joe Stalin, the father of the Motherland, did the world a favour and shuffled off to burn in hell for all eternity.

Meanwhile, back in England, I got born. Kaboom!

It turns out that I was the second little bundle of joy born to Albert and Vera, my big brother, Bobby having popped out four years previous. Albert and Vera had met in a pub halfway through the dark days of World War II. Vera was eighteen, a Paddy who'd grown up in London. The story goes that years of cowering in a freezing backyard bomb shelter, or worse, taking refuge down the local tube station sheltering from German bombs, had driven Vera out into the relative safety of a small village in Hertfordshire, some thirty miles north of what was left of London.

Details are sketchy but, as my stone deaf old mum yells it: 'Well, I walked into the Sow and Pigs one night with my friend, Edna, and there's this tall, skinny soldier in a baggy uniform and him and his mate are playing darts. 'Ere, but I had to laugh. They had a picture of ruddy old Hitler pinned to the dartboard and were taking potshots at it. I thought that was smashin', see, I hated Hitler and even to this day, I don't trust them Germans; even though me brother went off and married one after the war. And as for them Japs ... I'll never forget what they did to our boys ... !'

'Yes, yes, thank you. Time for your medication.'

Poor old Vera. In the years to come, not only did she have to welcome one of the dreaded Boche into the family but many years later my youngest brother, Clive, would fall in love and marry a Japanese girl.

'Ruddy 'eck!'

These days, Vera coos, happily besotted, over her Anglo-Japo grand-sprog. Cor blimey, mamma son!

Back in the Sow and Pigs, Albert and Vera struck up a conversation. Voila! Love at first sight. (It seems it was a lot easier to impress a woman back then. You didn't need a flash job, a Porsche, an Armani suit or a Platinum Visa card. Apparently, all it took was an ill-fitting uniform, some soldierly dartsmanship and you were in like Flynn. Of course, what with the world going to hell in a hand basket all around, I imagine one was a little less picky when it came to the selection of a potential spouse.) Vera only admits to swapping addresses on that first meeting and that's enough information for me.

Albert went back to the war and, with the help of General Montgomery and Spike Milligan, took on the formidable might of Field Marshal Rommel and his Afrika Korps in the deserts of North Africa. Like a lot of old soldiers, Albert never discussed what must have been a sheer living hell. Fishing for evidence of his heroic deeds and fuelled by post-war comic-strip propaganda in the Dandy and Beano, we would, as kids, pester him with wide-eyed fascination.

'What was it like in the war, Dad? ... How many planes did you shoot down? ... How many Jerrys did you kill?' (That one got us a whack around the ears. Worse if our German auntie happened to be visiting.)

My old man buried his head in books concerning every theatre of the war and his favourite TV show was All our Yesterdays, which featured grim and grainy black and white war footage. He would gladly discuss the history and tactics of various bloody battles but his own involvement remained a closed book. A no-man's-land buried deep inside, like a piece of jagged shrapnel. He would never open up about his war years. Hated being reminded of it. I never once saw him polish his umpteen medals and I don't think he ever attended any regimental reunions or functions. All he would ever admit to was being the most adept and fastest 'squaddie' in his regiment when it came to digging a bloody great hole and getting in it whenever enemy aircraft appeared – or, indeed, if any kind of action was imminent. And he would tease us with a wild claim that he had known and been a close personal friend of the Unknown Soldier.

With the war finally over, Albert and Vera's romance evidently blossomed and, after marrying in 1948, they decided to settle in the village where they had first met. Albert had grown up there and, presumably, Vera didn't take much convincing that a country life was for her, much of London having been reduced to a lunar landscape of bomb craters and rubble.

Albert had been conscripted into the army at eighteen and, after five long years of dodging bullets, all he was qualified for in civvy street was digging holes, so he went to work as a gardener. That's pretty much what he did for the rest of his life. He earned bugger all but in those days, a job on one of the big country estates brought with it a free house. A 'tied cottage'. Money was scarce but Albert and Vera and their young family at least had a roof over their heads. Best of all, ruddy old Hitler wasn't trying to kill them any more. After years of carnage followed by the hardships of rationing, life was good. The world turned and peace reigned supreme. Albert and Vera were in cloud cuckoo land.

One of my earliest recollections is that of playing on my farm. My 'farm' was, in actual fact, nothing more than a ripe and rotting compost heap where all the rubbish of the estate was deposited. The countless rats that scurried about were my farm animals.

The first house that I can remember living in was a white washed cottage with a rusting tin roof. I can recall bare, wooden floorboards throughout, uneven and unpolished, and this long before bare floorboards were, by any stretch of the imagination, fashionable. Back then, people only had bare wooden floorboards because they couldn't afford to cover them with anything. Albert and Vera did, however, splash out on some linoleum for the kitchen. With its cavernous fireplace it was the epicentre of the house and it was here, that the young family would huddle together on a winter's night. A roaring log fire keeping at bay the cold wind that shook against the old, oak door and rattled in the loose-fitting window frames. I don't remember a telly in those early years. As far as I can make out, families used to sit around and talk to each other. Just imagine.

Come bedtime, I would scream my tits off. I shared a room with Bobby but as he could stay up later than me, I would be left alone to contemplate the sounds of the night and the creaking, creepy old house.

There was an ancient and gnarled walnut tree in the garden outside my window. Its branches hung down over the tiny cottage and the howling wind would roll in off the dark fields and the old tree would sway and groan and thrash itself noisily on the tin roof.

This would start the bats chirping. The bats lived in the roof and they scared the bejesus out of me. An early bit of ill-advice from Vera warned to be very wary of bats. Apparently, with a kamikaze-like determination, a bat liked nothing more than to so entangle itself in a human head, that the only way to extract it would be to cut all one's hair off. I would scream and holler that the bats were coming to get me and eventually Vera (her hair covered by a scarf) would come into my room and comfort me. I don't know where she got such dingbat ideas but to this day, I can only get to sleep if my head is completely submerged under a duvet.

Vera had a huge catalogue of old wives' tales and superstitions. She would make the sign of the cross whilst putting the willies up me with dire warnings of the 'Banshee'. And she was convinced that goblins lurked in the bushes at the bottom of the garden. I never saw any and it was always a mystery to me as to why they would choose this particular locale, it being where the outside toilet was situated and nobody ever ventured near that reeking thunderbox unless absolutely necessary.

Crossing on the stairs was *verboten* in our house, as was placing shoes on the table or opening an umbrella indoors. Black cats were not permitted within a five-mile radius but if one crossed your path, it was good luck. Walking under a ladder was a definite no-no and stepping on a crack in the road was to be avoided at all costs. Strangely enough, if a passing bird decided to take a dump on your head, one was considered truly blessed. Christ Almighty, is it any wonder that, as an adult, I'm a minefield of nervous tics, paranoia and insecurities?

All this angst can be levelled at Vera's crazy Irish mother. I never knew the old girl; though she got to hold me as a baby then died of a stroke soon after. Family folklore has it that she had to hightail it out of Ireland with the rest of her clan when, during the 'Troubles', one of her brothers, not the brightest crayon in the box, had brought disgrace on the family by getting himself shot to death by the IRA whilst home on leave from the British Army. Evidently, he had been strutting around town, proud as a pillock, showing off his uniform and mouthing 'Rule Britannia' platitudes.

The white washed cottage with the rusting tin roof and the ancient and gnarled walnut tree in the garden was called, not surprisingly, Walnut Tree Cottage. Albert worked for the same big cheese for years and yet we were always on the move. Once a year, we would have to up and shift all our meagre possessions, including the linoleum, down the road to the next leaky hovel. The rationale for this was never explained but years later, Albert would surmise that it was the upper classes' way of keeping the hoi polloi in their place – by constantly keeping them on the move.

The toffs in the 'Big House', which had once been the country home of Prime Minister William Gladstone, owned most of the village – including its inhabitants. In a few short years, we moved from one tied cottage to the next. Walnut Tree Cottage. Chestnut Tree Cottage. Cherry Tree Cottage and Plum Tree Cottage.

Back in those days, there was never a shortage of visitors to whichever house we happened to be squatting in. There seemed to be a roving band of industrious folk who eked out a living by plying their wares from door to door. On alternate days, there was a butcher's van, a baker's van and a fishmonger's van and, on Saturdays, a converted bus would tour the village flogging fruit and veg. Real gypsies, which we called 'gyppos', hawked wooden clothes pegs and, now and then, a mobile tramp on an ancient motorbike would rumble into the hamlet and, for a few coins, hone everyone's knives on a circular sharpening stone. Best of all, there was a library van, for, in those bygone days, people read books.

The local doctor often made unannounced house calls just to enquire about the health of the family. Seriously! And the local clergy of both denominations were forever popping in for a chat and a free cuppa. Of course, there were always the less welcome visitors – the debt collectors. There was the electricity man who came to empty the shillings out of the meter and to check that it hadn't been tampered with. And, every fortnight, we were forced to hide when the dreaded insurance man came a-knocking; Albert and Vera rarely having the dough for 'the divvy'.

Everyone knew everyone then. People were always popping in, heralding their arrival with a 'Cooee! It's only me'. And it's true. People never locked their doors back then, in what must have been the halcyon days for burglars.

Things aren't quite the same these days, are they? I lived in my last pad for four years and, apart from an intimate knowledge of the hideous musical tastes of the ignorant bastards who lived across the hall (Motley Crue, Queen and Bon bloody Jovi), I didn't have a clue as to the identity of my neighbours. Making eye contact on the stairs was a major breakthrough in social communion. (And how come apartments are called 'apart-ments', when they're so fuckin' close together?)

Life, according to Albert and Vera, was, by far, more civilised in their day and violence virtually unheard of. Apart from the occasional world war, that is. And people didn't move around so much, then. Generations living in the same area for generations, only bothering to up and leave in time of global conflict. Then, when duty called, all the young men of the district would gladly join up together and march off, lemming-like, to die in the mud on some far-flung battlefield for God, country and one of Liz Windsor's rellies. Lest we forget, the names of the young men who gave up their lives are etched forever on a thousand village memorials.

In our village, the numbers are numerous but the surnames few as intermarriage produced families of clan-like proportion. The dire results of this inbreeding were evident in some of the gormless trolls that would plod about the neighbourhood. Knuckles dragging in the dirt, with a massive sloping forehead and drooling spittle down an oversized jaw, these harmless village idiots were a source of endless fun for us kids.

I recall one unusually hot summer's day, so stifling that the tar on the road was melting and had softened to a treacle-like consistency. I scooped up a large dollop of the goo and managed to convince one of these poor unfortunates that it was, in fact, a delicious helping of liquorice. Much to the delight of myself and some other little kiddies, the dopey clod believed me and attempted to stuff the sticky offering in his mouth. It was his first taste of hot tar and my first taste of the awesome power of my humour and the fun that can be derived from another's misfortune.

The village was only thirty miles from London but accents change from county to county in England, so the locals spoke with a definite country bumpkin inflection. Like most children, I picked up my speech patterns from my mother and grew up speaking with more of a cockney lilt. Consequently, I always felt a little different from the other kids. Like a Londoner misplaced in the sticks by mistake. Small for my age and with a razor-like wit delivered in true barrow-boy fashion, for better or worse, I never quite felt like one of the herd. I liked it.

EVENING HORSE RACING – with your host, *ARCHIE* – Come along and place your bets! 8.00 p.m. Main Lounge

SEASCAPE

Tuesday 4th December 1973 En route to Auckland

I crept up to my cabin, showered, changed out of my blood-soaked clothes and then went out on to the Crew Deck to take in the sights as we sailed up the harbour to the Heads and out to sea. Cradling my bandaged wrist, I thought over the mayhem of the past few days and how Sydney had lived up to its name as one of the world's most 'intoxicating' cities.

I went down to breakfast and was treated like a conquering hero. Fresh stitches, it appears, are a true badge of honour. Everyone had had a ball in Sydney and I lingered long to hear of the tales of debauchery and misadventures that had befallen my fellow shipmates.

Henri entered the mess and plonked himself down with a histrionic harrumph! Sulking over the bad behaviour of Bunger and me, he told anyone who was interested how we had embarrassed him in front of one of his oldest friends. I assured him I'd be paying for the damage and intended phoning Roland from Auckland to apologise and find out how much I owed him. But Henri is such an old drama queen. I think he's revelling in his supposed hurt and it's likely to be several days before he deems me worthy of forgiveness.

After breakfast, I crawled back to my cabin in the hope of catching a half-hour kip before having to man the games corner at eleven. I'd just lain on my bunk when there was a knock on the door and Pikey walked in. He informed me that Cocksakis had seen Bunger and me almost miss the ship from his perch, high on the bridge. Accordingly, we were both fined twenty bucks. Pikey, one of the good guys, warned me, for my own good, that it may be prudent for me to watch my step. At the time, I was past caring and just wanted to get my head down, if only for twenty minutes. I thanked Pikey for his help in getting us aboard and he turned and left.

Five minutes later, Paul came blustering through the door and, red-faced with rage, gave me a right bollocking. He said he'd been impressed how quickly I'd learnt the ins and outs of the job and was thrilled how popular I was amongst the passengers and most of the crew. But my increasingly wild conduct was bringing heat down from above and causing him grief.

'Don't take the piss, Maude,' he screamed.

With a pained expression, he warned me that if I couldn't behave myself, this first trip around the world would surely be my last.

'Don't blow it, Maude!' he yelled, as he stomped out, slamming the door behind him.

So much for a snooze. I was genuinely rattled after Paul's dressing-down and I hated the fact that I'd upset him to such an extent. The old darlin' had gone out on a limb to have me on board in the first place and now I was letting him down. I got up and, in an effort to disguise the stench of alcohol that was oozing from every pore, brushed my teeth, gargled several times with mouthwash and splashed half a bottle of Vetiver on my face and down my shirt front – Paul had commented mid-rant that I stank like a brewery.

After I closed the games corner at twelve, I managed an hour's shut-eye before a quick lunch followed by *Kiwi Show* rehearsals in the ballroom at two. Paul was still seething and, apart from the occasional withering glance and a shake of his peroxide mane, he ignored me.

Thankfully, I wouldn't be participating in the show as we'd got lucky and happened to have on board a professional troupe of Maori dancers and musicians who were travelling home after a European tour. Paul reluctantly handed over the choreography for the show and I was only on hand to help with costumes and props.

Bloodshot eyes down for a full house, I made it through bingo at four; then the best time of the day finally arrived. The quietest time on the ship when most passengers returned to their cabins for a late-afternoon siesta and left the hard-working crew a short respite from their daily grind. My next duty wasn't until eight, when I was due in the Main Lounge to host 'Horse Racing' (a game of chance whereby punters bet on wooden horses that are shuffled around a track based on the throw of the dice).

I laid up on the Crew Deck and watched the low hills of New South Wales fade into the sea haze. Tired as I was, sleep eluded me as I was worried about being thrown off the ship at the conclusion of the voyage. I was having too much fun to blow it and determined to, if not behave myself, at least keep my head down and cool it for a bit. Shape up or ship out!

After Horse Racing, where I easily recouped my twenty-dollar fine, I went to the cinema alone and watched the 10.00 p.m. session of *Paint Your Wagon*, then crashed out unusually early, just after midnight.

Albert's dad, my grandfather, lived alone in an old house at the end of a dirt track a mile or so outside the village. I don't remember him having a proper job but I think he helped out on one of the farms and so had his own tied cottage – nothing more than a large, wooden shed. It was a time-worn structure painted with black creosote and had been his home for donkey's years. The house was a very lopsided affair, with the walls going off at obscure angles and the flagstone floor a series of dips and slopes. Like all the old houses then, an enormous iron stove dominated the kitchen and, winter or summer, a fire was always burning as Grandad did all his cooking on this mammoth contraption. In the garden stood the obligatory tree and next to it, the obligatory outside lavvy. Dominating the garden was a large, murky pond, which was home to a family of squabbling ducks. The pond was not a natural part of the rural landscape but, apparently, man-made; created, that is, by an errant German bomb.

The story, according to Grandad Spinks, was that during World War II, Luftwaffe crews would, on their return from raiding London, drop any excess bombs willy-nilly across the countryside so as to lighten their load for the long trip home to *Der* Fatherland and their respective *fräuleins*. Late one night, one of these stray bombs came whistling out of the heavens, narrowly missing Gramp's shack. The resulting explosion obliterated the obligatory outside lavvy, blew all the apples off the obligatory tree and the considerable shock wave lifted the old house three foot in the air before slamming it back to earth in a topsy-turvy condition. Hey presto! Instant duck pond. Well, that was the story, anyway.

My grandfather was a gentle old coot and a fabulous pisshead. He liked beer. He liked beer a lot. Plus whisky, wine and just about anything he could get his shaky paws on. Often drunk, he sometimes didn't smell too good but he was always good for a laugh. He hadn't always been a lush; had in fact been something of an entrepreneur. He had owned one of the first cars in the district and he then bought several more and operated a successful taxi service. This would have been between the wars and life was rosy until, one day, his wife, my other granny whom I never knew, dropped down dead at thirty-two. The old boy took it hard and, in short order, hit the sauce and lost his fledgling charabanc business.

One of my favourite stories involving Grandad Spinks was that, during World War I, he had been a conscientious objector. I always thought how courageous this was of him in a time when it was every man's duty to willingly commit suicide for king and country. Refusal to do so meant being branded a traitor, a coward and a downright dastardly bounder, before being banged up in the slammer for the duration. But Gramps went to the war to end all wars – as a stretcher-bearer in the trenches. Ironically, while he was missing out on all the fun and exhilaration of taking potshots at total strangers, he was wounded by someone who wasn't. Shipped back to Blighty, once recovered, he served as a guard in a prisoner of war camp.

He evidently liked his new job and struck up life-long friendships with some of the poor wretches who were in his charge. He learnt to speak German whilst he was a screw and would piss Vera off no end by lapsing into a few guttural phrases when 'in his cups'. He'd also proudly show off beautifully-made wooden boxes and carvings given to him by grateful lags and when I was a kid in the sixties, he was still receiving Christmas cards from some of his old POW cronies.

Gramps loved animals, especially cats. At one time he had about thirty of the brutes living with him and his house stank to high heaven. When the numbers and the stench got too high even for him, he would tout kittens about the village, attempting to find them a home. When this failed, he would reluctantly drown them in a sack in the German-made duck pond in his garden.

Paying a visit to Gramp's pad was always a forlorn experience. Like stepping back in time. The old squalid hut he called home not only reeked of cats' piss but also the miscellaneous stench of stale beer, fags, old men's socks and the pungent aroma of something putrid forever bubbling away on his giant cooking stove.

Grandfather's grandfather clock tick-tocked mournfully away in a cobwebbed corner and on the walls hung the sepia-toned photographs of long-dead Victorian kin. Dressed in their starched Sunday best, their gaunt faces would stare out fiercely from ornate wooden frames, the glass filthy with decades of grime and fly shit. It always gave me the creeps to think that I was in some way related to these old relics and, young as I was, a blue mist would descend.

It was a family ritual that Gramps came to lunch (which we called dinner) every Thursday. Bobby and I would sit on the gate at the bottom of the garden and wait for him to come wobbling down the lane on his rickety-old bike. He had always been to the pub first and would be half-cut. It was the same routine every week. He would fall off his bike, grapple with his bicycle clips and then present Vera with a bottle of Babycham and a Walnut Whip. Bobby and I would wait patiently, as though it was a surprise, to be solemnly given a chocolate bar each and a bottle of Tizer to share.

Dinner (lunch) would be either egg and chips, sausage and chips, fish fingers and chips, beefburger and chips, spam and chips, or baked beans on toast. Or mincemeat on toast with fried onions. For a special treat, we sometimes had tinned stewing steak and mashed potatoes or Fray Bentos steak and kidney pie and mashed potatoes. Considering we lived in the country, I don't recall digesting too much in the way of fresh produce when I was kid.

Sometimes, Gramps would pay us a surprise visit when the pubs closed. Late at night, we would be awakened by the crash of dustbins and much loud cursing. The old boy would be sprawled in the road with his bicycle at his side. The only way he'd been able to stop was to collide with something. Whatever the hour, he was always welcomed by Albert and Vera. They'd pick him up, make him a cup of tea and listen patiently as he rambled on in half-remembered German.

As time passed, he got so old that he could only manage to ride his bike downhill so, in his twilight years, he was a regular at the Rest and Welcome a boozer conveniently located not far below sea level from his shack. He would spend a pleasant evening mooching drinks then lean on his trusty steed for the uphill journey home. His push-bike was a precursor to the wheeled walking frame.

He died a peaceful death aged eighty-two. He'd smoked like a chimney, drank like a fish and, as far as anyone could remember, he'd never had a day's illness in his life. It was Albert who found him. Gramps was sitting in his favourite mouldy chair with a purring cat in his lap, his callused hand still clutching a half-full pint of Guinness. At his wake, a raucous, cheerful occasion, one of his old reprobate drinking buddies commented that the only regret Gramps would have had, would have been to have snuffed it without finishing his pint. He was a good man and, apart from the death of a few thousand cats on his conscience, he never hurt a fly.

LOST:

One pair of Bifocal Reading Glasses. They were last seen in the Coral Dining Room, lunchtime at first sitting. If any passenger has found them would they please contact the B-Deck Purser's Office.

SEASCAPE

Saturday 8th December 1973 At Auckland

It took four days to cross the Tasman and I more or less stayed sober and behaved myself. No, really I did! I even left my stash stashed in its hidey-hole up on deck. By way of apology, I bought Paul a gold chain from the gift shop (Bunger gave me a substantial discount). The old queen's got tons of jewellery but he can't get enough of the stuff and, genuinely touched, he's forgiven me my misdemeanours and, once again, I'm his surrogate daughter.

Now that we're on the northbound voyage we've a whole new bunch of passengers, which means, of course, a fresh crop of crumpet to pursue. A far younger demographic than the southbound voyagers, the new passengers are markedly different with the ratio of Pommies to Aussies now reversed. Apart from a few disgruntled, homesick Poms, the majority are young Aussies off on an obligatory year-long tour of Europe. Going by the atmosphere in the bars and discotheque, the northbound is shaping up to be fun.

Not surprisingly, the Greek officers were out in force for the first few nights. Dressed in their finest 'whites', they strut the decks twirling worry beads yet have no worries when it comes to wooing the fresh crop of willing, vulnerable lovelies. For most of the young Aussie chicks, it's their first time away from home and, easy meat, they fall early prey to such oily Mediterranean charms.

I've met some good-looking girls but, to my disgust, I find myself missing the easy relationship I enjoyed with Annie and thus far, haven't come across anything that's a candidate to replace her. Oh well, early days. The best news of all is that we're carrying two hundred fewer passengers northbound. Paul's pulled a few strings and Sean's been given a single passenger cabin on Main Deck and I get to keep the four-berth crew cabin to myself.

With far fewer children on board, the morning deck games on the Sports Deck are far more subdued affairs. A couple of days ago, I was sitting in the sun enjoying a ciggie and watching a few Aussie kids scrapping with three Pommy brats when a seriously sexy woman of about thirty came and sat next to me and admonished me for smoking in front of the children. She was a short woman with a compact, very fit little bod packaged cutely in a flared dungaree suit. I was instantly attracted to her.

I stubbed out my fag and she smiled and introduced herself. Her name's Claire and she's travelling with her husband and young son back to England after a two-year stint in Australia, where hubby, some sort of engineer, was under contract to theAustralian government.

131

Claire blabbed on, in her snooty accent, about how she'd hated her time spent living in Canberra and was pleased to be heading home. We talked some more and she let on how much she loved children and was wondering if she could assist in the daily deck games with the kiddies. As I never know what to do with the little buggers, I was delighted. Not only that, I really want to get to know this woman.

We only stayed in Auckland for the day and, to keep the peace, I behaved myself and went ashore with Paul and enjoyed a very civilised lunch. Even on a Saturday there wasn't much in the way of distractions but, not to be deterred, after lunch, Paul took off on his never-ending search for trade and I was back on board by mid-afternoon.

I caught up with Sean in the mess; he'd had a far more exciting time. Claiming he'd been set upon by two large Tongans, he was sporting a black eye and a thick lip. We set sail for Tahiti at six.

10

Fire and Brimstone and Assorted Bollocks

I was five years old. I now had another brother, Liam, two years my junior and had joined my brother, Bobby, at school. There was a primary school in the village but I couldn't go there as it was Church of England and I was a Catholic. About the only condition that Vera had put on Albert before marrying him was that any resulting sprogs were to be brought up, or indoctrinated as it turned out, into the Catholic faith, a command handed down by Vera's stark raving mad mother.

Albert was C of E and very involved in his church. He sometimes read the sermon and delighted in tormenting the local blue bloods by preaching the word of God dressed in his gardening togs – complete with mud-splattered wellies. Aside from his church, he was a bit of an old commie really, and always took great pleasure in getting up an aristocratic hooter.

One day I was out with him in the local town. The place was festooned with banners and bunting and the streets full of excited townsfolk carrying little Union Jacks on sticks. A phalanx of police motorcycles roared down the main street, followed by a black limo with a big gold crest on the bonnet.

Sitting in the back, was a little old lady wearing a turban-like hat and going through the motions of what looked like swatting flies in slow-mo. The throngs of people lining both sides of the street went apeshit, jumping up and down, cheering and waving their little flags ecstatically.

The little old lady in the black limo with the gold crest on the bonnet turned out to be the Queen Mum. As the old duck sailed serenely past, my old man, still holding my hand, stepped out of the crowd and gave her the finger.

This incident would have taken place sometime back in the late fifties; a time when the teeming masses were expected to know their place, respect their so-called betters and never dare question the relevance or necessity of having such an archaic and pampered dynasty as leaders of the pack. Albert viewed 'the Royals' as nothing more than the pointy end of a class system that had kept England and the common man in the dark ages for far too long. He never had anything against them personally but he never missed a chance to stir the pot. Even so, I recall us having to skedaddle out of town a bit sharpish that day. I'm surprised he didn't get us both lynched!

As for his children attending Catholic school, he didn't seem to give a rat's arse. He loved his church but figured just so long as his kids received some sort of religious grounding, that was fine by him. As he explained to me years later, his certain philosophy was trying to live a good life on a day-to-day basis, denomination or dogma being of little consequence, even though he did concede that the Pope probably had the best hats.

And so it was that my religious brainwashing began. Over the fields, four miles and a couple of villages away, stood St Cuthbert's Catholic Primary School. A small, flint-stone building, it huddled under the twin spires of St Cuthbert's Catholic Church. All the better to ensnare the young mind.

Bobby took care of me on the journey to and from school and the trip across the hills, through farmland and forest, was an added bonus. Every school-day morning, an ancient bus would tour the district picking up clutches of Catholic kids and deposit them in a cloud of holy smoke outside the pearly gates of St Cuthbert's.

I enjoyed school from day one. I learnt my ABC and basic maths, which consisted of reciting, parrot-fashion, the ten-times-table. We had biased history lessons, where we were told of all the treacherous bastards who had invaded our island over the centuries but had never succeeded in enslaving its people for too long. For further evidence of England's might, we studied maps of the world – with special emphasis given to the all-important pink bits. I delighted in these early geography lessons. They coloured my dreams with faraway places and whetted my young appetite for a life-long love of travel.

Best of all, was art class. The teacher, Mr Greenstreet, was a bored, beatnik type who taught part-time. He would shuffle into school once a week, to sit at the head of the class and read a book whilst we busied ourselves making plasticine willies. One week, Mr Greenstreet failed to show up and Sister Veronica took the class, which wasn't half so much fun. The first thing the young nun did was confiscate our phallic creations. We were then made to kneel on the cold, stone floor and pray for the soul of our missing 'teach'. This had the effect of scaring the bejesus out of the whole class. What was going on? Where was Mr Greenstreet?

A few days later, the whole school knew the truth. Mr Greenstreet, it turned out, had committed one of the most heinous sins in the Catholic catalogue and gone and topped himself. As I've mentioned before, I'm a recovering Catholic and can't for the life of me remember if committing suicide is a mortal sin or a venial sin. I don't think it can be an original sin as there is nothing very original about gassing oneself in the oven – Mr Greenstreet's preferred choice of exit. Maybe it would have been original if he'd stuck his head in an electric oven. The most determined case of suicide in Christendom.

But never mind. Being a little kiddie at the time, I do remember being very frightened. I knew that Mr Greenstreet was not a bad man so I didn't think he'd be going to Hell. Then again, because he'd taken his own life, I knew there was no way he'd be allowed into Heaven. Unless, of course, he went to purgatory first. Or was it limbo? ... It was all very confusing. (As it happens, it still is.)

Religious instruction took up the bulk of our early education and, being Catholic, this meant generous daily dollops of fear and guilt. Hammered home to us with shaking fists were the many bloody sacrifices made over the centuries by a litany of misguided saints, martyrs and lunatics who gleefully got nailed up, hung, drawn, quartered, barbecued and boiled in the name of Jesus Christ, Our Lord. Amen.

It was drummed into us every day that Catholicism was the only way to go, the only gang to belong to; all other religious doctrine a rocky road to eternal damnation. It was all God-fearing and not much God-loving and I lapped it up.

It was fairy tales with blood and violence and I excelled at religious instruction, learning my catechism by rote and showing off in class by standing up and reciting Latin verse. I was such a little brown-nose that I won prizes for my religious zeal. The prizes usually took the form of picture books full of saints in various stages of *déshabillé,* being tortured by a horned bloke with a long, pointy tail and a scalding-hot pitchfork. Talk about S&M.

The best prize I ever received was for naming all twelve Stations of the Cross. For my efforts, I was presented with a plastic grotto in which stood a lime-green figurine of the Virgin Mary that glowed in the dark. Whichever house we lived in over the years, the glowing Virgin Mary in the plastic grotto was always placed, pride of place, on the mantelpiece, sandwiched between the Houses of Parliament in a snowstorm and a foot-high model of Blackpool tower with a thermometer in it. Later on, the Houses of Parliament in a snowstorm got smashed and was replaced with a framed picture of my dead grandad clutching a pint of Guinness. (When he was still alive, of course.)

I couldn't sing for shit and so never made it into the choir. But I did make altar boy, which was a much sought-after gig. It meant that I got off lessons to rehearse for weddings, christenings, funerals, and all kinds of jolly occasions. I served as an altar boy for four years, learning, religiously, the various rigmaroles and routines of the mystifying craft. In time, I worked my way up to the very important job of walking solemnly behind the priest, an angelic look on my face, and swinging a brass incense burner back and forth on the end of a long chain.

My fall from grace came one Sunday morning when, before mass, myself and my fellow altar boys were out back in the vestry, backstage so to speak, puffing on a dog-end we'd found in the churchyard. Father Quinliven, normally a benign old codger, went ballistic when he caught us smoking and apoplectic when he saw what we were using as an ashtray.

As I was in charge of the stupid thing, I took the full brunt of his fire and brimstone and was stripped of my altar boy robes on the spot. Sent home in disgrace, I copped a hiding from Albert and a flood of tears from Vera. I didn't feel as though I'd done anything that bad and from that day, my God-fearing ways began to unravel.

I must have been about nine years old when I began to have a sneaking suspicion that the whole thing might just be a load of old bollocks! Priests dolled up in gold-laced robes and silly hats droning on in Latin. The empty rituals of Catholicism and the dualism of being told that all other forms of religion were false because they worshipped graven images – then being forced on to our knees to pray to some dusty old statue of a long-dead saint who'd slain a few thousand barbarians before himself being strung up and hacked to pieces.

And I must confess that I never quite grasped the concept of confession. Still a relatively innocent little brat, I remember having to make shit up just to keep the silhouette of the creepy old priest on the other side of the wire mesh from nodding off. It was all harmless stuff: 'I told Vera a fib'. 'I beat the shit out of Liam'. 'I shot my pal, Joey, in the foot with an air pistol just to see what would happen'. (He leapt about ten foot in the air, screamed his head off and limped home to report me to his mum who went charging around to my house to report me to Vera, who reported me to Albert, who beat the living shit out of me and confiscated my piece.) Whatever the misdemeanour, it would be forgiven with a half-dozen 'Hail Marys' and a few 'How's your Fathers'. The slate wiped clean, one got to live another day with the liberating sense of having accrued a few more frequent flier points for the wings one would surely be awarded in the life hereafter.

There were some truly crazy priests and nuns, who should never have been let anywhere near the shaping of young minds but, on the whole, the majority were good, well-meaning duffers who dedicated their lives to helping others. One very popular priest was 'Loose Canon', Father Gleeson, whose nickname was 'Crunchie' because he was forever doling out these much-loved candy bars. ('Is that a Crunchie in your cassock or are you just pleased to see me?') He was always pleased to see us. Liked nothing more than to scoop a kid up in his arms, wrestle them to the floor in a frenzy of tickles and then bounce them up and down on a bony knee. (At least, I think it was a knee.) And he wouldn't hesitate to visit a sick child at home, sit by their bed, mumble a prayer or two and gently stroke a fevered forehead.

He liked to take groups of us on excursions to the local swimming baths, would even give us a good, vigorous rub-down after. One day at assembly, the headmaster announced that Father Gleeson had been hurriedly transferred to Africa for some urgent missionary work. We never saw him again. And he didn't even send us a postcard.

I was now a Big Cheese at the little school and, apart from being treated as though I were the Antichrist by all the religious zealots, I was a popular kid and, though not prefect material, I did score the popular gig of inkwell monitor. (It amazes me to think that I took my first tentative steps at written communication using nothing more than a scratchy old pen. These days, I'm slave to the keyboard of a recalcitrant laptop and if it crashes on me one more time, I'm throwing it out of the fuckin' window! Fuck it! I'm not kidding. For all the grief this thing causes me, I'd be better off with a fuckin' typewriter. Or why not a pen? Why not? The Bard wrote all that heavy stuff with a feather, for Christ sakes!)

So school was fun with the only bleak spot being my diminutive size. Being vertically challenged was no big deal in itself, except, that is, when it came to the selection of football teams for the umpteen matches forced upon us in all weathers. Lumped together with the fat kid, the callipered kid, and the spotty kid with glasses – and a note from his mother – was downright humiliating and, though un-geezer-like in the extreme, ingrained in me a deep and life-long loathing of the world game.

But to be a working-class kid and not like football was tantamount to heresy and, for a few years, I had to pretend to be as smitten by the stupid bloody game as the rest of my football-mad chums. It was only when, a few years later, I started to enjoy and excel at cross-country running, that I could safely admit to not being so enamoured of the game without being branded ... heaven forbid ... 'a pansy'.

PS I hate cricket, too.

10.15 a.m. LIFEBOAT DRILL FOR PASSENGERS AND CREW

At the sounding of the alarm bells and the ship's whistle, **ALL PASSENGERS** are requested to proceed to their assembly station wearing their life jackets. The assembly station for each cabin appears on a notice behind the cabin door. During the drill, all ship's offices, shops, bars, children's playroom and nursery, will be closed.

SEASCAPE

Monday 10th December 1973 En route to Tahiti

Last night after snowball bingo, I snuck up on deck and retrieved my stash. It was a beautiful night and I sat on deck for hours, getting ripped and listening in my cans to a new Doobie Brothers album I'd picked up in Auckland. I then passed out and had a disturbing wet dream featuring Claire.

For the sake of aerial and marine navigation, the world is divided into hypothetical parallels and meridians, i.e. lines of latitude and longitude. The parallels are concentric circles running parallel to the equator, which use the north-south axis of the globe as their centre. Proceeding north and south from the equator at equal distance ... blah, blah, blah ... we crossed the International Date Line during the night, which means today is also Monday the 10th.

The sky is hot and blue as we steam towards Polynesia, some six days distant across the South Pacific. Lifeboat drill this morning – what a farce. Still, bit of a laugh for the crew as we got to boss the passengers around, herd them to their muster stations and generally pretend that we'd know what to do in an emergency.

Next, I toured the ship flogging tote tickets, and then rushed up to the Sports Deck for kiddies' hour. I was early; Claire wasn't there so I had a quick ciggie. When she did turn up, she took my nicotined breath away. She looked about eighteen, dressed as she was in a tight, white singlet, a very short, pleated tennis skirt and simple, white pumps.

A dozen little kiddies showed up and Claire quickly organised a game of tag and soon had them running about like silly buggers. I was only too keen to let her take charge as it meant I could sit back and study her – and she's so beautiful. A burnished golden tan covers her small, taut frame and she has a gleaming bob of flaxen hair, sparkling, ice-blue eyes and flawless, very white teeth. Add to this the Milky Way of freckles that bless her perfectly pert nose, and she looks more like a young Nordic goddess than a thirty-something English mum. Oh dear, it's official. I'm in love.

Once the hour was up and the kiddies had buggered off, I had Claire all to myself and we sat in the sun and talked. She was very candid, telling me all about her hubby, who spends every night getting hammered and usually sleeps well past noon. His name's Terry and he's an Aussie who studied engineering in the UK. They met at university and married young when she fell pregnant.

Now I'm no marriage guidance counsellor but it's clear to see that they have a huge logistical problem in that hubby wants to move back to Australia permanently and the missus, quintessential English rose that she is, can't stand the place. Their son, Sebastian, is now twelve and is having the time of his life on the ship. He's fallen in with a few kids his own age and, unlike me, wants nothing to do with his mother. Poor Claire's pissed off, as the very reason for opting to take the long way home rather than fly was so the family could spend some time together.

I didn't quite know how to react to such open-faced revelations from somebody I barely knew. I felt both sadness for her lonely predicament and elation that she'd confided in me. I wanted to reach out to her. Embrace her. Feel her in my arms. Feel her arms around me. Stroke her hair. Kiss her kissable lips, long and slow. Drag her back to my cabin and ...

The usual request for help with the various shows had been run in Seascape and we were inundated with a bevy of volunteers this afternoon. Paul quickly weeded out the fat, ugly and unfashionable and we were left with a very attractive chorus line – including Claire, whom I'd persuaded to turn up and audition. *The Welcome Cabaret* is scheduled for tomorrow night so Paul has his work cut out whipping his new troupe into shape.

In 1963, a brand-new council estate was completed in the village and we were one of the first families to take up residence. The garden was barren and so, in the absence of the normally ubiquitous tree to name the house after, Albert dubbed our new abode Lava-Tree Cottage, as it was our first home with an inside toilet.

Prior to this step up to sumptuous opulence, getting caught short in the middle of the night was a nightmare, with only the chipped enamel pisspot under the bed for relief. Worse still, now that I was, in short, a big kid, I wasn't allowed to use it for 'Number Twos'. If nature called in the middle of the night, I had no choice but to drape a candlewick bedspread over my jim-jams and make my way down to the Tardis-like structure at the bottom of the garden. Keeping a wary eye out for any lurking goblins was spooky enough, but hovering over the evil-smelling abyss on a cold winter's night conjured up horrors to rival anything that I'd learnt in Bible class.

We loved our new home, considered ourselves rich and, as long as Albert coughed up the minimal rent each week, there was no reason why we couldn't live there for ever and ever. Back then, it seemed like a grand shining mansion but I don't know how we all fitted in, especially as there were now six of us, my youngest brother, Clive, having been born the previous year.

The house was a red-brick semi with a shared alleyway separating us from the house next door. The tiny kitchen was crammed with a cooker, fridge and an old-fashioned clothes boiler with a hand-cranked mangle. There was a coal-burning stove and our old mutt, Sam, was billeted in a basket under the sink.

Off the kitchen was a small dining room, or dinette, where we would all squash in to eat and argue, and listen to The Goons on the mammoth radiogram. Then there was the almighty front room, which Albert and Vera filled with a bursting sofa and two mismatching armchairs. These were strategically placed to face the new, black and white telly, 'paid for' on the never-never. Jammed in the front room was also an old piano that nobody could play and a vintage glass cabinet brimming with 'family heirlooms' ... tack, bric-a-brac and a plethora of shields and trophies that Albert and my football-mad siblings had won. The only trophy attributed to me was a small, silver-plated cup that I'd won by riding home the winning nag in a donkey derby whilst on a family holiday in Felixstowe when I was seven.

Upstairs was Albert and Vera's bedroom; next to that, another bedroom that I shared with Liam and Clive; and above the stairs, the tiny box room that Bobby had to himself because he was the eldest and really good at football. Then there was a small bathroom and, next to that, the luxurious toilet. Under the stairs was the glory hole – a large cupboard where we kept all the junk that we had no more use for but could not be thrown away. This was also where the electric meter was housed. It gobbled shillings and we always had to keep a good supply on hand as the power had a nasty habit of cutting out in the middle of a favourite TV show.

Cult classics such as the animated antics of salty, old sea-dog, *Captain Pugwash*, were always worth rushing home from school for. *Blue Peter* taught us how to construct a nuclear reactor out of toilet-roll holders and pipe cleaners and, one wonderful day, a nervous elephant rendered Valerie Singleton and John Noakes famously speechless when, under the full glare of the studio lights, it took a dump on live TV.

For more laughs, we turned to *Bootsie and Snudge, Hancock's Half Hour; The Rag Trade;* and *Steptoe And Son. Dixon of Dock Green* and *Z Cars* kept the streets safe. *Emergency Ward 10* and *Doctor Finlay* took care of our medical needs and *Doctor Who* did intergalactic battle with the dastardly Daleks and those other tinny troublemakers, the Cybermen. For a taste of 'glam' we tuned into *The Saint, The Avengers* and *Danger Man,* and the big deal of the week was *Sunday Night at the London Palladium.* More family favourites included American imports *Sgt Bilko* (whom Vera loved) and *I Love Lucy* (whom Albert hated).

The never-to-be-missed show for me was *The Lone Ranger,* though, as he was never seen without his faithful steed, Silver, and his devoted sidekick, Tonto, I could never work out where the 'Lone' bit came in. Especially as he was, more often than not, surrounded by a large tribe of pissed off Apaches all doing their damnedest to fill him full of lead.

Games of hide and seek were a complete waste of time in our house. It was so small and so cluttered that swinging a cat was out of the question. Not that we ever stopped trying. With four young boys to terrorise her, our poor old moggie, Wimple, had a terrible time. One day, Wimple disappeared – never to be seen again. Soon after, our old mutt, Sam, kicked the bucket; presumably to spend eternity in doggy purgatory because he'd never been baptised a Catholic. We didn't bother with another pussycat but Sam was soon replaced by a stray dog that turned up one day and stubbornly refused to leave. Mud-brown in colour, we named the new member of our brood an optimistic 'Rusty'.

Packed into our new home like sardines, we were in paradise compared to the friendly Irish family who moved into the same-sized house next door. The McCarthys had seven kids and, the walls being paper thin, we couldn't help but hear them going about their business and laughingly beating the shit out of one another.

Albert and Vera were proud of their new home and delighted to be out of the damp and dingy cottages that were now being 'tarted up and sold off to poshies', as Vera so eloquently put it. Why anyone would want to pay good money for one of those old dumps, when they could rent a brand new council house for next-to-nothing, was beyond her.

Albert and Vera set about decorating their new dream home. Linoleum was laid in the kitchen, of course, paint was slapped on walls and Vera ran up floral curtains on her foot-cranked Singer. But it was in the bathroom where Vera's interior design skills came to the fore. The wallpaper was a windswept seascape affair featuring sailboats and swooping seagulls. The ceiling was painted a searing sky-blue and, to complete the nautical theme, Vera came up with the brilliant idea of cutting out some of the gulls from the leftover wallpaper and sticking them in jaunty formation across the blue sky of the ceiling.

It seemed like a good idea at the time. But, alas, over the years, the steam from a thousand bath nights played havoc with the wallpaper and, in time, the corners lifted and curled. Meanwhile, on the ceiling, the flock of trapped gulls drooped their wings in submission. The unfortunate seabirds, supposedly driven insane by years of suspended animation, would eventually become completely unglued and, one-by-one, flutter down to disappear beneath the soapy waves.

The best thing about living on the new estate was the hordes of kids that moved there. My parents' generation didn't fuck about when it came to the procreation of the species, so there was never a shortage of kids to have fun and do battle with. We ran, laughed and fought through endless summers of cowboys and Indians. We rode our bikes, smashed windows and tortured cats. We climbed trees and explored rubbish tips, returning home at the end of the day with a set of prized pram wheels. We were so happy that we didn't even know we were poor.

The prized pram wheels were a vital component in the construction of billycarts – which we called 'trucks'. With no brakes and steering with a piece of rope attached to the front axle, we raced them down Windy Rise at breakneck speed. These races would be serious affairs and with up to twenty racers competing, it became necessary to instigate a Le Mans start.

Once, I almost came to serious grief in one of these gladiatorial duels when my pal, Stevie Piper, attempting to snatch the lead, snared his front wheel in my rear axle. Instead of pulling away, Stevie shunted into me and I slammed into the wire-mesh fence that was speeding past on my right, tearing off my rear axle and taking the whole back end of my speeding chariot with it. Stevie's front wheel disintegrated and he disappeared with a scream in my wake. Miraculously, I was still in control but slowed now due to the loss of my rear undercarriage.

The other racers sped past, whooping and hollering, and I momentarily relaxed, thinking I'd survived the crash unscathed. I heard a shrill cry from behind and turned in time to see fat Trevor Barker bringing up the rear as usual. Closing in on me out of the sun and totally out of control, he rode straight up the back of my cart and sent me tumbling into the air. I crash-landed, face down in the middle of the road, relatively uninjured but for a few scratches and a grazed knee. (It yielded an impressive scab that I had fun picking at for weeks.) Fat Trevor got off lightly, went on to race another day and would grow up to waddle in his fat father's footsteps and become a bus driver. Stevie broke his arm, the daft sod. Being out of the racing circuit for a while, Stevie used his time away from the track constructively and, always the entrepreneur, set up a nice little family business with his sister, Sharon. The business worked like this: a gang of us would traipse around to Stevie's house and shell out a precious three-pence a piece. Stevie would stow the cash in his sling, then, one-by-one, we would be led into his house and directed up the stairs to his sister, Sharon's, bedroom. Waiting inside, with the net curtains drawn, was the lovely Sharon, wearing only a thin, cotton night-gown. She would have been about thirteen at the time and though no beauty queen, she was very well-developed for her age. Most important of all, Sharon was willing to take her kit off for a few shekels.

With my heart in my mouth and my small willy straining in my dungarees, I was made to sit on the bed. The room appeared devoid of oxygen and I gulped air like a fish out of water. A cantankerous fly buzzed loudly, trapped behind the curtains. After what Sharon considered a dramatic pause, she slowly peeled the nightie over her head to reveal herself naked but for a tiny pair of pink knickers with a ladybird embroidered in one corner.

I had seen tits before but only in discarded Parade magazines that had been dumped around the back of the village bus shelter. These early, girlie mags featured pictures of heavily made-up women, flaunting huge, pendulous breasts with nipples like saucepan lids. Sharon's developing buds were firm and her nipples like tiny, ripe acorns. Then she pulled her pants down. My jaw dropped and my heart stopped.

'Blimey! So that's what a fanny looks like.'

All too soon, it was over and, gathering my bewildered thoughts, I was yanked off the bed, hustled out of the room and, with wobbly knees, shoved unceremoniously down the stairs. Sharon bade me farewell by yelling past me to her pimp brother, 'Next!'

The business boomed and swarms of horny boys came from miles around to get a geek at their first vision of female loveliness. A week went past, during which time I was locked in the lavvy, furiously wanking and desperately attempting to hold on to the ecstatic memory.

A few days later, Stevie turned up at school and, to match his broken arm, he was now sporting a black eye. Stevie's dad, a vicious drunk, had staggered home early from work one day only to discover that his house had been turned into a bordello. Sharon was branded a floozy and locked in her room for two days and Stevie copped a good hiding, resulting in the black eye.

Not to be deterred, Stevie would grow up to own a chain of massage parlours before going spectacularly bust in the mid-eighties and serving six months for tax evasion. Last time I banged into him, he was running a video store and due up in court for receiving stolen goods. Normally one step ahead of the law, Stevie never had his day in court and, soon after our chance encounter, I heard that he'd disappeared. His beaten-up Jag was found abandoned in Dover and knowing Stevie, right now, he's down in Spain on a nice little earner, running some horrible bar into the ground. The lovely Sharon pursued a career as an actress and was last seen waiting tables in a truck stop on the M4.

WELCOME ABOARD COCKTAIL PARTY
The Captain presents his compliments and requests the pleasure of the company of all passengers at this party, which is held in their honour. Main Lounge. First Sitting Passengers 6.00–7.00 p.m. Second Sitting Passengers 7.45–8.45 p.m.

SEASCAPE
Tuesday 11th December 1973 En route to Tahiti

I was doing my bit mingling with the punters when Claire entered the room on the arm of a chubby bloke in a tux, whom I presumed was hubby.

The Captain and his officers had to stand in line and press the flesh with all the passengers. They usually rushed them through like sheep but this time, I watched, with amusement, as Claire was engaged by each randy officer for a couple of minutes, thereby holding up the long queue.

Once inside the room, she made a beeline for me and introduced Terry, a jovial type though clearly well-oiled. She looked amazing in a shimmering silk gown. Black, low cut, and very chic.

Show time once more, I was with the rest of the troupe backstage in the small dressing room. They were all nervous apart from Claire, who treated the whole thing as exactly what it was – a joke. Sean, drunker than usual, was on fire tonight, and introduced Paul thus:

'Ladies and gentlemen, what can be said about this ... erm ... man that hasn't already been said by others who, quite frankly, should have a little more respect for the elderly. He asked me to give him a good plug before introducing him but as I'm not that way inclined, I'll bring him straight on. Ladies and gentlemen, please welcome to the stage the one and only ... thank God ... Paul Ravel ... and his lead-footed boobies.'

Paul's still not talking to him.

I, uncharacteristically, only drank mineral water at the after-show piss-up and, to further impress Claire, refrained from smoking. After the exercise of the show, she glowed, rosy-cheeked, and as I sat beside her on a costume trunk, I noticed, with growing excitement, the beads of perspiration that clung like jewels to her neck, shoulders and chest. She was only wearing a skimpy costume – not much more than a few sequins and feathers – and it was with great difficulty that I refrained from licking the sweat from her wet, glistening, heavenly body.

Claire saved me from embarrassment when she excused herself as she had to drag young Sebastian from the disco and get him to bed. Before leaving, she rewarded me with a peck on the cheek and thanked me for involving her in the show as she'd had fun. I was so flustered that after a quick, cold shower and a change, I sought out Sean in the Outrigger Bar where we drank Bacardi and Cokes till we were thrown out when the place closed at 2.00 a.m.

Time to remember the 5th of November. Guy Fawkes Night. The months leading up to this eagerly anticipated pagan ritual would see every kid on the estate working feverishly on the construction of a huge bonfire. Built on wasteland behind the houses, we would chop down trees and drag them for miles to create our monster. The adults, happy with an excuse for a clear out, would donate ruined sofas, soiled mattresses, old tyres and miscellaneous junk. Added to this would be countless bundles of newspapers and magazines that, before being tossed on the heap, would be carefully fossicked through in search of a prized Parade magazine.

As the magical night approached, we would make a life-sized dummy of Guy Fawkes, prop him in a pram and trundle him from door to door, begging pennies for the Guy. With the cash, we would buy an arsenal of fireworks and roam the streets tossing miniature incendiaries at one another, under parked cars, and into dustbins. Woe betide anyone who'd been too stingy to have made a contribution to our war chest for they'd be paid a late-night call and have a hissing banger shoved through their letter box.

On the 5th of November, the life-sized dummy of poor old Guy Fawkes would be bunged atop the bonfire, the whole village would turn out to see it lit and a kaleidoscope of fireworks would light up the night sky. The adults would get all puffed up about safety and take over the lighting of the rockets but everyone got to torch something or blow something up. Guy Fawkes Night brought the community together and the heady whiff of gunpowder had the wondrous effect of bringing out the arsonist in all ages. Even the little toddlers got to singe a few hairs and risk blindness as they gleefully waved a sparkler above their heads.

I remember that first Guy Fawkes night in our new home only too well. Vera, Bobby, Liam and Clive were out in the backyard oohing and aahing as Albert launched a few early evening rockets. I was alone in the kitchen and decided to impress little Clive with my pyrotechnic skills by firing him up a sparkler. The trouble was, I couldn't find anything to light the damn thing with as Albert and Vera were non-smokers and there was always a lack of matches in our house. However, on several occasions I had observed that when the ever-resourceful Vera needed to light a fire, she would roll up a piece of newspaper and stick it under the grill ... the electric grill. And that's how I lit the sparkler ... the metal-pronged sparkler!

The resulting electric shock raced up my arm and threw me across the kitchen, where I banged the back of my head on the larder door and slid to the floor. Rusty, our new mutt who'd moved in under the sink after Sam went to doggie purgatory, woke with a start and bit me on the hand, causing me to drop the sparkler on the floor. I watched, dazed, as it spat and fizzed and scorched the lino. I picked it and myself up, kicked Rusty in the ribs, then staggered into the backyard and handed the sparkler to Clive. As I did so, it spluttered and died. Then I threw up in the cabbage patch. Vera wanted to know what was wrong but, feeling like a total twat, I never let on. (I've been terrified of electricity ever since and to this day, am forever going about switching things off or, better still, unplugging every electrical appliance in the house.)

A few weeks later I was sitting in the bog, my head buried happily in an Eagle comic, when I heard the earth-shattering news that President Kennedy had been shot. To be honest, apart from a vague notion that he was some sort of hero who lived in America, I didn't really have a clue who he was. Vera was downstairs busily burning something for dinner. I heard the back door open and slam shut followed by the loud, hysterical voice of Mrs Titmuss from two doors down. The two women traded squawks for a few minutes then Vera, sounding uncharacteristically serious, was yelling up the stairs:

'Archibald, get down here, quick! President Kennedy's been shot!'

Oh shit! I only ever got called Archibald when I'd done something wrong, and my first thought was to do a bunk out of the window, hightail it across the shed roof, then shimmy down a drainpipe to freedom. But hang about, there was no way I could cop the blame for this one, as Albert still had hold of my air pistol. Had, in fact, taken it to work to cull a family of crows that had been getting in his gooseberries. Engrossed as I was in the extraterrestrial exploits of Dan Dare, I reluctantly threw the comic on the floor and ambled downstairs to the kitchen. When I walked in I was greeted with the strange and confusing apparition of Vera, clutching my squirming brothers in her arms and beseeching me to join them. This was all highly embarrassing as we were never a touchy-feely family. Physical contact was, in general, avoided at all costs. Vera was sobbing her old heart out.

*5.30 a.m. – SS KIONI IS EXPECTED TO ARRIVE AT PAPEETE PILOT STATION.*There is usually an interval of approximately 1 hour between arrival at the pilot station and the time when the vessel actually docksIn order to avoid congestion, passengers are requested to remain on the open decks, in the public rooms or in their cabins until an announcement is made over the public address system advising them when to proceed ashore.

SEASCAPE

Saturday 15th December 1973 At Tahiti

Tahiti has always meant different things to different people. For adventurers, seekers of truth and beauty, wanderers, and those of art and literature, there is a vast store of writings and paintings, research and histories about these beautiful islands. Unfortunately, all completely wasted on the crew of the good ship, Kioni. Tahiti meant a chance to get off the ship, eat some decent food and, of course, get completely shit-faced.

Mind you, approaching Tahiti from the sea is a truly awe-inspiring sight. The blue-green volcanic mountains loom large, with peaks reaching almost eight-thousand feet into the trade winds. White surf pounds the reef and, broken in many places, it rims the figure-of-eight-shaped paradise and lush tropical vegetation spills down over everything. Seven weeks ago I'd never set foot out of dreary-old England. I can't believe I'm here.

We were tied up in the little semicircular harbour of Papeete by 7.00 a.m. and the usual quorum of Don-the-Slot, Tiny-Tom, Bunger and myself, stepped on to the glorious copra-scented quay. Customs was basically non-existent so we'd taken the trouble to secrete a couple of dozen pre-rolled spliffs in camera cases and the like.

All along the tree-lined waterfront, colourful booths had been set up selling shell and pearl jewellery, wooden carvings and Polynesian craftwork. Bunger cut a rakish pose in a splendid pandanus hat. The smiling stallholders would soon be inundated with the swarm of disembarking passengers who, for now, were being hijacked by ship's photographer, Reg, and his mangy assistant, Dirty Charlie, for the all-important gangway shot.

We weren't due to sail for Acapulco until 2.00 p.m. the following day and had decided to splash out on a bit of luxury and check into a hotel for the night. Bunger led the way along the quay, where yachts from all over the world were tied up.

The main drag, the Boulevard Pomare, was abuzz with what passed for early morning rush hour. We ambled along, soaking up the atmosphere of the busy little town, past stylish boutiques displaying the latest Paris fashions. A gendarme halted traffic at an intersection and blew his whistle, and a parade of raven-haired Eurasian lovelies swivelled our heads as they sped past on whining scooters.

We plonked ourselves down at a pavement café, and Bunger ordered breakfast in flawless French (at least, I think it was flawless French; it could have been Outer Mongolian for all I knew) and, after stuffing ourselves with delicious fresh croissants and several cups of bitter coffee, Bunger overpaid the bill with American dollars and then led us around the corner to an Avis office where we hired a Mini Moke.

Don took the wheel and, top down, we roared up the street, waving to the hordes of passengers that were now flooding into town. Driving past the airport, Don nearly got us all killed when he hurtled around a traffic island the wrong way, narrowly missing a mini-bus full of locals. Turns out that Don had never driven outside Aus and an argument ensued before Tom wrestled the wheel from him, forcing him to pull over. Tom delivered us safely to our destination; a modern, pyramid-shaped hotel set in lush, tropical gardens of banana, breadfruit, papaya, guava, lime, orange, grapefruit and mango trees. Blimey!

After negotiating two double rooms, Bunger and I blew a joint on our balcony. The majestic beauty of Moorea, ten miles across the bay, made for a dramatic backdrop and, as the strong South African weed took hold, appeared to hover on the blue horizon.

We rendezvoused with Tom and Don by the pool and Bunger ordered the first round of the day. We were on island time now and it was a good half-hour later when an afro-haired waiter waddled across from the bar with what appeared to be four pint-sized fruit juices. As Bunger explained, the drink, called a 'May Day', was to be treated with respect as it was a concoction of several white spirits, dark rum, grenadine, umpteen different fruit juices, coconut liqueur and a splash of Grand Marnier for good measure (or something like that). Disguised as a healthful fruit punch, the stuff tasted harmless enough but after knocking back three more, we were all pissed as farts and languished by the pool for most of the day. We had the place more or less to ourselves, smoked dope openly, and, by mid-afternoon, we were sunburnt and completely wasted.

A brief siesta was called for before we met in the open-air bar at six. We'd hardly eaten all day so following one for the road, we piled into the Moke and headed off in search of sustenance. We drove for an hour before coming across an up-market joint called *Le* 'something or other', where we enjoyed a sumptuous dinner. Bunger, in his element, expertly worked his way through the expensive wine list and, having bunged most of the staff on our arrival, we were treated like VIPs. After settling the extortionate bill, the *maître d'* gave us complimentary balloons of cognac and recommended a nightclub just a few miles distant.

In spite of the state we were in, it was virtually impossible to get lost as, apart from a few dusty tracks heading off into the interior, there was only the coast road to negotiate and we took our Froggie mate's advice and headed off into the balmy night in search of the club. There was little in the way of street lights and Tom, an expert driver, handled the little car like a pro. The fat joint he had clenched between his teeth left a glittering stream of sparks in our wake.

We found the club, no probs. Loud disco music boomed from the palm-thatched building, which was built on stilts above a lagoon. Festooned with lights and open on all sides, with a central bar, the place was jumping and a loud cheer of welcome greeted us as we skidded to a halt out front.

Bunger bought a round of the local Hinano beer and we boogied through the throng of happy revellers and took up position at the edge of the dance floor. The club was devoid of tourists and, mercifully, none of the passengers had found their way to this remote part of the island. The majority of the punters appeared to be Polynesian, with just a sprinkling of French expats and soldiers, who sat chatting and smoking at the bar. The only other people from the ship were two English hosties and their Greek boyfriends, who waved and gestured for us to join them at their table.

Maggie is a scary-looking Mancunian who's a hoot of fun and can drink the biggest pisshead under the table. Tina, her equally scary friend, is from Cardiff. They've both worked at sea for a couple of years, are never short of boyfriends, and do all of their socialising going from one crew party to the next somewhere down in the bowels of the ship. In fact, apart from meeting them in a work capacity in the public rooms, this was the first time I'd seen them above decks since leaving Southampton.

Maggie's escort this evening happened to be a good friend of mine, the fabulously mad Yannis, who managed the Marine Bar and also happened to be one of the few Greeks I knew who smoked dope. Yannis introduced us to his pal, Thanos, who worked in the kitchens. It was obvious that all four of them were stoned off their heads and we were in good company.

We danced our legs off to a mixture of Euro-pop and Tahitian drum beats, drank gallons of alcohol, squandered a ton of cash, and made frequent trips to the beach to smoke dope and cool off in the dark lagoon. In spite of our best efforts, none of us managed to crack on to any local puss as the club was, in the main, full of couples. Bunger came the closest when he chatted up a tasty little French nurse. Unfortunately for him, her stroppy Legionnaire boyfriend turned up and things looked like turning nasty until my fast-talking friend disarmed him with patter and free drinks. Never mind. A long way from home, we all had a fuckin' ball.

At about one in the morning, the crowd began to thin and, guessing we were about halfway around the fairy tale island, we decided to keep going in the same direction and complete our sozzled circumnavigation. Our four shipmates, Maggie, Tina, Yannis, and Thanos, had arrived by taxi and were now stranded, so once we'd dragged Tom off the beach, where he'd passed out, all eight of us piled into the Moke.

Bravely taking the helm, Bunger steered our overloaded chariot into the night. With virtually no traffic on the road, the nearest we came to grief was when a startled islander came wobbling out of the dark on a bicycle and Bunger, horn blaring, was forced to swerve to the other side of the road to miss him. Apart from that little mishap, we only veered off the road a dozen more times and were approaching the outskirts of Papeete, when Bunger, in need of a break, turned down a side road and parked at Venus Point.

According to a memorial plaque, Captain James Cook had spent three months here in 1769, his mission being to observe the transit of Venus as it passed across the face of the sun. Here to do our own star-gazing, we staggered on to the black-sand beach, stumbled about gathering driftwood, and finally managed to get a bonfire going. Maggie never went anywhere without supplies and produced a litre-bottle of Vodka from a large string bag. We passed the bottle and the last of the dope around and talked bullshit as the fire crackled and sent sparks into the firmament above.

Showing off my climbing skills, I shimmied up a palm tree that jutted out over the lagoon and, reaching the top, suddenly lost my grip when a large coconut crab scurried from the palm fronds, ran up my arm and across my back, and then disappeared down a hole at the base of the trunk. It scared the shit out of me and I tumbled twenty foot into the water.

One by one, we passed out on the sand and I woke dehydrated and itching from umpteen sand fly bites. The fire was almost out, the sun was up and it was already promising to be another beautiful day in paradise. We had the crescent-shaped beach to ourselves, apart from a teenage couple playing in the surf. Their outrigger canoe was pulled up on the sand and placed artistically under a grove of gently swaying palm trees, the scene so achingly picture-perfect it could have been art directed by the lingering spirit of Paul Gauguin. Tiny-Tom opened his eyes, groaned, pulled himself to his feet and pissed on the dying embers of the fire.

Yannis urged us to get a move on as he had to open the Marine Bar at nine. Come to that, Tom was supposed to be on board to print the day's *Seascape*. Lucky for him, he had a very understanding Greek counterpart who hardly ever bothered going ashore and was always picking up the slack for his young English colleague.

After a reviving dip in the ocean, we drove, with caution, the last couple of miles into Papeete and dropped our pals off opposite the port. Continuing on to our hotel, we crashed by the pool for the morning before checking-out of our virtually unused rooms and driving back to town to drop off the trusty Moke. At two in the afternoon, we cast off for Acapulco, three thousand six hundred nautical miles across the vast Pacific blue.

11

Tongue Sandwich

With the arrival of winter, we donned duffle coats and wellies, scarves, gloves and scratchy balaclavas, which gave us the appearance of miniature terrorists. When the snow came, we took the pram wheels off our trucks and converted them into toboggans. We made snowmen, with lumps of coal for eyes, a carrot for a nose and a turnip for a knob. Snowball fights went on for hours and we turned the pavements into giant ice slides, causing havoc for little old ladies and home-bound drunks. Red-cheeked at the end of the day, we would bang in the door and, before being allowed to sit down for dinner (which we called tea), peeled off our wet togs and draped them over the clothes horse to steam and ferment in front of the fire.

And then it was Christmas. What with four boys, the Yuletide season must have been a hideously stressful time for Albert and Vera but come Christmas morning, the pillowcases that we'd left at the foot of our beds the night before would be chock-a-block full of presents. After ripping open our gifts and checking out who got what, we would race down to breakfast (which we called breakfast), which always began with half a grapefruit smothered in sugar. God only knows why, but we only ever got to see these exotic citrus fruits once a year.

Following breakfast, we played with our new toys some more and gorged ourselves on nuts and dates and other luxurious goodies seen only at Christmas. After stuffing an enormous turkey in the oven, Vera would drag us all, kicking and screaming, to morning mass at St Cuthbert's. The church was always packed on Christmas morning – the collection plate overflowing as lapsed Catholics, driven by guilt, turned out in droves to sing carols, press the flesh and generally feel good about themselves.

On our return home, we'd be assailed with the stench of over-steamed veggies that had been left to boil away throughout the long, drawn-out mass. We would again disappear to play with our toys, which was never as much fun as the batteries would be running low by now and we'd be obliged to turn to the less interesting gifts that aunties and uncles had contributed. A jigsaw puzzle of the Battle of Jutland. A Roy of the Rovers annual. (More bloody football!) A Davy Crockett hat. Several yo-yos. A couple of hula hoops. And a ball of string from mad Auntie Ethel (who, it was said, was 'resting' in the local bughouse). And there was always a compendium of games. A big box full of Snakes and Ladders, Chinese Chequers, Tiddlywinks, Ludo and Blow Football. (More interesting than the real game but made you dizzy after ten minutes of play.)

Vera would yell up the stairs 'Come and get it!', and we would once more crowd around the dining-room table for a huge blow-out Christmas lunch (which we called Christmas dinner). We'd pull crackers and put on paper hats and stuff ourselves on a scorched turkey full of stuffing, brussels sprouts steamed to perdition, Birds Eye frozen peas, which even Vera couldn't bugger up, and a ton of delicious roast potatoes, burnt to a crisp and smothered with lashings of lumpy gravy. There was always a fight over the wishbone, and then the Christmas pud would be brought out, whereupon another fight would erupt over the hidden sixpence.

In the afternoon, neighbours would drop in for a beer or a glass of Bols Advocaat, and Vera would get drunk on two glasses of sherry and her voice would raise several decibels. I don't remember Albert ever drinking much. Maybe it was because his old man had been such a piss artist. When he did drink, he usually ended up with a crippling migraine, which, along with his campaign medals, is the only thing I ever inherited from him.

In the evening we would squash into the front room to watch the Queen's speech on the box. We did this not out of respect but to take the piss. Her Majesty's message would be followed by a Disney film that we'd all seen umpteen times before and then we'd all be packed off to bed with a cup of cocoa, leaving Albert and Vera to count the cost of Christmas. I don't know how they coped.

The time came for me to sit my eleven plus; the exam that would determine whether I'd be going to grammar school or heading off to secondary modern. Apart from football, which I avoided, religious instruction, which I ridiculed, and maths, which seemed to induce in me a kind of numerical dyslexia, I consistently achieved good marks.

At junior school, the end of term results were an uncomplicated affair with marks out of ten given in each subject. These numbers were then totted up and a single grade awarded to each child. In the six years that I spent at St Cuthbert's, I never came less than fifth in class and should have been a prime candidate to receive one of the few scholarships awarded by St Edmond's College.

St Edmond's College was set in the leafy environs of a country estate, just up the road from St Cuthbert's. It was a dead-posh Catholic public (private) school for boys and – guess what? – I didn't stand a snowball's chance in hell of getting in.

As happened every year, the scholarships went, not to the highest achievers, but to the well-heeled children of the local landowners and landed gentry – the very children whose parents had no need of financial assistance. But these fat cats were friends with our headmaster, Mr Drinkwater, and well-connected with the clergy. It was all so phoney, so corrupt and so bloody Catholic. Of course, my coarse cockney accent wouldn't have done me any favours and my complete disinterest in the teachings of the Church most definitely blotted my copybook, if not my soul. The powers that be had my number and they were convinced that it was 666.

As it turned out, there were limited spaces to be had at the local grammar school, too, so it was explained to Albert and Vera, by Mr Drinkwater, that it would be a waste of time me even sitting the eleven plus. In his haughty opinion, I had no hope of passing and the best solution would be to enrol me at the nearest Catholic secondary modern school. Albert, with his distaste for the rabid class system, argued my case but, in truth, I think he had little desire for one of his sons to be corrupted by a decent education and was relieved that he wouldn't be required to shell out for the expensive 'poncy' uniforms that were *de rigueur* at the more 'salubrious' schools.

I was thrilled with the news that, along with the majority of my pals, I was to join my big brother, Bobby, at Cardinal Bourne Secondary Modern School. The big advantage was the fact that the school was situated some twelve miles away. That put it just about on the outskirts of London. This was, as I saw it, a far more exciting prospect than attending school in the country with a bunch of hoity-toity hooray Henrys.

And so it came to pass that I caught the 7.30 a.m. bus the five miles into town every morning and then connected with a coach that transported me the remaining seven miles to school.

Cardinal Bourne Secondary Modern School had only been open for four years, Bobby having been one of the first students to enrol. An ugly, sixties, glass-box edifice, the very best thing about the place, as opposed to the previous two schools mentioned, was that it was co-ed. This was a huge plus as I had stopped chasing girls to beat them up and was now pursuing girls to feel them up. It was soon after starting at Cardinal Bourne that I got my very first tongue sandwich.

I had the hots for Maureen Day who, in more ways than one, was in a different class from me. With her sparkling turquoise eyes, a mass of curly, blonde hair and a cute, freckled nose, she was considered one of the prettiest girls in school. We were too shy to speak but always making eyes at one another. Then one day I got lucky.

Bunking off football, I was loitering in the cloakroom when Maureen walked in. She was crying and dabbing at her gorgeous eyes with an embroidered handkerchief. I asked her what was wrong and, between sobs, she explained that she had been thrown out of domestic science class when Mrs Rumble had heard her say 'Shit!' when the cake that she was attempting to bake had stubbornly refused to rise. I took Maureen's hand and told her not to worry. I told her not to let the old girl get to her and tried to make light of what Maureen evidently considered a dire situation. Then, with a masterstroke, I proceeded to rattle off an impressive array of multicoloured profanities that put her 'Shit!' in the shade.

Having the desired effect, Maureen cheered up instantly and I was rewarded with a smile that confirmed in me, without any doubt, something that the Catholic Church had failed miserably to achieve ... the existence of a wondrous and benevolent Heavenly Father. Thanks be to God. Hidden behind a wall of duffle coats and anoraks, Maureen and I started snoggin'.

We'd meet in the cloakroom every day. I loved kissing Maureen and, sometimes, she'd let me feel her small breasts but when I tried to stick my hand up her skirt, she'd scream blue murder. One day, she failed to turn up for our planned dalliance and, later that afternoon, Maureen's best friend, Teresa O'Connell, informed me, spitefully, that Maureen was no longer my girlfriend but was now going out with Giuseppe Pelligrino. I was mortified.

Two years my senior, Giuseppe Pelligrino was a vicious little thug and godfather to a gang of Italian kids who wreaked mayhem throughout the school. The children of Sicilian migrants who came to the district after the war, this mini-Mafia ran card games in the playground and sold fags around the back of the bicycle shed after school.

Always moving in packs, they liked to fight and the odd knife attack was not uncommon. I got along fine with most of 'the wogs' as we called them. The best way to deal with the little gorillas, was to stand up to them and it was generally only the more dorky kids who came to grief.

Giuseppe Pelligrino, however, was a regular little Joe Pesci in the making so, preferring a broken heart to a broken nose (or a ballpoint pen in the neck), I gallantly accepted the realisation that my first true love was lost to me forever ... and fuck the pair of 'em!

The Sicilian girls were something else altogether. With smooth olive skin, large ripe breasts and childbearing hips, these exotic Lolitas, always earlier to mature than their English counterparts, oozed an earthy sexuality way beyond their years. Every once in a while one of these girls would mysteriously disappear from school and a rumour would quickly circulate that she'd fallen from grace and was 'up the duff'. The poor girl would be shipped back to Sicily in disgrace and, after giving birth to her bastard bambino, spend the rest of her days chopping wood and fetching water on her uncle's farm, high in the hills above Palermo. Least ways, she was never seen again.

DISCOTHEQUE
The Sounds of today! – with *ARCHIE* –11.00 p.m.–1.00 a.m.
Main Lounge

SEASCAPE
Sunday 16th December 1973 At Tahiti and en route for Acapulco

Half an hour after sailing, I was in the ballroom to rehearse for *The South Pacific Show*. A favourite amongst the old hands, who claimed it was Paul's most hilariously pretentious spectacle by far. Claire showed up looking gorgeous but sad, and we swapped stories of our very different time spent in Tahiti. Hubby only made it as far as the nearest bar and she was left to traipse about the shops with her son, who was bored stiff. What a waste.

Following rehearsals, I went up on the Crew Deck to catch some rays. In spite of The Stones blaring in my cans, I was half asleep when I sensed someone standing over me. It was Henri. As he spread out his towel and laid his wrinkled old body next to me, I noticed that something was troubling him. He can never keep a secret, loves to gossip, particularly enjoys boasting of his numerous conquests, and delighted in giving me a blow-by-blow description of his sordid sojourn in paradise, where he claimed he'd behaved like a whore.

As was often the case, his 'fiancé', Georgios, had to stay on board to work so Henri had joined Paul and another couple of queens and gone trolling for trade ashore. Henri could never be accused of being picky and didn't have to prowl far before snaring a bare-foot Tahitian dock worker, whom he dragged back to his cabin, conveniently vacated by Phil who was entertaining his current northbound bonk with a day trip to Moorea.

After doing the dirty deed, Henri's native friend had waddled off the ship in a pair of Phil's favourite Gucci loafers. The stingy Welsh hairdresser was very pissed off and convinced that Henri was involved in the theft. For Henri's part, he was revelling in the drama but, keen to come clean, was scared of Phil's wrath and asked me if I'd be present when he spilt the beans.

After dinner, I went to Henri and Phil's cabin and, over a beer, Henri told his sad tale and apologised profusely. The awkward silence that followed was eventually broken by Henri who, sitting on Phil's bunk, let rip with a loud, nervous and extremely moist fart. Then Henri stood, gingerly, to reveal what can only be described as a large splotch of ... anal leakage!

Phil stared at his soiled bunk and, calm under the circumstances, shook his head and muttered softly, 'Oh, for fuck's sake,' and Henri, mortified, ran out of the cabin clutching the back of his trousers and loudly proclaiming, between sobs, that he'd suffered yet another miscarriage. Gosh!

After bingo, it was my turn to spin records in the disco. You might think this sounds fun but it's not my favourite gig as I'm constantly bombarded with requests for all kinds of dross. You wouldn't believe some of the rubbish I'm asked to play – David Cassidy, Sweet, T-Rex, Slade, The Electric Light Orchestra, Suzi Quatro, dreadful Gilbert O'Sullivan, Bread, The Carpenters, and on and on. And don't get me started on Wings. What the fuck was Paul McCartney thinking?

Anyway, the good news is, I only have to man the disco every third night or so as I alternate with Romeo and Jerry, a couple of Filipino waiters who love the gig as it gets them out of clean-up duties in the dining room. Romeo lives up to his namesake and is always hitting on girls. As for Jerry, well, he's very good friends with Paul, if you know what I mean.

Pearls to swine, I'd just slipped *Mercy, Mercy Me* by Marvin Gaye on to the turntable when Claire walked in. She was looking for her son, who wasn't there, so I jumped right in and she accepted my offer of a dance.

'Just one,' she said coyly.

I rested a hand on her slim waist and as we shuffled around the floor, her soft hair brushed my cheek and I breathed in her scent and held her tighter. To be in such close proximity drove me wild with desire and I was forced to bend slightly at the waist to conceal the obvious erection that was straining in my tight trousers.

Just as the song was coming to an end, Claire suddenly pushed me away as she'd spied Sebastian standing with a group of friends in a darkened corner of the lounge. I leapt back behind the sound booth and grabbed *My Ding-A-Ling*, the Chuck Berry hit (certainly not my cuppa tea but the punters love it) and watched, with despair, as Claire disappeared out of the door with her son.

I finished the night with *Mouldy Old Dough*, the God-awful but much requested one-hit wonder from Lieutenant Pigeon and was packing up when I was surprised to see Claire smiling at me from the back of the lounge. I walked over to her and she apologised that she'd left so abruptly but was keen to get her son safely tucked up in bed. We both knew the real reason – that she'd felt awkward having him see the two of us dancing together.

The disco emptied out and Claire waited for me whilst I packed the records away and locked the sound booth. She declined the offer of a drink without stating the obvious – that she'd no desire to bump into her husband, who'd definitely be propping up one of the bars. Instead, she suggested a walk and we made our way out to the Promenade Deck and then up on to the Sports Deck, which I knew, at this time of night, would be deserted and in virtual darkness.

Wordlessly, we made our way to the bench where we'd first met. It was a warm night but I was shaking with a myriad of emotions new to me. We sat beside one another in silence. Time passed, then Claire gently took my hand in her lap and I dared to look in her eyes.

She ruffled my hair, smiled her beautiful smile, dropped her head and said, in a whisper, 'You know nothing can happen, don't you?'

My heart was racing so fast that I thought I'd faint and, in reply, only managed to croak a wan, 'I know that.' With that, she lifted her head, our eyes locked once again, and we were drawn together, out of control, kissing, passionately, with a burning, wanton hunger that I'd never felt before.

Claire was trembling in my arms and I knew she was experiencing the same intense rush of emotions as myself. She sat astride of me and I undid the buttons on her dress. She wasn't wearing a bra and I sucked on her small, perfect breasts. She arched her back, moaned, and wrapped her arms around my head and her legs tightly about my waist. We kissed more furiously. Weeks, days, hours, minutes passed, when, suddenly, she pushed me away, struggled to her feet, adjusted the dress that had ridden up above her waist, scooped up her shoes and ran, barefoot, from the Sports Deck, leaving me alone and panting, gasping for air.

I pulled a crumpled joint from my shirt pocket, lit up and, when my heart rate finally slowed, made my way to my cabin for a long, sleepless night.

The school was forever crying poor, begging funds for one thing or another and, looking back, I surmise that the majority of our teachers were on the bottom rung of the educational ladder and couldn't get a job anywhere else.

There was Mr McMurray-Jones, a truly violent and fucked-up Scot, who taught maths and technical drawing and was never seen without his pet T-square that he called Jimmy. Due to his savage behaviour, Mr McMurray-Jones commanded a great deal of respect but he was also looked up to for his wild sense of humour. He would have us in stitches as he gleefully poleaxed some poor unfortunate across the back of the skull with Jimmy.

English lessons were always a joy, taken as they were by Mr Hoffman. Mr Hoffman was a young, strangely passionate Austrian who's questionable command of the English language was more than compensated for by his enthusiasm for passing on his love of the written word.

I look back with a melancholic fondness to those far-off winter afternoons. Snow flurries swirling in the deserted playground and dark by three. The classroom, snug as a sauna, and Mr Hoffman, a tear in his eye, reciting Shakespeare to a spellbound and sniggering class.

'Unt gentlemen in Engaland now abed shall sink zemselfes accurzed zey were not here, unt holt zheir manhuts cheap vhiles any speaks zatt fort viz us upon Zaint Crispinz day.' Enter the Earl of Salisbury. Mr Hoffman did his best. He was a good teacher and instilled in me an early obsession with literature 'n that, innit!

Biology lessons were presided over by an ancient, toothless nun called Sister Isabel. With a face like a dropped pie and reeking strongly of mothballs, I find it incredible that this sour-pussed old celibate was the entity placed in charge of our early sex education. Her carnal knowledge only one step up from 'Mummy Bee meets Daddy Bee', she'd point, confusingly, at medical diagrams of the male and female genitalia. At pains to answer our many questions, she'd fumble with her rosary beads and suggest that we carve up a dead frog or a rabbit or two. It was farcical, sad and pointless – especially as we were gaining valuable, hands-on experience from the comely Sicilian girls around the back of the Woodwork Department at lunchtime (which, of course, we called dinnertime ... blah, blah, blah ... I think you get the picture).

The most popular teacher in school was the very hip Mr Phipps, who taught music and played in his own jazz band. In class, he strived valiantly and, alas, in vain, to turn us on to the likes of Beethoven, Mozart and Bach. But he'd also play us early Beatles hits and other pop songs that he deemed worthy of a spin. One day, he silenced the class and with obvious reverence, slipped a record on to the turntable, and we listened, in rapture, to *The House Of The Rising Sun* by The Animals. A bachelor who lived with his elderly mother, Mr Phipps was sacked one day for supposedly being over-familiar with one of his young prodigies who'd stayed back late for extra trumpet lessons. Mr Phipps couldn't get another teaching gig after that. His old mum died of the 'Big C' and Mr Phipps drank himself to death.

By far, the nuttiest teacher we had was Mr Cakebread, who taught science. I'm not kidding! This guy was the archetypical mad professor, launching into frenzied raves over nothing and throwing Bunsen burners, test tubes, and anything he could get his hands on all over the classroom. The only time he was ever calm was during a lightning storm, when he'd be rendered strangely mute and stand at a window staring out at a lone oak tree that grew in the middle of the playing field. It seemed that, for some strange reason only he would ever know, he lived for the day when the tree would be struck and erupt into a huge, apocalyptic fireball. It never happened and, one day, Mr Cakebread was carted off to join Auntie Ethel in the local bughouse. Poor old bugger. We never saw him again, either.

A lot of the kids I was running with at Cardinal Bourne were Londoners. This helped eliminate any trace of bumpkin in my accent and it took on a far more 'street cred' artful dodger lilt. I was having fun, the only drag being the twelve-mile journey that I had to endure to and from school every day.

Prior to boarding the 7.30 a.m. bus out of the village, I first had to complete my paper round, the only source of income for a struggling oik. This meant getting up at five-thirty to sort the bloody papers, then trudging around the village in all weathers, delivering my precious cargo to a news-hungry public. It wasn't so bad in the summer months but during the winter, it was a constant battle to keep the papers dry. When they did get wet, they weighed a ton and the punters would give me an ear-bashing and whinge about their soggy *Daily Mails* (as though the contents were any less sopping). On weekends, I could sleep in a bit but delivering the *Times* and *Observers* to all the posh houses on a Sunday was a nightmare – they weighed a ton. Even in good weather.

There was a big, old, stately Tudor home on my round. I would struggle up the long, winding driveway, past the manicured lawns, past the gazebo and past the apple orchard that Albert took care of for a few extra quid. On weekends, a small boy would often appear in one of the upstairs windows. He was a pasty-faced kid with huge glasses, which gave him the appearance of a startled owl – or a young Bill Gates. He was always delighted to see me and would give me a pathetic little wave. I would respond by giving him the finger. For some reason, this always tickled him pink and he would laugh his head off, affording me a look at his mouthful of metallic braces.

I felt a bit sorry for him, really. For one thing, he was the only kid that I knew who had to wear braces. I, like all of my pals, made do with fangs that grew every which way. And he missed out on all the fun in the village as he went to an ultra-snooty boarding school in London and, when home on weekends, was never allowed out of the house.

His name was Simeon Peacock. An only child, his father was a big cheese in the city and rarely, if ever, home. His mother was a very bossy lady who strutted about the village talking loudly to anyone who didn't see her coming first. She sat on a lot of committees and was always dressed in riding gear, though nobody ever saw her on a horse.

I was always greatly relieved after delivering to their house as my load would be considerably lightened due to the fact that they ordered just about every newspaper in the English-speaking world, plus a stack of boring magazines about antiques, cooking, country life, and all kinds of drivel. They ordered everything but comics for poor old Simeon, which, I presumed, was another avenue of pleasure denied to their cloistered offspring. The closest Simeon ever got to comic relief was a subscription to Look and Learn, a dull, pseudo-science rag, which, after leafing through it a few times, I deduced to be about as stimulating as a Parade magazine with all the pictures of tits torn out.

The Peacocks spent a small fortune on newspapers and magazines but they never paid their bill on time and they never gave me a tip at Christmas, as they'd be conveniently out of the country on a skiing holiday.

Something horrible happened to Simeon one day, though, at the time, I remember finding it piss funny. I first heard of Simeon's misadventure from Mrs Skaggs, who went to the bingo with Vera on Monday nights and was forever dropping around to our house to trade gossip and spread malicious rumours. Mrs Skaggs worked as a charlady, three times a week, up at the Peacock pile. Apparently, Simeon had been enduring his torturous braces for over two years and was due to have them removed. The big day finally arrived, along with a shiny red racing bike, a gift from his absent father. When Simeon came home from boarding school the following weekend, minus his braces, not even his commandant of a mother could prevent him from jumping on his new bike and making a desperate dash for freedom.

He tore off down the long, winding driveway, past the apple orchard that Albert looked after for a few extra quid, past the gazebo and past the manicured lawns. The great escape was going to plan until Simeon turned into the lane at the bottom of the driveway and slammed, head first, into the back of Mr Springate's milk float, which was parked in the road. Hilariously, Simeon emerged relatively unscathed – apart from losing all of his front teeth, bar one!

Simeon had to stay home for a long time after the accident and we became friends for a while. He was into all kinds of stuff that I had no interest in but he did have the best chemistry set that I'd ever seen. We spent hours in his attic laboratory, concocting all kinds of experiments that Simeon would engineer to climax in a flash of blue smoke and a minor explosion.

One day, Simeon's father ran off with a young bird, divorced Mrs Peacock and went to live in France. Mrs Peacock still got about the village in riding gear but she didn't strut so much and she didn't talk so loud any more either. She flogged the Tudor house to a Persian family and her and Simeon went off to live in Tunbridge Wells.

I bumped into Simeon years later at a wedding. Lucky for him, he hadn't grown up to look like Bill Gates, but he didn't look like Robert Redford either. Balding, and still wearing a pair of large specs, I couldn't help but wonder if his old mum wasn't still buying his clothes for him as he was dressed, badly, in a cheap beige suit, a pair of grey shoes and a pink, knitted tie.

The only good thing about weddings is the free booze and, as Simeon and I got progressively hammered, he told me all about the messy, legal bullshit he'd been forced to endure when his father had snuffed it. With the help of a battalion of lawyers, the new 'young' Mrs Peacock had done her damnedest to snaffle the lion's share of the old man's booty and Simeon had no choice but to fight back.

After many months of acrimonious wrangling, Attila the stepmother settled out of court and Simeon received a substantial inheritance. Over the years, he'd lived a charmed existence, basically sitting on his arse and adding to his windfall by dabbling in the property market.

With the *joie de vivre* arrived at only by the guzzling of gallons of complimentary alcohol, Simeon struck me as a happy, well-adjusted individual. A man in full. Then he went and stuffed things up when, after lighting my cigar for me, put the used match back in the box. I really hate it when people do that.

Simeon introduced me to his wife, Rachel, who, with the amount of piss I had on board, appeared to be a gorgeous-looking creature. I would have attempted to have a crack at her if I hadn't been so legless.

Madonna urged guests to '*Get Into The Groove*' and Rachel dragged Simeon on to the dance floor. They happily made twats of themselves, leaping around and waving their arms in the air like a couple of epileptic windmills. I watched them from the bar and wondered, not for the first time, why posh people can't dance for shit. Simeon looked over and gave me a pathetic little wave to which I responded by giving him the finger. Tickled pink, he didn't disappoint but laughed his head off, affording me a look at his set of perfect, pearly-white teeth. I'm not kidding! He had gnashers like a newsreader.

Still on my paper round, there was one house that made my laborious job eminently worthwhile. At number twenty-seven Belmont Avenue, lived a young housewife. Nay, a goddess! She would greet me at her door every morning, scantily clad in a minuscule gossamer night-gown. She was drop-dead gorgeous and made me so anxious I could hardly speak. I can still remember nervously handing over her *Daily Mirror* and then, feeling my cheeks flush, being forced to take a sudden interest in my scuffed monkey boots. As my eyes dropped towards the ground, I would dare to linger for a delicious second on the dark, mysterious triangle, clearly visible through the thin fabric of her nightie.

Her name was Mrs Foster. Mrs Belinda Foster. I had an awful schoolboy crush on this woman (along with Una Stubbs, Stevie's sister, Sharon, and Lulu) and she was placed in the top drawer of my early fantasy file. (When I got a bit older, Una Stubbs was ousted by

Felicity Kendal, Sharon got dumped and Lulu was traded-in for Olivia Newton-John. Mrs Foster, however, continued to be pulled from the top drawer for many years to come.)

She would take the paper from my trembling hand and I imagined she allowed her fingers to gently brush mine. And then, for a few agonising minutes, she would engage me in conversation with her ever-so-sweet angelic voice. It wasn't much of a conversation. She would enquire as to how I was doing at school. Ask whether I had a little girlfriend yet. I would just stand before her, mouth agape, trying not to faint. When the torturous ecstasy was over, she would thank me for the paper, tilt her pretty head and slam the door in my face. Dejected, excited and confused, I would be left to limp uncomfortably home, skip breakfast and rush upstairs to the toilet.

Years later, I met Mrs Foster on one of my many nostalgic jaunts back to the village. (Yes, I know. It sounds like I'm forever bumping into people from my past. It's very annoying and it happens a lot, and it happens to be true. More to the point, this is my story and I'll pad it out any way I damn-well please!)

She was sitting at the bar in the Sow and Pigs. I'd have been in my early forties at the time. That would have put her in her mid-fifties. I recognised her straight away as nature had been very kind to her and she was still something of a horn bag. I poured a couple of Chardonnays down her shapely neck and when we were both a bit tipsy, I let on how she'd driven me crazy as a kid and what an inspiration she'd been to me in my many hours spent thrashing away in the karzi. Another couple of drinks and she spilt the beans. She'd been fully aware of the devastating effect that she'd had on me as a nipper. What a bitch!

Better late than never, I was about to put the hard word on her when her hubby spoilt everything by having the audacity to turn up in the pub. Things went downhill fast after that as Mr Foster ('call me Frank') bored the arse off the pair of us by droning on about his rhododendrons and his new ride-on lawn mower.

PORTHOLES:

We would respectfully request passengers to assist by keeping their porthole closed as opening them causes the indoor temperature to rise. We thank our passengers for their cooperation in this matter.

SEASCAPE

Monday 17th December 1973 En route to Acapulco

Claire failed to show up on the Sports Deck this morning but she did rock up for rehearsals this afternoon. Mind you, she kept her distance, wouldn't talk to me and even avoided eye contact. I roamed the ship in search of her tonight but she was nowhere to be seen. What's going on?

The air conditioning has packed up again and my cabin is like a fuckin' sauna. God knows what it's like for the poor bastards down on the lower decks who don't have the luxury of a porthole. Anyway, along with Don-the-Slot, Tiny-Tom, Phil, Pikey and Brendan, one of the shore excursion boys, I dragged a mattress out on to the Crew Deck with the intention of spending the night camped out under the stars.

I was just nodding off when Pikey drew my attention to several strange lights that darted back and forth out to sea. Pretty soon, we were all wide awake and mesmerised by the mysterious spectacle. The lights, multicoloured but predominantly fluorescent-blue, would dance every which way then shoot up into the night sky before floating back down to hover and pulse in formation above the horizon.

Looking towards the bow, we could make out the silhouettes of an officer and a couple of sailors who were standing on the fly bridge scanning the weird lights. Brendan, an inquisitive type, couldn't contain himself any longer and I went with him to investigate. The Bridge is strictly out of bounds but, luckily, the officer of the watch happened to be a friendly Cretan called Vasilis, who invited us into the Wheel House.

We enquired as to the origins of the lights and, fidgeting with his worry beads, Vasilis laughed and told us there was nothing out there.

'No ships, no land – *tipota.*' (Nothing.)

Noting our puzzled response, he explained that there was nothing showing on the radar and the incident would not be entered into the ship's log. For further explanation, he walked us into the chart room and pointed out that the nearest land, the Tuamotus and Marquesas islands, lay way behind us and we were in an area of the Pacific devoid of even the smallest uninhabited atoll.

'There's nothing out there,' he repeated, with emphasis.

Vasilis has spent over twenty years at sea. His whole adult life. In that time, he claims to have witnessed many unexplained phenomena and, with a shrug of his shoulders, he walked back out on to the fly bridge and continued scanning the horizon. Brendan and I thanked him, left him to finish his watch and clambered back up to the Crew Deck.

The unearthly light show continued for a further ten minutes then, one by one, the lights appeared to sink slowly into the sea. Several joints did the rounds and we talked long into the night about UFOs, little green men from Mars, Ming the Merciless and assorted sci-fi twaddle. Inevitably, this led to a highly intellectual debate concerning *Star Trek.* Which is the best episode? Is Captain Kirk a good bloke or just a fat, posturing cunt in tights? Is Mr Spock a pointy-eared Vulcan poof? And, how come the crew of the Enterprise purports to boldly go where no man has gone before yet when they get there, there's always someone there? And we all agreed that we'd like to give that Lieutenant Uhura a good seeing to!

My paper round was my only source of cash and I squandered every penny on sweets, fizzy drinks and pellets for my air pistol. Albert had returned it to me on the proviso that I ceased using my playmates for target practice and promised not to take out any famous heads of state.

Then I turned thirteen. A teenager at last, I began to take an increasing interest in music and was forever on the hunt for funds to bolster my fledgling record collection. I could only afford singles and would act as DJ to my younger siblings, spinning my favourites, over and over again, on the faithful radiogram. *Bits and Pieces* by the Dave Clark Five was an early entry into my personal hit parade. It stayed in the charts for several months before being ripped from the turntable and smashed into bits and pieces by an enraged Albert, who was suffering one of his migraines.

I bought discs by the Swinging Blue Jeans, Freddie and the Dreamers, Brian Poole & The Tremeloes, Unit 4 Plus 2, Herman's Hermits, Gerry and the Pacemakers, Billy J. Kramer and the Dakotas, The Applejacks and Dave Dee, Dozy, Beaky, Mick & Tich. Thankfully, I soon graduated to The Kinks, The Spencer Davis Group, The Yardbirds, The Byrds, the Small Faces, The Rolling Stones, The Who, and on and on.

School was still a laugh but when the long summer break rolled around, it was time to get busy and make some serious money in any way that I could. Desperate as I was, I sometimes went potato-picking with my grubby and equally cash-strapped pals. We called it spud-bashing.

A lorry would pick us up in the mornings and deposit us in a large field. Buckets and sacks were issued, a plot allocated, then a tractor towing a plough would drive up the rows of plants, turning them over to reveal the spuds underneath. It would then be our job to scoop the 'tatties' into a bucket as fast as possible and dump the contents into a sack before the plough came back the other way, when the whole process would be repeated. At the end of the long, back-breaking day, the farmer would tot up each personal cache of sacks and pay us accordingly. It was a tough way to earn a few bob and only gypsies, tramps and struggling DJs stooped so low.

When there was no spud-bashing available, I reluctantly went to work at Stibby Ives' pig farm and root crop emporium. Stibby was a miserly old bugger who would always try and wheedle out of coughing up the agreed day's pay. And hoeing weeds from between his long rows of beetroots and swedes for hours on end was the most boring job imaginable and always made my head itch. Feeding his pigs was even worse.

For some reason, Stibby encouraged us to bond with his pigs. Simply filling their troughs wasn't good enough for him. He'd have us get into their pen and, with a slopping bucket of swill, we were forced to run like fuck to avoid being mown down by the vicious brutes. The pig pen was always knee-deep in mud and shit, which would suck your wellies off, and the underfed pigs wouldn't hesitate to take a bite out of your arse, either.

My career as a pig farmer came to an abrupt end one day when Stibby caught me and my pal, Ernie Wheeler, having a bit of fun with his precious swine. Standing outside a part of their pen that was partitioned off by an electric fence, we coaxed the pigs with a heaving bucket of delicious swill. Slobbering with hunger, the pigs took turns making charges at the bucket only to be sent reeling and squealing by jolts of electricity. We were having a fine old time until Stibby crept up behind us and went apeshit. Grabbing us by the scruff of our necks, he marched us off his property and used our crime as the excuse not to pay us for the three days that we'd already put in that week. With nothing better to do, we'd often seek revenge and sneak back on to his property with our air pistols and take a few pot shots at his pigs, his potting shed and his dilapidated greenhouses.

One summer, I scored a proper job working as a van boy for a large electricity supply shop in town. I got to ride all over the county, delivering washing machines, refrigerators and cookers. Lucky for me, the driver would take care of any installation requirements so I didn't have to worry about meddling with electricity. The job was fun but, with all the humping up and down stairs, I would be knackered at the end of the day, especially if we'd had to deliver great big six foot-long deep freezers to houses that had more food than they knew what to do with.

The owner of the business was Mr Sawyer, a cheerful, rapscallion entrepreneur who'd got his start in business when stationed as a sergeant in Italy soon after the war. He proudly boasted to me how he'd made a small fortune by flogging army supplies to the locals. As Mr Sawyer saw it, he'd done nothing wrong. Had simply grabbed an opportunity and seized the moment. Food, clothing, jeeps and firearms, it made no difference to him. 'Mark it up and sell it on,' was his war cry.

I liked Mr Sawyer and, taking him on his word, I was soon knocking stuff off from his store with little or no remorse. I couldn't move the big stuff but transistor radios, hairdryers and electric shavers bought me a nice little earner when fenced to a network of equally unscrupulous chums. The pilfered goods were never missed as Mr Sawyer ran a very shonky shop, with the only 'stock taking' being done by yours truly. On the odd occasion that I felt a twinge of guilt over my 'entrepreneurialism', I reconciled myself with the near certainty that a large proportion of Mr Sawyer's stock was hot in the first place.

Sometimes I'd be asked to stay back after work to help unload a truck. Mr Sawyer would always slip me a bonus but it was nothing like the thick wad of cash that the driver would receive. And I know for a fact that he'd buy factory-damaged and soiled white goods by the container-load, fix them up and sell them on as new. I know this because I used to help with the elaborate touch-up jobs that were performed behind closed doors in his lock-up late at night.

Country life didn't hold as much sway as it once had and, when not at school or work, I hung out in town. I'd been too young to be a mod like my big brother, Bobby, and so I became a skinhead for a while. Skinheads back then were a gentler breed than today's more dangerous manifestation of neo-Nazi thug. We were into shaved heads, braces and Doc Marten boots just the same but, apart from 'Paki-bashing', which came along later, our motivations for mayhem were rarely racial. There were even a number of tough, black kids and a few Asians in our clique.

On the whole, being a skinhead in the mid-sixties was just another dumb fashion statement. The music we favoured was Motown and reggae and, for the most part, all we did was hang out in various youth clubs, dancing to the likes of Marvin Gaye, the Isley Brothers and Desmond Dekker & The Aces.

Most of us weren't old enough to get away with drinking yet. We'd have to pool our money and draft bigger gang members to buy cheap bottles of port. We'd guzzle the horrible stuff down, get pissed quick, spin out, throw up, then do it all again.

Invariably during the evening, a spontaneous floor show would take place. The music would stop. The dancing would be halted. The lights would go up and the club would erupt as two tasty geezers in mohair suits attacked one another in a frenzy of flying fists. The fights were always over nothing – a bird or a favoured football team – and the bouncers would usually take their time breaking up a brawl unless a knife or a razor was pulled. Then, they would move in swiftly and pummel the two combatants to the floor before dragging them outside and giving them a good kickin'. Meanwhile, the lights would be dimmed, the music cranked up and things would go back to normal.

I loved being in a gang and I won't attempt to justify some of the stupid antics that we got up to as adolescents. Being part of a fraternity was exciting and empowering and I was spending less and less time at home and more time running wild in the streets. Being one of the smallest kids in the gang, I quickly learnt to avoid any serious beatings or abuse with bullshit and bravado and I made up for my diminutive size by exercising a very large and lippy mouth. I soon sussed that, so long as I was good for a laugh, I could getting away with all kinds of audacious shit.

Being one of the smaller kids had other advantages, too. With a two hundred-strong army of hooligans to call upon when a big rumble was imminent, we'd sometimes pull the whole crew together and bunk the trains down to the coast for a weekend of mayhem at the seaside.

In Southend, we'd join forces with other skinhead gangs and engage in huge, pitched battles on the muddy beaches with our arch enemies, 'the greasers'. The greasers rode motorbikes and were the younger brothers of the 'rockers', who had been in similar conflict with our elder brothers, the mods, a few years previous. Daft, isn't it?

The melee would spill on to the streets. Cars would be torched. Shop fronts wrecked. Then the coppers would wade in wielding truncheons. With the help of police dogs and a few coppers on horseback, the riot would finally be brought under control and hundreds of us would be lined up along the seafront. This is where my lack of height proved to be an advantage. Being logistically impossible to arrest us all, the coppers would simply march along the ranks of battered kids and pick out the biggest ones, supposing them to be the ringleaders. Okay, it wasn't exactly just, but my larger mates pulled more birds than me, so fuck 'em! All's fair in love and war. The majority of us not spending the night in the clink would then be frog-marched to the railway station and put on a train. Naturally, it would be totally trashed by the time we got home.

Some of my skinhead mates sporadically attended Cardinal Bourne and at morning assembly it was considered a badge of honour to be the kids most likely to have our names called out on report. Being on report meant the cane and the headmaster, 'Old Man Hicks', derived great pleasure from the dishing out of corporal punishment. His preferred instrument of torture was a thin, whip-like piece of wood and it hurt like hell! Six-of-the-best raised blisters on the hand. Twelve-of-the-best, and skin would break and blood would flow.

In an attempt to intimidate the sadistic old bastard, we'd try to look him straight in the eye and never, ever, show any sign of fear. When the ordeal was over, it was advisable to run your hands under a cold tap and then take a few minutes for a private blub in the toilet. Then you'd rejoin your mates and assure them that it hadn't hurt a bit.

SHIP'S TOTE:

Yesterday, the ship's run was 446 nautical miles within 24 hours. There were six winners who will collect $1.93 each.

SEASCAPE

Tuesday 18th December 1973 En route to Acapulco

Believe me. Don't believe me. It gets weirder. Don-the-Slot booted me awake.

'Quick! Quick! Get a load of this, Archie!'

A cloudless, pink dawn signalled the beginnings of another perfect Pacific day. I stood up and stretched and, looking down on the Boat Deck, was surprised to see the rails lined with passengers. Then I stared in amazement at the sight that had so many of them out of their bunks at such an ungodly hour. Dolphins.

Now I'm not just talking about the daily occurrence of three or four dolphins cavorting in the bow wave. And I'm not just talking about an unusually large pod of dolphins. What I'm talking about is what must have been thousands and thousands of the critters. As far as the eye could see, in every direction, the sea boiled to the horizon with leaping, laughing, somersaulting dolphins. People cheered and applauded the amazing, heart-warming spectacle and someone on the bridge, probably Vasilis, gave the ship's whistle a few blasts in appreciation.

They stayed with us for something like twenty minutes then, abruptly, as if on command, the whole massive herd disappeared as one, leaving the sea as flat and smooth as a mirror. It was a wonderful, though strangely spooky, experience, coming as it did only hours after the eerie light show. And, of course, there were those amongst us, including Pikey, a cynical bastard at the best of times, who couldn't help thinking that the two events were somehow connected.

Far-fetched bullshit? Crappy Hollywood bunkum? Hippy-dippy bollocks? Believe me. Don't believe me.

Cringe, here we go again. It's time for the enchanting, ethereal, and, in our case, highly embarrassing *South Pacific Show*, or, as it's known amongst the crew, 'The South Pathetic Show'. Some people live on a lonely island but they're the lucky ones who don't have to witness such drivel. To dress the boys in the chorus, Paul raided the sailors' quarters and we wore white trousers rolled up to the knees, white Cyclades Line T-shirts, and sailor hats. Complete with crêpe paper leis around our necks, we looked like a right bunch of plonkers. The girls didn't look half bad in grass skirts and bikini tops.

Poor old Rodgers and Hammerstein. What had they done to deserve such shabby disrespect? We waded through *Bali Ha'i*. We did *Happy Talk* and, accompanied incongruously by Evris on bizouki, a big, fat bird from Leeds absolutely murdered *Younger Than Springtime*.

There is nothing you can name that is anything like the lame excuse for a show that we spewed up tonight. Several crew squeezed into the back of the ballroom to witness our humiliation and waiters, waitresses and bar staff stopped serving drinks and huddled in groups, tears of joy in their eyes, pissing themselves laughing.

I felt sorry for the poor old Captain who, for PR purposes, is obliged to attend every show. I'm sure this is not what he had in mind when he ran away to sea at the age of fourteen and tonight, he sat, ashen-faced, as Paul took centre stage and sang *I'm Gonna Wash That Man Right Out Of My Hair*.

To ease the skipper's suffering, Sean and I offered up a bit of light relief with a balloon dance. Dressed in grass skirts and bikinis, with bread rolls for tits and wearing wigs, I think we saved the night. It's a mystery to me but the passengers, especially the Aussies, went apeshit at the sight of a fat Irish drunk and his skinny English sidekick prancing about the stage dressed as Polynesian maidens. We brought the fuckin' house down.

Claire's talking to me again. She thought the show was hilariously funny and, after putting her son to bed and enduring a barney with hubby, who was in his usual spot propping up the Smoke Bar, she joined me for a drink in the ballroom.

The ballroom, now transformed into a nightclub, swung to the sounds of Evris and his Athenians, who were doing their best to assuage the shame they no doubt felt following the dreadful show. To be honest, they're a talented bunch of musicians and a pretty-good band when they get to do their own thing.

It was obvious from our brief tussle on the Sports Deck, that Claire and I wanted one another but I was so besotted with her that she rendered me unusually shy and I didn't have a clue how to take things to the next dizzying level. A repeat performance of two nights previous was out of the question as a tropical downpour was lashing the decks. Then I was reminded of a favourite ruse that my wily brother, Bobby, had passed on to me.

Unless working, the majority of the expat crew have to vacate the public rooms by midnight. Of course, being on the entertainment staff, this rule doesn't apply to me. A fact that Claire was unaware of. Pikey entered the ballroom on his rounds, reminding various crew members that it was time to drink up and get off deck. I excused myself, telling Claire I had to answer a call of nature and, catching Pikey's eye, we met in the toilet.

When I got back, Claire was being chatted-up by a tall engineering officer called Theseus. He was none too pleased to see me, or the way in which Claire pulled me to her side. Looking daggers, he left us alone and I ordered another round of drinks.

The band was taking a break and, suddenly, there was a crash on the other side of the ballroom. My friend, Maggie, obviously pissed, had dropped a tray of drinks and was now swearing loudly at a table of equally pissed Aussie blokes who were laughing and pointing at her. Maggie doesn't take shit from anyone but I'm sure things would have blown over if only they hadn't started flicking coasters at her. Maggie stomped to their table, picked up a beer and threw it in the face of the largest bloke.

The girls always look after each other and her friend, Tina, who also happened to be on duty, and another girl, Sherry, grabbed her on either side and dragged her, screaming abuse, from the ballroom. Being so blatantly pissed on duty is a definite no-no and as several officers had witnessed the fracas, I knew that poor Maggie was in deep shit. She'd certainly be up for a hefty fine. Maybe worse.

Meanwhile, Claire and I were getting along famously and we watched with satisfaction as Pikey escorted the table of drunks from the ballroom. He returned twenty minutes later looking none the worse for wear apart from a spray of blood staining the front of his tunic and a missing epaulette.

'Don't think they'll be causing any more trouble,' he said, massaging a fist. Then, with a barely-concealed grin, said, 'Hey, Archie, come on, you know the rules, it's twelve-thirty, way past Cinderella time.' (Must remember, I owe him a bottle of Scotch.)

I explained my predicament to Claire and, shyly, without her eyes leaving mine, she said, 'What a shame.'

It was now or never and, gulping down the remains of my drink, I hesitantly suggested that maybe she'd like to see my cabin.

She wavered for a second and then took my hand, and said, 'I don't think that's a good idea.'

'It may not be a good idea but it could be fun,' I managed to blurt out nervously.

'Is it allowed?' she asked.

'No,' I squeaked.

'Good, let's go,' said Claire.

We took the shortest route via some 'crew only' stairs behind the bar and made it to my cabin in record time. The air conditioning was still on the blink and the cabin was like an oven as I'd closed the porthole because of the rain.

Claire walked the few steps to my bedside table and started rummaging through my tapes so I walked up behind her, laid my hands on her slim hips and buried my face in her hair.

'Have you got anything to drink?' she asked.

I had a bottle of Bacardi and some Coke on hand but wanting to do everything right, I licked her ear and whispered, 'I'll be right back', and dashed down to the mess to grab some ice.

Minutes later, pausing to get my breath, I opened my cabin door to the heavenly vision of Claire, sprawled, naked, on her back, on my bunk. My bunk. Claire, sprawled, naked, on my bunk. My bunk. Claire, naked! Legs slightly apart. Legs, apart! Naked! Claire, naked, naked, sprawled on my bunk, one hand fondling the golden triangle between her legs. The golden triangle between her legs!

I clicked the door locked behind me and Claire opened her arms and said, 'I want you so much, Archie. Make love to me.'

Who was I to argue? Dumping the ice in the small sink, I dropped to my knees, leant over her and gently lifting a delicate ankle, licked a foot and sucked on a succulent, tiny big toe. I worked my way up, ever so slowly, to her calf, her thigh, then down again to her other leg, her other delicate foot. Up again, calf, kiss knees, thigh, golden triangle!

Claire moaned, 'Oh, this is so naughty.'

She arched her body, reached down, yanked my shirt from my waistband and pulled it over my head. I paid no heed, lost as I was, my tongue exploring her wet, silken insides. I bit gently on her clitoris and she was wet, wet, wet. I licked the taste of her, breathed deep and drank her in. Reluctant to leave, I worked my way up slowly to her navel and paused for a moment to delve, deeply, then up to her soft breasts and nipples, erect, hard and delicious.

I licked her neck, her chin, then we were kissing, gently at first, then with a furious, teeth-gnashing intensity. I pulled myself from her grasp, stood up and quickly unzipped my trousers and pulled them off. Claire sat up, and pulled my pants down. I'd never known my cock to be so hard. So engorged, it felt like a hot lead pipe. Claire took me in her mouth and I grasped the rail of the top bunk and closed my eyes.

I caressed the back of her neck, ruffled her hair, pulled my cock from her mouth, took her in my arms and we kissed some more. She laid down on her front and I bit an ear, licked the back of her neck, then her shoulders, her back, one hand fondling a breast, the other stroking her wet pussy with two fingers probing inside.

The rain had stopped, the clouds parted and moonlight shone through the porthole illuminating her taut, sublime body. I worked my way down her spine and marvelled at the swirl of soft, blonde down that grew like a secret in the small of her back. I licked and gently bit both cheeks of her tiny, hard arse, alabaster-white in the moonlight in contrast to her honey-tanned, delicious body. She reached down and slapped me about the head, rolled over and I was eating her again but with less finesse and more hunger. She grabbed my hair, pulled me up her body, grabbed my cock, rubbed the sheath against her labia and with one long, slow, hard push, I was inside her.

Claire arched her back and came to meet me with a loud gasp. She seemed to have lost all interest in making love and now beseeched me, loudly, to fuck her. Fuck me! Fuck me! Oh, Fuuuck me!

She wrapped her legs around me and we fitted together perfectly. For extra traction, she braced her feet on the bottom of the bunk above. We parted for a second and she smiled up at me. I kissed her and she raised her arms above her head and gripped a pillow as I licked her arm pits and nipples, alternately. We came together in a sweaty crescendo of whimpers, gasps and moans. I banged the back of my head on the plywood support of the upper bunk and Claire laughed and banged loudly on the cabin wall. Panos, the purser who lives next door, banged back and cheered.

We lay intertwined in the hot bunk, giggling and kissing, then went at it again, but unhurried this time. This time we made love. By now it was something like two in morning and Claire got up, dressed and kissed me goodnight, promising to catch up tomorrow. When she'd gone I retrieved the few slivers of ice from the sink, poured myself a quadruple Bacardi and Coke, rolled a joint and smoked it with my head out of the porthole.

Oops! So much for behaving myself. Now I'm shagging a married woman.

12

Romantic Fool

Nineteen sixty-eight was a turbulent year and I couldn't help but wonder if Louis Armstrong had got it wrong when he topped the charts with *What a Wonderful World*. Mind you, I suppose it could have been worse. John Farnham was wowing them down under with *Sadie, The Cleaning Lady*.

Nineteen sixty-eight was the year of the Tet Offensive. There were riots in Paris and Russian tanks rolled into Prague. John and Yoko were busted and Jackie and Aristotle got hitched. Tricky Dicky was elected President, Martin and Bobby were both slain and poor old Tony Hancock topped himself in a Sydney hotel room. (No doubt driven to it by hearing *Sadie, The Cleaning Lady* just one too many times.)

Meanwhile, I was in my final year of school and didn't have a clue as to what I was going to do. It wasn't really a case of what I wanted to do but more a question of what my paltry education had prepared me for. Our school taught the girls to cook and sew as they were fully expected to do nothing more than get married as quickly as possible and start banging out Catholic sprogs. As for us boys, our choices were limited to the building site, the factory floor or a few years servitude in Her Majesty's armed forces.

I only excelled in one subject. Art was all I was really good at so, against the advice of the careers officer, I began to make enquires about turning my creative skills into a paying profession. I learnt that the local technical college ran a graphic arts course. After further enquires, I managed to secure an interview. I don't know what it's like nowadays but back then, getting into college was simply a matter of turning up on a given day and, after displaying a mild interest in the course on offer, one was enrolled. First come, first served with very few questions asked. So that was it, I was going off to college.

A school pal of mine, Mickey Hayes, desperately wanted to join the army. He was still too young so, with nothing better to do for the time being, he decided to join me at college. It was a joke. Mickey couldn't draw for shit but figured that college would be a great place to meet chicks and fuck around for a bit before signing his life away to Queen and country. Mickey was such a hoodlum that he only lasted a few months at college before being booted out. He mooched around for a bit doing various odd jobs before eventually joining the army. Evidently, he excelled, as every time he came home on leave he would have another little stripe on his arm. (A few years later, my pal, Mickey, was blown to smithereens by a huge car bomb in Northern Ireland.)

I left school at fifteen with little fanfare, no graduation ceremony and no speeches. Cardinal Bourne just wasn't that kind of school. The place only existed for some thirty years and was torn down in the late eighties to make way for a supermarket and a multi-storey car park. (What worries me is where the hell will they stick the blue plaque with my famous name on it when this book becomes a searing potboiler?)

I began college but money was still tight so I kept my paper round and, on Saturdays, continued to work for, and steal from, Mr Sawyer. College was very liberating after years of Catholic schools but I didn't fit in at first. The majority of the students were better educated and of the hippy persuasion whilst I was an uneducated skinhead ruffian. But slowly I made new friends and, dancing to a different tune, they turned my head around and turned me on to Cream, Led Zeppelin and Hendrix.

It was time for a change of direction anyway as I was getting a bit weary of my skinhead mates. The thuggery and violence was becoming less innocent and more mindless, climaxing horribly one night when one of our more psychopathic leaders stabbed and nearly killed a young cadet copper. He was sent to borstal for his crime and graduated to a cell in Brixton Prison when he was older. Pretty much overnight, I traded my braces and Doc Martens for a smelly Afghan coat and a set of plastic beads and embraced the peace and love philosophy of the swinging sixties. All I needed now was long hair.

Ours was not a fine arts course and we were not expected to go on and starve to death in a garret or worse still, grow beards and become art teachers. The majority of our tutors were burnt-out graphic artists from the advertising industry, now content to take things easy but earn far less by passing on their knowledge to us. We were taught calligraphy and hand lettering. We had lessons in photography and typography and lectures on print production. There was little emphasis put on illustration but we did attend life classes, which was very embarrassing for me as the large lady who came in to model for us lived in the village and was on my paper round.

Mrs Threadwell had a nice house and would have been paid a pittance for exposing her ample flesh, so I could only assume that she got a perverse kick out of getting her kit off. A very jolly, middle-aged fat lady, with massive knockers, several enormous stomachs and huge, hail damaged thighs, her Rubenesque credentials were never in doubt. The challenge in drawing Mrs Threadwell was knowing where to start.

One day, as she was waddling out of the door after class, she caught a glimpse of my sketch. It was a particularly grotesque rendering on this day and, exercising a little too much artistic licence, I'd represented her gargantuan boobs as a pair of exploding Hindenburgs – complete with Swastikas. Unfortunately, Mrs Threadwell failed to grasp the artistic symbolism and, henceforth, she never tipped me at Christmas.

MASONIC BRETHREN
There will be a meeting of Freemasons at 3.00 p.m. today in the Library.

SEASCAPE
Thursday 20th December 1973 En route to Acapulco

Claire did her disappearing act again yesterday and I combed the ship, searching for her in vain. I knew her cabin number but I could hardly rock up there for fear I'd drop the both of us in it. I must admit, I was getting a bit worried that her husband had got wind of our erm ... get-together and had done her in. Or, worse still, was drunkenly roaming the ship looking for me.

I finally tracked her down whilst flogging tote tickets down on Main Deck later that morning. Unbeknown to most of the passengers, there's a small deck that's situated on the starboard side of the aft foyer. And that's where I found her, lying on a lounger, wearing a simple summer frock, her pretty head buried in a magazine. There was nobody else on the secluded deck so I sat on the end of her lounger and reached out for her hand. Surprised by her reaction, it was as though I'd zapped her with a cattle prod and she looked at me over her large sunglasses, brushed my hand aside, swung her feet to the deck and stood up abruptly.

That Claire was less than pleased to see me was plainly obvious but I didn't have a clue what I'd done to upset her. Maybe she's just nuts. I stood, then grabbed her arm, but she shrugged me off saying, in a strained voice:

'Archie, I can't do this, I'm a married woman.'

'Claire, you've already done it,' was the best I could come up with, at which she burst into tears.

I reached out to her but at that moment, an old couple shuffled on to the deck and Claire pushed me away and started gathering up her things. Lowering my voice, I convinced her that we needed to talk and, before rushing off, she agreed to meet me in the relative safety of the cinema that afternoon at four.

'Fancy meeting you here, dear,' said the old duck.

It was Mavis and her husband, Ted, a couple of octogenarian Kiwi bingo fanatics. I flogged them some tote tickets and continued on my rounds.

We've re-crossed the equator so, once again, Sean got to put on a false beard and do his Charlton Heston impersonation and Paul got to humiliate a fresh crop of virgin line crossers. This afternoon we held a dress rehearsal for tonight's *'King Neptune Show'*. Claire was there and, though I couldn't tear my eyes from her, we didn't speak. Roll on four o'clock.

As I'd hoped, the Palm Cinema on D-Deck was virtually deserted for the afternoon matinee – a grainy copy of the 1964 comedy/romance *Sex and the Single Girl*. I got there early so as to secure a couple of seats in the back row and sat in the dark, anxiously awaiting Claire. Following her skittish performance this morning and having ignored me at rehearsals this afternoon, I didn't believe she'd actually show up but, ten minutes into the movie, she slipped into the seat beside me, took my hand and gave me a long, passionate kiss.

Tony Curtis was doing his damnedest to get into Natalie Wood's pants (and who could blame him?) but we ignored the on-screen action and talked in whispers, my arm around Claire with her head resting on my shoulder. Sleeping with me had totally freaked her out and she went to great lengths to point out that she'd never been unfaithful before.

'I don't know what I was thinking,' she whispered.

Claire was terrified we'd be found out and shuddered at the perceived repercussions that would follow. She explained the obvious, that she was in a loveless marriage, and confided in me that during their time in Australia, she and hubby had grown apart. She said she intended to do something about her situation on returning to England but, for now, she had to think of her young son and the hurt and confusion he would suffer if his mother's indiscretion was to come to light.

Claire also held concerns regarding our age difference. Worried that I'd be less than discreet if, by chance, the sex – which she admitted to having been mind-blowing – were to bloom into a full-blown affair. Between agreeing that this couldn't possibly happen, that the shenanigans of two nights previous was a one-off, we were both becoming increasingly horny and talking less and kissing more. By the time the closing credits rolled, Claire had my cock out, I had my hand in her knickers, and we had a result.

As it was patently clear that we had no intention of keeping our hands off one another, we agreed that it may be prudent if we exercised a degree of caution whenever our paths crossed in public. I was relieved that Claire was keen to continue helping out on the Sports Deck every morning. Not that we were ever likely to tear each other's clothes off in front of a bunch of kiddies and a clutch of mums, but you never know. Basically, the same applied for the shows and accompanying rehearsal sessions – always plenty of people around to prevent any hint of romance between the two of us.

But Claire was adamant that she didn't want us to be seen hanging out together in the bars or disco any more as she suspected her soon-to-be-teenage son already had his suspicions that there was a sexual tension between the two of us, had in fact almost given her a heart attack when he'd joked to his father about me being 'mum's boyfriend'. I had an unexpected ace up my sleeve there as, according to Claire, hubby had scoffed at the idea, convinced as he was that I'm Paul's pillow-biting boyfriend.

'Half the crew are poofters!' he'd laughed.

He got that bit right.

Just before the lights went up, Claire adjusted her underwear and with a smile and a parting kiss, left the cinema. I gave her a minute then zipped up my flies and skipped up to the mess for an early dinner before helping Paul prepare for tonight's show.

I met Judy at college and, along with the majority of students (male and female) and several of the more lecherous lecturers, I was fuckin' nuts about her. She was studying window dressing and I could tell by the way that she completely ignored me that she was equally besotted with me. I stalked her fruitlessly for several months, but it wasn't until my hair was beginning to creep over my ears and I was scruffy enough to appear what Judy considered to be respectable, that we became friends.

We would meet for lunch (which I now called lunch) in the college refectory and, over coffee, we would have long, deep and meaningful chit-chats on putting the world to rights. Judy would get very heated and prattle on about the war in Vietnam, the banning of bombs, apartheid, pollution, women's liberation, vegetarianism, gay rights, starving Biafrans, and Che-bloody-Guevara. All I knew about Che Guevara was that he wore a very cool hat and I couldn't help but wonder if he'd have become such a legend if he'd gone around wearing a beanie or a knotted hanky on his head. To tell you the truth, I didn't know what Judy was bangin' on about half the time. I just wanted to get in her pants.

But she was an angel who took me under her wing. She took charge of my literary preferences and I obediently ploughed through *Nineteen Eighty-Four, The Catcher in the Rye, On the Road, The Electric Kool-Aid Acid Test*, and other essential reading for the budding bohemian.

Judy was forever going up to London on some peace march or another and encouraged me to become involved and join her on these crusades. Of course, putty in her hands, I did as I was told and tagged along – just so I could be with her. With revolution in the air, I was pleasantly surprised at how much fun a demo could be and how much bonhomie I derived from my fellow peaceniks. Thanks to Judy,

I began to take a genuine interest in the rabid politics of the day and was soon plastering my shared bedroom with 'Ban the Bomb' signs and pictures of Ho Chi Minh.

I was completely gaga over Judy. She was a very switched-on hippy chick, who was always dressed magnificently in the flamboyant, top fashions of the time. And she was seriously cute. She had long-lashed almond eyes and the smoothest of olive skin with a shimmering mane of chestnut hair that reached to her slim waist. Alas, she was never really my girlfriend but we did hang out together and on nights when I could get enough cider into her, she'd let me stick my tongue down her throat. (I was such a romantic fool back then.)

Judy and I would go up to the Roundhouse on Sundays. A former railway shed in North London, the Roundhouse was hippy heaven, where, for half a quid, you could see bands play all afternoon and into the night. The atmosphere was very laid-back and friendly with people sharing wine and ciggies with all and sundry.

One afternoon I was digging the fuggy ambience and doing my best to look cool, when a jumbo-sized, badly made cigarette was passed to me. I was no dope and knew it was dope straight away, as Judy and I had been keen to get stoned for some time but didn't know how to go about scoring.

I took a tentative toke and predictably coughed my lungs up. With kindly instruction from an older, proper hippie, I tried again and, this time, managed to hold the smoke in for a few seconds. I took a couple more hits then passed the joint on to Judy who's reaction was much the same as mine had been. The marijuana didn't take long to take effect and pretty soon the band on stage began to sound a hell of a lot better than they had before. In fact, they started to sound fantastic! They sounded like the best band that I'd ever heard in my life! Even their daffy lyrics began to make sense. (I vaguely recall the band in question was called Spooky Tooth.)

I told Judy that I loved her and she burst out laughing. Not the response I had hoped for but what the fuck! I was laughing too. We attempted to stand but our knees had turned to blancmange and we sat, doubled up, laughing and pointing at one another's grinning mugs. We finally managed to get up and stagger down to the front of the stage where we attempted, with difficulty, to dance on a floor that appeared to have taken on the properties of a wet mattress.

The light show projected on to the back of the stage was previously of little consequence, being just the usual sixties fare of multicoloured blobs of oil swimming, amoeba-like, across a psychedelic background. But now, with my first hit of dope on board, the kaleidoscope of colour was one of the most awesome sights I'd ever seen. Judy and I were spinning in a purple haze, wheels on fire and spaced out of our young minds.

We started to come down a bit, pooled what little money we had and I took off in search of the proper hippy who'd introduced us to this wonderful new vice. He didn't have any dope to sell but he was well-connected and I followed him out into the foyer and was introduced to a tall, skinny freak with a long, curly moustache and a pointy beard. He looked like a wizard and was resplendent in a plum-coloured jacket with gold stars and crescent moons embroidered into the plush velvet. In place of the usual uniform of flared, faded jeans, he was wearing what appeared to be a pair of multistriped pirate pantaloons tied at the waist with a bright-red sash. On his feet, he wore what looked like court jester shoes minus the bells and several silk scarves were draped around his scrawny neck. Precariously balanced on his head, sat a floppy top hat with a feather in it.

'What do ya want, maaan?' drawled the Wiz.

I wasn't exactly sure, but he led me into the toilet and sold me a quarter ounce of Moroccan hash. My first 'big score'. Making our way back to Judy, my new best friend, the proper hippy, whose name was Howie, asked me if I had any skins. I didn't know what the fuck he was talking about but Howie, who was turning out to be a veritable font of wisdom, explained that skins were, in fact, rolling papers. I didn't have any but Howie did and he spent the rest of the afternoon and evening patiently instructing Judy and me on the very precise art of joint origami. Judy and I floated home on the last train and, still a bit out of it, she rested her lovely head on my shoulder and fell asleep in my arms. I walked her to her house and she let me kiss her, stroke her small boobs and give her tight little arse a squeeze. (I told you I was a romantic fool.)

I had to hitch home as there were no buses to the village on a Sunday. Hidden in my sock and wrapped in silver foil was the tiny lump of dope that I had remaining. It didn't stay there long for as soon as I got home, I sneaked into the garden shed, rolled myself a joint and smoked the bugger down to the roach. It had been a magical day and too wired to sleep, I went for a walk under a full moon that had never looked so fanfuckingtastic.

LOCAL CURRENCY IN MEXICO:

The unit of currency in Mexico is the Peso and the Centavo. One hundred centavos are equivalent to one peso. Approximately 12 pesos are equivalent to one US Dollar. However, the American Dollar is used in the same way as the local currency.

SEASCAPE

Sunday 23rd December 1973 At Acapulco

Now that we've worked out a routine of sorts, Claire's stopped stressing about being busted. And when we're not fucking one another's brains out, she seems to derive great pleasure from giving me the cold shoulder whenever we happen to find ourselves in the company of others. She won't tell me who but, apparently, one of her girlfriends in the chorus let on that she's got the hots for me. Claire told the girl to dream on as she knew for a fact that I was gay.

For my part, I'm having fun getting in touch with my effeminate side, camping it up whenever I encounter Claire's old man. Last night, after bingo, Paul and I were mincing through the Smoke Bar and, just as I'd expected, Terry was slouched at a table with a bunch of other drunks. He nudged one of his cronies and said something that I didn't quite hear but whatever it was, they all looked our way and fell about laughing. As Paul and I drew level with their table, I pursed my lips, smiled sweetly and, in a high-pitched girlie voice, lisped:

'Evening, boysss.' Paul raised a perfectly plucked eyebrow.

'Friends of yours, Maude?' he enquired, as we swished through the bar.

I lay, face down, on my bunk, breathing in the heavenly scent of Claire that lingered on my pillow. She sneaked up to my cabin last night – she sneaks up to my cabin every night, if you must know. What am I saying? She sneaks up to my cabin in the afternoons, too. And first thing in the morning.

Being a fitness fanatic, she rises at dawn to jog the decks and swim a few laps in the pool before the hordes descend. Well, guess what? Now she's got a new fitness regime and makes her way up to my cabin at daybreak to slip into my bunk for an hour of boisterous rutting. The woman's insatiable. I got out of bed, wrapped a towel around myself, shuffled off to the showers and painfully bathed my battered love trumpet. Ouch!

Just prior to breakfast, we sailed into Acapulco Bay. Owing to the lack of berthing facilities, we dropped anchor a mile from shore and passengers and crew are to be ferried in by local launches and the less reliable ship's lifeboats.

A chain of mountains ring the beautiful bay and high-rise hotels line the long curve of white-sand beach. As crew, we're usually first off the ship but, today, we've been instructed to wait until all the passengers have disembarked. A bloody cheek, if you ask me.

I stood at the Promenade Deck rail and watched a pod of Mexican kids who'd braved the swim from shore and now begged for coins as they trod water beside the ship. I spotted Claire stepping nimbly into a boat with her son, and husband, Terry, following unsteadily behind. They're off to play happy families on an organised tour whilst I'll be venturing ashore with my usual swashbuckling compadres, Bunger, Don-the-Slot and Tiny-Tom.

As this is strictly an A to B voyage and definitely not, by any stretch of the imagination, a cruise, the Kioni never hangs around long in port and we'll be sailing at midnight. We're all hanging out for shore leave after the long days at sea and we intended to cram as much mayhem into the day as possible.

We were ashore by nine and had a stroll around the excellent market, which was just opening for business by the quay – beautiful silverwork, pottery, hammocks, blankets, toys, handicrafts, onyx chess sets and '*tourista*' tack. All very nice I'm sure, but, as Bunger pointed out, it was time for a drink and we piled into a cab and headed off to the El Mirador Hotel, situated high above the Quebrada cliffs, famed for its high divers and put on the map by Elvis in his laughably bad flick, *Fun in Acapulco*. The next suicidal leap wouldn't be taking place for an hour so we sat in the shade of a thatched pool-bar and sampled several early morning *tequilas*.

The divers were mightily impressive, if not completely nuts, and, after snapping a few souvenir shots, we headed back down to the main drag and crashed out on La Condesa beach.

We'd just got comfortable when a young Mexican kid of about fourteen sidled up to us and said, in a perfect Cheech Marin accent, 'Hey, *gringos*, you wanna buy some marijuana?'

Don handled the transaction and took off with our new friend, returning ten minutes later with a cigarette packet full of Acapulco Gold.

We rolled joints under the limited privacy of a rented straw umbrella and were, in no time, grinning like goons, stoned off our heads. Nobody seemed to pay us any attention except for the umpteen vendors who trawled the beach flogging the same stuff as found in the market but for half the price. We bought chilled beer from a guy pushing a converted pram and feasted on tacos and burritos that were expertly cooked at a little hut just a short crawl up the beach. We were in fuckin' dreamland.

Bunger and Don hired a sailboat and Bunger, having learnt sailing as part of his rite of passage, expertly helmed the small dinghy out through the crystal surf. A strong sea breeze filled the sails, the boat picked up speed and the two intrepid adventurers headed out towards the Kioni, riding at anchor in the middle of the bay.

Tom encouraged me to have a go at parasailing and, bolstered by another spliff, I found myself literally higher than a kite as I was towed around the bay dangling from a flimsy harness. I flew over Bunger and Don's small craft, cried out to them and they waved back. Then, as I was swung high over the Kioni, I yanked out my camera and snapped a very surreal shot straight down the aft funnel; my two feet floating in air either side. I noticed boring Graham sunbathing, alone, on the Crew Deck and yelled out to him:

'Hey, Graham, you daft, sad twaaat!'

Imagine not bothering to go ashore in Acapulco.

Ten minutes later and the speedboat swung me over the beach and I dropped safely to the sand. Nearby, a couple of young, bikini-clad horn-bags were watching me and, making out I partook in such butch activities every day, I unclipped the harness, paid the boat boys and swaggered over to the girls.

To be honest, I didn't make much progress at first and it wasn't until I pointed out my large friend and chick magnet, Tiny-Tom, that

I persuaded the girls to decamp and join our party. Karen and Martha, two students from Vancouver, eagerly accepted our offer of a puff of primo weed and were soon off their exquisite tits.

Bunger and Don yelled from beyond the breakers and, hoping to impress our guests, headed straight for shore, close-hauled. Picking up a large wave, which greatly added to their momentum, the small craft began to weave unsteadily, increasingly out of control. At the crucial moment Bunger forgot, or was too preoccupied, to raise the daggerboard and the small craft struck the sand, the boat tipped over, the boom snapped off and the two hapless mariners were dumped unceremoniously in the shallows.

Once Bunger had overpaid for the damage, he limped valiantly up the beach to fetch more beer and, on his return, regaled the girls with a completely fictitious diatribe of bullshit and bollocks.

They may not have been impressed with his sailing skills but their stoned eyes lit up with the knowledge that they were in the company of a travelling rock 'n' roll band called 'Fudge Monkey'.

'We've just come off a particularly gruelling European tour and are currently enjoying a short sabbatical on that liner out there,' he said, waving a joint at a sleek Norwegian cruise ship that lay pretentiously upwind of our battered, rust-streaked tub. 'Then it's back in the studio. Care for a spot of lunch, girls?'

As we'd be at sea on Christmas day and most of the crew would be hard at work, Brendan, from the shore excursion office, had taken the initiative to organise a crew party and had pre-booked a restaurant for the occasion. The whole ship's company had been invited but, as I knew the Greeks don't give a rat's arse about Christmas, I was pleasantly surprised to see just how many had taken up the offer – any excuse for a piss-up, I suppose.

The large restaurant on La Costera Miguel Aleman – the main drag – was open to the street and teeming with two-thirds of the crew. Everyone was there from bridge officers and pursers, engineers, bar staff, waiters and waitresses, cooks and so on down through the food chain to Filipino dishwashers and Indian bog cleaners. And I was amazed to see my pal, Bossy, and some of his boys from the laundry as they got off the ship about as often as boring Graham.

A live band had been hired and Paul, Henri and half-a-dozen queens shimmied on the small dance floor and eyed the slim-hipped waiters, who were rushed off their feet with loud demands for 'more alcohol'.

Bunger slipped the *maître d'* a wad of cash and, with our attractive Canadian friends in tow, we were shown to an excellent table on the veranda overlooking the beach. Fellow crew sent drinks to our table or dropped by to bid us greetings of the season and the impressionable girls were, by now, so totally convinced of our star status that Martha claimed that a friend of hers had one of our albums.

Bunger, in his element, bunged the band a few bucks then paid a visit to the bemused kitchen staff, dolling out Christmas cheer and Yankee dollars as he went. A long, pissy lunch followed, crew were toasted, and a glow of camaraderie spread throughout the warm afternoon. Even Evris, our moody band leader, entered into the swing of things by joining the Mexican combo on stage and shipmates, regardless of rank or nationality, linked arms to dance around the restaurant, knocking over tables and chairs in their wake.

Pikey turned up and Karen took an instant shine to our barrel-chested friend, whom we'd introduced as our head of security. Martha was sitting on Tom's lap and it was clear that Bunger, Don and I, in spite of all our spadework, didn't stand a chance with the two girls. Not strictly fair as I'd 'discovered' them so, by rights, should have had first dibs. To tell the truth, I was only slightly miffed, totally besotted as I am with Claire who, in my opinion, wins hands down in the drop-dead gorgeous stakes.

After a few spins around the dance floor, Karen and Martha, by now totally out of it, dragged our two fortunate shipmates back to their hotel, just a few blocks along the promenade from the restaurant.

An hour later, Pikey and Tom returned, having left the girls, comatose, in their room. With a smile on his face, Tom joked that our fictitious claim to rock stardom was not the only thing the vulnerable girls had swallowed. Dirty, lucky fucker!

As the ship wasn't due to sail until midnight, most of the crew (much to the delight of the ecstatic *maître d'*, who catered to our every need) stayed on in the restaurant. We drank margaritas as the sun went down and then disaster struck as we realised, with horror, that our stash of dope was almost depleted. It was time to restock.

During a break in the music, Don struck up conversation with the band and returned to our table with the joyous news that the drummer could hook us up. He made a call on our behalf, gave us directions to a bar a few streets back from the beach and, with Pikey riding shotgun, we took off into the heart of old Me-hi-co in search of gold.

The backstreets of Acapulco turned out to be markedly different from the brightly lit tourist strip but we soon located the bar, a seedy joint with a collapsed awning out front and inadequately lit from within by candlelight. Pikey cautioned Bunger to desist from his usual flamboyant flashing of cash and warned the rest of us to watch our backs.

As the drummer had phoned ahead, the arrival of five gringos was expected and, as we ordered beers, a big guy with a face like an Easter Island statue and long, black hair tied in a ponytail introduced himself as 'our man'. He explained that he didn't have the grass on him but it was only a few streets away and, if we gave him the cash, he'd go fetch it for us. He assured us the merchandise was of top quality and added that we could trust him because he was 'our friend'. Yeah, right!

Things were shaping up decidedly dodgy but when 'our man' saw that the deal was in jeopardy of falling through, he conceded that one of us could accompany him. Bunger immediately volunteered but, for security reasons, it was agreed that Pikey was a better choice and we pooled most of the cash we had left – enough for a large score of Acapulco Gold plus (for research purposes) a quantity of mescal buttons that, after making a phone call, 'our friend' assured us was *'no problema'*.

Pikey left with the dealer and an uncomfortable half-hour passed; the decrepit bar was almost deserted apart from the sullen barman and a few down-at-heel patrons, who sipped their drinks in silence. An emaciated dog rummaged through the debris on the floor, stopping occasionally to chomp on a peanut or broken tortilla chip.

The patrons stared us down, the barman hissed at us to buy another round and Pikey burst through the door, his shirt torn and covered in blood.

'Quick, boys, we're out of here!'

Fuck! We dashed out of the bar and chased Pikey through the backstreets to the security of the well-lit promenade. Catching up with him, he explained what had gone down.

He was led through a maze of backstreets and, eventually, to an alley behind a warehouse. He sensed that something was not right but was unprepared when he was grabbed from behind and pinned against a wall by half-a-dozen assailants. He attempted to fight back and that's when he was stabbed in the shoulder – the gang relieving him of his fake Rolex and a gold sovereign ring. I'd seen Pikey in action before and knew he was like a raging bull once cornered and had no reason to doubt him when he told us that he'd managed to inflict serious damage on three of the gang before they fled with all of our cash.

Pikey's wound wasn't serious but he was furious and embarrassed at being jumped and, with all of our money gone, we began walking dejectedly back along the beach towards the quay.

The beach was virtually deserted compared to the crowds of the day and we tensed when approached by three dudes who emerged from behind a stack of deckchairs.

'Hey, boys, you wanna buy some marijuana?' said the taller of the three, foolishly waving a bag of grass enticingly in front of him.

Whack! Pikey dropped the guy with one punch and as he crumpled to the sand, Bunger wrestled the dope from his grasp. Out of the corner of my eye, I saw a second guy pull a knife. Tom stepped between us and the guy thought better of it, turned and legged it up the beach followed by the third guy.

'Nothing personal, mate,' Pikey said to the guy lying prostrate on the sand.

We hightailed it up the beach to the quay and caught a tender back to the ship. Apart from Pikey's flesh wound and a few ripped-off bucks, we'd had a great day ashore and celebrated up on the Crew Deck after sailing by sampling our ill-gotten grass. Pikey tugged on a joint, the glow illuminating the homicidal grin on his mug.

The dope did the rounds, Bunger took a hit, exhaled and said, with precision, 'Gentlemen, justice has been served.'

In 1969, Neil Armstrong took one giant leap for mankind and I turned sweet sixteen. For my birthday, Judy gave me a little red book written by someone called Chairman Mao. I never read the bloody thing, of course, but I carried it around everywhere. Albert was very pleased with my apparent leftist leanings but increasingly dismayed by my complete lack of interest in football. He and my brothers were fanatics. Albert had played in goal for donkey's years and, though he'd passed his use-by date, he still got out on the pitch every Saturday and ran around blowing a little whistle. He'd become a referee. He also managed the youth team, which Liam played for, and on Sundays, he'd watch Clive play in his kiddie team. Football-mad Bobby played for two teams ... one on Saturday afternoons and another on Sunday morning. He even got to try-out for Luton Town once. (Whoopee-fuckin'-doo!)

I was revelling in my role as the black sloth of the family but spending as little time as possible at home as the place was starting to drive me insane. I was pissed off at having to share a bedroom with my two younger brothers and felt very hemmed in by the tiny house in general. The place had become a tip and I was forever tripping over bleedin' football boots and having to fight for wall space for my growing collection of political posters. Albert and Vera never stopped hassling me about my long hair and hippy clothes. They also wanted to know why my eyes had begun to resemble two poached eggs on blood.

Of course, I was smoking a lot of dope and becoming increasingly popular at college as Judy and I saw it as our mission to turn-on as many of our friends as possible. We scored from the Wizard every week and I was becoming something of a connoisseur, with a preference for the more expensive, and far more potent, black hashish from Pakistan and Afghanistan.

My college friends needed little encouragement and, to feed their voracious appetites, I was having to score a bit more and a bit more and within no time, I was the main conduit of drugs coming into the college. It was crazy. The Wizard would give me a small discount for buying in bulk but because I took the precaution of only selling to friends, I didn't care to mark the stuff up much and, consequently, was making very little profit on the hazardous business. All that was in it for me was the satisfaction of bringing a little joy into people's lives. Trouble was, I was taking a huge risk in carting the stuff around and I began to get a little paranoid about getting busted.

The best tutor in college was a very hip dude named Neil Swift. Neil was only in his mid-twenties and, with a partner, had his own small art studio in Euston. Being very passionate about his craft, he enjoyed lecturing part-time and was the only tutor who gave us tight, realistic deadlines along with real briefs. In the unlikely event that one of our ideas made it through concept stage and went on to be used in an ad, Neil would make sure we were slipped a few quid.

Neil was also hip to the fact that half his class were permanently stoned and he took me aside one day and warned me that a scurrilous rumour had begun to circulate around the staffroom: that I was perhaps the person responsible for all the shiny, happy people about the place. He told me that I'd better watch my arse. I freaked out, warned Judy and we stopped dealing immediately. I thought everything was cool until one morning, a week later, I was summoned to the principal's office. I'm fucked!

Mr Windybank was a gentle, eccentric old duffer who was hardly ever seen. He avoided conflict like the plague and preferred to spend his days locked in his cosy, wood-panelled office, chain-smoking and making model aeroplanes from Airfix kits. He favoured baggy corduroy trousers, Hush Puppies and sensible cardigans with reindeer motifs, lovingly knitted for him by Mrs Windybank. At the end of a long, hard day, he would be spied shuffling towards his battered Morris Minor. It was usually the first car out of the car park, a good hour before college knocked off.

I tapped nervously on his door and, as I entered the smoke-filled office, he attempted to put me at ease with a gentle quip.

'Ah, Dr Spinks, the famed herbalist. Do come in.'

When he'd stopped chuckling and I'd stopped having kittens, he sat me down and offered me a cup of tea and a biscuit. He then went on to assure me that the purpose of my visit was for nothing more than a friendly chat. Then he came straight to the point and informed me that it had been brought to his attention that I was the kingpin of a drug smuggling ring and that Judy was somehow involved. Some friendly chat. I broke into a cold sweat. Seeing the impact his words were having on me, he paused for a second, then leant across his desk and offered me a Woodbine. Attempting cool, I sucked, hungrily, on the un-tipped ciggie then painfully pulled a sliver of skin from my top lip as I withdrew the soggy end from my mouth.

Mr Windybank strived valiantly to educate me on the dangers of drugs. He clearly had no idea what he was talking about and, having no stomach for hostility, soon lost interest. He then waffled on to explain (God love him) that, with little or no hard evidence against me, and a full confession unlikely, he was willing to let the matter drop. I was to make a solemn promise that I would cease dealing forthwith and never again bring drugs on to college premises. In short, if I gave my word as a gentleman, no further action would be taken. I was no gentleman but I gave him my word. Shit! I was so relieved I would have given the old bugger a forefinger knuckle shuffle if he'd asked for it.

I stood up. He remained seated but offered his hand. We shook and, just for good measure, I gave him my word again. As relieved as myself that the 'awkward business' was over, he thanked me and bade me good day. As I backed out of his office, he flicked some fag ash from his cardigan, dunked a ginger nut in his tea and went back to studying the half-built model Messerschmidt that was being readied for take off on his desk.

For an old codger, Mr Windybank was pretty cool but I could hardly believe that I'd escaped, scot-free, from some potentially serious strife. Talking over the incident with Judy at lunchtime, she put a different spin on our close shave. She agreed that Mr Windybank was cool, but she didn't think he was that cool. She acknowledged that, with nothing more than hearsay, there was little that the old boy could have done but believed that the main reason for our lucky escape was that Mr Windybank was close to retirement. The last thing he needed on campus was a raid by the Old Bill and the scandal that would surely follow.

When I gave it some thought, I realised that Judy was, as usual, correct. Old man Windybank liked the quiet life and in the interest of the peace and harmony of the college, it made perfect sense for him to sweep the matter under the carpet. Forget the whole thing. Ecstatic, Judy and I bunked off college and spent the afternoon getting ripped in a derelict boathouse down by the river.

Things settled down and, when I wasn't watching Judy's arse, I took my friend Neil's advice and watched my own. I concentrated on my studies and, at the end of the first year, I sat for my A-level art exam and passed, no worries. College broke up and I accepted an offer from Neil of a few weeks' work experience at his London studio. The training was invaluable and at the end of the first week, I felt I'd learnt more than in a whole year of college. When I mentioned this to Neil, he smiled and took me aback by suggesting that I pack in the course and get out into the real world earlier than planned. Neil assured me that I had the raw talent to make the grade and emphasised that getting a job in a studio was not going to be easy. Another year of college would make little difference to the kind of lowly position that I was likely to land.

Neil's business was booming and he could no longer afford to take a day off each week to teach. Plus, he was pissed off with the archaic teaching methods of the college and therefore would not be returning in the New Year. He urged me to consider what he'd proposed and promised to help me in any way that he could.

I was now faced with a dilemma. College was a great scene. I was having a ball but, unlike some of the more affluent students, I didn't have the luxury of fucking around for too long and was keen to enter the workforce as soon as possible and try and earn some real cash. Typically, it was Judy who made my mind up for me.

I met her the next day. I was secretly hoping that, when hearing of my plans, she would break down in a flood of tears, beg me to stay on with her at college and confess her undying love. I got the flood of tears alright. And a bonus hug. Then she dropped her own bombshell.

She told me that she loved me. How special I was to her. Her bottom lip trembled and she started crying. She told me that she loved me again then added the dreaded word ... 'but'. She lowered her lovely eyes, waffled on a bit more about how much I meant to her ... but ... but ... but ... our closeness was preventing her from becoming involved in what she called a 'real relationship', blah, blah, blah.

The grass-cutting bastard of her desire was a drippy rich kid and one of the few students who had his own car. But it wasn't a proper car as he wasn't old enough to hold a licence. His wheels, all three of them, sprouted from beneath a bright yellow bubble car that he could legally drive on a motorbike licence. His name was Julian. A tall, long-haired, serious twat with a wispy goatee that failed dismally to hide the lack of chin underneath. He was never seen without his guitar and would insist on playing the sodding thing at every opportunity. Trouble was, he only knew one tune and would sit, cross-legged, in the refectory and strum off-key to *Blowin' in the Wind*. To be fair, he did a passable Dylan in that his voice was as flat as a pancake, though with a far more annoying whine than even 'Uncle' Bob's. I was crestfallen by Judy's news. In a valiant attempt to heal the gaping wound in my chest, I swiped a bottle of vodka from Bobby's secret liquor stash and got horribly plastered. I tried to convince myself that she wasn't worth my tears. That I was better off without her. That she was a ball-busting bitch. Of course, I didn't believe any of it but I knew there was no way I could face college with my beloved slobbering all over her bubble car-driving beau.

A few days later, after I'd stopped throwing up, I phoned my friend Neil and informed him of my decision. He was delighted and, with his many contacts in the industry, quickly lined me up an interview at an art studio in Soho. I thanked Neil and he again stressed the importance of getting my foot in the door regardless of the position or salary.

The job on offer wasn't much and the studio manager who interviewed me made it clear that he didn't give a flying fuck that I had a year of college and an Art A-level under my belt. And, to add insult to injury, he openly ridiculed my portfolio. When he'd tired of taking the piss, he went on to explain that they already had a junior but because they were so busy, were looking for a junior to the junior … an under-junior. A glorified dogsbody to make tea, fetch sandwiches, clean brushes and rinse paint pots. When not performing any of these lofty duties, I'd be delivering artwork to ad agencies all over London. The salary was a measly eight pounds a week and the job was mine if I wanted it.

The Art Machine was in no way a flash joint. In fact, it was nothing more than a ratty old warehouse with twenty or so desks crammed around the walls. But the atmosphere seemed wonderfully chaotic with a colourful crew of geeks, who all appeared to be having the time of their lives. I'd decided to take the job on the spot but haughtily informed the studio manager that I had a few more offers to consider, thanked him for his time and said I would get back to him in a few days if that was okay.

I phoned Neil and told him how it'd gone. As I knew he would, he strongly urged me to grab the job, as The Art Machine was considered one of the best studios in London. Next, I had to persuade Albert and Vera that another year of college was a waste of time and I'd be far better off getting on-the-job training.

I put up a convincing argument. They acquiesced but pointed out that most of the minuscule salary would be chewed up by train fares, something I'd failed to take into account. I did the sums. I'd be forced to jack-in my paper round but if I continued to fleece old-man Sawyer on Saturdays, I could just about swing it. I never returned to college. I took the job and thus began my love-hate relationship with the turbulent and fickle world of advertising.

The train fare problem was solved simply by the fact that I rarely purchased a ticket. With a little care, it was easy to bunk the trains without too much strife as the majority of British Rail staff lived up to their disastrous track record and could be relied upon to be either half asleep, or AWOL. Unfortunately, bunking the tubes was a bit more of a challenge and, with the advent of automatic barriers, virtually impossible. All in all, it took me a couple of hours to get to work in the mornings. I caught the seven o'clock bus out of the village, jumped a gratis train ride up to London, a tube across town to Oxford Circus, followed by a short walk to the studio.

> The Captain, his officers and crew would like to take this opportunity to wish all passengers *CHRONIA POLA!* – *SEASON'S GREETINGS!*

SEASCAPE

Tuesday 25th December 1973 En route to Panama

It's a hot, sticky, overcast day and we're somewhere off the coast of Guatemala. Thank Christ Claire didn't visit me this morning as I woke with a gruesome hangover having had only a couple of hours' kip. She didn't leave my cabin until 2.00 a.m. last night and I've got furrows of scratches down my back and across my arse where she dug her fuckin' nails in. When she'd gone, I cleaned myself up, dabbed some Germoline on my wounds and went from one crew Christmas party to the next, finally crawling into my bunk at dawn.

The mess was unusually hushed this morning, the few crew that did turn out for breakfast sipping coffee and nursing their own hangovers. I wandered the ship flogging tote tickets and, grinning through my nausea, bid Merry Christmas to any passengers that I came into contact with. Then I caught up with Paul, who was in a right tizz, panicking because he couldn't find Sean, who was due to play Santa Claus in half an hour.

The last time I'd seen the obnoxious Paddy would have been about four in the morning when he'd lurched off arm in arm with Big Glenda, a stewardess. I rushed down to Sean's cabin; his door was unlocked but there was no sign of him. We had the Purser's Office page him several times and, when he failed to respond, I tracked Big Glenda down in the stewardesses' quarters, where she claimed that she and Sean had argued and she'd left him sculling whisky in his cabin.

I reported back to Paul, who was becoming frantic as, by now, there were only minutes to go before Santa's scheduled appearance in front of a horde of excited kiddies and their doting parents. With Sean nowhere to be found, Paul, almost in tears, made the staggeringly ridiculous decision that I should play the role of Father Christmas.

Sean is a fat bastard of fifty and would have filled out the moth-eaten Santa suit with aplomb. I, however, am a skinny, five foot nothin', fresh-faced brat and I looked completely ludicrous. Paul stuffed a few cushions under the costume, which padded me out unconvincingly, kissed me on the cheek for luck and then hooked a somewhat smelly false beard over my ears.

'You look gorgeous, Maude,' Paul said, patting me on the head.

Ho! Ho! Fuckin' Ho!

Paul dashed down to the Promenade Deck to announce the arrival of Santa to the gathered throng and I dejectedly made my way up to the Boat Deck where I was loaded into a lifeboat along with a sackful of goodies. The sailors who operated the antique winch were pissing themselves as I was lowered, creaking, down the side of the ship to the Promenade Deck below.

It was stifling inside the padded suit, the false beard itched and, with my hangover and the swaying of the lifeboat, I was fighting the urge not to throw up. As my head became level with the Boat Deck, I looked up in time to see Sean, who was leaning on the Crew Deck rail laughing his head off and waving an empty whisky bottle at me. I just had time to give him the finger before the boat descended to the Promenade Deck where, whipped up by Paul, a cheer of greeting erupted as the kiddies caught sight of the smallest Santa in the world.

The cheer quickly turned to groans of disapproval, then stunned silence and one of the lippier Aussie kids stepped forwards and snarled, 'You're not Father Christmas. You're that little Pommy, Archie.'

The boat was made fast to the side of the ship and Paul, acting the part of Santa's bigger helper, stepped through a gate in the rail and hopped aboard my seaborne sleigh. Keen to get this hideous duty over with as quickly as possible, we paid no heed as to who got what and, grabbing presents indiscriminately, we threw them across to the kiddies.

Several of the little girls ended up with a toy truck or a plastic machine gun and some of the boys got a miniature tea set or a doll. The contents of the sack were soon depleted and Paul hopped across to the safety of the Promenade Deck and attempted in vain to lead the kids and disgruntled parents in a farewell Santa wave and I was hauled back up the side of the ship to the Boat Deck above.

Once it was all over, Paul assured me that I'd made a splendid Santa, gave me a bottle of champagne for my troubles and promised to reprimand Sean for going AWOL.

My hangover had just about subsided by lunchtime and, though not a fan of the Yuletide season, I was surprised how much I enjoyed the on-board atmosphere of this, my first Christmas Day spent at sea. There was no organised entertainment planned for the day but Manolis, the head chef, and his team outdid themselves, putting on an elaborate buffet lunch out by the pool. The band played and passengers danced the afternoon away as the Kioni chugged merrily on to Panama.

Claire's old man, Terry, was right in the thick of it, swilling back the sauce with a few of his cronies and having a great time until he passed out in a deckchair. I tracked Claire down in the library and she followed me up to my cabin for a deliciously sweaty fuck in the tropical heat. Then we swapped Christmas presents. I gave her a silver ring that I'd bought in the market at Acapulco. It was too big for her but she said she loved it anyway and would get it altered once back in the UK. She gave me a beautiful hand-tooled belt. Then I had to go and fuck things up by telling her how much I loved her. Bloody 'ell. She went fuckin' loopy!

13

Paint Pots and Piss Artists

The decision to quit college and get a job turned out to be the right one. The Art Machine was better than I could ever have imagined and within no time, I was made to feel very much a part of the hectic and affable camaraderie of the studio. However, for the first few weeks, I was tested and teased mercilessly by my fellow co-workers. Being the lowest of the low, I was the brunt of a barrage of insults and practical jokes and, with reference to my diminutive size, I was immediately nicknamed 'Dwarf'. Not even 'The Dwarf'. Just 'Dwarf'.

The ribbing began on my first day when I was dispatched on a bogus errand to the art supply shop and told to purchase a skirting board ladder. I was so nervous and so eager to please that I failed to comprehend the phoney command and actually ran all the way to the store. On my empty-handed return, the whole place erupted in cheers, jeers and laughter.

Another day, as I was having a rare five-minute break, sitting on the toilet and studying a Playboy magazine, I half noticed a pool of water slowly begin to seep under the door. I didn't take much notice as the plumbing in the old building wasn't up to much and the small kitchen on the other side of the door was always awash with spilt tea and stagnant water. I continued to drool over the Playmate Pet of the Month as the water gradually turned to a puddle and crept towards my feet. What finally got my attention was the loud whoosh and accompanying fireball that suddenly shot up from the floor.

Throwing the Playboy in the air, trousers around my ankles, I shot out of the toilet like the proverbial rat out of a drainpipe and fell flat on my face in the middle of the kitchen. Standing over me were half-a-dozen guys, doubled up with laughter, delighted by my reaction to their dangerous prank.

As it turned out, what I had taken to be a harmless puddle of water had, in fact, been a pool of highly flammable industrial thinner, which was used in the studio for cleaning brushes. With hilarious results, the arseholes had crept into the kitchen and poured the stuff under the toilet door before igniting it.

My safety was most at peril on Fridays. Workload permitting, the whole studio would empty out and the guys would take off on a pub crawl around the West End and return, mid-afternoon, in various states of inebriation. Bernie Sauvage was the one to be given the widest of berths following these monumental benders. Bernie was a photographic retoucher and one of the sweetest guys you could ever wish to meet. Until he got on the turps, that is. Drunk as a skunk, a change would come over him and he would metamorphoses into 'Bernie the Biggest Bastard in the World, Arsehole to One and All', and demonic ogre to small, struggling art studio juniors. Indeed, it was said of Bernie that he was Sauvage before lunch and savage after.

Bernie's idea of Friday lunch being of the strictly liquid variety, meant that the drunken clod wouldn't have eaten a thing and, to soak up the booze, he'd snarl at me to fetch him a sandwich. Hearing this, the rest of the sozzled bums would suddenly realise that they, too, were famished and I'd be inundated with orders for fifty different varieties of sandwiches and rolls, cakes and sticky buns, doughnuts and crisps and every brand of ciggie on the market. Oh yeah…and a packet of wine gums for Shirley on reception.

One Friday, Bernie wrongly accused me of stuffing up his order.

'If I'd wanted Branston fuckin' pickle on my toasted ham and cheese sandwich, I'd have asked for Branston fuckin' pickle. I hate Branston fuckin' pickle, you little fucker!' Bernie screamed.

Egged on by the other piss artists, Bernie ranted and raved. Working himself into a frenzy, he wrestled me to the floor, picked me up by my feet and shoved me, head first, into one of the large plastic dustbins that stood in the middle of the studio. The lid was slammed on and secured with gaffer tape then, for a bit of extra fun, the dustbin, with me playing the part of human bowling ball, was rolled up and down the studio for ten minutes or so until Shirley got the shits and came to my rescue.

But it was all good, clean, harmless, blokey, male bonding, rite of passage bullshit and never to be taken seriously. The cuts, bruises, humiliation and third-degree burns that I suffered seemed a small price to pay, for when not being tortured I was being tutored by some of the most talented artists in the business.

The Art Machine was made up of four expert illustrators who spent their days churning out visuals and TV storyboards. There were two lettering artists, Bernie the Bastard on retouching and a dozen or so paste-up artists ('lick and stick jockeys'). A couple of pasty-faced photographic techs ('togs') banged out negs and prints in the small darkroom and there was an office for the half-dozen 'reps' who took the briefs, four of whom were the owners of the company.

Art studios back then were very male-dominated and the only woman in the firm was the very tough Shirley, who manned the phones and saved my life on more than one occasion. At the bottom of the ladder, just half a rung above me, was my fellow junior, my *uber-*junior and good mate, Sid.

The ringleader at the centre of this mad circus was the studio manager, Alan Cleary, the guy who'd hired me. Alan was a thin, lanky, cigar-chewing streak of piss whose favoured state was panic. He possessed a strange, loping gait and, when he walked, his head would bob back and forth like a chicken. In moments of high anxiety (which for Alan were about every two minutes), he'd run up and down the rows of desks, flapping his long spindly arms and screaming, 'Quick! Quick! Quick! ... It's urgent! ... Quick! Quick! Quick!' He looked and sounded like a large flightless bird trying in vain to get airborne.

The pace at the Art Machine was fast and furious and the hours long yet erratic. Some days we'd sit around with nothing to do but play cards, read magazines and compete with one another for the filthiest joke. Suddenly, at five o'clock, just as we were preparing to head home, a rep would burst in the door with a new business pitch that would require the whole crew on deck to meet the critically tight deadline. Alan would go into a flap and do his bird impression and I'd be dispatched to fetch food, beer and fags for the long, mad night ahead.

Doing an all-nighter was always preferable to merely working late as, having missed the rush hour express trains, the journey home would take forever. If I was forced to catch a late train I would spice up the long, tedious trip and, prior to boarding, find a secluded spot on the platform and have a few surreptitious tugs on a pre-prepared joint. This had its drawbacks as, already dead on my feet, the combination of the dope and the rocking motion of the train would render me completely unconscious and I'd more often than not sleep past my station and sail on, oblivious, to the end of the line. By the time I'd managed to hitch home it would almost be time to head back to work again.

The upside was that, whilst not flush with money, I was pulling in enough overtime to jack in my Saturday job at Sawyer's. The old boy was genuinely sad to see me go and I felt a bit guilty accepting the two quid bonus he gave me on my last day. Especially as I'd just filched a fiver out of the till whilst he was busy giving the hard sell to a couple of young home-buyers ogling one of his shop-soiled refrigerators. We shook hands and I reconciled my guilt with the thought that his profits would be a lot healthier after my departure.

I was now free to spend Saturdays in the peace and quiet of an empty house. Albert, Bobby, Liam and Clive would be, more often than not, chasing a football around a muddy field and Vera would be at the flicks with her friend Bridget.

Vera felt sorry for Bridget, who'd lived alone since her hubby ran off with the next door neighbour and was now 'living in sin' in Ipswich ... or some such drivel. I wasn't listening, or not to Vera, that is. I was stoned off my head and playing the air guitar to Frank Zappa and seriously thinking that it was high time I split and got my own pad.

With Judy out of the picture, my Sunday jaunts to the Roundhouse were not so much fun and usually made me feel a bit sad. I only bothered making the weekly pilgrimage to get out of the house and, of course, to score dope. One week, the Wizard didn't show up and a disturbing buzz went around the place that he'd been busted. Another freak quickly moved in to fill the gap in the market and this dude was the purveyor of some very exotic herbs. Black hashish from Nepal and, occasionally, hash oil – a very convenient little product, indeed. Almost odourless, you simply spread a few streaks of sticky goo on to a normal, tailor-made cigarette and, 'Hey Presto!', you had yourself an instant, innocent-looking joint that could be smoked more or less in public.

One week I scored some Thai sticks. Grass was rarely seen in the UK then as I guess it was a lot more difficult and bulky to smuggle and this was the first time that I'd got hold of any. The stuff was so powerful it should have come with a government health warning as a couple of tokes rendered the smoker into a gibbering, giggling goon in a matter of seconds. Ye gods! This could well be the elixir I've been searching for. I couldn't get enough of the stuff. Unfortunately, neither could anyone else and so I hit upon the brilliant idea of growing my own from the dozen or so seeds that I'd kept.

I placed the seeds on some blotting paper, poured some water over them and left them on the windowsill above my bed. To my surprise, a few days later, three of the little seeds had germinated and I took the shoots and put them in a small plant pot, which also went on the windowsill. Lo and behold, a week later, one of the shoots had clawed its way through the dirt and into the light. Voila! I now had my very own half inch-high dope plant.

Nobody noticed my fledgling herb, hidden as it was amongst the clutter of a bedroom shared by three boys. I'd only ever attempted to grow the wee thing for the heck of it and, watering it sporadically, didn't anticipate being self-sufficient for some time to come.

I continued to score at the Roundhouse and good news came of the Wizard. He hadn't been busted. Word that the drug squad was on his case had reached him in time and he'd skipped the country to hit the well-worn hippy trail across Europe to Greece and Turkey, on through Afghanistan, Pakistan and down to India. Fuck me! I wonder what the locals made of him.

WARNING!

We warn all passengers intending to go ashore at Cristobal that they must be careful as on many occasions in the past, passengers have been robbed and lost money, documents and valuables from their pockets and bags.

SEASCAPE

Thursday 27th December 1973 At Panama

The epic story of the Panama Canal goes back more than four centuries. The idea of joining the mighty Atlantic and Pacific oceans through the narrow isthmus was born soon after the New World was discovered … blah, blah, blah.

Twenty-four hours out from Panama and the pristine ocean starts clogging up with garbage and the sea turns from a sparkling azure blue to quagmire brown. Welcome to Central America.

We arrived at Balboa, the terminal port on the Pacific side of the Canal, and, after picking up the pilot, stood off to await instructions from the US Canal authorities before transiting the Canal. As we'd arrived early in the morning, we wouldn't be docking at Balboa so I wouldn't get to sample the delights of Panama City on this trip. Bit of a bummer, really as, according to my crew mates, it's a wild town with many deviant distractions awaiting the weary mariner. Oh well, hopefully I'll pass this way again.

The good news is there's no entertainment scheduled today as the passengers are happy enough to be left alone to sunbathe or snap away at the passing jungle and the umpteen shanty towns that cling to the muddy banks of the canal. I spent the day slurping Bacardi and Coke on the Crew Deck and marvelling at the fifty-mile trip and the engineering feat that made it possible.

The outstanding part of the traverse through the canal was going through the umpteen locks and the raising of the Kioni to a height of eighty-five feet above sea level with no perceptible motion or disturbance. By midday, we'd entered Gatun Lake, the largest man-made body of water in the world. Next, we passed through three more locks, which lowered the ship to the Atlantic side of the Canal, no probs. It took thirty-four years to dig this trench and over thirty thousand people lost their lives in the process.

The Kioni took ten hours to traverse the Canal and we docked at Cristobal at five in the afternoon. I went ashore with Henri, Georgios, Phil, Don-the-Slot and Reg, the photographer. There wasn't much to see in the dangerous little town but we had a few beers and managed a few laughs in a run-down bar, where we were constantly hassled by a bunch of butt-ugly hookers. Though not easy on the eye, they were harmless enough but Henri got spooked and insisted we leave when a big fat old thing sat on Georgios' lap and refused to budge until he bought her a drink. Following a horrible Chinese meal, we were back on board by nine.

Some of the passengers had a far more adventurous time of it and, though they had been warned of the dangers, several of them were relieved of cameras, jewellery, handbags and the like. The few lasting memories of my first trip to the Canal Zone were the oppressive heat, the poverty and squalor, lots of machine-gun-toting cops, cockroaches the size of small rats and rats the size of small dogs.

We didn't hang around long in Cristobal and had set sail for New York by 11.00 p.m.. I caught up with Bunger in the mess and he raved on ecstatically about his few hours ashore. Having headed straight for a casino, he'd happily relieved himself of three hundred bucks at the roulette table then, hero that he is, had scored a couple of grams of fine Peruvian cocaine off a taxi driver.

'We've got to cool things down, Archie,' said Claire.

She'd ducked up to my cabin soon after sailing and we tore each other's clothes off and jumped in the sack. As for cooling things down, I didn't quite know how to respond, considering she was sitting on my face at the time.

I was cruising down Carnaby Street one day when I bumped into a guy that I'd been at college with. We hadn't exactly been friends but we got chatting and he told me what he was up to work-wise, which was basically the same as me. In short, he'd left college early and was now a dogsbody in an art studio in Shaftesbury Avenue.

Colin was only sixteen, the same age as me, and that's about all we had in common. He had no time for the music, fashion, drugs or any of the fantastic events that had shaped our decadent decade. All that Colin cared about was his girlfriend, Cheryl, who he'd been going out with since he was about twelve. They'd recently run away together and were shacked up in a love-nest in the very unromantic hamlet of the Elephant and Castle.

Colin went on to explain that the flat had a spare bedroom and, as he was struggling to pay the rent, wondered if I knew of anyone who was looking for a place to crash. The prospect of living with Colin and Cheryl didn't exactly thrill me but the thought of having my very own room and not having to spend half my life travelling to and from work was enough to propel me over to the Elephant that night to check the place out.

For those not familiar, the Elephant and Castle is not one of London's more salubrious suburbs and its only claims to fame are the two famous sons it's sired. Charlie Chaplin was born in the area and the Elephant was also the childhood stomping ground of cockney hero, Michael Caine. The funny man and the talented thesp' have long since buggered off and, if you've ever dared venture into the borough, you surely wouldn't blame them.

Colin and Cheryl's hovel was situated on the second floor of a crumbling, Dickensian row of flats whose tenants were predominantly crumbling, Dickensian pensioners. Sad old kippers with fading memories, who wheezed out their last days with nothing more than a pussycat called Tiddles and the loom of a black and white telly for company.

The flat itself was a dump. Two bedrooms and a living room-cum-kitchen opening on to a small balcony, which overlooked a depressing, rubbish-choked courtyard. There was a tiny bathroom with a dingy bath and an ancient toilet with a broken wooden seat and a piece of string dangling from a mould-covered cistern. So desperate was I to leave home that I decided to take the place as a stopgap measure before finding something better and I moved in the following weekend. The rent for the small room was a staggering four pounds a week, half my basic salary, but I figured, what with all the overtime I was clocking up, I could scrape by just so long as I went without a few luxuries ... such as food.

Albert was either glad to see the back of me or too embarrassed to say goodbye for, on the day of my departure, he slunk off to football extra early without saying a word. Vera went all Irish on me, making the sign of the cross and beseeching God to watch over her wayward child. Then she turned on the waterworks full blast as I was the first of her brood to fly the nest.

It was just after Christmas when I moved to the Elephant. There was no heating in the flat and I immediately regretted not having nicked a fan heater from Sawyer's when I'd had the chance. The only source of heat came from the gas stove so, to stave off the sub-Arctic temperature, the three of us would huddle around the open oven door.

Colin and Cheryl were as skint as me and we existed on a diet of baked beans, beer, fags, coffee and fish and chips when we were flush. Following our evening repast, Colin and Cheryl would retire to their fetid bedroom and I'd be left to my own devices. If I happened to have some dope I'd get stoned, crash out and come up smiling the next morning. On the nights when I had nothing to knock me out,

I'd lie alone in the dark and be assailed by the sounds of boisterous bonking and complaining bedsprings as the two young lovebirds tore into one another next door.

My small room looked like it hadn't been decorated since Queen Vic' sat on the throne so, with nothing better to do, I went about fixing up my solitary coop. The Art Machine had recently had a deep purple paint job done throughout and I purloined some of the leftover tins of paint. There wasn't quite enough to cover the faded flock wallpaper in my room so I filled the gaps with whimsical Roger Dean posters and a few movie posters that I found discarded in Wardour Street.

Another day I came across half-a-dozen carpet sample swatch books in a skip. I hauled them back to the flat, pulled the books apart and laid multicoloured carpet squares on the bare wooden floorboards. The effect, though aesthetically bilious-inducing, did help to insulate the room from the bitter cold.

I had no furniture, not even a bed, and crashed in a sleeping bag on the floor, with my faithful Afghan coat providing a little extra comfort. A piece of wire nailed up and strung from one corner to another served as a clothes rack and an upturned orange crate made do as a bedside table. It wasn't much but it was home sweet home for now.

Things were going well for me at work. I enjoyed my delivery duties and got to know London like the back of my hand. Running errands all over town also brought in a few extra shekels as, once I'd sussed out all the short cuts, I found that I could leg it around the West End a hell of a lot quicker on foot than by pissing about on public transport. With kindly instruction from my pal Sid, I fiddled my travel expenses accordingly, pocketed the cash and nobody was any the wiser.

With little reason to rush back to the Elephant, I hung back at work most nights. I needed the overtime and I enjoyed the laughs as I slowly learnt the tricks of my chosen trade. The guys knew of my lack of funds and, now that I'd more than proved myself in the piss-taking department, I was constantly being treated to lunches and dinners so I didn't really starve to death for too long. And if ever things did get a bit desperate, I would bunk a train home for the weekend and a delighted Vera would fill me full of fry-ups and burnt offerings.

I had left the dope plant at home as I hadn't yet worked out how to transport it to my new digs. It had surpassed all my expectations and had continued to thrive on the weak winter sun and the humid conditions of the messy bedroom. Clive had been watering it in my absence and on my previous visit home, it had appeared very healthy and was almost six inches high.

A month later, I was home again and eager to see my little Thai chum. After being welcomed by a worried Vera, who cackled on about how thin I looked, I rushed upstairs only to discover that the plant was gone. As soon as Clive came home from watching Bobby's team lose, three-one, to 'a bunch of wankers', I pulled him aside and gently grilled him as to the whereabouts of my missing weed. He wasn't making much sense so I loosened my grip around his neck and listened in horror as he spluttered the disturbing explanation. These were innocent times and though the majority of teenagers were permanently stoned out of their heads, (or certainly the ones I knew), the older generation had little clue as to what we were on about. They had even less idea of what a marijuana plant looked like.

Vera had been on one of her rare dusting expeditions in the bedroom when she'd noticed the plant. Clive informed her that it belonged to me. Delighted that I was taking such an interest in horticulture she'd passed the joyful news on to Albert. He'd checked the plant out, fortunately failed to identify it, but, feeling it looked in need of a little TLC, had decided to take it to work and put it in his greenhouse. Oh fuck! The 'Big House', where Albert had worked for years, prided itself on its prize-winning gardens and often flung open the gates to allow the public to swan about and see how the other half lived. In fact, a spring carnival was scheduled for the following weekend. I had to get the fuckin' thing back. Pronto!

That night, I slipped out of the house, commandeered Liam's bike and cycled the two miles to the 'Big House', my progress severely hampered by my flares, which kept getting snagged in the front wheel spokes. I wobbled past the main gates of the mansion, carried on a further half-mile down the road, turned on to a public footpath that circled the estate and chucked the bike in some bushes.

Midnight found me standing over my little dope plant with a torch in one hand and a bottle of weedkiller in the other. I'd had to hike through the woods in the pitch fuckin' dark, and then sneak across the tennis court and through the kitchen garden at the rear of the estate before forcing the lock on the greenhouse. I'd then spent another half-hour locating my plant amongst all the ferns and shit. This wasn't made easier by the fact that I was ripped off my tits, having smoked a large joint to bolster my courage for the covert operation.

My plan had been to simply swipe the fucker then beat a hasty retreat. Then I figured that Albert might become a bit suspicious if it just vanished into thin air. No! There was only one thing for it. The plant must die, and good fuckin' riddance for all the trouble it had caused me.

I plucked a few souvenir leaves from the eighteen-inch-high plant before administering the coup de grace. Giving the bugger a good blast with the weedkiller. I breathed a sigh of relief. Mission accomplished. It was then that I heard the dogs. Shit! I'd forgotten about the dogs.

I knew that there were six of the brutes. They lived on the estate and were friendly enough during the day but at night they were allowed to roam free – and they took their sentry duties seriously. At night they became 'The Hounds of the fuckin' Baskervilles'.

I dashed out of the greenhouse, legged it through the kitchen garden then shot across the tennis court like a skinny white javelin. Diving blindly into the woods, I became momentarily entangled in a blackberry bush, and then kept running as the dogs drew closer. I was disorientated and, though I knew I was heading in the wrong direction, stumbled on until stopped short by a narrow but fast-running river.

I paused to get my breath and promised God that I'd give up the fags if he spared me from being mauled to death by the pack of 'hell hounds' that now sounded too close for comfort. The river gave me an indication as to my whereabouts and I was about to set off in the direction of the footpath, when a snarling form flew out of the woods and sank its slobbering fangs into my arse. The forward motion of the gargantuan beast caused me to lose my footing in the soft earth of the riverbank and I tumbled forwards into the icy water. When I surfaced, a few feet from the bank, all six dogs were baring their teeth above me and one determined show-off launched himself into the water. I managed to punch the brute in the snout and he whined in pain, turned, and scrambled up the bank to join his mates in their barking frenzy.

The strong current swept me downstream but I eventually made it to the safety of the opposite bank. As I hauled myself out of the freezing black water the dogs slavered and snarled in protest. I gave them the finger as I took off towards the footpath, retrieved Liam's bike, rolled up my soggy, mud-covered flares and cycled quickly home before I froze to death.

The next day I caught the train back to London and, apart from a mangled arse and the beginnings of double pneumonia, I was none the worse for wear. I heard no more of the incident until a few days later when I phoned home. Vera informed me that there had been some sort of attempted break-in at the 'Big House'. Nothing had been stolen but tragically my little plant was no more. Apparently, it had succumbed to the cold when 'the burglars' had left the greenhouse door open. According to Vera, 'it was all a ruddy mystery'.

So much for being self-sufficient. I wisely decided to continue feeding my growing dope dependency by the far safer mode of scoring at the Roundhouse or buying from one of the huge Jamaican dealers who hung around outside the tube at the Elephant.

> *$ SNOWBALL BINGO $* – With Archie –The Snowball now
> stands at $28.00. Please note that all proceeds go to the
> Seaman's Mission.5.00 p.m. Main Lounge

SEASCAPE
Saturday 29th December 1973 En route to New York

Shipboard life continues its crazy course as we meander through the Caribbean *en route* to New York. Gertrude, the Dutch nurse, was telling me at breakfast this morning that, as usual, half the below-deck crew had picked up a little souvenir from the Canal Zone prostitutes and, since leaving Cristobal, she's been doing a brisk trade in penicillin jabs.

'My Got! I'fe nefer seen so many shrifelled cocks,' she squealed, handing me a piece of toast.

I hope she'd washed her fuckin' hands.

Meanwhile, Claire seems to have forgotten all about 'cooling it' and we're 'at it' night and day. Conveniently, her old man, Terry, bored out of his wits with the voyage, appears to have upped his sauce intake and doesn't seem to give a rat's arse what his wife gets up to. Consequently, Claire and I are spending even more time together. She rarely leaves my cabin until 2.00 a.m. and is sliding back into my cot a few hours later at daybreak. I'm loving it, and I'm loving her but, Christ, I'm only twenty, give me a break – I think I've put me back out.

The little time that I have had to myself has been spent helping my friend Bunger demolish half his coke. Like a lot of things that have happened to me over the past couple of months, snorting coke is a first. When I left England, the stuff was just starting to creep on to the scene but it was extortionately expensive and, up until now, I'd never even seen any. As for the purity of Bunger's score, I have nothing to compare it to. All I know is that a couple of lines are enough to freeze the whole face numb and a rapturous, jaw-gnawing feeling of well-being envelops the soul. Then the verbal jousting begins and, for the next half-hour, it's yackety-yak, yackety-yak, yackety-yak, with every utterance a hilarious and brilliantly observed load of old bollocks! Oh yeah, and I find that chain-smoking is delicious and absolutely essential when one is snorting coke.

We were in my cabin enjoying a pre-dinner snifter when Bunger, suffering a rare bout of sanity, suggested we may want to think about easing up a tad.

'The trouble is, old boy, this stuff is extremely moreish,' he said, decorously. 'And what with New York coming up in a few days, we're forced with the dilemma of either making piggly-wigglies of ourselves or of putting a bit by for the trauma of the Atlantic crossing,' he added.

We had another snort and mused on our conundrum for a moment before Bunger made his decision.

'I fancy we should stash the bugger. Let it cure for a few days. Give our olfactory fibres an opportunity to regroup,' he said, before hoovering up another line.

I took a hit next and then Bunger sealed the remaining gram in a plastic bag and wrapped an elastic band around it for good measure.

Being a lot easier to conceal than a large bag of grass, Bunger didn't see the point in clambering up into the superstructure to squirrel the coke away in his usual hiding place and, as I followed him out into the corridor, he indicated a small hole in the corner of a ceiling panel.

'That'll do perfectly, old boy. Close at hand in case of emergency.'

Once we'd checked that the coast was clear, Bunger handed me the gear and I clambered on to his back and shoved the goodies through the hole. As I did so, I detected a sucking sensation on the other side of the panel and, with horror, I watched the little bag disappear, with a pop, into what I imagined was some sort of air-conditioning duct.

'Oh fucking hell! That didn't sound good,' said Bunger.

A cabin door swung open at the other end of the corridor and Stefan, the baggage master, emerged wrapped in a towel.

'*Kalispera*,' he said, heading for the showers.

Bunger and I ducked back into my cabin, wondering whether it was the last we'd seen of the Charlie.

Man oh man! And I thought the *South Pacific Show* was as bad as it could get. Sadly, I was wrong as we outdid ourselves this evening with a Greek tragedy billed as *Hellenic Night*.

What with the Greeks' love of dancing and the fact that they make up the majority of the crew, it's a complete mystery to me, as to why, when it comes time to showcase a bit of national pride, I, along with several other nationalities other than Greek, was press-ganged into performing the many dances that made up the boring show. Maybe it has something to do with Paul's unorthodox choreography. Or it could have something to do with the silly bloody costumes we were forced to wear?

The girls, wearing headscarves and long dresses, looked like those panhandling gypsy women who harass tourists outside the Tottenham Court Road tube station. As for us blokes, we had to dress in the official Greek warrior costume, which comprised of a floppy, felt beanie, puffy shirt and embroidered waistcoat. We slipped on white tights and wore some sort of goatskin moccasin on our feet, a black pom-pom embellishing each pointy end of the bizarre footwear. Then, of course, no self-respecting warrior would be seen dead going into battle without the cheeky *Fustanella* – a pleated, white skirt.

I felt like a right pillock as we opened the show with a stirring, though slipshod, *Kalamatianos'* – the national dance of Greece.

If there was a highlight to the long, drawn-out evening, it was when the girls performed the *Kariatides* – the virgin's dance. They got to ditch their drab costumes and as the lights dimmed and the stage was lit only by fluorescent tubes, they made their dramatic entrance. Now resplendent in what appeared to be nothing more than thin, white nighties, the girls, a *papier mâché* urn balanced on one shoulder, snaked alluringly across the stage.

I watched the ancient prick-teasing ritual from the wings and Claire winked at me as she bent to pour imaginary water from her urn. As she turned and tippy-toed back across the stage, I smiled at the very idea of her performing the virgins' dance. I had a raging hard-on under my skirt, too.

Led out on stage by Paul, who made for a very unconvincing warrior, we closed the show with a foot stomping *Hasapico* – the famous Greek knees-up better known as Zorba's dance.

Up in my cabin later that night, I had Claire reprise her virginal act by dressing in the skimpy, white robe. It didn't stay on long, I can tell you.

14

Oh ... oh ... ah ... ah ... sorry

A new decade had dawned and Rolf Harris topped the charts with *Two Little Boys*. Apart from that, life was good. There was only one troubling dilemma for me – I was desperate to get my leg over. The guys at work were forever grilling me on my non-existent sex life and I was fast running out of bullshit and spin.

Returning home late from work one night, I held the door open for a young woman who, as it turned out, lived in the flat above mine. She was one of the few residents I'd seen in the building who didn't have one foot in the grave and I guessed her to be in her mid-twenties. I saw her on a number of occasions and started to keep an eye out for her in the street. When I saw her coming, I'd dash out on to the landing to 'bump into her', accidentally on purpose.

'Bumping into her' one night, I helped her up the stairs with her shopping and she invited me in for a cup of tea. Her name was Sarah and she welcomed me into her small flat, which was very feminine and cosy and a world away from the slum that I lived in only one floor below. We got talking and, concerned that I was living away from home at such a young age, she insisted that I stay for dinner.

Sarah was no supermodel but there was something very sexy about her and I couldn't take my eyes off her bum as she wiggled deliciously about the kitchen in a tight little miniskirt. We ate dinner in front of the telly, which we took little notice of as, both starved for company, we were too busy jabbering. Sarah gave me her life story in about ten minutes flat.

Born in Manchester ... came to London to study nursing ... met Dave ... whirlwind romance ... married Dave ... honeymoon in Benidorm ... marital bliss lasted all of five minutes ... Dave turned out to be an arsehole ... always drunk ... lazy bum ... doesn't work ... abusive ... started using her as a punching bag ... Dave fucked off one day ... good riddance, Dave.

I listened with interest before casually enquiring as to the possibility of Dave turning up unannounced. Sarah assured me that this was highly unlikely as she'd seen neither hide nor hair of him for over a year. Had indeed moved to the Elephant to cover her tracks.

Sarah and I enjoyed each other's company and I started going up to her flat to eat several times a week. No prizes for what happened next, though at the time, it came as a complete shock to me.

One night, after a few glasses of plonk, we were sitting on the couch watching *Till Death Us Do Part* when Sarah leant against me and slipped her tongue in my ear. We started kissing and, in short order, she undid my fly and wrapped her hand around my cock. I was so young and inexperienced that I didn't know what to do so, not having much say in the matter, I simply surrendered and let Sarah take charge. I was like a wide-eyed kid let loose in the cockpit of a 747. Excited, but too scared to touch anything in case I caused a calamity and was asked to leave.

She slithered down the couch and, in one deft move, pulled my jeans and pants off and started sucking, hungrily, on my old chap. Hallelujah! 'Look, Mum. No hands!' She stood up, dragged me into the bedroom, we kissed some more, and then she pushed me on the bed and tore the rest of my clothes off. I leant back and watched as Sarah quickly undressed herself. Then she lay down beside me and guided my hand to her tits, then down between her legs.

The unexpected wetness aroused me some more and the silkiness of her pussy drove me wild as she guided my cock inside her. Then she stuck her tongue back in my ear and whispered, huskily, in her ever-so-sensual Mancunian accent, 'Fook me ... foook me ... foooook me'. I did as I was told and lasted all of ten seconds before collapsing on top of her.

In the coming weeks, Sarah and I fucked each other's brains out and, thanks to her expert tuition, my personal best times quickly improved. Sarah worked shifts and sometimes she'd knock on my door when I was getting ready for work and drag me up to her flat for a brisk fuck and a bowl of cornflakes. 'Breakfast of Champions'. Fuckin' lovely!

With all the fucking going on it was only a matter of time before she became pregnant: Cheryl, that is (Sarah was mercifully on the pill). Colin was over the moon, unlike Cheryl's parents. When they found out, they hit the roof and ordered their wayward daughter home. Poor old Colin was lost without his true love and within a matter of weeks, he'd schmoozed Cheryl's folks and the dreaded death knell of wedding bells was in the air.

Colin announced that he'd given notice on the flat, which suited me fine as I needed an excuse to be moving on. The sexual education I was acquiring from Sarah was invaluable and fantastic but, because of our age difference, we both knew that we were never destined for a long-term relationship. Sarah was relieved when I told her I'd be moving on. It turned out she had plans of her own and had been working up the courage to tell me that she'd soon be heading back to Manchester. She'd completed her studies, was filing for divorce and wanted to move back home to be near her aging mum, who was starting to lose the plot. I had two weeks to find new digs.

The Captain, his officers and crew would like to take this opportunity to wish all passengers
KALI CHRONIA! – HAPPY NEW YEAR!

SEASCAPE

Tuesday 1st January 1974 At New York

Once we'd cleared the Bahamas and were on a Rhumb-Line for New York, the weather changed dramatically. The sun disappeared behind a freezing fog and the ocean turned a cold slate-grey. The wind blew, the seas grew and the officers reluctantly stowed their tropical whites and, for the first time in almost two months, donned their less glamorous black, cold-water uniforms.

The drop in temperature did nothing to dampen last night's festivities and passengers and crew alike saw in the New Year in fine form. After I'd called a bumper snowball bingo session, I had to help Sean compere the fun and games in the ballroom. Sean was pissed out of his head and I was stoned but nobody seemed to notice or care as we cajoled passengers to compete in limbo contests, knobbly-knee competitions and the like. It was all very naff but as I was so ripped, I actually had a laugh. Sean handed me the microphone and let me lead the countdown to midnight. Happy New Year!

Balloons rained down from the ceiling and Evris and his Athenians struck up *Auld Lang Syne*. Friends and strangers hugged and kissed and, with my duties over for the evening, I sought out Claire and we scurried up to my cabin to see in the New Year in our own deliciously depraved manner.

When she left me, battered and bruised, a couple of hours later, I went to a piss-up in the nurses' quarters, where I found Bunger looking unusually morose.

'Alas, old boy, I fear that fine gram of cocaine has vanished forever,' he yelled, over the din of the party.

He was sitting on a bunk, one arm draped listlessly around Gertrude who, completely paralytic, was perched on his lap. Her head lolled from side to side, her mascara had run, her usually crisp, white uniform was covered in splotches of red wine and one of her black stockings was torn off at the foot. Bunger was wearing her hat.

Gertrude looked up at me, her crazed eyes rolling in her head as she attempted to focus. She managed a sloppy grin, then grabbed my hands and placed them roughly on her impressive knockers.

'Archie, I know you luff *Elf en Twaalf* but do you haff a fafourite?' she enquired, offering up first her left boob then her right for inspection.

'I fancy Miss Bloemfontein has rather overindulged,' said Bunger, shoving Gertrude off his lap.

Her knees buckled and she slithered to the floor, tipped backwards, banged her head on the cabin wall, laughed maniacally and, wedged between the bunk and a writing desk, promptly passed out.

I sat down beside Bunger on the bunk and he told me his tale of woe.

'See, it's like this, old boy,' he began.

It had been all of forty-eight hours since we'd had a snort of coke but, with the passing of midnight, Bunger's nose had begun twitching and his thoughts turned to the stash that hopefully lay dormant behind a ceiling panel in the corridor outside my cabin.

' … after all, old boy, when one thinks about it, one hasn't indulged oneself since last year,' he offered up, by way of justification.

The upshot is that, sometime after midnight, he'd dragged a chair into the corridor and foraged, unsuccessfully, for the gram of coke.

'I fear some dastardly rodent may have swiped it,' he sniffed, glumly.

I handed my friend a consolatory joint and he cheered up a bit.

'From the racket emanating from your boudoir, I surmise you were entertaining the Home Counties vixen,' he said, lighting up.

So, on a freezing-cold New Year's morning – hangover or not – I stood on the forward observation deck and took in my first sights of the home of the brave. It was all there, just as I'd seen in a thousand picture books and movies. We sailed past the Statue of Liberty and Ellis Island then, with the Goodyear blimp hovering above, sailed up the Hudson River to gaze in wonder at the skyscrapers of New York City. The sun burnt through the early morning fog and lit up the splendid art deco spire of the Chrysler Building. Then there's the Empire State, majestic and proud but now forever dwarfed by the massive twin towers of the newly-completed World Trade Center.

We were tied up at Pier 57 by 9.00 a.m. and I couldn't wait to get ashore. Unfortunately, as soon as we'd docked an announcement came from the bridge that all crew were to remain on board as the US Coast Guard had decided on a crew safety drill. Happy New Year and bollocks to you, too!

I was standing at my lifeboat station, freezing my arse off, when the Captain, a couple of officers, including Cocksakis, and half-a-dozen uniformed Yankees came stomping along the Boat Deck. The group stopped in front of our boat and one of the coastguards indicated that a rope ladder at his feet should, in fact, be dangling over the side of the ship. Cocksakis rattled off a command in Greek and Pippo, the sailor in charge of our boat, shrugged, bent down, picked up the ladder and dutifully heaved it over the rail. Unfortunately, the ladder wasn't attached to anything and, after hitting the water with a loud splash, momentarily floated on the greasy surface like a dying sea serpent, then sank without trace into the murky depths of the Hudson.

Cocksakis went fuckin' nuts and had to be restrained by the coastguards who, along with the rest of us, were pissing themselves laughing. The hapless sailor gesticulated wildly, jabbered back and forth with Cocksakis, and then Captain Tsakos, who had remained calm throughout the whole debacle, stepped forwards and, to the obvious shock of the US Coast Guards, silenced Pippo by slapping him hard across the face with the back of his hand.

After that little embarrassing episode, the coastguards decided to detain us further and insisted on seeing how we performed when launching a lifeboat. Thankfully, they chose the boat next to mine and the crew, including a terrified Henri, was ordered to clamber aboard. After much grunting and swearing from the sailors operating the winches, the boat was eventually lowered, in jerky fits and starts, down the side of the ship. Poor Henri knelt in the stern, tears in his eyes and arms splayed, beseeching Cocksakis to allow him to go down with the ship.

When the lifeboat finally made it to the water, commands were issued via walkie-talkie to start the engine, and the little craft, looking vulnerable and frail when viewed from the height of the Boat Deck, was ordered to perform a series of manoeuvres before being allowed to chug back to the side of the ship.

Henri threw up several times on the long ascent and, once safely aboard, collapsed theatrically on the deck. The coastguards shook their heads, made a few notes and, mercifully, the group moved on to inspect another part of the ship.

We waited around for a while and then more bad news came down from the bridge. The boys from US Customs who, like their coastguard colleagues, were also presumably on double time, decided on a thorough search of crew quarters. Of course, we had nothing to fear as any illegal substances had long been stashed at various locations throughout the ship but everyone was pissed off at being held up some more. And Pikey had a particularly hairy time of things.

Turns out that last night he'd busted a rowdy passenger party on D-Deck and scored himself a KitKat-sized block of hashish into the bargain. He'd stuffed it down the side of his mattress and forgotten all about it, only remembering the stuff as he was escorting some of New York's finest around our particular part of the ship. As the coppers were snooping about in an engineer's cabin opposite his, he'd ducked into his cabin, retrieved the dope and deftly shoved it under his cap. He conducted the rest of the tour with the large block of hash balanced precariously on his head. Thank Christ there were no sniffer dogs in attendance.

Eventually, we were told we could go ashore but by now it was almost noon and we were due to sail at five in the afternoon. Mind you, I suppose we were lucky to be allowed off at all as our Chinese and Filipino colleagues were refused entry visas and the poor old Indian crew, considered the highest risk of jumping ship, were locked up in the kiddies' playroom for the day.

Bunger had an old school chum who worked on Wall Street and was meeting him for lunch so I went ashore with Don-the-Slot and Tiny-Tom and we hired a cab for a whistle-stop tour of the Big Apple.

With limited time, we managed to take in the Brooklyn Bridge, Chinatown, Greenwich Village, Fifth Avenue and Harlem before being dropped off in Times Square – the heart of the city and hang-out of some of the sickest junkies I've ever seen. We took refuge in an Irish pub, sculled a few Guinnesses and then cabbed it back to the ship. Shortly after five, the Kioni set sail on the last leg of her epic voyage. Southampton, 3,254 nautical miles across the cold, grey Atlantic Ocean.

I'd now been working at the Art Machine for six months and was spending less time delivering artwork and more time preparing it in the studio. I learnt basic paste-up, line drawing and helped the guys in the darkroom when necessary. Sid was promoted to his own drawing desk, another junior was hired and my salary went up to a whopping twelve pounds a week. I felt very grown up and gleefully took an active roll in the initiation and persecution of the new oik, whose name was Martin. The poor sod didn't stand up to the daily beatings and insults too well and it soon became clear that he was a bit of a wuss. He was also a bit of a klutz.

One fine day, Martin was trimming out some artwork with a Stanley knife. Suddenly, he let out a loud howl of pain as he expertly sliced three quarters of an inch off the top of his pinkie finger. Alan swooped down from his perch at the other end of the studio and screamed at Martin not to get any blood on the job. But he soon changed his tune when he saw the seriousness of the accident and, wrapping Martin's damaged digit in a tissue, rushed him off to hospital. Twenty minutes later came an urgent call from a nurse – with instructions to pack the bit of chopped finger in some ice and get it to the hospital quick smart as it might be possible to sew it back on and make poor Martin whole again. Oops!

A strange and evil force who went by the name of Dennis had retrieved the bloody finger tip, painted the nail black and stuck it on his anglepoise lamp where it bubbled and slowly burnt to a crisp from the heat of the bulb. God knows what Dennis' parents had done to him as a child. Maybe his bizarre behaviour had something to do with all the acid he'd dropped over the years. Whatever, his frazzled nerve-ends made him do the weirdest things and he was a very sick puppy, indeed. But Dennis always cracked me up and, being the talented artist that he was, had become something of a hero to me.

Martin never returned to work. I heard he got a nice, safe job working in the kitchens at the Royal Garden Hotel in Kensington (I just hope they never let him near any knives). Another, more hardy junior was hired and passed his first few months of terror with flying colours.

Dennis, my strange friend, mentor, burnt-out acid freak and painter of pinkies, lived in Ealing with his wife and two kids but spent most of his time, out of it, at his girlfriend's pad in Earls Court. Her name was Christine but she insisted on being known by her self-invented sixties pseudonym of Crystal. An original flower child, Crystal had a mass of frizzy hair and a ditzy personality to match. She wore long, flowing dresses, tasselled calf-skin jackets and embellished her deathly-white pallor with a ton of hastily applied make-up, which made her look like Alice Cooper.

Crystal and Dennis were a match made in hippy heaven and she was always nagging him to leave his wife and kids in the burbs and move in with her. Dennis, permanently stoned and ever the pro-crastinator, often promised to but never quite got around to it.

I was hanging out with Dennis more and more and would frequently end up back at Crystal's pad, lying around on a bean bag bombed out of my mind listening to the Moody Blues, King Crimson and Floyd. Crystal was the matriarch of the flat and lorded it over the other freaks who called the place home. There was Miriam, Crystal's equally freaky younger sister, who had a room to herself, and two Spanish cousins, Diego and Alberto, who shared a larger room.

Diego and Alberto were in London studying hairdressing at Vidal Sassoon and paid their way by dealing weights of hash to all and sundry. Consequently, there was a never-ending flow of dope fiends dropping in at all hours so, with the etiquette of the day demanding that one hang back and share a few joints before splitting, there was always a party going on.

The large flat took up the entire top floor and the rest of the house was split into four small bedsits, which shared a communal bathroom and toilet. As luck would have it, a room became available for a fiver a week and I grabbed it and moved my few belongings from the Elephant to the just as shabby but far more 'happening' Earls Court.

As a parting gift, I gave Sarah a Joni Mitchell album and she reciprocated by 'fooking' my brains out one last time ... God bless her. She buggered off back to Manchester and I never saw her again.

I wasn't invited to Colin and Cheryl's nuptials but I bought them a lava lamp as a wedding present. I heard later that, with the help of Cheryl's folks, they put a deposit on a dream home in Enfield and presumably lived crappily ever after. Best wishes, etc.

This was more like it. I felt as though I had truly arrived. The bedsit wasn't much but it was in the right part of London and a palace compared to my depressing digs in the Elephant.

There was an old army cot, a built-in wardrobe and, tucked behind a curtain, a Baby Belling – for cooking. Best of all, a large bay window looked out on to Earls Court Road, which made the small room bright and airy. I tacked the usual posters on the walls, covered the cot with a very trendy Union Jack bedspread and, as my fortunes improved, furnished my new home with a stereo and a second-hand electric guitar and amp. I never learnt to play the guitar but would crank up the stereo and sit in the window for hours making a God-awful noise playing backup to Carlos Santana.

I missed the regular rumpy-pumpy with Sarah but I was having fun and I wasn't starving to death any more. And I was living in the heart of swinging London with a growing number of new and very hip friends. If I wanted to party (which was all the time), score some dope (ditto) or get a haircut (rarely), I only had to pop upstairs to Crystal's pad. And Earls Court had loads of cheap eateries and a plethora of clubs and bars that didn't appear to give a stuff that I was only sixteen and looked about twelve.

In the room opposite mine lived a seriously cute Japanese student named Akiko. The only English she knew was, 'Herro. How getting are you?' and, 'Yes, I am not speaking Engrish.' I attempted to chat up Akiko at every opportunity but it was an exhausting exercise. Christ, I had enough trouble with Pommy chicks but getting into Akiko's no doubt luscious pants would require the patience of a very determined saint. I persisted for a month then gave up and just nodded to her and mumbled 'Herro' whenever our paths crossed. Akiko was not the first, and certainly would not be the last woman to have failed to understand me.

The room next to mine was occupied by a crotchety old Russian dame who was forever complaining about all the noise and comings and goings of the many visitors to the house. She was ignored as much as possible.

The other room was home to Kirsty. A pretty Irish girl who was nineteen but looked the same age as me. Kirsty worked in a record shop in Chelsea and never had much dough so I'd shout her dinner at the Hungry Years – a hamburger joint in Earls Court Road. She repaid me with swiped records.

I liked Kirsty a lot but was wary of becoming involved with her as she lived next door. But I needn't have worried, as she was a very independent little thing and, having just split from a four-year relationship, was loath to become involved herself. However, our friendship grew and, though we both saw other people, we would end up in bed together several times a week. Fucking perfect. No complications. No pressure. No tears. There should be more of it, if you ask me.

HOT DOGS!
Available daily from the Marine Bar (weather permitting) – ONLY 25 cents.

SEASCAPE
Thursday 3rd January 1974 En route to Southampton

For the umpteenth time in her epic life, the Kioni headed out into the great Atlantic pond for the long, hard slog to England. January storms battered the gallant old tub mercilessly, rusting plates bent and creaked, rivets popped and several low-lying portholes gave way causing chaos, fear and minor flooding below decks. Giant green waves broke over the bow, sending tons of water crashing up and over the bridge, and plumes of sea spray rained down, turning the decks to fast-running rivers before pouring out the scuppers and back to the sea. Spookiest of all was when the stern would pop out of the water every so often and expose the screws, which would then cavitate and cause the ship to stop in its tracks before shaking violently like a great, metallic pooch.

Up until now, the northbound passengers had been blessed with calm seas and plain sailing but now the majority, too ill to venture out, stayed locked and miserable in their cramped, leaky cabins.

Waiters skittered and slid along the vomit-strewn passageways delivering unwanted stale sandwiches and beakers of lukewarm bouillon to the cabin-bound voyagers. Many of the Greek crew hailed from the impoverished mountainous areas of Greece and had only happened upon a life at sea as an economic necessity to escape a dreary existence of herding goats or eking out a paltry living growing *souvlakis* or whatever? Never happy when conditions got rough, these affable characters were as frightened and miserable as most of the passengers and did little to assuage any anxiety by going about their business mumbling incoherently, clutching worry beads and, worse still, wearing life jackets.

For the hardy expat crew, the inclement weather meant reduced duties – i.e. party time! And, with the added melancholic atmosphere of journey's end that pervaded, a shindig was never too far away and I roved about the ship from piss-up to piss-up. The stewardesses' mess was the place to be for a mid-afternoon drink and then, for after-hours cocktails, the favoured venues were the nurses' quarters or the Beauty Salon. Late at night, we mustered for a smoke in the evil-smelling photographers' darkroom, and then it's on to a Chinese banquet with Bossy and the boys in the laundry, which is where I caught up with Bunger last night.

'Got the bugger,' said Bunger, wiping crumbs of white powder from beneath each nostril.

He grabbed my hand and steered me into the heads, where he pulled a package from his pocket and quickly proceeded to chop up a couple of generous lines on the grimy toilet lid.

'It took a bit of doing,' he said, between snorts. 'Had to rip half the fucking ceiling down. Tuck in, old boy,' he said triumphantly.

When I eventually crawled back to my cabin in the middle of the night, I was stunned to see that Bunger hadn't been exaggerating with his wild claim of devastation. Indeed, half the fuckin' ceiling was missing and, evidently working fast, he hadn't bothered to cover his tracks as the whole passageway was littered with broken and torn ceiling panels. About to throw in the towel, my deranged friend's tenacity was eventually rewarded when the bag of coke was located, wedged behind some wiring at the far end of the corridor.

15

Escape from Devil's Island

If you can remember the sixties, you weren't there – or so the saying goes. I do remember the sixties, no problem, though I must confess that the early seventies remain a bit of a mystery, shrouded in time and a thick haze of marijuana smoke. Stoned as I was, I worked hard at the Art Machine and became a valued member of the team who, being always hungry for cash, could be relied upon to work whatever hours were required. I worked a lot of weekends and thrived on the challenge of all-nighters, which reaped 'double-bubble' overtime. In short, I was soon earning a fortune for my age and joyfully blowing the lot on clothes, booze and drugs. I seemed to be able to function on very little sleep and, when not working or partying at Crystal's, I was out on the town in search of adventure.

My big brother, Bobby, meanwhile, had been a very busy boy indeed. From an early age he'd set his sights on a career at sea and, after leaving school, had sat for the entrance exam to the Merchant Navy training college at Greenwich. There were few places available and he dismally failed the exam. In hindsight, considering Bobby's growing thirst for alcohol, wild times and dope, this was a good result for the world's oceans.

With his dream of growing up to become a danger to shipping scuppered for the time being, Bobby reluctantly signed up for a five-year printing apprenticeship. He hated the job and, with his eyes still firmly fixed on distant horizons, learnt that most cruise ships carried at least one printer to produce the daily newspaper, menus and entertainment programmes. Bobby applied to P&O and was, mercifully, knocked back by the up-market carrier. Undeterred, he checked out a few of the less posh cruise lines.

Towards the end of his gruelling tenure, a work colleague drew Bobby's attention to an ad in an industry rag and dared him to apply. The job on offer was for a ship's linotype operator with the Greek-owned Cyclades Lines. Bobby attended an interview at their London office and landed the job. Two weeks after completing his apprenticeship, he shipped out on the good ship Kioni, bound for Australia by way of the Canaries and Africa.

Bobby and I had had our differences as kids but, in our teenage years, we had become very close and, though I was excited for him, I missed him like hell. He returned home three months later but, as his ship was only docking at Southampton for a few days, he would be spending his shore leave visiting Albert and Vera in the village. That weekend I joined the rest of the family for Bobby's triumphant return. When he finally turned up in a taxi at midnight, we barely recognised him for he was covered from head to foot in something rarely seen in England in those days ... a suntan!

Bobby emptied out his suitcase, chock-a-block full of exotic souvenirs from his travels. African masks, a boomerang, a grass skirt from Tahiti, several cool T-shirts from the Caribbean, plus an impressive collection of trophy knickers. Albert got a litre bottle of cognac. Vera, some perfume. Liam and Clive each received a New York Yankees cap and I got a carton of duty-free fags.

When the rest of the family had finally gone to bed, Bobby dove into the lining of his suitcase and extracted an envelope full of a pungent, rust-coloured weed. The stuff turned out to be a fine ounce of the legendary and lethal Panama Red. We sat up all night getting mega-stoned and he regaled me with wild stories and flashed photos of the many beauties that he'd defiled.

I took the following Monday off work and accompanied Bobby down to Southampton to say farewell to him and get a look at his ship. The Kioni was a world-weary old tub. Over six hundred feet long, she was no spring chicken, having been launched in America way back in 1932 as the SS Pacific Queen flying the Mattison Line flag. Since 1963, she'd flown the Greek flag and, these days, plied between the UK and Australia, Cyclades Lines having the contract to ship thousands of Pommy migrants down under.

She was due to sail that evening so the day was spent following Bobby from cabin to cabin to meet and drink with his shipmates. At the end of the day, I was, predictably, blind drunk and the only conversation I could recall was with a guy called Kostas, who'd given Bobby his job.

Kostas was a very dapper Greek queen in his mid-fifties. He'd spent a lifetime at sea but had recently taken up a position in the London office where he was in charge of recruiting the many English staff required on-board. I asked Kostas about my chances of getting a job on board and he laughed when he learnt that I was a graphic artist and didn't see how he could help. Over the next few years, I would meet Kostas on several occasions in Southampton and would always hassle him for a job. He would just laugh and tell me to dream on.

The years flew past and in the blink of a bloodshot eye, it was 1973. Whilst Bobby sailed the seven seas, Tricky Dicky was sworn in for a second term and Lyndon Johnson snuffed it; as did Betty Grable, Bruce Lee and Picasso. Princess Anne got hitched to Captain Mark Phillips and her mum bludged a free holiday when she journeyed down under to open the Sydney Opera House. The IRA exploded bombs in central London and Little Jimmy Osmond stormed the charts with *Long Haired Lover from Liverpool.*

I was more than happy with my lot at the Art Machine but Bobby's postcards made me restless and I yearned to travel. I was hunched over my drawing desk one late summer afternoon and dreaming of faraway places when I took a call from Kostas. Without beating about the bush, he asked if I could drop everything and ship out on the Kioni the following Monday. I was stunned but didn't hesitate and said emphatically yes, even before he'd explained the position. He said if I was serious, to jump in a cab and get to his office post-haste.

It turned out that he was in a bit of a bind as one of the entertainment staff had dropped out at the last minute and he only had a few days to fill the spot. When I pointed out the obvious fact that I had no experience whatsoever in the line of work on offer, he reminded me of how much I'd nagged him for a job over the years and assured me that I was more than capable of filling the post. The on-board entertainment director had been consulted and informed of my lack of experience and was keen to train me up. Apparently, he was sick to death of dealing with ex-Butlins redcoats or being up-staged by a bunch of prima donnas.

Kostas went on to explain that the job entailed nothing more taxing than calling bingo, organising deck games and helping out backstage during shows. The money on offer was half what I was then earning in London but tax-free and, with all on-board costs taken care of, it was the chance of a lifetime. I was given the address of the company doctor as I would require a medical and Kostas also told me to get a haircut and buy a couple of suits. Then he shoved a contract under my nose and, just like that, I signed up for a three-month round the world voyage.

I only had a few days to get my shit together and that included securing a passport. As luck would have it, I had a friend who worked in the passport office at *Petty France* and I acquired a passport within a couple of days.

Considering that I only gave two days' notice, the guys at the Art Machine were fantastic. They wished me well, threw me a huge, messy shindig and just for old times' sake, shoved me head first into a dustbin. I gave most of my belongings away to friends, paid the remaining rent on my bedsit and an all-night bash ensued in Crystal's pad.

Bobby wouldn't be shipping out with me as he'd signed-off for the summer and taken off to Greece on a drinking and shagging tour of the islands. Last I heard, he'd taken up with a young Danish filly and, meandering through Europe in a combivan, wouldn't find out I'd gone until he returned home in a couple of weeks. I said farewell to Albert and Vera over the phone and, on a wet Monday morning, caught the early train to Southampton.

Reading this, you probably think it's utter bullshit that I scored a job on a cruise ship with no experience whatsoever. Believe me, half the crew had landed jobs simply because they knew somebody who worked on-board, with their only 'qualification' being a desire to be paid for seeing the world. And, get this ... a few years after I shipped out, my brother Liam got a job as ship's masseur. Apart from pounding flesh, his duties also required him to spend several hours a day lounging around the ship's swimming pool acting as lifeguard. He had zero qualifications as a masseur and, as for him being a lifeguard, I kid you not, he couldn't fucking swim!

I was completely unaware of any of this at the time and, as the train neared the coast, I became increasingly nervous. I didn't know what the hell I'd let myself in for. But there was no turning back so I figured that if things didn't work out, if I made a complete tit of myself, I could jump ship some place and fly home.

**SALE OF SPIRITS FOR PASSENGERS FINALLY
DISEMBARKING AT SOUTHAMPTON**

There will be a sale of bottled spirits in the A-Deck Midships
Foyer between 4.00 p.m. and 6.00 p.m. today. The following
spirits will be available:

WHISKY..US$2.30
METAXA BRANDY (Three Star)..US$1.60
GIN...US$1.60
VODKA..US$1.60
VERMOUTH...................................US$1.60

SEASCAPE

Sunday 6th January 1974 En route to Southampton

Mid-Atlantic and the weather's foul. Haven't seen the sky for days,
the seas are huge and it's knacker-cracking cold on deck. Just getting
about the ship is hazardous, the elevators are out of action and ropes
have been strung across foyers. The majority of the passengers
remain out of sight and so I, like most of the crew, continue to enjoy
reduced duties.

Poor old Pikey, however, has been knockin' his pipe out. He had to
break up a near riot in the Outrigger Bar the other night and got his
fuckin' head kicked in for his troubles. And Cocksakis has been riding
him to uncover the culprit responsible for the mysterious vandalism to
our crew quarters. Added to that, he's had to deal with two deaths in a
matter of days. First off, an old biddy lost her footing, banged her head
and carked it; Pikey did his thing and tossed her overboard early
yesterday morning. Then there was the tragedy of old Demetri.

Old Demetri was the ship's upholsterer and, two days ago, he was
found slumped over his sewing machine ... dead as a dodo. Having
worked at sea for forty years, this was to be his last trip as he was due
to retire to spend the rest of his days with his wife, his children and
his umpteen grandchildren – photos of whom he never tired of
showing off. With a ready, gap-toothed smile, he was a popular
member of the crew and a surrogate papa to many, and a collection
was taken up at the news of his passing.

It turns out that the doc had been treating Demetri for a dodgy ticker for some time. Indeed, had in fact counselled the old man that, for the sake of his health, it was time for him to sign off for good. With Demetri's chest pains becoming more frequent and debilitating, it appeared that he'd foreseen his own demise as a note was discovered amongst the old man's belongings with instructions on what to do with his body in the event of his death. Apparently, he was terrified of being bunged overboard and, due to his long service with the company, he thought it only right and proper that his mortal remains should be repatriated back to his home island of Lefkada for burial.

Respecting his wishes, the Captain wired head office in Piraeus, who promptly replied with an answer to the negative, reiterating that it's not company policy to ship stiffs home and the body should be disposed of in the usual manner.

Least ways, this was the sorry tale that was doing the rounds amongst the crew. Everyone was pissed off about the situation but, in the end, nothing could be done. Demetri's body was subsequently wrapped and readied for a burial at sea and, just after midnight last night, he was cast off the aft Rope Deck. After the short ceremony, I bumped into Pikey who was sitting in the mess, white as a sheet, downing glass after glass of Metaxa brandy. Poor bastard. He looked like he'd seen a fuckin' ghost. As it happens, he had.

The aft Rope Deck, situated directly above the screws, sits only about forty feet above the surface of the ocean and is not the place to be in a rough sea at night. As the old upholsterer's body was commended to the deep, a huge wave lifted the bow of the ship and the stern dropped into a trough. With a following surge, another huge wave picked up the weighted corpse and the ghostly-white shape stood upright, reared out of the tumult and almost surfed back on board. Pikey admitted to being freaked out by the spooky apparition but, according to him, the Greek officers and sailors who were in attendance fuckin' lost it. A superstitious lot at the best of times, they fought their way off the Rope Deck and disappeared, yelling and screaming, down a companionway.

I left Pikey in the mess, clutching his brandy and mumbling over and over, 'Thirty ... he was number thirty. Old Demetri number thirty ... and he didn't wanna go.'

Lugging my brand new vinyl suitcase behind me, I clambered up an aft gangway and found my way to the Purser's Office on 'B-Deck forward'. The Kioni wasn't due to sail for another ten hours and yet the place was jam-packed with irate passengers – all howling and yowling to any poor sod in a uniform.

The majority of the complainants were Pommy migrants, doing the bolt from Blighty for a new life down under. Trouble was, most of the poor buggers had never moved counties, let alone countries, so they were agitated and jittery and a bleating, herd-like mentality had taken hold.

The heady aroma of shared fear mixed uncomfortably with the rancid pong of Greek cooking that wafted through the creaking air-conditioning system. The bored officers who manned the Purser's Desk had added to this cloying olfactory soup by dousing their swarthy chops with gallons of Brut 33 and Paco Rabanne.

They'd heard all the complaints a thousand times before and did their gallant best to put the passengers at ease by shrugging their shoulders and feigning no understanding of English. I had a gruesome hangover and, feeling a tad queasy, was none too pleased with the ugly mood that was developing in the claustrophobic confines of the foyer. Fortunately, I was saved from the bedlam by Don-the-Slot, who came weaving towards me through the crowd.

Don-the-Slot was a good pal of Bobby's and I knew him from many a piss-up. Don was the casino manager, 'the casino' being the grandiose name given to a corridor full of twenty or so slot machines – hence Don's *nom de plume*. Don had seen me come aboard, informed me that it was unnecessary to check-in at the Purser's Desk with all the riffraff and, grabbing my case, cut a swathe through the whining mob. We rode up five floors in the elevator to a foyer full of suitcases, turned right past the Radio Room and stepped outside on to the Boat Deck.

The deck was wet and slippery from the morning drizzle and I wobbled uneasily in my brand new snakeskin boots with the four-inch heels. Half a dozen sailors in grease-smeared boiler suits were manhandling a lifeboat from its derrick and, as we tottered past, Don rattled off a few words in Greek. This raised a laugh from the sailors and one, a sleazy old coot with several gold teeth and a drooping moustache, pursed his lips, winked, and blew me a kiss. A simple good morning would have sufficed. Mercifully, Don shoved me through a door marked 'Crew Only'.

Don was an Aussie from the northern beaches of Sydney and, with his laid-back surfie twang, explained points of interest along the way – who bunked in which cabin and so on. We ducked into the officers' mess and Don swapped a few *yiasous* and *kalimeras* with the dozen or so dishevelled crew who were enjoying a late breakfast. A half-empty bottle of Metaxa brandy stood amongst the debris on the table.

We continued on our way, up a set of metal stairs, down a labyrinth of corridors, and on past some evil-smelling heads until finally Don flung open a door and ushered me into a cramped, four-berth cabin.

'Home sweet home, ya big galah,' he chirped.

As I took in my new surroundings, Don went on to explain a few facts of shipboard life. The Kioni, apparently, was a veritable floating UN when it came to the multitude of nationalities that made up the six hundred or so crew. Along with the Indians, Sri Lankans, Filipinos and Chinese, who did all the shit jobs, there was a sprinkling of Brits, Aussies, Kiwis and a few Europeans, who held the more prestigious positions on-board. Hairdressers, shop staff, photographers and shore excursion staff to name but a few … plus three nurses, half-a-dozen female pursers and, of course, a Pommy printer. Last but not least, the Kioni never sailed without at least one 'Brit' or 'Aussie' Master at Arms (ship's cop/bouncer).

Due to our privileged position, we were deemed as petty officers and subsequently billeted in a small, private township situated on the top deck behind the aft funnel. Don let me in on some more good news in that, as I was part of the ever-so-elite entertainment staff, I would be sharing the four-berth cabin with only one other soul. Don spelt out that, with the ship's band and a cocktail pianist, there would be just three travelling troubadours to entertain and amuse almost seventeen hundred passengers on their four-week voyage to Australia. Musing on this titbit of information, the queasy sensation that I'd felt earlier was fast spiralling to downright nausea.

The cabin had plenty of storage space, a small sink and, best of all, a porthole. Initially a bit peeved to learn that I'd have to use the communal bog and shower at the end of the corridor, I later discovered that my accommodation was akin to a suite at the Ritz compared to what some of the Pommy migrants would be shown to that day. The ones who'd drawn the shortest straws would be shoved somewhere down in the bowels of D-Deck aft. A stifling six-berth metal box with no porthole and close enough to the engine room for the twenty-four-hour vibrations to make sleep virtually impossible.

Don made to leave, with instructions to join him in the Main Lounge in half an hour as he and a few shipmates were going on a last bender in town before the Kioni sailed at six. I'd planned on exploring the ship but figured I'd better do as I was told for the moment. As far as I was aware, I didn't have to report to anyone until after sailing so I commandeered a wardrobe, stowed a few clothes, dumped my case on the bottom bunk furthest from the door and took off in search of the Main Lounge.

I got hopelessly lost and ended up back down on B-Deck where the same chaos ensued outside the Purser's Office. After studying a deck plan, I ducked down a corridor and bumped smack into Kostas. He was delighted to see me as he was keen to introduce me to the guy who was to become my shipboard boss, mentor and fairy godmother – the entertainment director, Paul Ravel.

Paul had worked at sea for donkey's years and on the Kioni for the past two. He had himself a nice little home away from home up in the chief officer's quarters situated directly behind the bridge. A gold star embellished his cabin door. Kostas knocked and walked in.

I'd been warned about Paul but nothing could have prepared me for that first sight of 'her'. Very tanned, very blond and very effeminate, he was sitting on the floor dressed in a silk kimono and busily painting his toenails. At the sight of Kostas he leapt theatrically to his feet and the two queens hugged one another and kissed on both cheeks.

Paul noticed me standing behind Kostas and, with an exaggerated swoon and a manicured hand to the heart, screeched, 'And you must be Maude'.

Kostas introduced me then the two old fudgers bantered back and forth for a few minutes, doing their best to put me ill at ease. On learning that I was Bobby's younger brother, Paul threatened that he would do his very best to bring Bobby back a sister. This comment sent the pair into another round of raucous shrieks and cackles.

Paul produced a bottle of champagne from a small fridge, popped the cork and poured a glass for Kostas and myself. I was later to find out that Paul never touched alcohol but was a genial host who always had a ton of booze stashed in his cabin; gifts from grateful passengers or left behind by a retinue of hairy suitors.

As he dressed, he traded gossip with Kostas and, having applied a liberal covering of rouge to his leathery-old dial, the two friends decided on heading ashore for a day on the razzle. I couldn't help wondering what Southampton had to offer two old sodomites in the way of entertainment on a wet Monday. Emboldened by the champagne, I enquired as to their plans. With a disturbingly impish leer, Paul informed me that he and Kostas would no doubt spend a lovely day 'cottaging' and I was more than welcome to accompany them if I so desired. I didn't have a clue what the hell 'cottaging' was all about but, naive as I most certainly was, something told me that it had nothing to do with real estate.

I thanked Paul for his kind offer, informing him that I had a prior engagement. Paul snatched the glass from my hand, dismissed me somewhat cattily and told me to report back to his cabin at seven-thirty that evening. Kostas shook my hand and wished me luck and I thanked him once again for the opportunity he'd afforded me.

I found Don-the-Slot in the Main Lounge where he introduced me to Tiny-Tom, the ship's printer, who'd taken over from Bobby. Tiny-Tom was a six foot four gentle giant from Newcastle with an unruly shock of coal-black hair and a face like a King Edward potato. I'd always thought him an ugly great bastard but, for reasons I could never fathom, I was to discover to my chagrin that women couldn't get enough of him. For all the pussy he got, he could have replaced his cabin door with a fuckin' turnstile. A couple of years older than me but looking thirty-five, Tiny-Tom was larger than life, had no enemies and was to become one of my best buddies.

Tiny-Tom was busy giving me a blow-by-blow description of the fine young Aussie chick who'd been his northbound squeeze when we were interrupted by a gaunt, elegantly-wasted looking chap with an upper crust accent so terribly clipped, that he made the Duke of Edinburgh sound like an East End spruiker. Fresh from an all-night poker game with Bossy and the boys in the laundry, he stank like a brewery and was obviously still drunk.

He yelled to anyone who could hear: 'Once again, I have been fleeced by those Oriental dhobi wallahs ... the blighters took me for a monkey.'

His name was Barrington Towers but was known to all and sundry as Bunger.

Bunger enthusiastically worked various scams from his head-quarters in the duty-free gift shop, and made a pile of cash on each voyage. With even greater enthusiasm, he pissed the whole lot up the wall or lost it, gambling. Like Tiny-Tom, he was also only a couple of years my senior. Unlike Tiny-Tom, Bunger looked about ninety.

THE LONDON WALKABOUT CLUB is beneficial for all visitors to London. Accommodation, free coach service to the capital, employment and European travel. So come along and meet Kelvin **NOW!** A-Deck Midships 10.00 a.m.–12.30 p.m. and 4.00 p.m.–6.00 p.m.

SEASCAPE

Wednesday 9th January 1974 En route to Southampton

Last night was the Captain's farewell cocktail party. The weather hasn't let up since leaving New York but it's amazing how the promise of free grog managed to coax hundreds of the passengers out of their cabins.

Claire's old man, Terry, was blind drunk and busily slurping away in one corner of the Main Lounge whilst I chatted to his gorgeous missus on the other side of the cavernous room. The giant chandeliers swayed with the motion of the ship and as my pal, Maggie, the hostie, staggered uphill with a tray of cocktails, she banged into me and, indicating towards Claire, whispered, 'Skinny Bitch' in my ear.

Dirty Charlie, the photographer, was doing the rounds and he slunk across the room dragging his camera gear with him. He looked his usual slovenly self, like he'd just dragged himself out of bed, which, no doubt, he had. Dressed in a very mouldy-looking tux, shiny from wear, food stains on the lapels and cuffs frayed, Dirty Charlie never ceases to amaze me in that he's completely unfazed by his appearance or the various noxious odours that he gives off.

Dirty Charlie leered at Claire and, speaking directly to her cleavage, asked if we'd care to have our photograph taken. He'd outdone himself this evening in that his breath was even worse than its normal paint-peeling quality and would have made a pathologist puke. Claire batted her long lashes and backed into a corner. I put my arm protectively around her and Dirty Charlie snapped off a couple of photos. Looking over the filthy photographer's dandruff-dusted shoulder, I noticed Terry glaring at me from the other side of the room. He downed his drink and grabbed another from Maggie's tray. Maybe he's not that blind, after all.

Show time for the last time this trip. Sean opened with his usual retinue of insults and lame gags and then Paul took the floor and launched hysterically into the Tom Jones classic *It's Not Unusual*. What was unusual about Paul's performance was that, instead of playing up to any female members of the audience, he would sidle up and gyrate his crotch in the face of any young guy who happened to be unlucky enough to be seated in the front row. Paul finished the number by jumping up on stage with the band and wrapping himself around Dionysus, the young bass player.

Captain Tsakos blanched but, as usual, the old biddies lapped it up and Paul, ecstatic to once again be hogging the limelight, grabbed a pair of maracas, wiggled his arse and urged Evris and his Athenians to 'shake it up'. I thought the old poof would never get off the stage and, for the next ten minutes, he disgorged a medley of gruesome pop songs that included *Lily the Pink*, *Chirpy Chirpy Cheep Cheep* and *Little Arrows*. The band did a valiant job keeping up with him and he finally left the stage completely drained after dishing up his horrible pièce de résistance, *I'd Like to Teach the World to Sing*.

The show dragged on and then it was my turn to make a complete twat of myself. Up until now I'd been getting away with taking care of the props and handling the lights and only ever appeared on stage hidden amongst the chorus line. But, in his infinite wisdom, Paul had decided to stretch my repertoire to breaking point and, for the past few days, he'd been coaching me every afternoon in the ballroom.

The Lionel Bart musical, Oliver!, had been a huge hit on stage and screen and, for his own nefarious ends, Paul had nabbed a few numbers and bunged them into one of his awful shows ... and who better to play the Artful Dodger than yours truly?

I was quaking with fear backstage and accepted, with gratitude, a few nips of whisky from Sean's ever-ready hip flask. Then the band struck up the first few bars of *Food, Glorious Food* and I skipped on stage followed by my troupe of urchins, pickpockets and chimney sweeps. God knows how, but we made it through *Consider Yourself* and *I'd Do Anything* and, to my complete surprise, left the stage in triumph with the buggers wanting more. I know – it's amazing. I think these people have been at sea too long.

Paul was dead chuffed with my performance and patted me fondly on the arse as I came off stage. I had a feeling that the old bugger was testing me and, sure enough, he pulled me aside after the show and, to my great relief and joy, informed me that, if I cared to, he'd be delighted to have me on the next voyage. I was only supposed to be fill-in crew but I'd been pestering Paul for weeks about the prospect of me signing on for the next trip and, up until now, he'd kept me guessing.

I thanked Paul with a kiss and headed down to the Outrigger Bar to celebrate. Sean was propped in his usual spot, bludging drinks from passengers in exchange for a hackneyed joke or two.

I must admit to being surprised that Sean's managed to keep his spot, considering how he and Paul are not exactly the best of buddies. When I broached the subject, Sean assured me that his position was secure as he and Paul were, if nothing else, professionals and, in a strange way, respected one another (not that you'd notice).

Sean's lackadaisical work ethic and his maniacal mood swings apart, we've become good friends and I was shocked when he blew up on hearing I'd be staying on for the next trip. He went fuckin' ballistic, advising me to get off while I could and pursue my more secure career in the graphics caper. And, as the evening wore on, he went all Irish on me, cried into his beer and said he didn't want to see me become a floating pisshead like him and, indeed, most of the long-term crew.

The four of us caught a cab into town and settled into a greasy spoon for a great big, horrible fry-up breakfast. We all had hangovers of varying ferocity and, with nothing better to do, drank gallons of coffee, chain-smoked and traded bullshit until the pubs opened at eleven.

As we got progressively sozzled on what were to be our last pints of flat Pommy beer for a while, my new best pals lectured me on the many dos and don'ts of shipboard life. Top of the list was 'don't screw crew' – evidently a fate worse than death. What the boys were referring to were the forty or so female stewardesses and cashiers who worked in the various bars and restaurants on board. Comely young ladies no doubt, once tempted by one of these sirens, a young man could find himself stuck with the same piece of arse for weeks on end. Or, horror of horrors, an entire voyage! No, far better to home in on the hundreds of female passengers who were, apparently, all gagging to get their hands on a member of the crew.

We guzzled more beers and Tiny-Tom broached the subject of the umpteen gays who delighted in a life on the ocean waves. He advised me to put the word out quick that I was hetero, assuring me that if I did this I'd never experience any hassles. I was to take his sage advice and, as things turned out, some of the old queens became like surrogate big sisters. And I needn't have worried as most of them happily had their hands, gobs and orifices chock-a-block full with a *smorgasbord* of willing trade below decks.

Last orders were called and Don-the-Slot and Tiny-Tom took off with Bunger to one of his favourite haunts – a restaurant whose congenial host would allow them to drink the afternoon away. I got a cab back to the ship.

My hangover had completely disappeared for, by now, I was smashed out of my skull and, not wanting to push my luck, I figured an afternoon nap was in order. I somehow made it back on board and located my cabin. I was just nodding off, when the door burst open and a huge figure ricocheted in the door frame. My cabin mate had arrived in the shape of a fat, florid-faced fifty-year-old Paddy pisshead by the name of Sean Tierney.

A trouper of the old school, Sean had been born in a circus and, apart from a stint in the army where he'd learnt to fight like a bastard, had spent his entire life in show business. For the past twenty years, Sean had eked out a brave but paltry living working as a stand-up comic. Sadly, his 'shtick' was so ancient that some of his jokes could have been carbon dated to the Pleistocene epoch. His ship to stardom had long since sailed without him and, for the past few years, he'd plied his nefarious trade on the high seas. This was to be his fourth trip on the Kioni.

Of course, I was to discover this, and much more, later. For now, all I knew was that I was being rudely awakened by a huge and terrifying apparition who was bearing down on me, bellowing in a Belfast accent:

'I don't know who the fuck you'se are but you've got five seconds to get your scrawny arse out of my bunk – you little shite!'

Like most of the crew I'd met that day, Sean was completely plastered. I dutifully did as I was told and quickly relocated my scrawny arse to the lower bunk closest to the door – all the better for a quick getaway if things turned really nasty. Sean sat down heavily on his reclaimed bunk, retrieved a bottle of Johnny Walker Red from a holdall, unscrewed the cap, took a long swig and then handed the bottle to me, insisting that I join him.

Between swigs, Sean asked me several questions to which I endeavoured to deliver the correct answer. He made it clear that he was none too pleased with my youth and extravagant clobber but was relieved to know that he wouldn't be sharing a cabin with a 'King Lear', as he so delicately put it.

We were getting along fine until Sean began drilling me on my previous 'showbiz' experience and he was horrified to learn that shipping out on the Kioni was to be my first gig. I did my best to appease him, explaining that it wasn't exactly my fault. That Kostas should shoulder most, if not all of the blame, for giving me the job in the first place. I tried to explain that I was merely a last-minute stand-in for the guy who was supposed to have taken the job. Indeed, I had ended up on board by mistake.

'Straight up, mate, I was virtually press-ganged.'

Nothing I could say would placate him and, lazy fat bastard that he was, he was very pissed off, figuring he'd have to do more than his fair share of work.

Sean lay back on his bunk and continued slugging morosely on his whisky. I unpacked some more clothes and, in an effort to sober up, took off for the showers at the end of the corridor. When I returned to the cabin, Sean was flat on his back, clutching the whisky bottle to his chest and mumbling incoherently into it as though it were a microphone. Between snores, he laughed, maniacally. I dressed quietly, left Sean on his bunk to dream of storming Vegas and headed off to the mess for my first trepidatious sampling of Greek cuisine.

Generally, the food on board was bloody awful but, being crew, we could at least choose from a larger variety of ways in which to poison ourselves. For starters, we had a choice of the passenger menu or, if so inclined, we could eat the Greek food that was prepared for the majority of the crew. When I'd been on-board a few weeks and had got to know my way around, I found there was an even greater choice. For instance, if you got on good terms with Bossy and the boys in the laundry, you could join them for excellent and authentic Chinese food whilst simultaneously being fleeced at poker. Then there was the Indian crew mess, where you could have your head blown off by some of the hottest curries this side of Calcutta – or Bradford.

That first night I was too excited to eat much and just had some unidentifiable gruel, which had been lovingly garnished with a thick, black hair. The stuff tasted so bad that I experienced a momentary pang of homesickness, for it instantly reminded me of dear old Vera's questionable culinary skills.

Three-quarters of the crew were old hands, shipping out for the umpteenth time. They knew one another intimately and the only reason I was paid any attention was that several of them knew Bobby.

Sitting next to me at dinner was one of the three on-board nurses. Gertrude Bloemfontein was Dutch, very cute and knew Bobby very well indeed. I had the inside track on young Gertrude as Bobby, not one to abide with the 'don't screw crew' rule, had bedded her on a round-the-world a couple of years previous. I must confess to being somewhat ill at ease when meeting Ms Bloemfontein in the flesh as I remembered her from several Polaroid photos. Stark naked and in various athletic poses, they had been presented to me by my dirty brother in much the same way that normal people show off baby snaps.

She was an extremely fit little thing with a set of wonderful knockers that strained to be set free from the crisp white confines of her uniform. Gertrude was obsessively proud of her knockers and rightly so. So proud in fact that she had a pet name for each. For reasons never explained, Gertrude referred to her tits as '*Elf en Twaalf*', which, on enquiry, I was to learn meant 'Eleven and Twelve' in Dutch. From where I sat I had a breathtaking view straight down the cleavage of her sensationally ripe young boobs. *'Elf en Twaalf* jiggled mischievously whenever Gertrude laughed, which, due to the fact that she was as crazy as a bedbug, averaged about every ten seconds.

The ship's whistle blew and announcements crackled through the public address system for all visitors to disembark as the ship would shortly be sailing. The old hands paid no attention and carried on eating, drinking and gossiping. I excused myself and, with some of the other new recruits, ventured out on deck to witness all the goings-on of departure.

5.00 a.m. SS KIONI IS EXPECTED TO ARRIVE AT NEEDLES POINT PILOT STATION

There is usually an interval of approximately 3 hours between arrival at the pilot station and the time that the vessel actually docks.We advise passengers that there is currently a ban on overtime operating in Southampton Docks. A mass meeting of stevedores is due to take place at 8.00 a.m. this morning and, depending on the duration of the discussions, some delay may occur in the reporting time of the stevedores for work to discharge baggage from the ship. We shall keep passengers informed by announcements and look forward to the cooperation of everyone should a delay occur.

SEASCAPE

Friday 11th January 1974 At Southampton

Well, we don't have to worry about being in contention for the Blue Riband. The Atlantic crossing took nine days. The Queen Mary did it in just under four days and that was in 1938. Mind you, in defence of the Kioni, the weather has been horrendous. I was chatting to Staff Captain Cocksakis yesterday morning and he reckoned it had been the worst conditions he'd seen in years. Then he went on to take the piss out of me and told me that he'd done his utmost to have me thrown off the ship in Southampton. But he laughed, shook my hand and wished me luck. He's flying home to Greece for a few weeks and then he'll be joining the Austral Star as skipper. I congratulated him on his promotion and I think we parted friends.

I spent most of yesterday afternoon snuggled up in my bunk with Claire. Though long overdue, her old man, Terry, is starting to become suspicious and has been grilling her on where she disappears to all the time. Past caring, Claire has told him that she wants a divorce when they get home.

With the end of the voyage in sight, we were both a bit morose as we realised that there was no future for the two of us. In fact, it's highly unlikely that we'd ever see one another again. Oh well, I feel all the richer for having known this magnificent woman. She taught me a lot, that's for sure, and I've got the bruises, scratches and teeth marks to prove it.

There was a massive party in the mess last night. The coke's long gone but we did our damnedest to smoke up any remaining dope. I sadly said farewell to some of my chums who are either being booted off the ship or leaving for the sake of their sanity. To nobody's surprise, Maggie, the hostie, is being kicked off. As is Reg, the alcoholic photographer, who's spent the past week in the hospital with a tube up his arse. According to Gertrude, his liver's packing it in. I went to visit him yesterday and was shocked at his horrible, deathly pallor. Poor old bugger.

Phil, the hairdresser, has done two years straight and is getting off for a break but will be back next trip. Henri is heartbroken. Not because of Phil but due to the fact that his beloved fiancé, Georgios the plumber, is being called back home to Greece for a stint in the army. Slut that he is, I'll be interested to see how long it takes Henri to find another boyfriend.

And, much to everyone's relief, Boring Graham is signing-off to marry his bird, Brenda, from Blackburn. Nobody's gonna miss that twat!

But the majority of crew are eager to stay on board for the next trip out is shaping up to be a doozy. Following a four-day turnaround in Blighty, we set off on the usual cattle run down to Aus'. Once we've dumped all the Pommy migrants and returning Aussies off, the Kioni is scheduled for two five-week cruises. The first, a jaunt across the Pacific to LA and San Francisco via Tahiti, the Marquesas islands and Acapulco, and then it'll be back to Australia by way of Hawaii, Samoa, Fiji and the New Hebrides. Then we're off on a five-port call of Japan via Guam and back by way of Hong Kong, Singapore and Bali. But wait. What am I thinking? It's January in England. Think I'll stay here. Ha!

We'll be away for almost six months and I'd have been really pissed off to have missed out. And, though I'm looking forward to getting home for a few days, the thought of spending winter in

England sends an Arctic shiver creeping up my spine like the wizened hand of a defrocked bishop.

We arrived off the Needles Point pilot station sometime in the early hours of the morning and should be tied up in Southampton in a few hours. I'm lying in my bunk listening to Tony Blackburn twittering away on Radio 1. I haven't missed that jerk, I can tell you. Right now he's coming over all phoney and twatting on about his latest tip for the top. Something called *Solitaire* by the Yankee crooner, Andy Williams. Claire just left in tears after a final farewell fuck and, once again, I'm all on me lonesome.

My loose plan is to head up to London for a couple of days of partying with the Earls Court gang and the boys at the Art Machine. And I'm gonna try and hook up with Judy. Last I heard she was working in the props department at Elstree Studios in Borehamwood and was shacked up with a sound technician called Trevor. Then I suppose I should whizz down and visit the folks. Then we're off again.

We were tied up at berth 38 by nine o'clock and, after breakfast, I queued up outside the bank for my pay. Paid in a cash lump sum at the end of the voyage, I collected a healthy wad – even after all the fines and subs were deducted. Cashed up, tanned and happy, I went in search of Bunger, Don-the-Slot and Tiny-Tom who are catching the train with me to Waterloo.

The majority of the passengers appear to have disembarked in record time, though, according to Pikey, they needn't have bothered as they've got a long wait in the Customs shed for their luggage.

I sauntered down a deserted passageway, walked past the Beauty Salon on A-Deck and, as I turned the corner into the foyer, I banged straight into Terry.

'You Pommy bastard!' he screamed.

Before I had time to react, he'd grabbed me around the throat and head-butted me smack on the nose.

At least I think that's what occurred. Just like in the cartoons, I saw stars and tweety birds sang. Fuck! I didn't know he had it in him. As my knees buckled and the lights went out, I remember thinking, nonchalantly, oh well, that'll teach me.

Did it bollocks!

Back then, travelling to Australia was a big deal for most people – akin to blasting off to an unknown planet. The majority of migrants didn't know when the hell, or if ever, they would be seeing their homeland again.

Several of the Pommy passengers were bawling their eyes out and clutching little coloured streamers. These were strung across to weeping friends and rellies', who crowded the observation deck above the Customs shed. After much hullabaloo, the last gangway was taken away and, with another blast of the ship's whistle, the Kioni was slowly pushed and pulled into the River Test and out into Southampton waters.

A young girl stood alone at the rail. She was sobbing, clutching a small teddy bear to her breast and waving to a young guy on the observation deck. Tiny-Tom sauntered along the deck, now dressed in a white boiler suit, which identified him as crew. He walked up behind the girl, put his arm around her and yelled at the guy on shore.

'Don't worry, mate, we'll take good care of her!'

The girl, lost in the moment, nestled into her giant protector and continued to wave at her distraught boyfriend, now frothing at the mouth and shaking his fist at Tiny-Tom.

The friends and rellies left behind waved and hollered frenetically and, as the gap slowly widened, their parting words grew fainter, eventually stolen by a cold, uncaring wind. Many became frantic, jumping up and down, growing hysterical. The shipboard Pommies put a hand to an ear and hollered back across the void. 'What? What? I can't hear ya! What ya say?' Some of the friends and rellies held up hastily scrawled cardboard signs bearing sad, chin-up messages: 'Good luck, Malcolm, Jean and the kids down under.'

The Kioni blew a long, last, mournful blast of farewell. This final eruption causing a cloud of soot to descend on to the desperate passengers like a sudden flurry of fine, black snow. A large, oily dollop came to rest on the shoulder of my white Afghan coat. But what the fuck! What a hoot! We were on our way.

The tugs pulled the Kioni further into the Solent and, when they'd done their job, dropped astern and disappeared into the night. I'd just turned twenty. I was off to see the world.

Giddy-up!